W9-BPM-499

THEY CALLED IT *TERRA INCOGNITA*—THE UNKNOWN LAND—AND NOW, IN A CENTURY OF DARING DISCOVERIES, THESE COURAGEOUS MEN AND WOMEN FOUND WHERE IT EXISTED: OUT THERE ACROSS THE SEAS AND DEEP INSIDE THEIR OWN HEARTS.

TOM OF BRISTOL—His handsome blond looks and sky-blue eyes make him an emperor's pet in a kingdom no European has ever seen. Here, as Chin Mao, his every wish is fulfilled, except the one he wants the most—to go home.

LAN-YING—As lovely as a lotus blossom, she is a royal concubine trained in the arts of love. She will be given to Tom as a gift, but one that is his only as long as the emperor desires . . . or as long as Tom never tries to leave.

SANDRO CAVALLI—His noble birth nearly forgotten, two years as a galley slave have almost robbed him of hope. But as hate for the brother who betrayed him has kept him alive under the lash, so love for a beautiful young woman will give him new reason to survive in an Arab land.

**MARINA**—A Greek beauty sold into the slavery of a pasha's harem, she is just beyond the reach of Sandro's arms. Yet in the end it may be her Christian faith that tears them apart . . . and sears his soul forever.

**THE TURK**—This scarred giant has been shackled to Sandro by slavery's chains and bound to him by a friendship no power on earth can break. Unbowed by the lash, he stands tall, ready to fight for the freedom he and Sandro must soon win . . . or die.

**PEDRO DA COSTA**—Once a mere peasant, he is now a master seaman, drawn by an irresistible desire to sail unknown seas and discover new lands . . . if only he can convince his prince to let him take the terrifying risk.

**INÊS ALVES**—Cheated of her inheritance, robbed of her good name, she is a fragile gentlewoman given two choices, neither of which she is likely to survive: to be thrown into a dungeon . . . or to be sent to help colonize Madeira.

LOBO—Huge, ugly, and quick with a knife, he is a rapist and murderer freed from the dungeons by royal decree. He takes women as he wants them, and now, on Madeira, he wants another man's wife.

PRINCE HENRY THE NAVIGATOR—Possessed by an obsession to explore, he will use a nation's wealth to create the greatest fleet of discoverers ever launched ... but he himself is driven by the treacherous winds of whim and vision.

CHENG HO—A eunuch in China's imperial court, he is one of history's greatest shipbuilders and sailors, but he must fight intrigue to carry out his life's ambition: to sail around the tip of Africa with a hundred ships and a dream.

ZARCO—Having led the expedition that discovered Madeira, he could destroy it with the prisoners he brought to colonize it. He never suspected that among them is the child of his best friend ... a young girl he once adored.

BANTAM BOOKS BY PAUL KING

*The Dreamers*
*The Voyagers*

# THE VOYAGERS

Paul King

BANTAM BOOKS

NEW YORK • TORONTO • LONDON • SYDNEY • AUCKLAND

THE VOYAGERS

*A Bantam Book/January 1994*

*All rights reserved.*
*Copyright © 1993 by Paul King.*
*Cover art copyright © 1993 by Ken Laager.*
*No part of this book may be reproduced or transmitted in any*
*form or by any means, electronic or mechanical, including*
*photocopying, recording, or by any information storage and*
*retrieval system, without permission in writing from the publisher.*
*For information address: Bantam Books.*

*If you purchased this book without a cover you should be aware*
*that this book is stolen property. It was reported as "unsold and de-*
*stroyed" to the publisher and neither the author nor the publisher*
*has received any payment for this "stripped book."*

ISBN 0-553-29830-5

Published simultaneously in the United States and Canada

*Bantam Books are published by Bantam Books, a division of Bantam*
*Doubleday Dell Publishing Group, Inc. Its trademark, consisting of the*
*words "Bantam Books" and the portrayal of a rooster, is Registered in*
*U.S. Patent and Trademark Office and in other countries. Marca Reg-*
*istrada. Bantam Books, 1540 Broadway, New York, New York 10036.*

*PRINTED IN THE UNITED STATES OF AMERICA*

OPM  0 9 8 7 6 5 4 3 2 1

# CHAPTER 1

A caravan from the south had deposited another load of returning hajjis in the streets and alleys of Gaza, placing a further strain on the already overcrowded inns and eating places. The pilgrims were everywhere, many still wearing the togalike garments of restriction, chattering to one another about the wonders they had seen in Mecca and competing in accounts of their acts of piety at the sacred Well of Zamzam and the three pillars where the devil was stoned, and their exploits on the day of the Standing.

Sandro Cavalli hung around Goliath's Well, waiting for the Turk to return from his expedition to the waterfront, moving frequently from place to place so that he wouldn't attract the notice of Gaza's aggressive street hawkers, or invite conversation from some overtalkative hajji.

He kept an especially sharp eye out for the flimflammers and confidence tricksters who preyed on the pilgrims passing through. The hajj gave them an annual flock of sheep to be sheared. While the majority of pilgrims were destitute at this stage of their journey, quite a few had managed to hang on to some portion of their travel money. The local confidence men were adept at separating them from it on one pretext or another, and the special danger from them was that they became professionally inquisitive about their quarry in order to find a wedge for swindling them. Sandro knew he could not stand close scrutiny. On the other hand, he did not think he provided attractive game for a flimflam artist. In his shabby and threadbare cloak he didn't particularly look like one of the hajjis who was likely to have any money left.

His eye wasn't sharp enough. He'd let his attention stray to the clear blue bowl of the sky and the bracing salt smell of the sea breeze with its promise of freedom beyond. A shifty one-eyed fellow sidled up to him and said, "I guess you'll be anxious to get home now, hajji."

"What. Uh, oh, yes."

Sandro knew, unhappily, that he had failed to react to the honorific the way most fresh, new hajjis did—like a cat purring over a bowl of cream.

"Salaam, hajji," the man said. "I'm Achmed—*al-Ayn*, as they call me."

"Uh, salaam, Achmed, uh, al-Ayn. I'm Ali, uh, bin Yusif," Sandro said, making a botch of the name he had been using on the flight from Damascus.

Achmed the Eye pounced. "Ah, Ali. Are you a Shi'ite, then?"

"Uh, no . . ." He added hastily, "Though of course we all revere Ali. No offense."

"That's all right. I'm not a Shi'ite either. But we're all Moslems together, aren't we?"

"Yes, yes, very true."

Achmed's single eye roved over him, stopping here and there. "I can't place your accent, brother. Where did you say you were from?"

"Oh, I've lived in a number of places. I, uh, spent some years as a child in Tunis."

Sandro took care to place himself as far away from Damascus as possible, though his life in Jaybir's household had made him familiar with Damascene ways and doubtless affected his Arabic pronunciation. But Tunis was safe, in case he had to fend off more questions. He had visited there as a small boy with his father, after all, and corresponded with the House of Cavalli's factor there.

"Ah, Tunis," Achmed said. "I've had the opportunity to perform services for many pilgrims from Tunis." His eye came to rest on Sandro's hands, still thickened and callused by his years as a galley slave, despite his subsequent soft service with Jaybir. "You look as if you've had a hard life, *ya*

Ali. But all must be well now, if you've managed to attain the blessings of the hajj."

It was too late to hide his telltale hands from this unsavory little man. In Saracen lands a galley slave was likely to be a Christian, just as in Christian lands one was likely to be a Saracen, and in the far-reaching territory of the sultanate there were bounties for escaped slaves.

"I was captured by the Franks during a sea voyage a long time ago," Sandro said with assumed candor. "They made me a galley slave, may God destroy their race. But, praise Allah, I was able to escape when the Franks were attacked by one of our corsairs."

"That explains your accent," Achmed said. "Living among the cursed Franks all those years."

"Yes," Sandro said. He moved to get away, but Achmed plucked at his sleeve and held him fast.

"Do you have a place to stay in Gaza, *ya* Ali?"

"I don't have money for an inn," Sandro said to squelch his interest. "I just slept in a doorway last night."

That was true enough. The majority of pilgrims passing through Gaza wrapped themselves in blankets in the streets or pitched tents on the outskirts.

"I can arrange a bargain for you on sharing a tent with a group of hajjis from Fez," Achmed persisted. "Very fine people, very pious."

"Thank you, *ya* Achmed," Sandro said, trying politely to disengage himself, "but I won't be here long enough for it to matter."

"Ah, then you've got passage on a ship. Are you with a group?"

"No," Sandro said. "That is, I was with a group, but I got separated. I'm traveling with another pilgrim now. . . ."

"Where can I find you later, if I can come up with something to your advantage? I know all the captains. I can get you aboard a pilgrim vessel at very low rates, taking the place of one of the charter passengers who died on the hajj." He struck a virtuous pose. "I swear to you, as Allah is my witness, that I don't want a single *dirhen* for commission. It's enough for me to know that I'm doing a service for God by helping one of His holy pilgrims."

"I . . . I won't need passage," Sandro floundered. "I may . . . that is . . . I may just walk."

"Walk?" Achmed exclaimed in horror. "You've done

enough walking, my dear brother, by the look of those sandals." A glint of interest came into his eye. "How far?"

"To . . . to Egypt. Only as far as Suez. There are pilgrim
ships there."

"Oh, then you're going west. Not north or east, say to
Baghdad or Damascus?"

"No," Sandro blurted. "Not north or east."

Achmed gazed at him speculatively. "*Ya akhi*, my dear
brother. I love you as I love my own hand. You won't find a
ship any cheaper in Suez than I could arrange for you right
here. I'll look for you tomorrow. Will you be here again, at
the Well?"

"Uh, I don't know where I'll be."

"I'll find you. In the meantime, if you're short of money,
do you have any souvenirs of Mecca you'd like to sell? A vial
of holy water from the Well of Zamzam? Or a pebble from
the Stoning?"

"No."

"No souvenirs. That's too bad. Most hajjis have something
or other. Well, it's what we take away in our hearts that's important, eh, *ya* Ali?"

"Yes," Sandro said.

He finally got rid of the man when the little sharpster
spotted a prosperous-looking pilgrim who had two slaves to
attend him. The pilgrim tried to brush him off, but Achmed
the Eye kept circling around in front of him till he finally
stopped. Sandro could not leave the vicinity of Goliath's
Well when the Turk would be looking for him there, but he
made a wide detour and came around the other side, where
he could lose himself in a dense fringe of vendors' stalls
with hundreds of people milling around them, and still keep
an eye on the tumbled masonry basin that was Gaza's chief
tourist attraction.

The Turk returned shortly before noon and spotted
Sandro after a quick scan of the crowd. He motioned Sandro
to meet him in a side street, and after a few moments joined
him there.

"I've got us passage to Granada," he said. "We're part of
a big, prepaid pilgrims' tour group with three ships. Some of
the passengers have switched accommodations to be with
friends they made in Mecca, so the hajjis on any particular
ship aren't necessarily familiar with all their shipmates. The
captain wasn't averse to making a little extra money on the

side. Here's your boarding pass. It belonged to an old man named Kazimi from Málaga who died on the voyage out. Don't show it to anyone but the boatswain—he's in on the bribe. But there'll be passengers who'll remember Kazimi."

He handed Sandro a small wooden tally with a name and a number painted on it in Arabic script.

"We sail tomorrow morning," the Turk said. "Till then, keep your head down and don't talk to anybody if you can help it." He looked Sandro over critically. "You may get by, Venetian. The sun's burnt you dark enough these last weeks. You were getting fishbelly white, playing the scribe for the old scholar. Just don't let anyone see your *zib*—though that may be hard to manage on shipboard."

"Don't worry about me," Sandro said. "I won't give us away."

The Turk scowled. "You'd better get rid of that Christian idol of yours. Now—right away. You won't be able to keep that hidden during a sea voyage. I was a fool to let you go back for it."

The Turk had had little choice. Sandro remembered how crazed he had been on the morning of their escape. He had refused to leave without his late wife's icon, and had risked capture for both of them by taking the time to dig it up from the corner of the stable where he had buried it.

"No," he said. "I'll be careful."

"You've rowed a load of Christian pilgrims. You know how a habit of thieving attacks even honest men at sea, for some strange reason. And it's always trifles—handkerchiefs, pens, a spoon. You turn your back for a moment, and it's gone—under the robes of someone you've just been talking to."

"I'll keep it on me all the time. I'm not crazy enough to leave it lying around."

"What about when you're sleeping? There are hands feeling around for purses."

"I'm a light sleeper. Remember? It's a habit we acquired on the rowing benches."

"By Allah, you're still as stupid as ever. I ought to take it away from you."

"Try it and I'll kill you." Sandro's hand stole to the dagger under his cloak. It was a fine, sharp weapon that had belonged to Hassan the Knout.

The Turk studied him for a long, tense moment, his face growing darker with fury. Sandro's grip on the dagger handle tightened. The Turk, for all his rational talk, was capable of anything—even starting a scuffle in the midst of a crowd of pilgrims.

Then the bulging veins subsided and the Turk laughed. "I believe you would, Venetian. You're mad. They say that God looks after madmen. I hope that's so."

They walked on down the narrow, crowded lane. "We'd better buy some supplies," the Turk said. "There's still some of Hassan's money left, though I didn't let that villain of a captain see it. We're supposed to have our keep during the voyage, but it's never enough. They feed these pilgrims swill you wouldn't give to a dog."

"All right. Give me some of the money. I'll get some flour and beans and a little cauldron we can share. Some dried meat and some fruit for the first few days. We can get more whenever we make port. And a water cask. We each ought to bring aboard our own water cask."

The Turk drew them into a doorway and counted out coins. "Meet me in the alley where we slept last night," he said. "If anyone's taken that niche in the wall we used, I'll throw them out. It's a good spot—hidden from the ends of the alley, but you can see anyone coming from either direction."

"You're too suspicious, *Turkeeya*," Sandro said. "We got away, didn't we?"

The Turk bared his teeth in a jagged smile. "Maybe," he said.

A rattle of armor awoke them before dawn. The Turk grabbed his arm. "Listen," he said.

Voices were coming from the head of the alley, low purposeful voices speaking a language that was not Arabic. A horse whinnied and someone quieted it. Sandro caught the words, *"Burada bekleyiniz."*

"Mamluks," the Turk said. "My old comrades in arms."

The soldiers moved down the alley, leading their horses. The horses' hooves were muffled, by the sound of them— probably wrapped in burlap. They stopped at one of the sleeping forms that lined the alley and shook it awake. Sandro heard a voice of protest, then someone saying, "He's not one of them. Go back to sleep, fellow."

Another voice whined, "Give me my bounty now. You promised me a bounty."

Sandro's insides curled up as he recognized the voice as that of Achmed the Eye.

"You'll get your bounty when we find the men, rat-face," someone answered. "After you point them out to us. If they're what you say they are."

"They're looking for runaways," the Turk said. "Look at those silks and plumes. They're a Damascene regiment."

"It's us they're after," Sandro said. "It's my fault. We'd better get out of here."

They disentangled themselves from the water casks and provisions they'd curled themselves around to protect and started to get up.

"Wait," the Turk said.

More soldiers were coming from the other end of the alley, blocking that route of escape.

"I hope you're ready to die, Venetian," the Turk said. "I'm not going back."

"What can we do?"

"Wait till they get here. Kill one if you can. That'll throw them off. Don't try to break through that lot coming from the other side. Then we'd have one lot chasing us and another lot to block us. Go the other way. That way they'll tangle with one another and get in one another's way. When we reach the head of the alley, we'll run in opposite directions. They won't know who to follow for one or two seconds, till the officer tells them how to split up. We'll meet at the ships, just before boarding—if we're still alive."

It was all delivered in a crisp military tone. The strategy was professional. The Turk seemed fresh and years younger—almost happy. Sandro caught a glimpse of the formidable soldier the Turk must have been before life had swatted him with misfortune. That part of him had been buried in the darkness within him, but it hadn't died.

They pretended sleep, wrapped in their blankets like the other pilgrims lining the alley. Sandro's hand was on his dagger. He knew that the Turk had a short-sword hidden under his rags; it had been a relic of Hassan's own military service. All during the dusty trek from Damascus, the Turk had sharpened it on stones whenever he had a chance.

The footsteps stopped. Sandro sensed someone standing over him. He opened his eyes a slit and saw boots, flaring pantaloons, a short robe. A soldier bent over the Turk and shook him. "Hey, fellow, wake up!"

The Turk suddenly grabbed the front of the man's robe and yanked him down. Before the soldier hit the ground, the Turk had him skewered. A powerful leg shot out and sent a water keg rolling under the horses' feet. The horses shied and whinnied, knocking against the soldiers who held them. The Turk leapt to his feet like an uncoiled spring, jerked his sword out of the dead man, and slashed at the soldier nearest him.

Sandro, at the Turk's first move, had whipped his blanket at the eyes of the man standing over him and, while the man clawed at it, sank his dagger into his belly. The horses were still pawing the air, their hooves flailing at the Mamluks who were fighting to hold onto the reins. The second group of soldiers at the far end of the alley had started to run toward the action. Sandro got past the flank of a bucking horse. He saw the Turk take a moment before fleeing to cut the skinny throat of Achmed the Eye. "Here's your bounty, cockroach!" he heard the Turk snarl.

Then he himself was running for the mouth of the alley. All was confusion behind him, with the sound of clashing horses and cursing men all in a tangle. As he reached the corner he flung a look backward to make sure that the Turk had broken free and saw him pounding after him, the bloody sword held straight out where it could be swung in an arc at any pursuer who got too close. Sandro veered to the left and headed for another opening in the maze of alleys. Dawn was breaking with a great rosy splash, and the sleepers in the streets were beginning to stir. Sandro saw people sitting up to stare at him and realized he was still holding the dagger. He thrust it out of sight beneath his cloak and turned his run into a fast walk. He ducked through a crevice in the row of mud walls and found himself in a narrow, shuttered defile. Goggle-eyed women stared at him from the roofs, and a man's angry voice shouted at him. He took several more turns through the maze, eventually emerging into a minor thoroughfare where sleepy shopkeepers were unshuttering and the proprietors of a few rude eating places were crawling out of their holes and setting up matting on the ground and unfurling patched canopies.

He stayed off the well-trafficked streets and kept to the side streets and back alleys, killing time. He bought some fruit and a skewer of lamb for breakfast with some of his remaining coins. On further thought he bought a grimy blanket and a worn pilgrim's scrip from a ferrety little urchin who had probably lifted them from a sleeper and filled the scrip with bread and fruit so that he wouldn't be conspicuous when he went aboard the ship. He regretted the loss of the water casks and the other provisions, but he had gone hungry and thirsty before; the captain, no matter how cheese-paring, would not let his passengers starve. Once he saw a troop of Mamluks crossing an intersection he had been about to enter; he turned his back and studied a rug seller's wares until they had gone by.

At the appointed hour he went to the beach where the ships were anchored. Sailors were rowing boatloads of pilgrims out. Two or three hundred hajjis, their possessions piled next to them, stood about on the sands, waiting their turn. Sandro looked for the Turk and didn't see him.

He made himself known to the bribed boatswain, who gave him a sidelong look and said in a low tone, "Where's your friend?"

"He'll be along soon," Sandro said. "I'll wait here till he shows up."

He surrendered his wooden tally, and the boatswain pretended to check off his name and the name of his father in the register. The tally disappeared under the man's clothing, but Sandro was given a boarding tag to hang around his neck. He lost himself in the crowd of waiting pilgrims; he was sure the Mamluks were out looking for him, but even if they rode by this beach, he didn't think they'd recognize him. They wouldn't expect to find an escaped slave in the midst of a tour group where people were supposed to know one another.

He waited through the morning while the sun climbed higher and the sands grew hotter. The crush of pilgrims dwindled. It was down to just a few more boatloads now, and the Turk still had not come.

A hajji standing next to him offered him a drink of water from his bottle. Sandro accepted with thanks.

"I don't remember you from this ship, brother," the hajji said. "Were you on one of the other vessels?"

"Yes," Sandro said.

"It was marvelous, wasn't it?" the man said. "Did you visit the sacred cave?"

"No."

"Ah well, that's not required, as long as you perform the *wuquf* and your other duties. You stoned the devil, didn't you?"

"Yes," Sandro said.

"Of course," the man apologized. He laughed. "I myself was able to squeeze into the cave—I'm skinny enough—but there was one fat merchant from Gibraltar who got stuck, and it took all the rest of us to pull him out. Not that there's anything to see in the cave, but just think—the Prophet saved from his enemies by a spider!"

"Yes, it's wonderful."

"Still, I'll be glad to get back to my little orange grove in Almería. Travel is interesting, but there's no place like home. When I think of the discomforts, the dangers we've undergone . . ." He shook his head. "The rest of the world isn't as civilized as Granada."

"No."

"Gaza, especially. I'll be glad to get out of this place of violence. Just think, only this morning, not very far from where we're standing, an escaped slave killed two soldiers and an innocent businessman of the town."

Sandro stiffened. He hoped his face hadn't betrayed him. So word had spread so soon. It made things more dangerous for the Turk. It was fairly safe here on the beach among the hajjis, but everyone in the town must be looking for the escapees and scrutinizing every passing face. That must be why the Turk hadn't shown up yet. He was probably holed up somewhere, waiting for a good moment to make a dash for the ship.

But he didn't have much time. Sandro looked out at the anchored galleys. The ship's boat was coming back again. There couldn't be more than one or two loads of standees left on the beach.

"I can see you're as impatient to leave as I am," the hajji smiled indulgently. "I don't blame you. But there's nothing to worry about. The slave didn't get far. They caught up with him and killed him."

The House of Cavalli ranked as one of the greatest of the mighty Venetian merchant houses, its far-flung commerce carrying the Cavalli name to the various ports of Europe and throughout the Moorish lands. Alessandro Cavalli, the handsome younger son of the powerful and wealthy Girolamo Cavalli, had been born in a gilded marble palace within sight of the Grand Canal. But fate had turned Sandro's life from one of remarkable privilege into one of utter privation.

Because Sandro's unscrupulous older brother, Matteo, had cared little for anything but his own base pleasures, their father had chosen to ignore tradition and train the younger Sandro—who had a keen interest in the business as well as a keen mind—as his successor as overseer of the Cavalli enterprises. But Signor Cavalli had underestimated the boiling malice spawned by his decision. When the elder Cavalli unexpectedly died, Matteo had told Sandro that the youth was suspected of having poisoned Girolamo and was to be brought before the ruling Council of Ten on charges of parricide, a judgment that would mean certain execution. Sandro had been shocked by such a terrible accusation, but before a trial could take place, the perfidious Matteo had snatched control of the family power and fortune by arranging for Sandro's abduction by an equally unprincipled Genoese trader.

Thrown first into a fetid dungeon and then into the rat-infested bowels of a merchant ship, Sandro, then barely eighteen, his hands accustomed to a pen or a lute, had been forced to labor for two years as a galley oarsman, chained to his seat day and night, slaving under unimaginably brutal conditions. When by an odd twist Sandro had finally learned of his brother's treachery, he had vowed to escape and exact revenge—and try to regain what was rightfully his. With the help of his benchmate, a powerful and dangerous Turk whose own endurance was fueled by rage, Sandro had nearly succeeded, but the two of them were taken prisoner by Barbary pirates and sold at a slave auction.

Their new owner had been an Arab scholar, a stern master but kind enough in his absentminded fashion. Jaybir al-Sumit had rescued Sandro from the stables and the lash of the overseer—had rescued him from the galleys, when it came to that—and had given him as decent a life as a slave could hope for, teaching Sandro about astronomy and map making and even permitting him to marry a fellow slave he had fallen in love with, a beautiful Greek woman named Marina. But Sandro's relative good fortune lasted only a

year, and then the hand of fate had lashed out with another
blow when Jaybir died and his odious nephew, Murrwan,
became the new householder. Sandro had been thrown back
into the stables, his marriage—one between "infidel
slaves"—declared invalid and his wife, Marina, tortured into
renouncing her Christian faith as a prelude to her being included in Murrwan's stable of women. But Marina had
quickly put an end to her physical and spiritual agony by
killing herself, and the Turk, dealing his own blow, had
killed the brutal stable overseer. Sandro and the Turk had
fled the compound and escaped to Gaza—where they now
awaited the next turn of the wheel.

*Qismah.* Fate. The Arabs were great believers in fate.
One's lot in life. It was Sandro's *qismah* to be there. Venice
was a shadow, Maffeo a ghost. The marble palace near the
Grand Canal, his little sister, Agnese . . . they were gone, as
a dream is gone when one opens one's eyes. The past three
years had erased nearly every trace of the high-born, advan-
taged youth; in his place stood a man hardened and
strengthened by travail and pain—a man capable of anything.

The Moorish kingdom of Granada was a shrunken rem-
nant of the centuries of glory, when the caliphate of Córdoba
had ruled almost all Spain. Today its boundaries were re-
stricted to a two-hundred-mile stretch of the southern coast
of Andalusia, from Gibraltar to Cuevas, and it paid tribute to
Castile. But even after the Reconquest it still was the most
brilliant kingdom in Europe.

Sandro, squatting on his heels to tie up a bundle of firewood, paused to look across the river at the splendors of the
Alhambra—the Red Castle—rising on its hill. Its soaring
towers and mile of walls, its lavish gardens, the intricate
traceries of its courts, made it one of the wonders of the
world. The old caliphs had done themselves well.

He hefted the load of firewood to his shoulder and started
walking. It was his fourth trip of the day. That bastard,
Mokhtar ben-Aziz, wouldn't let him use the donkey.

The streets of the lower town, the Quarter of the Falconers, teemed with activity. Sandro's progress was slow. Shops
lined the streets—goldsmiths, coppersmiths, jewelers, per-
fumers, leather workers, furniture makers, dealers in silks.

The signs of luxury were everywhere. But these Spanish Moors set as much store by culture as wealth. In Granada, a gentleman was known by the size of his library.

Sandro passed the corn exchange, its bold horseshoe archway filled with gesticulating men in silken robes. Even a commercial building like this was a wonder of geometric filigrees and ornate vaulted ceilings.

The scene was not quite so glittering a little farther on, where half-naked men in chains, Christian prisoners, labored to repair a section of the quarter's ancient walls. Christians were treated harshly in Granada these days. The Moors couldn't help but resent their own steadily diminishing hold on Spain during the five hundred years of the Reconquista. The border clashes had grown more frequent of late, and there was a rumor that this year the sultan, Abu al-Hasan, would refuse to pay the annual tribute to Castile.

That would be a mistake, Sandro thought. The tide of Islam might be rising in the east, where the rich prize of Constantinople waited for the Turks only to decide to take it, but here in Spain it was receding. Granada could not endure as a Moorish state for many more generations.

He walked past the chained men as quickly as his heavy burden would allow him, not looking too closely at them. The sight was a hard thing to endure. The voyage from Gaza to Granada had been even harder—sailing as a passenger in the familiar stink of a galley and watching Christian slaves pulling at the oars, not daring to show his sympathy. When he had arrived in Granada, he had gone at once to the labor exchange. It would have been easy for him to get a job as a laborer in a quarry—workers of his size and strength were not easy to find. But then he found that the bulk of the hardest and most dangerous work was done by Christian slaves, like these miserable wretches he saw toiling on the walls, and he did not dare to be around them, where he might give himself away, particularly when the permanent marks of his floggings remained incised on his back to betray him if he were ever careless enough to take off his shirt.

But he had found employment as a porter at an inn in the old quarter. Mokhtar ben-Aziz was a stingy cur who didn't pay much, but Sandro was allowed to sleep in a corner of the stable, and the job was enough to sustain him until he could make some sort of plan.

The inn had a bad reputation. It not only served illegal

*nabidh*—made from raisins that had been allowed to ferment more than the two days allowed by the Prophet—but it served wine as well. Consequently, it attracted a raffish clientele—the dregs of society and the dissolute cream. Its advantage for Sandro was that nobody looked at you too closely here, or wanted to be looked at too closely themselves. The Mozárabes—the "almost Arabs"—came here for the wine, and nobody could gainsay them. As Arabized Christians living under Moorish rule, they might be persecuted from time to time, but they had not been required to give up their religion. As long as they paid the *zakat*—the tax on unbelievers—they enjoyed limited rights of citizenship.

It was a different story for the *Muladíes*—those whose Christian forebears had been converted to Islam, and who professed Islam themselves. There were many backsliders among them. Sometimes whole families practiced the Christian faith in secret for generations, keeping even their own children in the dark until the children grew old enough to be trusted. The law was sterner for them. In Islam, the penalty for apostasy was death. Sandro wondered how many of the patrons who came here to sip the bootleg *nabidh* had spent their lives looking over their shoulders for *ez zulmeh*, the "men of violence," as the arresting officers were known, to drag them off to the authorities.

The men of violence hardly ever came sniffing around Mokhtar's inn, however. He paid them off regularly. A good part of his clientele were nobles of the Falconers' Quarter, al-Bayyazin, who found the place a handy refuge for their nights on the town, and the authorities didn't bother such folk.

Sandro entered by the stableyard and added his load of firewood to the pile he had brought previously. It looked to be enough to get the inn through the evening. It had better be; Mokhtar didn't like spending money, but if the firewood ran out, it would be Sandro who got the blame.

"Where have you been? What took you so long? Hurry up and finish your chores here. I'll need you to help with the serving later."

Mokhtar ben-Aziz had come up behind him while his back was turned. He was a sour-looking man whose face rested on a sagging double chin that hung like a napkin beneath his real chin. The fat had stretched the space between his whiskers to make them look sparse.

"Yes, *ya* Mokhtar, right away. I'll hurry."

The bastard didn't have enough servants to do the work of the tavern. On busy nights, which came at least three or four times a week, Sandro had to shuttle between caring for patrons' horses in the stable and waiting on tables, squeezing his porter's duties in between.

He built the fires but did not light them, delaying that till the customers arrived in order to save money; mucked out the stable and spread fresh straw; then helped Rushd, one of the two servingmen, to make a fresh batch of *nabidh*.

"I hope that will be enough," Rushd said as they strained the last of it into earthenware jugs and put it away in the storeroom. "We'll have to mix it with the ripe stuff to stretch it out tonight. Those Christians drink like fish."

"Are we having a large party of Christians tonight, then?" Sandro asked. "They usually drink wine."

Rushd spat. "Out-and-out Christians do. They have nothing to hide. But these aren't Mozárabes. They're stinking Muladíes, trying to pass themselves off as sons of the Faithful. I can always tell. They're afraid to ask for the wine—when even an honest Moslem will imbibe, particularly if he's a gentleman, and pray for forgiveness the next day. But not the Muladíes. They're always holier-than-thou. They always dance around—order *nabidh* and hint for the aged stuff."

"You shouldn't be prejudiced, *ya* Rushd," Sandro said, playing his role. "All brothers in Islam are equal in the eyes of Allah."

"I can smell a secret Christian a mile away," Rushd said, looking Sandro square in the eye.

Sandro would not let himself be rattled. "Who is it?" he said. "One of the regulars?"

Rushd dropped his gaze. "It's that Said ben-Gamal," he muttered. "The one who works for the old Jew, Ezra the physician, who's said to be an astrologer like so many of these Jewish doctors. It's a going-away party for him."

Sandro recalled Said, a short, thick man with a nervous air. He had served him a number of times when the inn was busy. Said always chose a place near the door, and though he seemed standoffish at first, tended to become overtalkative as the evening wore on. Once he had ensnared Sandro in a bibulous discussion of astrology he was having with a colleague, and Sandro, caught off guard, had realized afterward that he had betrayed more knowledge about the use of astrolabes than a porter in a disreputable inn should have. Said had tried to draw him into conversation a number of times since, but Sandro had been wary. And perhaps it had been a good idea to be wary, if Said had Christians in his family tree, as Rushd had suggested. A person with convert origins, whether or not he himself was a secret practitioner, might be more sensitive to some small clue in Sandro's behavior than a real Moor would be.

"He's going away?" Sandro said. That was a relief. He wouldn't have to worry about him anymore.

"Yes, he sails with his master the day after tomorrow, may Allah be thanked for ridding this inn of his presence. The Jew Ezra is taking up a post in the court of a Christian prince who fancies astrologers and such learned men."

"Who is this prince?"

Rushd spat again. "Dom Henrique of Portugal, may God roast him in hell. He who conquered Ceuta and placed that jewel of Islam in the infidel crown."

Sandro remembered Ceuta, of course. He had been a boy of thirteen when the wonderful news had come that a Portuguese prince had extended the Reconquest to Africa itself, planting a Christian presence across the Strait of Gibraltar. Venice had talked of nothing else for months.

"The one they call the Navigator?"

"The very same."

"May God roast all Christians," Sandro said judiciously.

The inn began to fill up shortly after the sunset prayer. The usual assortment of workingmen and al-Báyyazin businessmen arrived and were given places more or less in accordance with their status. A party of young noblemen staggered in, already drunk and bringing their own musician with them, and amidst much hilarity ordered wine. They had spent the day in falconry, and Sandro had to leave his duties to attend to their horses, but, thank God, they had sent the cadgers home with the birds, and Sandro didn't have to be responsible.

Said and his friends arrived an hour or so later, and Mokhtar put them up in the balcony, where they would be out of the way of the noblemen. They kept Sandro and

Rushd busy passing up *nabidh*, and soon the farewell party was going very well indeed.

"Pay more attention to the gentlemen," Mokhtar told Sandro. "See that they have everything they want."

"Yes, *sidi*," Sandro said.

The noblemen wanted a feast on the spur of the moment, and Sandro and the servants were soon sent scurrying back and forth to the kitchen to bring it to them. In addition to his other duties, Sandro was put to work preparing side dishes, cutting up lamb and putting it on skewers, and stuffing pigeons. Then one of the noblemen, a slender young man with a curled and perfumed beard, decided that the horses should share in the feast. Sandro assured him that he would take a platter of cracked wheat and vegetables to the stable as soon as he had a chance. Privately he decided to stow the dish away for the supper he had missed and see that the horses were watered. It had been a long hot day for them, and he hadn't dared to let the sweating beasts drink their fill when they first arrived, for fear of colic.

It was past midnight by the time he had a chance to tend to the horses. A number of patrons—workingmen who had to be up early, and those with little stamina—had already left, but the two parties were still going strong. They had tended to merge a bit, despite the difference in social station. Said's well-wishers were enjoying the benefit of the musician the noblemen had brought with them and had advanced from mere eavesdropping to active appreciation. He, on his part, had half turned toward the balcony to include them in his audience, and was even taking requests from them. The songs were getting bawdier, occasioning some good-natured exchanges between balcony and ground floor.

The sound of the lute and the raucous voices carried to Sandro in the stable as he hauled buckets of water to the horse trough. He was achingly tired and wished only that the merrymakers would decide to call it a night and go home.

One of them was in the stableyard now, relieving himself; Sandro could hear the splash of urine against stone going on a long time. The man finished and came through the stable, adjusting his clothing. It was Said, flushed and weaving.

"*Ahlahn*, friend Ali," Said blinked. "How goes it?" He staggered, and Sandro caught him.

"Let me help you back inside," Sandro offered.

"*Lah'za*. In a minute. We never got a chance to talk."

"There's time," Sandro humored him. "You'll be here to-morrow, won't you?"

"Tomorrow, yes. Then I sail. Never come back."

He sat down heavily on an upturned keg.

"I hope you'll be very happy where you're going," Sandro said tactfully.

"Portugal," Said supplied. "To the court of the infante Dom Henrique at Sagres. A generous man, they say."

"Then your future's assured." Sandro tugged experimentally at the man's arm, but it was like trying to shift a rock. "Come on, your friends will miss you."

"My master's an em . . ." He had trouble with the word. ". . . an eminent Jewish doctor, you see. Ezra ben-Abraham. Perhaps you've heard of him."

"I think so."

"Prince Henry collects eminent Jewish doctors, you see. He's surrounded himself with them. That's because medicine and astrology go together."

"That's very interesting."

Said winked at him slyly. "Come on, friend Ali. You know more about astrology than you let on, don't you? How else would you be so familiar with astrolabes?"

"You're mistaken, *sidi*."

"You see, the stars and the navigation of ships somehow go together," Said continued blearily. "Don't ask me how. That's what Ezra ben-Abraham told me. And this Portuguese prince is very interested in navigation. He's paying great salaries to astrologers . . . and instrument makers and mapmakers. If you know anything about such things, you should go to Portugal yourself. It's not healthy for you here."

"I don't know what you're talking about."

Sandro wanted to be rid of the man. But he didn't dare let him go now. Not in his drunken, blabbing state. First he had to find out what he knew.

Said stared at him out of eyes that seemed suddenly less bleary. "You're a Christian, aren't you?"

"No, *sidi*, I swear it."

"We could call a constable and find out if you're circumcised."

"No, *sidi*, don't do that."

"Then admit you're a Christian."

There was no way out. "All right." Sandro began to consider how he could shut the man up. He couldn't let him go back to the party. He looked around the stable for something to hit him over the head with.

"I thought so." Said caught the look in Sandro's eyes. "Don't worry, I won't give you away. I'm a Christian myself."

So it was true, what Rushd had suspected. "I don't want to know such things," Sandro said.

"It will be a relief to live in a Christian country, among fellow Christians, and not have to look over my shoulder anymore. I've been living a lie all my life, and my father lived a lie before me. I was circumcised by a mullah as a small boy, but it wasn't till I was sixteen that I was told we were Christians. I take care to go to mosque every Friday and to say my prayers every day. One more day, and the lie's over."

"Why are you telling me this?"

"Because you're a fellow Christian. And because I'll be safe the day after tomorrow. Otherwise I wouldn't have the courage. You mustn't stay here much longer. Sooner or later, Mokhtar will find you out. He's a sneaky cur. He'll turn you in for the bounty. I know he already suspects you. I heard the servants talking."

"The servants suspect you, too," Sandro said with an effort.

Said laughed. "I'm safe enough. If Mokhtar started turning in all the Muladíes customers that his servants suspected, he'd have no business left. Word would get around. But you're another story."

"How could you tell?"

"We crypto-Christians have a sixth sense. We have to, to stay alive."

"Thank you. I'll keep your warning in mind."

"Don't wait too long."

Said rose unsteadily to his feet. His legs were not as much under control as his tongue had been. Sandro helped him to the door.

"Back to the celebration," Said grunted. "The Portuguese ship's anchored at Málaga. It'll be there for a week. If you decide to take my advice and leave Granada, you could come with us. Ezra ben-Abraham's a good sort. He might even take you on as a servant, if you don't have passage money. If you want to get out of the country, Portugal's the safest bet. It's too far overland to get to the Castilian frontier, and with the recent trouble the border's a hornet's nest anyway. Think it over, and let me know tomorrow."

"All right," Sandro said. "I'll speak to you tomorrow."

But Said didn't appear the next day. Sandro wondered aloud to Rushd where he was.

Rushd took his time about answering. "The men of violence came after dawn prayers to take him away," he said, picking his teeth.

"But . . . how?" Sandro said, stunned.

"He was a secret Christian, just as I said he was. Someone informed on him." There was a look of sly satisfaction on Rushd's seamy face.

"Who? You?"

Rushd raised his tangled eyebrows until they almost hit his turban. "Me?" he said innocently. "How would I dare to take the liberty of going to the authorities about one of Mokhtar ben-Aziz's valued patrons, even if it were the satan himself? He'd skin me alive for interfering with his business. No, it was Mokhtar himself who informed on the apostate."

"But why? If it's bad for business?"

"Mokhtar ben-Aziz knows how to bide his time. He waited until the last day. Our other patrons will think only that the backsliding dog departed for the land of the Franks, as he was supposed to. And he took care that the man was not arrested here. If he loses the business of a few fearful Christian dogs over it, the reward will more than make up for the loss."

"He'll wait a time before he does anything like that again?" Sandro said.

"Long enough to lull any other infidels," Rushd gloated.

Sandro said nothing further. After the last patron left, and Mokhtar and the servants had gone to bed, he went to the corner of the stable where he slept. He dug away the straw and uncovered the hiding place where he had buried Marina's icon and the coins he had managed to save so far. He could tell from the refolding of the cloth the items were wrapped in that the hiding place had been disturbed. But it hadn't been a thief. A thief would have taken the coins. Whoever had done it had simply covered everything up again.

Sandro did not hesitate for an instant. He gathered up the coins and the icon, got his few things together, and left quietly within minutes. Málaga was not far. He could walk there in less than a week.

He wondered if Prince Henry, the patron of astrologers and other learned men, had heard of the *kamal*.

# CHAPTER 2

"She's shut herself up in her room, and she's having a fit," Miranda da Cunha confided, her twelve-year-old lips curved in a smile.

"Oh, the poor child!" Dona Beatriz Alves said. She turned a timorous gaze on her daughter Inês. "Go to her, *cara*. She's your cousin. Maybe you can comfort her."

"Huh! Inês is the last person she wants to see," Miranda said. "She hates her."

"Don't talk like that, *sobrinha*," Dona Beatriz told her niece in a strained voice. She fanned herself furiously.

"She remembers all the times Dom Sebastião smiled at Inês, or paused on the way in to the family to ask after her music," Miranda said, purring with satisfaction. "She called Inês a viper in her bosom and said Father should never have taken her in."

"What a thing to say!" Dona Beatriz gasped, looking faint.

"And you too," Miranda said with bright malice.

"Oh!" Dona Beatriz's face drained white and her hand flew to her mouth.

"She didn't mean anything by it, Mamãe," Inês said, touching her mother's arm. "She's just in a state, and she'll say anything." She shot Miranda an angry look.

Miranda had more to impart. She chose her words with relish. "She threw things at the servants. She broke her little hand mirror, and the glass cut Juanita. The blood had to be stanched by the barber."

"You should go to her," Inês said to her cousin. "Maybe you can do something with her."

"Not me," Miranda simpered. She gathered up her skirts and scampered from the room.

"Poor Helena," Dona Beatriz said weakly.

"Poor Helena, *de nada!*" Inês said. "She brought it on herself. She pushed too hard and scared him off."

Dona Beatriz fanned herself. "You shouldn't be unkind, *filha.*"

"Don't worry, Mamãe." Inês put her arm around her mother's waist. "I'll go see her. After she's had a chance to calm down a bit."

"It must have been a terrible shock."

"Yes."

The note had come that morning, delivered by a footman in the livery of the count's household. That it had not been one of Dom Sebastião's personal servants showed that the *condessa* must have had a hand in it. In the note Dom Sebastião expressed his regrets at being unable to call that evening. A sacred duty called him elsewhere, it seemed. He had joined the expedition of Fernando de Castro against the Canary Islands and was occupied with preparations for sailing.

The note hadn't said so but made it delicately clear that the engagement, if there ever had been one, was off. Staying clear of any reference to a real or implied bond between them, the note was couched in terms of the glory of Christian endeavor and duty to king and country. The future was uncertain—who could tell how many might return alive from such a peril-fraught mission? in the meantime, he praised Helena's excellence and wished her all good fortune in her life.

It was all very correct and very cautious. If there had ever been any "understanding" that an engagement was imminent, it had all been on one side. Certainly Dom Sebastião had never said anything that could be construed to be binding under law; not even the cleverest lawyer could find anything that would be actionable.

"Dona Florbella set her cap too high, that's all," Inês said. "The *condessa* didn't want Helena as a daughter-in-law.

Why would a family like that want to make an alliance with a family of codfish aristocrats like the da Cunhas?"

"You forget yourself, *filha*," Dona Beatriz said nervously.

"Oh, Mamãe, you know it's true. Pai used to say so. You've said it yourself."

"Dom Rodrigo's come up in the world since then."

"He's still *novo-rico*. It doesn't make him the equal of the great folk. And that's why he's going to swallow this. He'll put a damper on Helena and Dona Florbella and pretend nothing ever happened. He doesn't want to hurt his prospects with the *nobriza* by making trouble."

Dom Rodrigo, his pride hurt, had stormed through the house when the note had arrived. But he had nobody to vent his anger and resentment on, nobody to challenge. He could not even say anything outside these walls without making a fool of himself.

"You'd better stay out of his way for a while."

"Don't worry, I'll make myself small." She hesitated. "You know, Mamãe, Dom Sebastião never had the slightest interest in me. I don't think he even knows my name. He was just polite. He had a word for the servants, too, when he came to call. Once he heard me playing the clavichordium. He complimented me, just to have something nice to say. That's when Helena started imagining things."

"I know, *filha*, but all the same . . ."

Inês cocked her head. "I don't hear any caterwauling. Maybe she's cooled down by now. I'll give her a few more minutes, then I'll go see her."

"Yes, *cara*. That's best. Go and try to mend your bridges."


Truth to tell, Inês Alves didn't particularly care whether she mended any bridges or not, but she knew she had to keep things harmonious. She wished she didn't have to. She wished she could tell her cousin exactly what she thought of her—that Helena da Cunha was a manipulative, thieving little shrew, and if Dom Sebastião had ever actually had the slightest notion of making her his intended, a short amount of time spent in Helena's presence would quickly cure him of that foolhardy notion. But Inês would have to hold her tongue. Especially for her mother's sake.

Inês sighed. Every once in a while she questioned why it was that things had happened as they did. Just eighteen, she was at an age where she should be having eligible suitors asking for her hand from her father, the landowner Dom Martim Alves e de Aragao. Except her father was dead, his land had been taken by his conniving brother- and sister-in-law in payment for some supposed debt—stolen, in Inês's eyes; she was certain that the debt had been fabricated by her avaricious relatives—and she and her mother had been torn from their family home and taken in like stray dogs by those selfsame relatives.

It wasn't supposed to have been that way. Her father's plan had seemed so logical. Three years before he had gone to Prince Henry's court at Sagres—splendidly attired in garments lovingly sewn by Inês and her mother—to listen to a mere squire named Dom Joao Goncalves, known to all as Zarco, paint a glowing picture of sailing off to discover new lands. But convinced by Zarco's words, Dom Martim had decided to join the expedition, scraping together every *soldo* he could lay his hands on to go shares with Zarco. Under Prince Henry's patronage the voyage had taken place, and the gamble had at first seemed to pay off better than anyone had dared hope. The explorers soon returned to report the discovery of an island where no island was supposed to be—a paradise that they had named Madeira. Prince Henry had been overjoyed and proposed colonizing the island immediately, so Inês's father had sailed back to Madeira in a three-ship fleet laden with seeds, tools, and servants to build houses and plant a crop. When that was done, he had told his family, they would join him there.

But the paradise had turned into a hell, and Dom Martim, his body strained to bursting from laboring so hard, had died. Instead of recouping the Alves family fortunes, he had plunged Inês, and her mother deeper into misfortune. Where once the Alves family had had a dozen servants to attend to their every need and a majordomo to manage them smoothly, now they were treated like servants themselves, at the beck and call of the entire da Cunha family—especially the two spoiled daughters.

Inês sighed again. What good did questioning do? There were no answers. What good did it do to think about the past? The past was forever gone. And at that particular moment her future, God help her, seemed to rest in the hands of her cousin Helena.

• • •

"Go away!" Helena screamed. "Go away, go away, go away!"

She flung herself face down on the bed and began snuffling in great whooping gulps, all the meanwhile beating on the embroidered pillow with her fists. The pillow, which Inês had spent so many hours on, sewing by candlelight with red eyes and stiff fingers, was a soggy mess, and so was the marvelous coverlet with the coat of arms and the seed pearls that had been supposed to impress the *condessa* with Helena's prowess as a seamstress.

"There, there, *coitada*," Inês said. "Don't take on so."

A heavy pall of perfume hung in the room. Inês located its source: the smashed remains of at least a dozen of the little glass jars in which Helena had kept her scents and powders and gum benzoin, and which no servant had had the temerity to sweep up yet. The contents of the chest that had contained her trousseau were scattered over the floor as well, and Inês could see that an earnest attempt had been made to rip some of the fine, embroidered pieces apart.

"I want to die!" Helena squalled, kicking her feet like a swimmer.

"No you don't, *querida*," Inês said. "Things will look better tomorrow."

She bent to start picking up some of the scattered things, folding them and putting them back in the chest. The torn ones she put aside. She could go through them later and try to mend some of the least-damaged ones.

"Don't touch those!" Helena ordered shrilly. "Those are *mine*! It's *my* trousseau, you pathetic little churchmouse!" Then, contradictorily, "Take them away! I don't ever want to see any of it again! I hate it! I hate it all!"

Inês ignored the outburst and continued putting things away. "You don't want to say that, Helenazinha," she said soothingly. "It's not the end of the world. You'll have another *noivo*, one you'll love, just wait and see. And then you'll need your trousseau again. These are fine things, expensive things. Any girl would be thrilled to have them."

"Take them! Take them all! I don't want them!"

"You'll feel differently tomorrow."

She clucked to herself over a short-sleeved corset of Byzantine silk that had been crumpled up and flung to the floor, and smoothed out the wrinkles before storing it away. She had made that herself for Helena and, wistfully, had tried it on in front of a mirror before relinquishing it. It gave her a pang to see fine material treated that way.

And then her heart jumped as she picked up something she'd almost forgotten about. It was the *crespina* veil trimmed with the precious leftover scrap of Flemish lace that Helena had stolen from her that day long ago, before her father had died on Madeira.

With only the slightest pause, she folded it neatly and put it back in the chest with the rest of Helena's things. It didn't matter. She never would have had a chance to wear it anyhow; poor relations did not go around flaunting fine clothes. In fact, she thought magnanimously, it was a waste and a pity that Helena had never worn it either—just squirreled it away and probably forgot about it herself.

"There," she said brightly, patting the last piece of linen in place and closing the heavy lid, "at least they won't get stepped on."

"Get *out* of here!" Helena blubbered. She whipped around to a sitting position, her face puffy and her eyes swollen, and gave Inês a look of pure hate. "Get out, get out!"

Inês pursed her lips. "All right, *querida*. I'll take these torn things with me. Maybe I can do something with them."

As she left, she heard the sound of broken glass behind her.


Helena did not come down to dinner that forenoon. Dona Florbella told a servant to go up and ask if she wanted a tray, and the servant, showing some trepidation, tiptoed upstairs, returning a few minutes later to report that the senhorita was not in her room.

"Nonsense!" said Dona Florbella. "You were just afraid to go in, weren't you? Go up again, and knock louder this time."

"I looked inside, and no one was there," the servant insisted.

"Go again, I said, and don't argue with me."

This time the servant returned to say that the senhorita was there now and showed signs of appetite. A tray was loaded in the kitchen with roast beef and savories, and an abundance of the sweets that Helena was so fond of.

"Make it attractive for her," Dona Florbella told the cook.
"Serve it on the gold plate." The cook did this, and for good
measure served the wine in one of the jeweled goblets that
were Dom Rodrigo's pride and joy.

Dom Rodrigo was not present at dinner, for which Inês
was grateful. He had been in a foul temper when he had finally stamped out of the house at about tierce. Inês was not
supposed to know it, but it was hard to keep secrets in a
house full of gossiping servants, and she had found out that
Dom Rodrigo had gone to visit the moneylenders; he had
been counting on the earnest money that a *nobre* of Dom
Sebastião's rank would have paid upon the signing of the
*carta de arras* settling the terms of the marriage.

Inês was glad to be safely back in the little room she
shared with her mother when Dom Rodrigo finally returned. She could hear him barging around the house, looking for trouble. It must have gone badly with the
moneylenders. He still hadn't looked in on Helena an hour
later, when Dona Florbella must have given him an earful.
Inês could hear the nasal voice nagging him, a growl of a reply, and then Dom Rodrigo's heavy footsteps as he climbed
the stairs.

He was only halfway up when a piercing scream came
from Helena's room. The footsteps broke into a run, and
then a door opened on a lot of hysterical quacking from Helena, with impatient interruptions by Dom Rodrigo. They
were joined a few minutes later by the scolding voice of
Dona Florbella, and then the door slammed, muffling further gabble.

"I wonder what *that* was about?" Inês said.

"Never mind," her mother said. "It's nothing to do with
us." She continued sewing, keeping her head down.

Inês went back to her own sewing. She was pleased with
the way it was turning out. A damask pillowcase that she
thought Helena had ripped beyond repair had mended
nicely, and some decorative stitching that would continue
the design was going to make the restoration unnoticeable.

A few minutes later the door to the room burst open without benefit of a knock and Dom Rodrigo was standing over
her, breathing hard. Past his shoulder, framed in the doorway, Inês saw the puffed triumphant face of Helena.

"*Bom dia*, Dom Rodrigo," Dona Beatriz said in a small,

genteel voice that was the sum of whatever courage she could muster to protest the intrusion.

The feeble intervention checked him to the extent of extracting a tight-lipped, "*Bom dia,* Dona Beatriz," from him, but did not deflect him. "So you've rewarded my kindness by stealing my daughter's things!" he bellowed at Inês.

"*Ai!*" Dona Beatriz moaned.

At first Inês thought confusedly that he was referring to the mending she'd taken with her. "No, senhor," she stammered, holding up the pillowcase in her lap, "I only brought this here to sew up a tear."

"Look in the chest, Daddy," Helena said.

Inês stifled a protest as Dom Rodrigo went to her *arca* and flung open the lid. With a feeling of dizziness and unreality, she saw, lying on top of her things, the corset of Byzantine silk that she'd put away for Helena not three hours since.

"So!" Dom Rodrigo said, holding it up for all to see, "this is what jealousy can do!"

"I . . . I didn't . . ." Inês faltered, unwilling to accuse Helena.

"I suppose it got here by itself."

"See if there's anything else, Daddy," Helena said.

Dom Rodrigo rummaged through the chest. Inês noted dully that the neatly folded contents had been previously disturbed.

"Aha, what's this?"

He held up the *cancioneiro,* the illuminated songbook that had been her father's gift to her. She had kept it in the chest for a long time now, ever since Dona Florbella had forbidden her to play Helena's clavichordium, once in a great while taking it out and humming a few measures of a song to herself.

"Is this one of the books from my library?" Dom Rodrigo said.

He didn't even know what books he had in his library. They had been bought like trophies from a commission agent and displayed to impress callers, but he didn't trouble to read them.

"No!" she cried. "That's mine!"

"Where would you get a book like this?" he said. "Did you steal it from someone else?"

"Dom Rodrigo . . . Dom Rodrigo . . . she's telling the

truth . . ." Dona Beatriz quavered. "Please . . . where's Dona Florbella?"

"I told Dona Florbella to absent herself. This is very upsetting for her—her own sister's daughter."

"Please, Dom Rodrigo, I implore you—"

"Remember yourself, senhora!" Dom Rodrigo said sharply, and Dona Beatriz subsided, her chin trembling.

He continued pawing through the chest, throwing Inês's clothing aside, and came up with more items that Helena informed him were from her trousseau. At the bottom, to clinch it, was Dom Rodrigo's jeweled goblet, wrapped in the purloined *crespina* veil.

Inês tried to speak, but Dom Rodrigo silenced her. He spoke with controlled fury to a Dona Beatriz whose face had gone white as flour. "That's what comes of being charitable to one's wife's relatives," he said, his nostrils flaring. "Out of regard for the fact that you are Dona Florbella's sister, senhora, you may continue to have a home here. But I cannot tolerate a thief in the house."

"Get along, you," the jailer said, pushing her.

Inês stumbled on the stone step, then regained her footing. She wrapped her shawl closely around her; it was cold and damp below ground here on the women's side of the Limoeiro, the prison that fronted the big square that did double duty for bullfights and executions. The only light came from narrow grates above, through which, if one craned, one could see the feet of passers-by in the *quarto,* or the faces of men and boys trying to get a glimpse of the women.

"If you please, senhor," Inês said in her smallest voice, "when will I be taken before a judge?"

"Oho, the little *ladra* can't wait to be stripped to the waist and stretched!" the jailer said. "I wouldn't be in such a hurry, little miss. Count yourself lucky to put off the day of examination." He paused, licking his lips. "Although I don't think their Honors would bother to put small fry like yourself to the question as long as you admit your guilt freely."

The jailer's words terrified Inês, and she began to cry.

"I suppose you were going to tell them you didn't do anything," the jailer said. "The Lemon Tree is full of prisoners who didn't do anything. Take my advice and don't make them any angrier with you. You're in enough hot water around here already."

He took her by the elbow and propelled her down the corridor.

"But why?" Inês managed through her misery. "Tell me, senhor, for mercy's sake."

He stopped at a bend in the corridor and backed her up against a wall. "Your people didn't tip anybody, for one thing. How do you expect to eat?"

"I . . . I don't know, senhor."

"You don't expect the prison officials to feed you out of charity, do you?"

"N-no, senhor."

His tone softened a little. "The brothers of the Misericórdia come around to provide assistance to destitute prisoners—bread, soup, a bit of meat. But there's a thirty-day waiting period. What're you going to do till then?"

He had her pressed against the wall. She turned her face away from the garlic on his breath. "I don't know, senhor."

"Do you have any money on you? A coin or two?"

"No, senhor." Sometimes she had handled money in the old days, but she had not seen so much as a copper *dinheiro* since she had gone to live in Dom Rodrigo's house.

"What's that?" He was poking at her shoulder.

"It's only a little clasp, senhor," she said, frightened by him. She had had the plain silver fastening since she was a little girl and never thought anything of it.

"Give it to me," he said. "It'll do for now."

Obediently she unpinned it and handed it over. He pocketed it and released her.

"It won't last you long, mind you," he said. "When your people come to see you, ask them for money."

Inês could not imagine her timorous rabbit of a mother coming to the bullfight square and getting down on her hands and knees to peer through the Limoeiro's grates, or, having located her, tossing coins down. Besides, her mother had as little access to hard money as she had.

The jailer stopped in front of a heavy, iron-bound door with an enormous lock. He produced a large key.

"We'll work something out though, eh, little one?" he said. His hand slipped around her and squeezed a breast roughly.

Inês gasped. Before she could squirm away, he swung the

door open and pushed her inside. "Here you are, ladies, a little fresh meat," he said. "But mind how you behave; she's quality."

A flurry of obscenities answered him. He laughed and slammed the door shut on her. Inês heard a rattle of tumblers falling into place.

She turned to face the women in the room. It was a cold gray chamber of irregular stone, opening up on a gallery of what might have been individual cells in the days when it had been a fortress's dungeon, but which now were merely doorless alcoves that enlarged the principal space. A dingy light came from above, and she glanced upward in time to see a grinning boy's face appear at the thick bars and a grimy hand make a brief, lewd gesture.

"Quality, is it?" came a voice out of the gloom. "Have you come to lord it over us, *princesa minha*?"

"No," Inês said, confused and red-faced. "I'm not ... I'm not ..."

There were forty or fifty women in the cells. Some lay on straw, propping themselves up to have a look at her; some crouched against walls or moved through the dishwater light like aimless wraiths. As her eyes adjusted, Inês picked out individual forms—a ragged, sallow blonde woman nursing an emaciated baby at an elongated breast; a horrid rouged and powdered creature of the streets who was old enough to be a grandmother; a quick, feral, black-eyed girl her own age in the soiled remains of what had been the sequined gown of a rope dancer or jester's *soldadeira;* a country girl with the broad, patient face of an ox; a stringy-haired, half-naked slattern who was looking at her with too much interest.

"Look at the shawl, Sancha," said a sharp-faced *companheira* of the stringy-haired woman, nudging her. "I'll wager you've never worn wool that fine."

"And the dress," said another jade. "Have you ever seen such sewing?"

"Shut up, you sluts," said the woman called Sancha. To Inês, she said, "Well, *menina,* are you going to pay us our *propina?*"

"I ... I don't know what you mean," Inês said.

She heard a chorus of jeers, like the hissing of cats, from all sides.

The woman's eyes narrowed. "Everybody new has to pay their dues, see?"

The other women took up the cry. "*A propina, a propina!*"

"I don't have any money," she said nervously.

"What? Don't tell me that bastard of a turnkey, Gaspar, cleaned you out before you got here? Think now, were you stupid enough to give him your last coin?"

"No . . . I mean . . . I didn't have any money to give him, either."

"What then?" cackled a toothless crone whose only garment was a coarse woolen shift that sagged across a narrow width of bony chest. "Did you scabbard his sword for him on the way?"

"Sword?" guffawed a blowsy woman with unhealthy red patches on her cheeks. "Not Gaspar! Pocketknife's more like it!"

"Better not have taken the edge off him, little miss," put in the sharp-faced woman next to Sancha. "We count on making him grateful, d'you understand? The benefit's not going to go to some snip of a *moca* who's just arrived."

"I didn't . . ." stammered Inês, her cheeks hot as she remembered the hand on her breast. "I mean . . . I gave him my silver pin."

The rouged old wreck of a *meretriz* whom Inês had first noticed spoke out from the pile of straw she sat on. "You're wasting time, *idiotas*. Can't you see she doesn't have anything? You'll have to take her clothes for the *propina*."

The younger women surrounded Inês and pressed in on her. "The shawl's mine," said Sancha's sharp-faced friend. Hands plucked at Inês's clothing, jostled her about. She tried to fend them off, but there were too many. The shawl whipped away, then they were pulling off her dress, her hose, her shoes. In the end she was left with nothing but her shift.

She huddled, bare-armed and shivering, against the far wall. They left her alone after that. She was too miserable and defeated to compete with the others for the food that the turnkey and a pair of *mocos de prisão* brought when evening fell, though everyone seemed to be getting a share despite what the turnkey had said. Light gradually faded from the cellar, and she tried to burrow into the thin pile of straw for a little warmth.

The sounds around her in the darkness subsided after a

while, and she could hear snores and some scattered whispering from the corners.

A little while later somebody came near her, and she was able to tell by the dim and indistinct outline she could see that it was the young dark-haired rope dancer in her cheap spangle-encrusted costume.

"Here, I brought you a manchet of bread," the girl said. "I dipped it in oil and got you a few beans from the soup on top."

"Thank you," Inês said. She wanted to cry, but she didn't dare start. Then she discovered that she was hungry, and she began tearing off pieces of the bread and devouring it. The oil that it had been dipped in bore traces of garlic, giving it flavor.

"I'm Mafalda," the girl said. "I was with a troupe. We had a juggler and a dwarf and a *jograi*. My master was caught stealing—or so someone said. He's to be hanged in the square."

Inês told the girl her name. She said nothing about why she was there, and she was not pressed.

"They're not so bad," Mafalda said with a shrug in the dark toward the other women. "There are one or two you have to watch out for, but most of them have good hearts when you get to know them."

Inês finished the bread. "Thank you," she said, and then she did cry.


A rain of stones came from the cliffs above. "Watch out, *filhos*, or you'll get brained!" the friar cried, reining in his horse and raising his sword to call a halt.

Pedro Costa ducked just in time as a rock the size of his head missed him by inches and bounced down the slope. The knights riding in the forefront were not so fortunate. Pedro heard a rattle of stones against metal armor and a scream of pain as one fist-size missile, hurled with unusual force, hit a *fidalgo* hard enough to dent his cuirass and knock him from the saddle.

The mass of horse and men fell back, in a hubbub of shouts and whinnies. Pedro scurried to the fallen man, and he and another sailor dragged him back out of effective range. The *fidalgo* had lost his helmet, but they made no effort to retrieve it; he was heavy enough, even in half-armor.

"There's one of them now!"

A naked man painted in green and yellow scrambled up the cliffside, effortlessly dodging a hastily thrown ax. He must have been the one who had been bold enough to throw at close range the rock that had done in the *fidalgo*.

"I trow, these Canarian savages are as nimble as their own goats!" swore the knight whose ax had missed.

"That's because they've been interbreeding with them so long," put in a squire. He added a few coarse elaborations that drew ribald laughter out of the bone-weary men around him.

The laughter died down as Fray Goncalo approached, his face grim and the naked sword still in his hand. Despite the heat, he was wearing full armor and a tabard emblazoned with the emblem of the Order of Christ.

"Don't underestimate these savages," the friar said sternly, sitting like a steel statue atop his horse. "They may be as naked as Adam and have nothing but stones and clubs, but they're wonderfully agile and their aim is deadly. They can break a shield with those clubs, and you've seen what their stones can do."

Pedro followed his gaze to the clifftop, where a dozen Canary Islanders stood unconcernedly, staring back at the Portuguese force. They were a strong, well-formed race, taller than most of the Portuguese, with light skin and, many of them, with fair hair. "Guanches," they called their kind, it had been learned from captives who, though they spoke no known language, communicated readily enough with gestures. Like the man who had bounded up the cliff, they were stark naked, except for one huge fellow in a green-and-red-daubed goatskin, who seemed to be a leader. The others had contented themselves with painting their bodies in stripes of vegetable dye.

For the moment they had given up hurling rocks, though two of them were busy levering a boulder to the edge of the cliff in case the Portuguese started up again.

Fray Goncalo's eyes moved to meet those of Pedro, who was crouched over the injured man, trying to loosen the straps of the dented cuirass.

"How is he, *moco*?" the friar said.

Pedro swallowed hard before replying. The *fidalgo* was unconscious, breathing harshly, his face starchy white. Pedro knew him. His name was Dom Sebastião and, so Pedro had heard, he was the second son of a count, but the sailors took him for a nice-enough gentleman who didn't put on airs.

"Not so good, senhor," he said reluctantly. "There's blood at his lips. I think there's something broken inside."

Fray Goncalo frowned and looked up once more at the Canarians standing about at the top of the cliff. "Teach them a lesson," he said to a crossbowman.

With a grin of complicity, the crossbowman put a foot in the stirrup of his weapon and cranked back the cranequin until the trigger was engaged. He raised the stock and took aim, while the natives watched without apparent alarm. There was a twang and the whir of flight, and one of the natives fell with the vanes of a quarrel sprouting from his chest.

The other Canarians disappeared at once, before the crossbowman could wind up his weapon again.

"Now they know about crossbows," someone said. "We won't have that easy a target again."

"They ought to be used to crossbows by now," said someone else.

"These animals are slow to learn. Maybe word didn't spread to the tribes on this side of the island."

Fray Goncalo's second-in-command rode up to him, the visor of his helmet thrown back. "Shall we continue the advance, Dom Goncalo?" he asked breathlessly.

"No," the friar said. "I don't want to risk ambush halfway up. We'll go round by another route."

He gave orders for the wounded to be taken back to the ship. Besides the unconscious Dom Sebastião, there was a knight with a broken arm and a pikeman with a smashed kneecap. The broken arm was able to walk; Fray Goncalo detailed four able-bodied men to carry the other two on litters and sentenced a grumbling squire to lead back the riderless horses.

Pedro picked up his pike again and joined the march. They set off in some semblance of order once more, the mounted knights and squires in the lead, followed by foot soldiers in odd pieces of armor, and then the sailors, armed with pikes, cutlasses, hatchets, or whatever they had been able to acquire. Fray Goncalo skirted the base of the cliff until he found a gentler slope, and the company under his command struggled upward.

Some hours later they stumbled onto the Guanche village.

It was nothing but a collection of primitive huts with thatches made of palm leaves. As soon as the Portuguese appeared, people erupted from the huts and began fleeing madly in all directions. The knights tried to ride some of the painted men down, but they got away into the underbrush, where the horses could not follow. A few of the *cavalieros* dismounted and clanked around in their armor to no avail. The foot soldiers, less encumbered, gave chase and were able to catch a few of the Canarians—mostly women and old people. They led them back to the village, holding on to them tightly.

Fray Goncalo watched, tight-lipped, as his soldiers searched the pathetic huts. Apart from a number of abandoned babies, they found nothing except baskets of dried figs and grain; evidently the Canarians had not the art of grinding grain into flour. Cries of rage came from the surrounding underbrush as the soldiers dumped the baskets on the ground. The Canarians were out of sight, but they were watching.

"They mix the grain with a little goat's milk or water and eat it that way," a foot soldier said contemptuously to Pedro. "How does Fray Goncalo expect to make Christians out of people who don't even know how to bake bread?"

Another soldier had his eye on one of the naked women. "Who cares if they're Christians, *homem*? I'd like to get my hands on the big one, there. I wish Fray Goncalo would give us leave."

"She's swallow you up, *moco*. Anyway, look to your soul."

"It's not my soul that's standing up right now."

Pedro turned away, disgusted. The Canarians might be savages with neither bread nor wine and with no religion but the worship of sun, moon, and planets, but they were people who bled when they were wounded and who fought for their homes and children just like Christians. Quite possibly one of the crying babies in the huts belonged to the woman the soldier was so eager to rape. Prince Henry had forbidden the taking of Canarians as chattels; he wanted them converted, not enslaved. He had even gone so far as to return captured Canarians to their islands and scolded the raiders who had taken them. But raiders continued to ignore Prince Henry's prohibition; selling slaves was often the only way for them to recover their expenses, and the De Castro expedition of which Fray Goncalo was a part was no exception.

"*Voltamos*," Fray Goncalo ordered. "We return." He made a sign, and the trumpeter sounded the retire.

"That's all?" a disgruntled man-at-arms spat. "Just like that?"

"What were you expecting, *homem*?" said the man riding next to him. "Plunder and noble ransoms?"

Pedro fell in with the others and began the weary march to the beach. There was little to show for the foray: a few palm-leaf baskets of figs that had been taken along by some of the soldiers and a handful of miserable captives. Perhaps, Pedro thought, the friar could convert one or two of the old men to Christianity and send them back to preach to their fellows.

The soldier who had been greedy for the woman was holding forth on Guanche customs; he was a veteran of the campaigns on the other islands, and a great expert. "The friar shouldn't be so strict," he was telling the other pikeman. "There's no great harm done. They're used to it. None of their maidens can get married until they sleep with their chief. But first they're fattened up with milk until they're suitable for him. Then, after they're married off, any man can take them."

Pedro did not believe half of it. He trudged on, keeping a wary eye out for the natives who had vanished. He knew how he would feel if he had a wife and someone came along and led her off with a rope around her neck.

He looked ahead at the captives. They were going willingly enough, as if it were beneath their dignity to resist. They walked like kings and queens, holding themselves straight and tall, astonishingly surefooted on the difficult slope, while their captors slipped and stumbled in the loose shale.

"Careful there," he heard Fray Goncalo's voice up ahead. "The path's treacherous here."

The soldiers and horsemen bunched up as the path narrowed before going around a curve. All of a sudden the Canarians were among them, swinging their clubs and chucking stones.

Pedro met the rush of a huge painted fellow who was coming at him, and parried the club with his pike. A shock went through his arms and shoulders as the head of the pike snapped off. He brought the splintered butt up in reverse and rapped it smartly against his opponent's shins. The Canarian howled, but it didn't seem to slow him down. He barged past Pedro, whirling his club at the shield of his next opponent.

Horses snorted and neighed as knights tried to wheel their mounts around to face the foe. Lances were out of the question here, but most of them had freed a sword arm and were looking for someone to hack at. A shield rang like a bell as a club struck it, and Pedro heard a cry of rage. Near him a pikeman had unlimbered a short-sword and was striking out with it, but a stone thudded against the steel cap he wore, and he crumpled to the ground. All around him Pedro caught confused flashes of red-and-green-striped bodies, milling horses, pikes bobbing in the air like a wheat crop.

Then the Canarians, just as suddenly, were gone. There were no more targets to strike at. The press of men and horses expanded and contracted as the troop tried for some sort of order.

The prisoners were gone, too. There was no sign of any of them, except a naked and painted old man with a spear sticking out of his back.

The Portuguese took stock of their own. Armor had saved most of them, though there were a couple of broken shields, as Fray Goncalo had warned. The pikeman Pedro had seen struck in the head by a rock was alive, but he would have to be carried. As for the rest, there were a lot of limps among them, assorted bruises, and no doubt some cracked ribs.

Fray Goncalo got them moving toward the beach again. The men were sullen, quarrelsome. "We'll never subdue these cursed islands," groused the man marching next to Pedro. "Two thousand men, a hundred and twenty horses, and we can't get the better of a lot of naked *primitivos*. They say the transport alone cost the infante forty thousand gold *dobras*. If so, he's not getting his money's worth. What a wasted day's work this was! No booty for us, no souls for the friar, good men injured! And now, not even a slave or two to show for our trouble!"

• • • •

Pedro said nothing, but in fact he did not particularly care whether they got booty, souls, or slaves. The adventure itself was sufficient reward for him. How far he had come in the last five years—and how incredible the journey! The son of a simple fisherman in the small coastal village of Sagres, Pedro had had his life radically altered, his destiny irrevocably changed, by one of the most renowned men alive, Prince Henry, third son of the well-loved John the Bastard.

In 1420, five years earlier, when Henry, the hero of all Christendom since his victory over the Moors at Ceuta in 1415, had returned, covered with fresh glory, from North Africa, he had declined to bask in his celebrity. Refusing the honors of the Pope and the crowned heads of Europe, he had decided to retire in obscurity to the bleak and windswept promontory of Sagres, where the world ended and the chin of Portugal jutted out into the Ocean of Darkness. He had swooped down on poor startled Sagres with only a skeleton household, and as there hadn't been enough servants to do the work, local labor had been recruited for the rougher tasks. A well-muscled youth, Pedro Costa had been hired as a kitchen boy whose usual task was cleaning fish in the scullery—though he had been far more comfortable pulling an oar or hauling his father's nets than pussyfooting around the high and mighty.

As a simple kitchen worker Pedro never encountered any of Henry's minions, much less the great prince himself. But one day he had by chance been pressed into service to bear Prince Henry's food on a tray to his room, where it was to be left outside the door. Bartolomé, an old soldier who had fought beside Henry at Ceuta and who had been given the job as the prince's household constable, was impressed by young Pedro's diligence and shrewdness. Bartolomé had enthralled the youth with stories of past battles against the Moors and suggested that he, too, might well become a sailor in Prince Henry's fleet and have a chance at adventure.

Bartolomé had quickly been proven right, for later that day Pedro had in turn met the prince and, providentially, one of Henry's squires, João Goncalves—called Zarco—who had been in attendance to convince his prince to back an expedition that would sail into the Sea of Darkness and find the legendary Isle of the Saints, a paradise *toda madeira*—covered with wood. Henry had agreed, and Zarco had taken

Pedro aboard as a ship's boy for his first voyage, bestowing the embellishment of "*da* Costa" to his surname, and promising that if he proved himself, he would be promoted to ordinary seaman for the next voyage.

And so Pedro, nearly dizzy with his good luck, had sailed off on the first of his voyages into the dangerous, exhilarating unknown—this latest of which had landed him on an inhospitable island to be attacked by painted savages.

Like the other captains of the De Castro expedition, Fray Goncalo had bivouacked most of his force on the beach, leaving only a small complement on board to defend his ship. But the sailors, with their normal duties still to perform, returned to the big two-masted *nau* at night to sleep. Pedro paused at the water's edge to sniff the air. He smelled roast goat—someone had bagged fresh meat for the pot. Regretfully he clambered into the longboat with his crewmates; for them tonight it would be salt pork and hardtack.

As soon as his watch was finished, he went aft to inquire after Dom Sebastião. The *fidalgo* was still alive and had regained consciousness, he had learned. They had carried him to one of the tiny cabins that were reserved for officers in the sterncastle. A few knights and squires were lounging about, polishing their equipment. Pedro stopped short of them and, cap in hand, inquired timidly after Dom Sebastião.

"He's fine, just a few broken ribs," one of the knights said brusquely. "What's it to you, *moco*? Be off."

"Thank you, senhor," Pedro said. "I just wanted to see if he was all right. He didn't look so good when I first got to him." He turned to go.

"Is that the sailor who dragged me back to safety?" came a voice from the open doorway of one of the cubbyholes. "Send him in."

Pedro, a little flustered, entered. It was dark inside—no candles were allowed on the ship except one for the captain and one for the compass—but enough of the afternoon's dying light diffused through the opening for Pedro to make out the interior after his eyes adjusted.

"They told me how you risked your neck to pull me out of range of the rock shower—I owe you a debt of thanks for

that, my friend," Dom Sebastião said. He laughed, somewhat weakly. "But why didn't you go back for my helmet? I
paid a master armorer in Lisbon good money for it."

He was half sitting up on a narrow straw pallet. The surgeon had stripped him to his codpiece, and his torso was
wrapped tightly in bandages. Even in the dim light Pedro
could see how pale he was, but there was no blood on his
lips, at least.

Pedro began to stammer an apology for the helmet. "I'm
sorry, senhor, but everything was happening so fast. . . ."

Dom Sebastião, like the gentleman he was, acted at once
to end Pedro's embarrassment. Changing to a solemn expression, he said, "Don't take me seriously, *meu amigo*. I was
only joking. I'm glad to be alive."

"I thought you were done for, senhor, when I saw blood
at your mouth," Pedro said, relieved. "I thought that *ladrão*
had crushed your chest for certain."

"The *cirurgião* who came to bind me up told me I'd bit-
ten my lip through—that's where the blood came from.
When my ribs heal, I'll be as good as new. If I hadn't been
wearing a cuirass, though, I'd have been a goner."

Pedro nodded. "We've lost some good men, trying to take
these islands. We may not be fighting against swords and
crossbows, but it's a dangerous business all the same."

"Still," Dom Sebastião said, his smile coming back, "I'd
rather be here facing Canarian warriors than be in Lisbon
facing the mother of a certain girl who wants to be married
to me. I escaped just in time."

"That's fortunate, Vossa Excelência," Pedro said, uncertain
of how to respond to the confidence.

"The mother's a dragon and the father's a conniver—he
even tried to buy into the De Castro expedition for commercial profit, thinking he could ingratiate himself with Prince
Henry that way. If I'd stayed in Lisbon, they'd have had me
plucked, stuffed, and delivered to the altar by now."

Pedro defended the unknown gentleman. "Perhaps he
thought the Canaries were the same case as Madeira. Many
fine *cavalhieros* are investing in Madeira now—the infante
encourages it."

Amused, Dom Sebastião said, "What do you know about
Madeira, son?"

"I served on the ship that discovered it," Pedro admitted.

"You were with Zarco?" Dom Sebastião said, raising his eyebrows.

"*Sim, senhor.*"

"You're a young man to have been part of such a large piece of history, my friend. What do you plan to do when this Canaries expedition is over?"

"I'm just a sailor, senhor."

"Come, come, don't be modest. You know what you want to do."

Pedro flushed. Trying to keep the pride out of his voice, he said, "Fray Goncalo Velho promised Prince Henry that he would attempt the passage of Cape Non for him. I think I have a good chance of being part of his crew."

"Well said! But you may have to wait a while. First we have to clean up these islands. If it doesn't go well, there may be a further delay before Fray Goncalo can afford to mount a dangerous expedition down the coast of Africa. He's poured a considerable amount of his own money into this ill-fated Canaries venture, and he's overextended. He was counting on a generous reward from the infante, and if the expedition fails and that isn't forthcoming, well . . ."

"Do you think it will fail, senhor?"

Dom Sebastião shrugged, and showed by an immediate grimace that his ribs regretted this insult to them. "You know as well as I do that our supplies are running low, and that so far we've shown no results to speak of. The Canarians resist being converted as stubbornly as ever—and now a prisoner taken by one of the other captains claims that the chiefs are planning to raise five thousand fighting men from all the islands to converge on us here. The captains are meeting tonight with De Castro aboard his flagship to decide what to do."

Pedro thrust out his chin. "Dom Goncalo won't break his promise to Prince Henry. I was there when he gave it, and I know."

"No, he's a dedicated man," Dom Sebastião agreed. "But if there's a delay while he licks his wounds, what will you do then?"

Pedro thought it over soberly. "I can always go back to Zarco. He's still trying to populate his island. I can always get a job as one of his ferrymen."

"I've heard it said that Zarco's been given leave to empty the prisons if he has to. Is that true?"

"Yes, senhor. I heard the infante say so with my own ears."

"That would be something. *Degredados* for colonists."

Pedro said nothing. There were a few *degredados* aboard De Castro's fleet. Having no rights, they were expendable. They were always given the most dangerous jobs—including being human bait when necessary. Pedro had seen some of them commit acts of bravery that would have done credit to a *fidalgo*. Perhaps they had been criminals once, but he thought no less of them for it.

Dom Sebastião was showing signs of fatigue. He tried to shift his position and drew a sharp breath at the pain. Pedro helped get him settled more comfortably, then said, "I'd better go now, senhor. You need your rest."

"Thanks, *filho*." He managed a tired smile. "Don't be discouraged by my pessimism. Perhaps you won't have to become a ferryman for convicts if we're lucky. We may all go home with a scrap of glory yet. It all depends on what the captains decide tonight."

The meeting was a long one. It was well into the midnight watch when Fray Goncalo was rowed back to the ship. Pedro, curled up on deck in his accustomed place but unable to sleep, saw him come aboard. His face was grim. He swept past the captain of the watch without a word and closed himself in his cabin.

By morning rumors were all over the ship. Fray Goncalo did not appear for the dawn prayer, which was unusual. The captain of the watch, after waiting a few minutes, led the men in a ragged recitation of the paternoster and Ave Maria. Fray Goncalo emerged while they were still assembled amidships. He had spent a sleepless night, to judge by the hollows under his eyes.

"You've fought well, *filhos*," he told them, his face hard as iron. "But it was not God's will to grant us victory. Dom Fernando has cancelled the expedition. We sail for home tomorrow."

# CHAPTER 3

"No traitors," Zarco said.

The warden pulled at a protruding lower lip. He was a swarthy, corpulent man with a vulture's beak of a nose—a well-to-do tradesman who had bid successfully for the office of jailer in return for the privilege of collecting fees from the prisoners and forwarding a percentage to the *alcaide-mór,* the official responsible for policing the city.

"We have a very fine traitor in the dungeons at the moment, Your Excellency," he said. "A *fidalgo* of good family. His treason wasn't serious—just an affair of young hotheads and a few words uttered carelessly in a tavern."

"No," Zarco said with finality. "I want no one who was convicted of treason, theft, or any offense against religion."

"What about murderers, senhor?" the warden asked.

"Murderers, all right, as long as they're honest," Zarco said. "But we can't afford thieves or traitors in a new colony."

"Debtors? Beggars? Rapists?"

"Debtors are fine. I'll take beggars if they're able-bodied. As for rapists, they won't have much opportunity on Madeira. We're short of women."

The warden laughed. "In that case I'll give you a fellow named Lobo I'd like to get rid of. He's a murderer *and* a rapist."

"Is he able-bodied?"

"*Sim.* A very strong man. But incorrigible."

Privately he was thinking that the arrival of this Zarco, who bore the fishy title of "Count of the Chamber of Wolves," but who brought with him a bona fide order from Prince Henry for the release of any prisoners he could use, was a heaven-sent opportunity to cull out prisoners like Lobo, from whom fees could no longer be extracted. But he had no intention of giving up his more profitable prisoners.

"That doesn't worry me," Zarco said. "We'll take him in hand."

"I don't know how much help we'll be in alleviating your shortage of women, though. They're mostly trulls and trollops. But I can show you a few respectable types." He brightened. "We've got a fine healthy murderess waiting to be hanged just now—poisoned her husband. They were going to try her as a witch, but it became obvious that it was just a civil case."

"Let's go see the men," Zarco said. "Then I'll have a look at the women."

A hammering came from above, through the grate. Mafalda, the rope dancer, leaned closer to Inês and whispered, "That's the carpenters building the scaffold for poor Gabriela. Pretend you don't notice."

Inês could not help stealing a glance in the direction of the condemned woman. Gabriela herself, if she was distressed by the sound, did not show it. She was a large, handsome, forceful woman with heavy black brows, still neatly clad, despite her long incarceration, in a decent wool dress and shawl. She sat, a little aloof, sipping her bowl of soup as calmly as if she were in her own kitchen and ignoring the respectful stares that were coming her way.

"They're going to hang her in a sack, for decency's sake," Mafalda confided.

"Don't tell me any more," Inês said.

She made herself finish her own soup, though she had little appetite for it. She knew the hunger would come later if she didn't. The brothers of the Misericórdia came only three times a week to supplement the rations of the needy. Otherwise there was only the inadequate provender grudgingly allowed by the prison authorities—though the position of those without funds was not quite as bad as the warders painted to newcomers when they tried to extract money from them. There was enough bread to keep body and soul together and usually a thin cabbage soup with a few broadbeans or lentils in it. Then, too, some of the better-off women would sometimes stand a treat when their friends outside had been generous. Most of the women here, whatever kind of life they had lived, weren't bad sorts, once you got to know them. The ritual of the *propina* had to be gone through by newcomers, but after they'd been plucked, even Sancha and her gang left them pretty much alone. Inês had even acquired a dress to replace the one that had been taken from her; it was a tattered thing that no one wanted, from the meager chest of castoffs brought around on occasion by the good brothers, but it kept her warm at night and spared her the leers of the turnkeys.

"Her husband raped her daughter," Mafalda said. "That's why she killed him. But she shouldn't have used poison. She's lucky not to be burned."

Inês blushed. Mafalda's conversation left a lot to be desired. But Inês didn't have the heart for a rebuff. The seamy side of life was all the gypsy girl knew, though she was no older than Inês. Mafalda was impressed by her breeding and her virginity and had taken it upon herself to look out for her.

"My father sold me to the *jograis* when I was nine," Mafalda went on, "but first he had me himself. I was lucky, though. The minstrel who owned me never treated me as a common *meretriz*. He never sold me to a man I said I disliked, or let anyone hurt me, the way some of them like to do. He knifed a man once to protect me—we had to leave that town in a hurry!"

Now Inês really was blushing, and Mafalda noticed. She put a hand on Inês's arm and said, "I'm sorry, *santa*. I shouldn't talk of such things—and to a *virgem* like yourself!"

"It's all right, *cara*," Inês said in a strained voice.

Mafalda became lively. "Look, Sancha's sending wine to Gabriela!"

Inês peered through the gloom. Sancha and her cronies had been having a little party of their own, and now one of her satellites was carrying a jar of wine over to the condemned woman and offering it to her. Gabriela looked up with a steady expression, showing no reaction, gave a little shrug, and accepted the jar. Holding it with both hands, she took a swig, set it down, wiped her lips on the back of her hand, then picked the jar up again for another drink. Sancha's hanger-on hovered uncertainly, but when Gabriela showed no further sign of noticing her, she went back to the group of slatterns she had come from. Sancha raised her frowzy head and called out, "Drink up, *minha*! I'll see that you get another jar before they take you away."

"She's not such a bad soul," Inês said. "She has a good heart in spite of everything."

"Maybe," Mafalda said doubtfully.

There was a noisy rattle of bolts at the door, and the turnkey scuttled inside, falling all over himself to bow in the warden and an important-looking gentleman who was dressed flamboyantly in a scarlet cloak, gold-embroidered doublet, and multicolored hose, with a heavy gold chain around his neck and a jewel-hilted sword at his side.

. "Holy Mother!" said Mafalda. "Who's he?"

Inês stared wide-eyed at the handsome, reckless face with its weathered features and startling blue eyes and almost stopped breathing.

It was Zarco.

At the sight of the *fidalgo* in his splendid attire, the assorted strumpets in the dungeon set up a din. One old crone pulled her chemise open to uncurtain her withered breasts and cackled, "Come to have a look around, my fine *cavalheiro*? Don't pay any attention to those cheap trulls, Your Honor—old Clara knows how to show you a fancy time!"

"Shut up, you sluts!" the turnkey shouted. He shook a fist at the crone. "Keep your mouth shut, Clara, or I'll give you a knock on the head."

The *fidalgo* was frowning. The warden, a large fleshy man, turned to him with an ironic smile and said, "You see how it is, Vossa Excelência. Well, let's cull them out."

Inês shrank against the damp wall, her heart pattering at high speed. Mafalda said, "What's the matter? Aren't you feeling well?"

"I'm all right," Inês said, her breath coming short. She was ready to die of shame. Her mother hadn't thought much of Zarco—though Inês had never been able to understand why. He had been her father's captain on the two voyages that were supposed to have saved the family fortunes, after all, and she had thought him a dashing figure. It was too much to bear, that he should see her like this, bringing disgrace on the Alves name. She didn't know what she would do when he recognized her.

"You're white as a sheet," Mafalda said. "Are you going to faint?"

The dungeon dimmed and swung in great circles around her. She wanted to faint, but she fought her dizziness; fainting would only make Zarco notice her that much sooner.

"Listen to me, ladies," the warden said, looking around him with his hands on his hips. "This is Dom João Goncalves, the count of Camara dos Lobos, but you can call him Zarco because of those baby blue eyes of his. He's come here to do you a favor—some of you, at least. You can stay here in this hellhole if you want, or, if you're strong and willing and able to bear children, you can be free women, and get married and live in a paradise."

Zarco stepped forward. He had a wide, compelling smile. "I can guarantee husbands for everybody, at least," he said. "Now let me tell you about Madeira. . . ."

Inês hardly followed what he said. The details blurred together in Zarco's deep, persuasive voice. But she absorbed the outline of it. It was her father's old dream—but gone bad. She could be a colonist on Madeira—marry a *degredado,* one of the exiles who were being let out of the prisons. Women would be at a premium, outnumbered by the *degredados* ten to one. You could choose a good man, work hard, get rich.

Zarco finished. It had been a rousing little speech. The women crowded around him, clamoring.

"Not too close!" the turnkey shouted. "Get back!" He struck with his fist at a woman who had been clawing at Zarco, and knocked her sprawling. The rest of them fell back a little.

"None of that," the warden said. "Go sit down. Senhor Zarco will have a look around. He'll be the one to decide." He turned to jeer at the old crone who had bared her breasts. "What are you hanging around for, Clara? Think anyone's going to believe that shriveled old womb of yours could bring forth babies? It's been dried up since before Gaspar here was born."

"Maybe that's why he keeps trying to crawl into it," the crone jeered back, and the turnkey smiled weakly.

Zarco made his rounds swiftly and impersonally, his charm popped back into its bottle and corked now that his speech of exhortation was over. He looked briefly into faces and ran his eyes dispassionately over figures, rarely speaking to the women directly but instead turning to ask questions of the warden. Gabriela was one of the first women he chose. Inês saw her nod gravely, then stand up to show her readiness.

"*A Virgem Santíssima!*" Mafalda breathed. "My prayers have been answered. It's a miracle. She won't die after all."

Zarco was showing signs of impatience and dissatisfaction by the time he got around to the cranny where Inês and Mafalda were sitting. There were not many more women to go, and out of the whole ward he had collected barely twenty, even including Sancha and her drabs, whom he had taken as a body.

"See what I mean?" the warden was saying as they approached. "There just aren't that many who are suitable, even if you lower your standards and take some of the younger sluts whose offenses were religious. Like that girl with the big *peitos* who blasphemed against the saints. What does something like that mean when it's done in the heat of a brawl in a brothel? It's not as if the girl denied the saints with the intention of abjuring her faith. It's only a case of the free expression of the emotions of the moment. If she were a noble, she'd get a fine for it. Even a peasant would get off with a needle through the tongue and a whipping at the pillory. The magistrate must have had a sour stomach that day to remand her here for burning. She's been here a month. She's repented ten times over already. Look at those hips! She'll make lots of babies for you on Madeira."

Zarco stopped in front of Inês and Mafalda. Inês turned her face to the wall. Zarco took her by the chin and with surprising gentleness turned her face toward him.

"What's this one in for?" he said.

The warden hesitated. Inês could tell that he was deciding whether or not to lie. Finally he said, "Thievery, Your Excellency, but it was only an affair of a handkerchief. It was a relative who brought the charge. A family matter. You know how such things can get blown up. You can see the girl's of good family. With the collection of trollops and harpies you're taking with you, you can't afford to pass up one like this."

Inês sat rigid with fear. Zarco had not recognized her—had not connected her with the young girl with whom he had had a conversation in her father's fig orchard so long ago. She had grown since then, and in her present surroundings, with her straggly hair and torn dress and a face that was thin with hunger, she must have changed greatly in appearance anyway.

"Hmmm." He looked more closely at her, frowning to himself. "What's your name, girl?"

Her teeth chattering, she tried to talk. But her tongue would not utter the Alves name, the name of her father, that she had shamed.

"Her name's Inês, Your Honor," Mafalda volunteered. "She's a little shy. She's a real lady."

Zarco switched his attention to Mafalda. "What's her offense?"

"Rope dancer, Vossa Excelência," the warden replied. "Harlotry, causing a public disturbance, staying in a town longer than the three days allowed to *soldadeiras*—you name it. The rest of the troupe slipped through our fingers, but we caught up with this one."

"She looks like a strong girl," Zarco said. "Send her along with the others."

"Don't send me into exile, Your Honor," Mafalda pleaded. "I wouldn't know what to do."

Zarco appeared not to have heard her. "I'll take both of them," he said.


Lisbon's bright blue harbor, formed by the widening of the Tagus River on its way to the sea and broad enough to itself be given the name of the Sea of Straw, sparkled in the shafts of sunlight that were starting to pierce the early-morning mists. Beyond rose the hills of the city, spilling red-tiled roofs down to a busy waterfront. The river current tugged at the cables of Zarco's fleet, slapping gently at the sides of the three ships. They were big ships this time—bulky three-masted *nāos* with two decks and lofty sterns—a far cry from the small open *barchas* in which Zarco and Teixeira had sailed when they first made their discovery.

Pedro tossed a line to the coxswain in the bobbing craft

below and helped make him fast. The boat was full of women—women in tatters of clothes—and sailors were crowding the rails to have a look. Some of the women had made an effort to make themselves decent and presentable in the mended remnants of old gowns, but others were in a pitiable state. Pedro averted his eyes from one woman who was clad in little more than drawers and a shift, only to encounter the frank stare of a tangle-haired hoyden—a gypsy girl by the look of her—in a filth-encrusted ruin of a spangled gown that was slit to the hip, showing all of a lean brown leg. He colored and turned away.

"We're going to have the very devil of a time keeping the men away from them," said a ship's carpenter standing next to Pedro. "Those jailbirds down there will be through that barrier like rats gnawing through a cupboard unless we watch them every minute."

Pedro had worked through the night with him to help erect the oak partition below decks that would separate the male convicts from the women. Zarco had decreed that all chains be removed, to give them a start at being colonists, though they would be locked up except for exercise periods.

The male convicts who had so far been taken aboard were in as bad a condition as the women, but Zarco, with the help of the brothers of the Misericórdia, had made arrangements for fresh clothing to be distributed to the needy of both sexes on arrival in Madeira.

Pedro waited at the top of the boarding ladder with a couple of other sailors to give the women a hand. One woman with a baby was unable to climb with her burden, and a sailor in the boat sprang to take it from her and pass it up to Pedro; even then, the mother needed help, and she thanked Pedro with a wan smile when he handed the starveling infant back to her. The gypsy girl swarmed up the rungs, as limber as any man, and tossed her matted hair at the watching sailors before following the others below. After her came a pretty thing with dark hair and delicate features, in an old torn dress that she had mended skillfully—against what handicaps of borrowed needle and thread painfully unraveled from rags Pedro could only guess at.

"*Obrigado, senhor,*" she said as she took his proffered hand. Her voice startled him; she spoke in the refined accents of the privileged class, the middle nobility at least, and he could not imagine what she was doing among all these unfortunates.

"*De nada, senhora,*" he stammered, and she rewarded him with a warm smile before hurrying ahead to catch up with the gypsy girl.

Zarco sailed on the ebb tide. Aided by the pull of the river current, he did not hoist the *não*'s big square sails, but maneuvered with only the small lateen sail that Morales had rigged on the mizzenmast. It was an idea derived from the success Morales had had with the small standing lugsail that he had rigged for the *barcha*. Prince Henry had been enthusiastic. "We must think of new ways of doing things, now that we are venturing out into the Sea of Darkness!" he had boomed, darting an imperious glance around his audience hall to make sure that all the noble hangers-on and loitering hopefuls were taking in the import of Morales's ideas. "Some day we will know its winds and currents as well as we know those of our familiar waters, but until then we must be flexible. Yes—a combination of square sails for running before the wind, a lateen rig for close-hauled work." He gave an approving nod. "A lateen sail with a short luff makes a fine fore-and-aft sail for maneuvering in unfamiliar waters. With the leading edge tilted forward sharply on the spar, the greater part of the triangle is behind the mast, and the dangers of coming about are less pronounced. And by placing it on the mizzen instead of forward, with the greatest spread of canvas reserved for the square sail on the mainmast, we won't have the ship wallowing with its nose in the sea when the running is good!" He favored Morales with a man-to-man frown. "I grant you that a *não* is a clumsy ship for such an innovation, but still, the principle is sound, and perhaps some day we will design another sort of vessel— with a lighter, cleaner hull—that will handle better with such a rig. In the meantime it's important not to be hidebound, eh? At least we're gaining experience all the time."

Pedro was pleased to be sailing with Morales again. It gave one a feeling of confidence to have the squat, ugly Spaniard at the helm. It was to Zarco's credit, fine gentleman though he had become, that he still retained his respect for superior talent where seamanship was concerned.

He watched Morales now, standing by the mizzenmast where he could shout orders down an open hatch to the burly helmsman who was working blindly below, throwing his weight against the huge rudder tiller on command, while at the same time he could watch every flutter of the lateen sail to keep it in perfect trim. Not a puff of breeze or a surge of the Tagus current was wasted. Pedro felt the pure pleasure of seeing an artist at work.

It was not until the three ships were far enough out to sea to be free of the land breeze that Morales ordered the two square sails unfurled. Pedro saw him catch the first whiff of the prevailing northeasterly before anyone else did, raising his grizzled head to sniff like an old cart horse discovering a familiar track. *"Leva as velas redondas!"* Morales bawled joyfully, and Pedro sprang with the others to obey.

Only when the little fleet was settled on its southern course and tackle set did Zarco allow the *degredados* to come out on deck for fresh air and exercise. By that time only a few hours of daylight were left, and Zarco limited them to half-hour outings in groups of twenty-five to give everyone a chance. A sort of waist-high pen had been constructed amidships to keep them confined. The convicts kept trying, by one means or another, to get past the barrier, and Zarco was forced to station a number of sailors armed with belaying pins to keep them confined. Pedro, pressed thus into service, found himself glad of the barrier and the sea breezes. Sailors were apt to be fragrant, but he was used to his shipmates, who at least slept in the open air, with the occasional rain shower or accidental drenching from a heavy sea to keep them from becoming overripe. But the *degredados*, with the prison aroma still clinging to them, were more pungent still, even after only one day at sea. It was going to get worse during the ten days or two weeks that the voyage would require. Being shut up in the stifling space between decks in the tropical heat, with the bilge sloshing below to add its effluvium, was going to be hell. He felt sorry for them, villains though they might be.

He watched them now as they gambled with dice, cracked fleas, paced the deck as they must have paced their cells, or just stared out to sea. Well, it would be a new life for them. Perhaps they would make something of it.

Astern, across a heaving sea, Pedro could make out the square foresail of Teixeira's ship, emblazoned with the bold red cross of the Order of Christ, and behind it the sails of the ship carrying most of the tools, livestock, and seeds. Teixeira was transporting the free settlers—mostly ordinary

people from the Algarve with a sprinkling of additional nobles whom Zarco had recruited—in somewhat greater comfort. There were almost as many of them as there were
*degredados*. Zarco and Teixeira had promised the
*degredados* that they would make no distinctions in the
colony—once on Madeira they would be judged only by
their ability to work hard. Pedro's eyes sifted through the
crowd to try to pick out those who might have been laborers
or peasants, fishermen or craftsmen before running afoul of
the law. Zarco would need them.

"Psst, *moco* . . ."

Pedro turned warily to confront a shaggy-haired, shelf-
browed customer with shifty eyes.

"How about letting me through to pay a visit to the after-
deck garden?"

Pedro was alert to this dodge. During the first shift Zarco
had allowed the convicts out of the pen one or two at a time
so that they could use the wooden seats hanging over the
taffrail, only to find that they were wandering through the
ship to steal any small objects they could lay their hands on,
or to get into the wine casks. He had put a stop to it by having some planks and rope handholds suspended from the
amidships bulwarks that adjoined the pen.

"You've got your own garden over there to starboard
now," Pedro said.

"Have a heart, *moco*," the shaggy-haired man said. "A fellow could fall in."

"Didn't I see you on deck with the first group? And
weren't you one of those allowed aft to the garden then?"

"What of it?" the other said sullenly. "This stinking hulk
would give anyone loose bowels."

"Use the amidships planks," Pedro said. "Or if you don't
want to do that, go below and use the buckets. And how did
you get a second turn on deck anyway?"

"You're too smart for me, *homem*. All right, I'll tell you
the way of it. Let me past and I'll make it worth your
while."

"*Chega*. Get going. Don't try to bribe me."

"Listen, I can get you one of the women tonight."

"They're not yours to sell. Get going, I said."

"Or you could find a knife between your ribs after we get
to Madeira."

The man gripped the barrier with two hairy paws and

made as if to climb over. Pedro took a step forward. The man looked at the width of Pedro's shoulders and the thickness of his forearms and took his hands off the rail.

"All right, *moco*," he said, baring large yellow teeth in a snarl. "Remember what I said about the knife."

He sauntered off. A moment later Pedro saw him pause to talk to two dice players. He didn't like what he was hearing, because he grabbed a handful of one man's hair, forced his head back, and with his free hand helped himself to the winnings. He flicked a contemptuous finger against the man's face and walked away.

A sailor named Lucio came up to Pedro and said, "I saw Lobo pick you out for a chat. Did he try to bribe you?"

"Lobo?"

"That's what the other *degredados* call him—wolf. Shows you what kind of man he is. They're a pack of wolves themselves, but he moves among them as if they were a flock of sheep, taking what he wants."

"Is that how he got an extra turn on deck?"

"I wouldn't doubt it. Intimidated some poor devil, or beat him up. I shouldn't say they're all wolves. Some are just whipped curs."

"He tried to bribe me, all right."

"With what?" Lucio's plain face showed frank curiosity.

"I don't know. Then he tried to sell me a woman."

"You turned him down on both counts?"

"Yes."

"You were wise, *moco*. Lobo's bribes are worthless. He only tries them when threats won't serve."

"He tried those too. He offered to slip a knife between my ribs."

Lucio smiled without humor. "That, I'd take more seriously than one of his offers of a bribe. He offered Barros a gold ring to let him through after he'd already been out once and escorted back by a petty officer who found him sniffing around one of the cabins. Barros, like a fool, took it, and then it developed that one of the *fidalgos*, Dom Gonzalo, was missing a gold ring." Lucio looked around to see who was near and lowered his voice. "What could Barros do? The ring was worthless to him. He didn't dare be caught with it on him. I told him to drop it somewhere on deck when no one was looking. Then Dom Gonzalo would think it just turned up. Or whoever found it would keep it, and it would become *their* problem. But he was afraid. So he threw it into the sea."

Pedro was growing uncomfortable. He began to edge away; he did not want to know about such things. Lucio detained him with a hand on his arm and a last remark.

"Lobo's someone to stay away from. He's trouble."

When the next party of *degredados* made their way to the deck a little while later, Pedro saw Lobo among them again. He was rubbing his knuckles. Some other, weaker convict had lost his turn in the fresh air again. Pedro watched the shaggy brute try to suborn another seaman, but the officers were watching closely, and he had no luck. Lobo prowled the deck restlessly, and at last squatted down among some men who were passing around a bottle. They all looked to be drunk. Lobo took the bottle from the man who had it and helped himself to a long drink. He wiped his mouth on the back of one hairy hand and gave back whatever was left. He tried to get their drunken attention and, finding it insufficient, gave one of the men a series of small, quick, light slaps on the face. The man finally responded and roused himself to follow Lobo to a spot by the rise of the poop that offered relative privacy after Lobo drove off a man who was lounging against the rail. There they transacted some business that involved a third man and the passing of another bottle of wine that appeared somehow from a hiding place. Pedro kept an eye on Lobo during the rest of the shift, but the beetle-browed convict seemed to have given up further attempts to talk his way out of the enclosure for the time being.

Perhaps Lobo had had enough fresh air. He did not appear on deck with the next two batches of male prisoners, and Pedro forgot about him. Daylight was almost gone by then, and it was time for the female convicts to have their airing.

Half an orange sun sat on the western horizon, casting a shimmering path across the wrinkled sea. Though the sky was still too light for stars, Venus was already out, a brilliant white point to the right of the drowning sun. The wind was beginning to shift with the approach of nightfall, and Morales had changed the set of the yards to adjust the windage of the square sails the few necessary degrees.

It was good that there was nothing much to do at the moment, because every sailor who could do so without deserting a post had positioned himself where he could see the emerging women. Pedro, still on guard duty, was one of the lucky ones. He found himself standing shoulder to shoulder with Lucio at the rail of the convict enclosure while an officer shooed away idle men.

"Stand back," the officer said. "Here they come. Get away from here. Don't you have anything to do?"

The women struggled up the companionway one by one. There were about thirty-five of them. They were more cooperative than the men. They had organized themselves to help one another. Pedro saw them pass the baby up the ladder to the sickly woman who was its mother. The slop buckets came up the same way, and a couple of women, with no fuss or complaints, went about the business of emptying them into the ocean. There was no question of any of the women using the outboard seats, despite the lewd surmises Pedro had been hearing from his shipmates all day; even the aft garden hung under the curve of the poop for the crew didn't offer enough privacy.

"Excuse me, senhor, could you find us a rope so that we can lower a bucket and draw seawater?"

Pedro almost jumped out of his skin at the soft voice that had come unexpectedly from his left while he was staring in the opposite direction.

"But certainly, senhora," he stammered.

It was the girl he'd noticed before, the one with the genteel accent of the middle-class nobility, whose ragged gown had been repaired so neatly. She was embarrassed at the nature of her errand and had left the slop bucket by the bulwark.

Pedro found her a length of rope and a piece of iron to weight the bucket. "I'll get you a new bucket, senhora," he promised, "so you won't have to use the same one to draw water."

"You're very kind, senhor," she said.

They faced each other awkwardly for a moment, not sure of what more to say. Finally Pedro offered hesitantly, "You won't mind Madeira, senhora. It's a beautiful place."

An instant later, at the thought that he should not have alluded, however obliquely, to her condition, he blushed furiously.

She blushed too. "Have you been to Madeira before, senhor?" she asked.

"Yes," he said, trying not to let the pride show. "I was with Zarco when he discovered it."

Her reaction was not what he expected. Instead of acting impressed—or even unimpressed, which he would have understood—she acted almost as if she were frightened by the information. As he watched, she visibly made an effort to recover her poise. "What's your name, senhor?" she asked.

"Pedro," he said. He hesitated, then gave his surname with the embellishment that Zarco had bestowed on it. "Pedro da Costa." He stood grinning stupidly until it occurred to him that under the circumstances it would not be too bold of him to ask her name too.

"Inês," she replied. Again there was that peculiar struggle in her face, and she added after a moment's hesitation, ". . . de Faro."

It might have been a name, or she might have been telling him where she came from. Pedro knew Faro, the big port farther east along the Algarve coast; he had put in there once with Zarco, the time Zarco had been afraid to face Prince Henry after the fiasco with the rabbits on Porto Santo, but he had been there only a week, while Zarco chased bandits with the local landowners and gathered his courage, and he had never gotten farther than the waterfront taverns that his shipmates frequented during the wait. He wondered if this Inês, with her obvious breeding, could be connected with some family of *cavaleiros-vilãos*—gentlemen farmers—in the vicinity.

"Are you . . . that is, are your people . . . from Faro?"

"From nearby," she said.

She was in such obvious distress that Pedro dropped further inquiry. "Be sure you snub the rope before you lower the bucket, senhora," he said briskly. "It's easier than you think to let a rope slip through your fingers at sea. Here, let me show you a few simple knots that will hold safely. . . ."

And for the next few minutes he had the pleasure of having a pretty girl hang on his every word while he demonstrated the mysteries of clove hitches and half hitches, figure eights and square knots.

"It's just like one of the knots one uses in sewing," she exclaimed delightedly when he showed her a reef knot. Pedro made a small witticism comparing sewing and sailing, and they laughed together over it.

An officer interrupted them. "No talking to the women. Go about your duties."

"He was only giving us some help," Inês said with spirit. "I asked him."

"They're all eager to help," the officer said sarcastically. "The captain doesn't want any of that kind of help on board ship. On your way, *moco.*"

Pedro was embarrassed that she had to hear that kind of talk. "I'll get you the bucket tomorrow," he said.

"Thank you, Senhor Pedro," she said.

"Get going, *moco,*" the officer ordered.

Pedro moved off. From a little distance, he watched Inês go to retrieve the bucket. She tied a knot quickly and smartly and lowered the bucket over the side, no nonsense in her movements. If she had ever been of gentle birth, she was doing her best to get over it.

Lucio sidled up to him with a broad wink. "Nice going, *filho,*" he said. "That's a fine piece of goods. Did you fix yourself up for later?"

"She's not that sort," Pedro scowled.

"All right, all right, don't bite my head off!" He grinned. "All the same, there's going to be plenty going on tonight. If you want to get left out of it, that's your business."


A hand shook Pedro awake. "On your feet, *moco.* You've been chosen to stand guard below.

Pedro rubbed sleep out of his eyes. He heard the creak of the masts in a light breeze, saw stars spilled across a cloudless sky. Sailors snored on the deck around him. It was some time during the graveyard watch.

"I just came off my watch at midnight," he said.

White teeth grinned in the darkness. "Zarco thinks you can be trusted with the women. Don't ask me why."

Pedro stretched until his joints cracked and followed the other man below. His fellow guard was a grizzled salt from Estremadura whose name was Cerejeira, an old settled married man with grandchildren. It was hot and suffocating below decks; Pedro did not want to think about what conditions must be like within the walled-off slices of hull where the male and female convicts were confined. The sweat started to roll off his body as soon as the deck closed in above him. The stench was bad enough here, but it would be twenty times worse on the other side of the barriers.

There was just enough of a sickly yellow light to see by; Zarco had stretched ship's rules to allow a horn lantern for the benefit of his keepers. As Pedro and Cerejeira approached the source of the glow, they saw the dim shapes of the watchmen they were to replace, lounging against the roughly carpentered bulkhead that stretched the full width of the ship.

"What goes?" said the Estremaduran.

One of the sailors had his ear to the bulkhead. It was a freckled fellow named Solis who, from what Pedro had seen of him, was adept at finding soft duty for himself. Still, Zarco must have thought him trustworthy enough for the job. He rose slowly to his feet and said with a sly grin, "The little mice give a squeak from time to time, but otherwise no trouble. Gets a man bothered, thinking about what's on the other side of this wall."

"Don't think about it, then," the Estremaduran said, settling comfortably down in his place. "Go topside and help yourself to a snack. The cook won't mind. Tell him I sent you."

Solis made a face at the thought of awakening the cook, an excitable man who, though the voyage was young, had already made a dent in a sailor's head for getting into some sardines that he had set aside for grilling.

"It's topside where this vigil should be set, *amigos*," he said.

"What do you mean?" said Cerejeira. "With my own eyes I saw the carpenter nail down the hatch to the women's part of the hold for the night."

Pedro's eyes strayed with Cerejeira's to the improvised bulkhead. There too, a panel had simply been nailed in place, with no nonsense about padlocks; Zarco was taking no chances of having his untrustworthy passengers wander about below decks, either.

"Never mind, old man," said Solis. "Have a listen, if you want, but keep your snoot out of it." He laid a finger alongside of his nose. "A word to the wise."

He left with the other sailor, after a final nod and wink. Cerejeira turned to Pedro.

"There's a man I can do without," he said. "Likes to act

as if he knows a lot. Settle down, *mojo*. We can help keep each other awake. It's a long time till breakfast."

Pedro was loath to use the bulkhead as a headrest after Solis's prattle about eavesdropping. He sat down and stretched his legs with his back against the starboard flank of the ship. Even so, it was impossible not to be aware of scurrying movement on the other side of the barrier, and the sound of lowered voices.

"Little mice is right," Cerejeira said. "They're not asleep in there."

"That was a man's voice in there," Pedro said, suddenly alert.

"No, no, you're mistaken, *mojo*," the Estremaduran said. "The sound must be carrying from the men's section beyond."

All of a sudden there was a feminine squeal, and a male voice raised in anger. Other voices came into it, and then there was the sound of a quarrel, a scuffle, and then abrupt silence, as if someone had put a stop to it.

"I'd better get the ship's marshal," Pedro said. "And a crowbar."

He left Cerejeira standing next to the bulkhead while he climbed the ladder to the deck. He made his way past the bodies of sleeping sailors to officers' country aft and mounted the poop to find the cubicle where Dom Antão, the marshal, slept. He was afraid of blundering into the wrong cabin, but at least there was no danger of intruding on one of the wives; Zarco and the other *fidalgos* had put their families on board Teixeira's ship so they wouldn't be exposed to the *degredados*.

Dom Antão woke up with no fuss and listened to Pedro. He didn't bother with hose, but dressed quickly in shirt and drawers and buckled on a sword. Crossing the waist of the ship on the way to the hatch, he kicked a couple of stout fellows awake and said, "Come with me, lads."

Down below, Cerejeira came to meet them, carrying the horn lantern. Dom Antão cut him off when he tried to tell what he had been hearing in Pedro's absence, and motioned the others to silence. He listened at the bulkhead for a minute or two. Pedro could hear clearly what he was hearing—a drunken male voice and some giggles. Dom Antão gestured Pedro over and whispered, "Off with the hatch, *moco*, and quickly."

Pedro inserted the pry bar and levered the hatch loose on all four sides, trying to be as quiet about it as possible. The carpenter had used long nails. When one of them gave an unearthly groan coming out, the marshal made motions to Pedro to finish the job. Pedro inserted the pry bar all the way and hauled back on it with all his strength, his foot braced against the partition. One of the sailors sprang to help him, and with a backbreaking wrench, they pulled the panel free. It fell to the deck with a clatter, and Dom Antão clambered through, the Estremaduran behind him with the horn lantern.

Pedro followed as soon as he got his balance back and was in time to see a scramble of male forms—nine or ten of them—detach themselves from shadowy females and race for the opposite bulwark. There was a gaping square there, about a foot and a half across, and the men collided with one another in their eagerness to wriggle through it.

"Stop!" shouted the marshal.

He ran to intercept them, waving his sword, with Pedro and the other sailors at his heels, but it was dark and crowded, and he tripped and stumbled over the human obstacles in his way. He managed to catch only one of them, a bandy-legged fellow who was handicapped by having his breeches down around his ankles.

As the marshal led his captive to the lantern's light, Pedro was surprised to see that it was not one of the *degredados*, as he had thought it would be, but a sailor.

"How much did you pay them to smuggle you in?" the marshal demanded furiously. "How many other sailors are involved?"

He shook the sailor, but the man was too drunk to answer.

The marshal bit his lip and glanced at the dark square that led to the *degredados'* evil-smelling warren. It would be worth a man's life to squeeze through that inky hole. It had taken some determined characters to set up the racket with the sailors, and they were likely to be among the more dangerous elements. At any rate, although the derelict seamen could be identified on sight, it would be futile to try to ferret out the guilty parties among more than a hundred and twenty desperate ruffians.

As the marshal grasped the situation he abruptly thrust his drunken catch at the Estremaduran and shouted, "Take this man in charge! The rest of you follow me! If there are any more *malandros* like this one, they'll have to go out the same way they came in. We'll nab them on deck as they pop out of the hatch!"

Pedro had time for a confused glimpse of a dozen naked or half-naked female bodies—the participants in the debauch—in the flickering light of the lantern. Some were scrambling to retrieve clothes; others, drunk, had not tried to cover up, and one was tipsily holding out her arms in invitation. The other women in the hold were dim figures shrinking against the walls. He could not locate Inês among them.

Then he was running after the marshal and the others under the low overhead, dodging past the sacks and kegs of the stores, and clambering up a ladder at the risk of getting a foot in his face.

But they were too late. By the time they reached the deck, the fleeing sailors, if there had been any, were dispersed among the slumbering crew. With an exclamation of disgust, the marshal walked over to the hatch that opened onto the *degredados'* cage. The last man out hadn't taken time to replace the hatch cover; it lay on the planking where it had been pushed aside. Pedro managed a good look at it. The shackles that clamped it down had been tampered with so that it could be opened easily by a light push from below.

"I'll have the hide of the man who did that, if I ever find him," the marshal swore.

In frustration, the marshal began prowling among some of the nearer sleepers, stooping over to listen for fast breathing or other signs of wakefulness.

"You!" he said, prodding a prone figure. "I saw your eye open then. You've been billygoating down below, haven't you?"

"No, senhor," the man protested. "Someone stepped on me and woke me up, that was all."

"Aha!" the marshal pounced. "Then you saw who it was. Point him out to me."

"I didn't see where he went. It was just someone taking a piss."

The marshal turned aside in a fury. The first face he happened to see was Pedro's. "And that's all I'll get out of any of them," he said. "I ought to keelhaul this one on general principles. Well, what do you think?"

Pedro spoke cautiously. "We can't be sure how many of

the men we saw were sailors. Maybe there were only one or two."

"Did you recognize anybody?"

"No, senhor."

"And you wouldn't tell me if you did, would you?"

Pedro said nothing.

"So that's how it is, is it?" The marshal clamped his jaw angrily shut.

A tall figure in a billowing shirt was striding across the half-deck toward them. As it descended to the ship's waist and drew closer, Pedro saw that it was Zarco.

"What's all this, Dom Antão?" Zarco said.

The marshal explained tersely, pointing out the open hatchway. Pedro saw Zarco becoming angrier as the story unfolded.

"So this is how they repay me for trying to rehabilitate them!" he said tightly. "But I refuse to believe that all the *degredados* are ravening wolves—we'll just have to keep an eye on them and try to pick out the bad apples among them."

"The sailor that we caught . . ." began Dom Antão.

"Yes, yes. It's bad enough that they're pimping for one another, but we can't have them corrupting the crew. In the morning we'll have the carpenters construct another bulkhead to separate the men's and women's sections, and we'll post a permanent guard in the space between. For tonight, we'll just patch up the hole on the women's side and keep two reliable men standing by to keep an eye on it." His eye fell on the tilted hatchway and his expression grew grimmer. "Put that back and have a man with a sword sit on it for the rest of the night. As for the jackrabbit you caught with his pants down, in the morning we'll make an example of him."

At the first crack of daylight, Zarco assembled the crew and a first batch of forty *degredados* on opposite sides of the four-foot barrier that ran across the deck. Everyone knew something was up, because he cut the dawn prayers short, allowing time only for a hasty paternoster. Then he stood aside while the marshal and two *cavaleiros* dressed in armor for the occasion brought out the unfortunate prisoner from the previous night's adventure.

In the cold light of dawn he was a miserable spectacle—a

bedraggled little man who on top of everything else was suffering the miseries of hangover. His wrists were bound in front of him, and he stumbled as he was prodded to the mast by the point of a sword. A gunner seized him, passed a rope between his wrists, and hoisted his arms above his head until he stood on tiptoe.

Zarco, resplendent in scarlet hose and slashed velvet doublet, coldly surveyed the scene from the half-deck rail.

"Until we arrive at Madeira, you're all under ship's discipline, exiles as well as crew," he said. His eyes flicked wrathfully over the *degredados* crammed into the pen. "If I ever discover who was responsible for last night, I'll hang them. You know who you are, you sons of bitches. I tried to give you a chance at a decent life and you betrayed me before we even got started. As for my sailors, you're good lads, most of you, and I won't blame you for the actions of a few. But I'm putting you on notice—I won't have men under my command behave like animals." He paused, and the men below followed his flashing gaze to the mainmast, where the prisoner was strung up by the wrists. "You're here to witness the punishment of Juan Chaves. I hope you learn a lesson from it." He nodded to the marshal. "For his offense he's sentenced to four *vintena* of lashes."

A stir went through the crew at the severity of the sentence. "Poor Juan," said Lucio, standing next to Pedro. "He's all skin and bones. He can't take eighty strokes."

Zarco smiled bitterly at the murmur. "You think it's too much? Very well, I'll divide the number of lashes by the number of guilty parties who confess. If only one culprit comes forth, he and Chaves will get forty lashes apiece. If three step forward, that's only twenty apiece." His tone became scathing. "What, no volunteers? What's the matter, *mocos*, don't you want to help a shipmate?"

"He can't get at the others," Lucio muttered, his face pale, "so he's taking it out on Chaves."

Pedro wondered how much Lucio knew. He glanced around at some of the other nearby faces. Solis—who, he was sure, had been paid off by the convicts—was watching the proceedings with a guilty expression.

"So," Zarco said scornfully, "you're going to let Chaves take the blame all alone?"

He gestured to the gunner, who ripped Chaves's shirt

down the back to expose his skinny spine, and took a backward step to get a good swing with the tarred rope.

The punishment had been split into four parts, so that all the convicts could witness at least a part of it. After the first twenty strokes, as Chaves hung moaning, the gunner splashed a bucket of seawater on him and waited while the *degredados* were herded below and a new batch sent up. By the time the third batch arrived on deck, Chaves was unconscious, his back a bloody pulp. But the *despensero*, who doubled as doctor, ruled that Chaves was fit enough to have the punishment continue, and another bucket of seawater was thrown on him to revive him. The *despensero* was an arrogant *fidalgo* named Dom Guilherme, whom Pedro didn't like. He couldn't help thinking that Senhor Alves, his old *despensero* on the voyage that had discovered Madeira, and who had died there before he had a chance to collect his share, would have been more humane.

The last group to be brought up on deck was made up of the women. They emerged one by one into the sunlight, gathering their skirts, some looking frightened, some making an effort to be bold and brassy. Pedro saw puffy faces and bruises among them; there had been rough customers among last night's visitors—or perhaps the one who'd done the pimping had had to bully them.

"Whores!" Lucio said bitterly. "*Meretrizes!* They're the ones who ought to be flogged!"

"They're not all *meretrizes*," Pedro disagreed. "Some of them must have been forced. And there are decent women among them too, who had nothing to do with it."

"Decent?" Lucio gibed. "You mean murderesses? Swindlers? Defaulters? Beggars? Thieves?"

"Some of them are just women who are down on their luck. Like some of the men."

He turned away from Lucio and located Inês in the mass of women. Her oval face was chalk-white, and she clutched a thin shawl around her as if it were cold instead of as hot as the inside of an oven. She was standing against the rail, a little apart from most of the others.

Pedro grimaced. It must have been horrid for a senhorita of her quality to have been exposed to the events of the night before—to say nothing of the fear she must have felt for her own safety when the men on the other side of the bulkhead broke through and started marauding. And surely she had never seen a man flogged before. She was doing her best not to look at the lacerated scarecrow hanging from the mast, but her eyes, huge with apprehension, could not keep from straying in that direction, and the stunned look on her face changed to pity. Pedro saw her friend, the gypsy rope dancer, come up to her and put a hand on her arm. The gypsy girl had a big, shiny black eye.

From below came the sound of hammering; the carpenter and his helpers were finishing the new barricade. There would now be a two-foot aisle between the bulkheads, and some poor *moco* would be posted by the marshal to stifle there for the remainder of the voyage.

Another splash of cold seawater jerked Chaves back to consciousness, and the gunner picked up the stiff length of tarred rope to administer the final twenty lashes. Pedro, looking at Inês's pale face and at the gypsy girl's black eye, found it hard to feel sorry for him.

Zarco himself stopped the flogging when there were still ten lashes left to go. "That's enough," he said. He addressed the women with biting words. "That will give you some idea of the trouble you've caused. If anything like this happens again, there'll be more trouble for everybody—you included. How do you expect to find good husbands on Madeira when the better men see you selling yourselves so cheaply to the trash? If you have any trouble with the hard customers, come to me about it. That's what I'm here for—to protect you."

The women were allowed to stay on deck to finish their exercise period after Chaves was untied and taken below to have his wounds dressed. The sailors drifted back to their duties. Zarco, with a final shake of his head, went aft and shut himself up with a few cronies.

The officer of the watch, seeing Pedro standing about with nothing to do, put him to work splicing rope. Pedro placed himself amidships and sat down on a keg with a marlinspike and some coiled odds and ends of line, and waited for a chance to speak to Inês.

He was not at all sure that she would want to talk to him again. He reflected that she might feel too embarrassed at having been present at the scene of debauchery that he had helped the marshal break up—though heaven knew she could in no way have helped being there! Still, a fine senhorita like her would feel compromised in front of a lowly *moco de bordo* like himself, who would know that her eyes had seen what a decent woman's eyes should not be exposed to. He considered sparing her that final mortification by staying out of her sight for the rest of the voyage.

But in a way, that would have been worse. She might imagine that he was lumping her in with the *degredadas* who had been involved. He could not avoid her entirely in the close quarters of the ship, and when they arrived at Madeira, everyone would be thrown together anyway.

What decided him was the thought that she was alone and unprotected in her present circumstances, and that perhaps it might help for her to see a friendly face, even though it belonged to a sailor, an ordinary man of the *povo* class who was miles below the station in life she had been born to.

As it happened, it was she who came over to him when she saw him. He scrambled to his feet and approached the chest-high barrier, his awkward hands wanting to remove his cap and stopping themselves. She smiled shyly and said, *"Bom dia, a Senhor Pedro."*

*"Bom dia, a senhora,"* he said.

She twisted a corner of her shawl in her fingers, not knowing what to say next.

"I didn't forget your bucket," he said. "See?" He ran to retrieve the leather bucket he had left in the corner formed by the barrier and the starboard bulwark. "I rigged up a light line from the bottom, so you can tilt it and rinse it out without having to haul it all the way up."

He showed her how it worked.

*"Obrigada, senhor,"* she said, the stiffness disappearing. "I wasn't sure you'd want to, after . . ."

"What are you saying?" he exclaimed. "Of course I want to." Impulsively, he added, "It must have been terrible for you last night. You weren't harmed?"

She showed her starch by answering forthrightly, without attempting to evade the question, though her face flushed red. "No. Some of the men who came into our quarters were very drunk, and they tried to molest some of the women who weren't . . . who weren't . . ."

She stopped, not knowing how to say it.

"Who weren't willing to receive men?" he supplied.

"Yes," she said, her face burning a deeper red. "One of them tried to drag me away with him, and I kicked at him and hit him . . . but he said he had paid to have a woman, and he was entitled to have any one he wanted . . . and one of the other women, a friend of mine, scratched him and showed him . . . showed him a knife . . . and he left me alone and went to one of the willing ones. . . ."

"The gypsy girl?" he asked. "The one in the *soldadeira*'s gown?"

"She's a good person," Inês said.

"Yes, yes, of course she is," Pedro said hastily.

"And she's not . . . not a *soldadeira*. She's a rope dancer."

It was one and the same thing, but Pedro did not argue the point. "The man who tried to molest you—was he a sailor?"

"No. He was a *degredado*. He said . . . he said he had paid someone named Lobo to . . . to gain admittance."

"Lobo?"

"Do you know him?"

"Yes," he said slowly. "He's a bad one—one to watch."

She shivered. "Zarco says he'll protect us. Do you think he means it?"

"Yes. He doesn't intend to run a penal colony. He's brought his wife and children with him this time. They're in the other ship with Teixeira's family. He wants a normal, law-abiding settlement for them to live in—lawlessness would reflect on his noble title, after all. Life at sea has its own rules, but once we disembark, things will be different. He'll give the *degredados* a chance—he said he'll wipe the slate clean for them. But he'll be strict with wrongdoers from now on. Prince Henry's given him the full power of a governor, with all legal authority except the sentence of death or mutilation—those have to be reviewed in Lisbon."

"Will you . . . will you stay?"

"Zarco's asked me to," Pedro said uneasily. "He's offering plots of land to any members of his crew who want to settle down."

He stared moodily out to sea, thinking of Fray Goncalo Velho and his promise to Prince Henry to attempt the passage of Cape Non. That expedition was up in the air at the moment, and there was no guarantee that it would ever be revived. But if plans ever were resumed, there would be a place in the crew for Pedro. Fray Goncalo had as much as said so.

Pedro's mouth went dry as he thought of the glory that

was waiting for the men who finally conquered the dreaded cape—the last obstacle to the exploration of Africa's mysterious coast. The life of a landlubber could not compare with that.

"Is anything wrong, Senhor Pedro?" Inês said to him.

"What?" he said. He shook his head to clear it of its vision.

"You were saying that Zarco offered you a plot," she prompted.

"Eh? Yes." He smiled at her. "I think I might try the life of a colonist. For a while."

# CHAPTER 4

"Watch out, she's coming down!"

At Pedro's shouted warning, the two convicts jumped hastily aside. Pedro, the sweat rolling down his bare back, wrenched his ax free from the deep notch where it was embedded and joined them a safe distance away. The mighty tree, taller than a cathedral, gave a groan of tortured wood and began leaning into the notch, its upper branches trembling.

"She's not going to go," one of the convicts said after several tense moments. "We'll have to give her a few more whacks."

"Are you crazy?" said the other. "That's how Ribiero lost his arm yesterday. We'll have to get ropes and blocks to bring her down."

He tossed down his ax and started to head toward the beach, where even at this distance the busy sounds of Zarco's improvised sawmill could be heard.

"Hold on a minute," Pedro called.

The tree made creaking sounds. Birds screamed in the leafy canopy overhead, and there was an outraged explosion of flight. The enormous trunk leaned farther and farther over, and a tremendous crack was heard, like a cannon shot. Slowly, as if in a dream, the giant toppled and fell with a thud that shook the earth.

One of the convicts came over to stand next to Pedro, a

quiet steady man named Heitor who had been a quitrent farmer before a dispute with his former master had landed him in prison. "There's never been such a tree," he said admiringly, leaning on his ax. "At least not in Portugal."

"It's had a long time to grow," Pedro said. "We'd better start trimming branches. It's too big to be dragged. It'll have to be milled here."

He sprang to the upper side of the trunk and began swinging his ax. Heitor joined him. The third man, the one who had wanted to go for tackle, stayed where he was. Heitor frowned over his shoulder at him but didn't say anything.

"You two can kill yourselves if you want," the man said, "but I'm taking a rest. Zarco can wait for his wood."

Pedro, braced for another swing, paused. "It's for our own benefit, Brito," he said mildly. "We've all got to pitch in to get the colony started. When the land's cleared, all of us will get grants of land that'll belong to us provided we improve them within five years."

"It's Zarco who gets all the benefits," Brito said. "He has the rights to all the grain mills, the lumber mills, the bread ovens, and if anyone else wants to start in business, they have to pay Zarco for the privilege."

Pedro frowned. The royal charter had been read to all of them when they landed. It was hard to understand, with a lot of *whereas*'s and *item*'s and *furthermore*'s, but it clearly gave Zarco the hereditary rights to the lion's share of Madeira, with another, smaller domain carved out for Teixeira on the northern side of the island, plus the barren Ilhas Desertas off the coast. Perestrello, the document affirmed, was welcome to Porto Santo and its rabbits.

"The conditions were reasonable," Pedro said. "Only two planks a week from anybody starting a lumber mill, and Zarco has to give ten percent of those to the Prince."

"Where does all this fine lumber go, I ask you?" said Brito, kicking the trunk of the tree. "To that fine new house Zarco is building for himself. *We* live in daub-and-wattle lean-tos while we're breaking our backs for him."

"The beams that a tree this size will give will go to the church he's building here in Funchal Bay—Nossa Senhora do Calho, Our Lady of the Flints. It's for all of us."

"A church made of wood," said Heitor. "Who ever heard of such a thing?"

"There's never been so much wood since the world began," Heitor said. "Why not make churches out of it?"

"The gentry in Lisbon are starting to build their big houses out of the wood that's being shipped from Porto Santo, instead of building them out of stone," Pedro said. "It's something new." He laughed. "Perestrello's getting rich after all, in spite of the rabbits. Zarco will be even richer, and if we all show good faith, we'll prosper too."

He turned to contemplate the primeval forest behind him. It was so thick that it formed an impenetrable green wall at a distance of only a score of yards, a wall shimmering with the emerald light that filtered through the tall treetops. The air was incredibly fresh. And on the entire island, there were no dangerous beasts to contend with, nor dangerous men, as in the Canaries. Eden, the *fidalgos* called it. One of them, Dom Gonzalo Ayres Ferreira, had even announced that he would name his firstborn children Adam and Eve.

Heitor was studying the dense growth too, his manner stolid and thoughtful. "It'll all have to be cleared away, if we hope to farm. I don't know how we'll do it. It's been raining leaves and dead matter for so long that you can't even find the forest floor."

He poked with his ax handle at the springy carpet underfoot to demonstrate.

"Farming," said Brito contemptuously. He was a city man, a petty criminal of some kind from Oporto. "That's all an ox like you can think of. You'll muck in the earth to grow vegetables while the real riches of this place will go to the gentry, as usual."

Heitor refused to be baited. "Wheat," he said goodnaturedly, "that's the crop I know. And a few grapes. With a climate like this, Madeira is bound to be good for wine."

Pedro heard a crashing in the underbrush and saw a glint of gorgeous color through the trees. "You'd better look lively, *homem,*" he said to Brito. "Here comes the gentry now."

Brito grabbed his ax and sprang to attack a branch of the fallen tree. When Zarco and the small party that followed him about emerged into the small clearing, he was working harder than any of them.

"You've done well, men," Zarco said, surveying the scene with his hands on his hips. "There's enough wood in that tree to build a ship from stem to stern—and you've made a good start at clearing a plot of land in the bargain. I just wish all the labor parties were as hardworking as you three."

One of the *fidalgos* with Zarco sniffed. "There's barely a quarter acre cleared here, Dom João. At this rate we won't get a crop in this season."

Zarco's eye singled out Heitor. "You're a farmer, fellow. I remember your papers. What do you say?"

Heitor removed his cap and said deferentially, "In a fertile climate like this, senhores, the growing season is year-round. We can plant any time. With God's blessing, we might get two—even three—crops a year." He hesitated, twisting his cap. "Still, it chafes a bit to wait when your hands are itching to get into the soil."

"You see, Dom João, your peasants are getting impatient," the *fidalgo* said with a supercilious smile. "If there's further delay in allocating land and parceling out wives for the men, you're liable to lose control of your colony."

"There's something in what you say, Dom Ruy," Zarco frowned.

Another of Zarco's companions, a knight named Dom Francisco, who had been one of those to lose his investment in the Porto Santo fiasco, raised a hand in protest. "Get the wood out first, that's what I say. The clearing of the land will take care of itself."

"There's plenty of wood—more than we can ever use," drawled Dom Ruy. "Too much of it is only an inconvenience. Why, the woods are so thick that I can't get through to the patent of land I've been granted only five miles inland."

Zarco nodded. "It would be nice if we could clear a great tract in a hurry. I'd like to get started planting the Malmsey grapevine stock the infante obtained for us from Cyprus."

Dom Francisco shook his head. "You'll just have to be more patient. It's not just a question of chopping down the trees. There's the layer of decayed vegetation that's been accumulating for who knows how many thousands of years. How are you going to clear *that* in a hurry?"

Zarco waved a hand expansively at the forest. "Burn it," he said.

A sheet of orange flame, whipped by a sudden gust of wind, billowed out over the stream. Pedro, standing thigh-deep in water, felt its blistering heat on his face. Beside him, Inês gave a small dismayed cry and stumbled. Pedro caught her and held her up until she regained her footing on the stream's bed of pebbles.

"Careful," he said. "Try to stay on your feet."

She turned a soot-blackened face toward him. "I'm sorry," she said. "We've been standing in this stream for two days and a night. My strength's giving out."

"The fire's burning its way inland," he said. "When the wind shifts, we might be able to go ashore for a while."

All around them the inferno still licked at the sky, but now a belt of charred and smoldering land that was at least two hundred yards deep stretched along the shore of Funchal Bay. The ashes contained tools, supplies, the charred remains of Zarco's fine house, the uncompleted frame of the ambitious church, the incinerated carcasses of livestock. But miraculously, not one person had died in the flames.

Pedro splashed a few yards downstream to where a boulder offered support, pulling Inês after him. "Here, lean against this," he said.

From where he stood, to the next bend in the stream, he could count at least seventy-five or a hundred people wading or standing up to their hips in the water, or sitting submerged on the streambed with only their heads showing. A few terrified animals had been rescued too—wild-eyed cows and bleating goats bracketed by determined men who were holding tightly to their tethers.

Zarco was among the refugees, as bedraggled and miserable as everybody else. Pedro spotted him farther downstream, braced against the current, carrying the smaller of his two daughters on his shoulder while the other girl clung to his leg. His wife, Dona Constanca, a plump pigeon of a woman in a sopping-wet gray gown whose long fashionable sleeves trailed in the water, was being supported by her son, a handsome boy of twelve who was dressed as a miniature *cavaleiro* with a three-quarters-length sword. Pedro had to admit that the Goncalves family, for all their new pretensions, had grit.

Inês was staring downstream too, her eyes wandering among the survivors, trying to pick out women she knew. "Thank God no one's drowned, as far as we know," she said fervently.

"It must be worse for those standing in the sea," Pedro said. "They've been without fresh water."

The fire had split the party of settlers into two groups and cut them off from each other. By the second day, some of those who had initially rushed for the beach had come wading upstream, but the deep pools and treacherous tidal eddies near the stream mouth made it difficult for most. Now though, with the fire peeling back from the devoured land, it was beginning to be possible to skirt the bank of the stream for short distances when the wind was blowing in the right direction, and more people were willing to try it.

"Look!" Inês cried. "There's Mafalda!"

The wiry little rope dancer was picking her way toward them, holding the rags of her skirts up almost to her hips, her clever feet feeling their way underwater from stone to stone. "Oi!" she said as she saw Inês. As she came closer, Pedro saw that her face was blistered, and that the hair on one side of her head was singed.

"If I'm going to go to hell," she said, looking at the roaring wall of flame around them, "at least I've had a taste of what it's like."

"Mafalda!" Inês said, shocked. "Don't talk that way!"

"What are conditions like down at the beach?" Pedro asked.

"It's possible to camp on the beach for short periods of time, senhor," she replied. "But you should see them scamper into the water every time the wind changes its mind."

"What about food? Supplies?"

The ships had been mostly unloaded before the fire started. Pedro ground his teeth at the thought.

"Gone, senhor. There's nothing left. And all the boats that were pulled up on the beach were burned too, so that we can't reach the ships and they can't reach us. I could hear sawing and hammering across the water, though, so the carpenters must be building new boats."

Pedro said with fading hope, "The seabirds are so tame you can catch them by hand. And there are fish in the surf. Isn't anyone doing something about organizing things?"

"There's no one to keep order." She wrinkled her nose. "The *fidalgos* keep aloof. The others have gone wild. They're fighting over the few scraps of food that are caught. And there's been a rape already."

"Madre Santa!" Inês said, coloring.

"You're safe, little one, with this great hulking sailor around. The other men think he's chosen you." She gave Pedro a quizzical look, then went on quickly, "But there's not enough women to go around. If a woman isn't spoken for, they're not willing to wait."

It was Pedro's turn to color. "Things are getting out of hand, then?"

Mafalda touched a bruise on her cheek. "Zarco had better get down there and take charge of things. Some of the worst element have begun gambling over the division of the women. If he doesn't put a stop to it soon, there's going to be a knifing."

Zarco must have come to the same conclusion. New arrivals from the beach had been filling his ears all morning. Shortly after noon he gathered a few of his lieutenants around him, and they held a conference standing in the water. Then the word went out for everyone to wet themselves down thoroughly. The flames were eating their way farther inland, and it had been hours since the standees in the stream had been subjected to a flare-up near enough to singe them. It looked safe enough to try walking seaward along the burnt-out bank of the stream.


It was hot underfoot. The desert of ashes they walked through seemed cool on top, but Pedro kept kicking up live cinders. Every once in a while there was a shower of sparks from above, as a wind gust drew a puff of flame from the burning forest. But only twice during the long exodus was the file of blackened scarecrows forced to take refuge in the stream.

"The land will be fertile underneath, at least," said Heitor, trudging along beside Pedro and the two women. He addressed all his remarks to Pedro. He was too deferential to speak directly to Inês, and he was embarrassed by Mafalda. Mafalda, for her part, was on her best behavior, and refrained from teasing the plodding farmer.

Pedro's foot dislodged a spongy clump, and a little tongue of flame licked at his ankle. He slapped at it and skipped ahead.

"It will have to cool down before any planting can be done," he said. "It's burning deep down like peat."

"Leão, our strongman, saw a forest fire like this once in

Beira province," Mafalda said. "He said it burned underground for months."

Heitor blinked. Still addressing Pedro, he said, "Zarco's determined to put seeds in the ground right away anyway. I heard one of the *fidalgos* say he's going to put us to work scraping out plots as soon as the ship carpenters can make some rough rakes and hoes."

"Where's he going to get the seeds, *querido*?" the gypsy girl said.

A flush rose from Heitor's thick neck to his square face. "He's sending one of the ships back to Sagres for more seeds, tools, everything."

"Just like a *cavalheiro*," Mafalda said. "He runs out on us when things get difficult."

"No," Heitor said earnestly. "He's going to stay behind with his family."

"He'll go hungry then, like everybody else," Inês said.

"There are still provisions aboard the ships," Heitor pointed out.

"Sea biscuit," Pedro said. "Salted flour, salt pork, chickpeas, sardines for the crews on the return trip. It won't go far."

"It's crazy!" Mafalda burst out. "*Louco!* The whole island's burning up! Why doesn't he give up and take us back to Portugal?"

Pedro kicked aside another cinder. Behind them the sky was a solid red glare. "The Prince isn't going to like it," he said gloomily. "First the rabbits. Now this."


For the next week the survivors led a precarious life on the beach, retreating to the surf when things got too hot. Zarco brought order with a few floggings, and the worst of the troublemakers lapsed into a sullen obedience, biding their time. Teixeira sailed a ship all the way around the coastline and reported that the entire island was ablaze; he would be unable to claim his domain for the time being. In the meantime, his own contingent of settlers and *fidalgos* mingled with Zarco's and pitched in to participate in the grim business of survival.

Perhaps there were isolated stands of wood farther inland, cut off by streams and still unburned, but they were unreachable. For now the refugees had to improvise what rude shelters they could from materials stripped from the ships. Zarco himself, with Dona Constanca and the three children, was living in a lean-to patched together out of tarpaulins, planks, and broken spars. Pedro, along with most of the sailors, slept in the open, counting himself lucky to have scrounged a piece of old canvas to wrap himself in.

Morales sought him out. "You heard that I'm to sail back to Sagres for help, Pedrozinho?"

"Yes."

"We're to dismantle one ship for its timber and fittings and keep one ship in reserve so these bare-bottomed pioneers won't be stranded. The big *não*'s the one I'm sailing back. I'm trying to round up a crew for it."

"I can't run away." He hesitated. "Before the fire, I told Zarco I'd be a colonist."

"You're not running away. You can do the colony more good by bringing back help. There's nothing to do here that any strong back can't do. But I want the best sailors for my crew."

"I . . . there's someone here I don't want to leave alone."

"The little miss with the good manners? She'll be all right. Zarco's laid down the law. As long as it's known you're coming back, it's hands off. There won't be any pressure put on her to choose someone—all she has to do is say she's waiting for you and say no. Have you declared yourself to her?"

"Uh . . . not yet."

"Better do it. Don't wait too long. We sail in four days. We'll be absent a month at most. She'll be all right till then."

For the rest of that day and the next, Pedro worked to exhaustion with the seamen and *degredados*, building shelters and hacking away at the scorched earth with the crude tools made by the ship's carpenters. Heitor had been right about the rich soil to be found under the layer of ashes—black, virgin soil, enriched by the rotting vegetation of millenia. When the vast fire finally burnt itself out, Madeira would be a cornucopia. For the present, though, all the frantic labor was done against a backdrop of towering flames that turned the steep slopes into one enormous pyre whose column of smoke, Morales averred, would provide a navigational beacon that could be seen all the way to Portugal.

Machin's giant cross was gone, Teixeira had reported— vanished back into the legends from which it had emerged.

The meadow of fennel that had given Funchal Bay its name had been devoured too, leaving a barren expanse of smoking ash. There was no fodder except seaweed for the few animals that had been saved; Zarco sent men in a boat to the Desert Islands to cut hay for them.

On the third day, Pedro worked up enough courage to speak to Inês. "I'm sailing with Morales, you know," he said.

"Yes," she said. "Mafalda said you would."

"Does Mafalda know everything?" he said, a little crestfallen.

She gave a strained little laugh. "Sometimes I think she does, where I'm concerned."

Pedro shifted his feet uncomfortably. "We'll be back in a few weeks, maybe sooner. Zarco's sending a deputation of *fidalgos* to Prince Henry to do his pleading for him. You know that when the prince decides to move, he doesn't waste time. If all goes well, we'll return as soon as more ships can be found."

"I know you have to go, but I wish . . . I wish . . ."

"What, senhora?"

Her fingers plucked at her shawl. "I . . . I wish you a good voyage, senhor. . . ."

Pedro struggled with his tongue. Finally he managed, "I wish I was staying."

The breath sighed out of her. "I'll . . . I'll look forward to your return."

They stood staring into each other's eyes. The activity on the beach going on a short distance away—the unloading of a boat, the stacking of ship's stores, the shouts back and forth—faded from Pedro's consciousness. His heart was racing. He could dimly understand the effort that it must have taken Inês, against all her upbringing, to say something of that sort to a *moço* like himself.

For himself, though he had not brought himself to the point of making a declaration in so many words, there was the sense that the thing lay between them.

He forced himself to be audacious. "You're kind to a poor sailor, *minha dona*."

"No, it's you who are kind to me, Senhor Pedro." Her eyes flashed. "I haven't forgotten what I am and why I'm here. You made me feel I was worth something again. I'm proud to have you for a friend."

"No, no, *dona*, you mustn't say such things about yourself," he said in some distress. He would have taken her hands then and there if he and Inês had not been in full view of every sailor and *degredado* on the beach. As it was, he could only stare earnestly at her, like a puppy.

She smiled at him, breaking the tension. "All right, I won't. If you promise not to call yourself a poor sailor any more."

He smiled too. "I promise, *dona*."

"And no '*dona*,' either. Just call me by my name."

He struggled to match her sudden lightheartedness. "If you'll stop calling me 'Senhor' Pedro."

"That's settled then. Come on, let's walk up the beach a little way, and you can tell me about yourself."

She put down the skein of fishing tackle she had been mending and gave him her arm quite naturally. After a moment's hesitation he took it, just as if he had been a *fidalgo* escorting a fine lady. Her bare feet and pitiful rags did not detract in the slightest from her gravity. Feeling like an imposter, he strolled with sober dignity down the long curve of the pebbled beach with her, unreasonably certain that the eyes of his grinning shipmates were boring into his back.

As they got farther from the populated part of the beach, he began to worry about what it looked like. Often enough now, one saw some horny *degredado* and a jade slip furtively into the fire-blackened wasteland together—under the circumstances, Zarco had been forced to relax shipboard discipline as long as public decency was not too blatantly offended—only to be greeted with ribald jeers when they returned in scorched disarray from their tryst.

But Inês, just as naturally and unaffectedly as she had taken his arm, observed the proprieties by stopping while still within sight of the makeshift camp on the beach.

Gulls wheeled overhead in a smoky sky. The two young people stood facing each other while the warm surf nibbled at their toes. Pedro did not know what to do with his hands. The moment stretched. He marveled at the oval perfection of her face, found himself astonished by the huge dark eyes that smiled up at him with total acceptance, found a throat-constricting poignance in the small, straight, slim figure hung round with tatters.

He had painted such a golden blur around her that it came as a jolt when the poignant vision spoke to him in a forthright, conversational tone. "You're more important around here than you think," she reproved him. "I've heard that Morales sets great store by you, and when Morales talks, Zarco listens."

Pedro mumbled a protest.

"You're going to amount to something on Madeira," she went on matter-of-factly. "Some day you'll be a freeholder with horse and arms, a *cavaleiro-vilão*."

"No, no," he said, smiling in spite of himself, "that's not for me."

"Why not? It's a new world here. Even Zarco was only a squire once—and now he's lord of a country, the Conde de Camara dos Lobos."

Pedro's pleasure faded to a paler hue as the gulf between them opened up again. He had been brought up to regard an *escudeiro* as an exalted being, but to Inês, Zarco was "only" a squire.

She sensed the dip in his mood and said quickly, "Accomplishment is what counts with Prince Henry, and that's why he elevated Zarco. And I know that Zarco feels the same way—he respects seamanship. How did you come to sail for him?"

Inês's grave attention drew his life story from him in fits and starts. He told her of growing up as a poor fisher boy from a village on the rocky shore of Cape Saint Vincent, of being taken by his father and the other men into the dark green waters as soon as he was old enough to bait a hook or handle a corner of the communal net, while around him plied the bright crescent-shaped boats whose upcurved prows were painted with eyes for finding the fish. The memories flooded back as he spoke, and he dredged up one of his earliest—a pair of strong arms handing him up into one of those staring prows and a warm voice saying, "That's a sturdy one, eh? He'll soon be pulling his weight on an oar."

"But it seemed you weren't born to remain a fisherman, were you?" Inês said softly.

He had never thought of fate before, but now he reflected on the strangeness of life, on all the separate events that had had to be connected to bring him to this place where he was today. He struggled to express it in words.

"It was being hired to work in the infante Henrique's household," he said. "Every boy from my village was hoping for that bit of luck, but it was me and two or three others that the seneschal from Lisbon chose. And it was the victory over the Moors at Ceuta, and the disappointment of having no great deeds to accomplish after that that brought the prince to establish a household at Sagres and look for a sign from God as to what to do next. And then, like *destino*, Zarco and Teixeira arrived with Morales to tell the story of the island and Machin's cross. And I happened to be there that day, and Zarco needed seamen, and I caught his eye."

"See," she said. "It was meant to be. And it won't stop there."

He knew she meant Zarco's promise of freeholds to those colonists who were willing to work for them, and he hesitated before divulging his ambition to sail with Velho Cabral beyond the barrier of Cape Non.

But pride got the better of him, and finally, trying not to boast, he told her of Fray Goncalo's half-promise to him.

"It doesn't seem very likely at the moment, though," he admitted. "He's in financial difficulties after the failure of the Canaries expedition, and the Prince doesn't seem inclined to throw good money after bad."

Was that relief on her face? "Don't be disappointed," Inês said. "There's plenty to do on Madeira in order to make a success of it—and one day, when you're rich and important, and can afford to leave your property in the hands of your servants while you sail off for a few months, there'll be time for you to be a sea explorer." She smiled at him indulgently. "You're very brave, Pedro. I know that some day that dream will come true for you."

Pedro was pleased that she seemed to understand his hopes and feelings. "It's in the lap of God," he shrugged.

Inês spoke of herself in generalities and isolated fragments of warm memories—a favorite kitten, the color and excitement of a saint's day, a songbook she had once owned, herself as a little girl learning to sew, a funny anecdote about a neighbor. Pedro scarcely noticed that no coherent story of her life emerged from these few glowing shards. Enough leaked through for Pedro to gather that her father had been a *cavaliero* of the old sort—but he had assumed that already; that he had died; that the family had come on hard times. Of the incident that had made her a criminal there was no hint.

The tide had been coming in while they talked, and little by little they had retreated from it without consciously noticing that they were doing so, until finally they were sitting side by side on some smooth boulders at the high-water mark.

"But that's enough," she said, cutting short a reminiscence about some pet rabbits her father had given her. "The past is done. There's no point talking about it." She looked up at the sun. "I'd better go," she said. "I promised Gabriela I'd help gather kelp for our cow. The poor animal would starve on the ration of hay that's been brought over so far from the Desert Islands."

"Gabriela?"

"The big woman with the bushy eyebrows who keeps herself so neat. I share a lean-to with her and Mafalda. Zarco gave us a cow to take care of. We're each to own a share if we can keep her alive. We've named her Blossom—the poor thing was terribly burned on one side, but she's healing. Some of the men wanted to butcher her—she's dry, as you'd expect, but she'll give milk once she's freshened, and the colony will need every calf it can get."

Pedro knew about Gabriela—she was the murderess, the woman who had poisoned her husband. Zarco had won her a reprieve from hanging. She was handsome and imposing, and the men snickered about her attractions, making jokes about dying happy. Pedro would not have cared himself to live in close quarters with a poisoner, but he kept his thoughts to himself when he saw the look of glowing happiness on Inês's face as she spoke of the shared cow.

She sensed his reservations and said quickly, "Gabriela and Mafalda are good protection—nobody wants to trifle with them, especially as it's known that Mafalda has a knife. But I don't know for how much longer it will be. Gabriela has a suitor, a little dried-up man who comes around and says flowery things. And Mafalda has her eye on your friend Heitor. She says it's because he's a farmer, and that's what will offer security in this new life here on Madeira. But I think she's really sweet on him."

Pedro brushed aside all the nervous talk about Gabriela and Mafalda. "Protection?" he said. "Against whom?"

She was evasive. "Oh, there are men who come around and bother the women. Some of them don't want to take no for an answer."

"What men?" he persisted.

She looked down at her lap. "It's . . . it's the one they call Lobo." When she saw the red flush rising to Pedro's face, she added a flurry of words. "He hasn't . . . that is, he hasn't tried to put his hands on me, or anything like that. But he's very insistent. He has a way of talking that . . . that frightens me. He says there aren't enough women to go around on Madeira, and he's made up his mind to have me. Then he smiles as though he knows all sorts of things that no one else knows. He's very sure of himself. He says I'd do well to choose him, because then I'd . . . I'd belong to someone whom nobody dares to cross."

"What did you tell him?" Pedro said.

She colored. "I told him no."

"Good," he said. He rose to his feet. "I'll have a word with the fellow."

"Oh, Pedro . . . be careful."

"No," he said. "*He'd* better be careful."

He found Lobo sitting with half a dozen confederates around a fire made from the charcoal that was now Madeira's most abundant product. The other *degredados* were scruffy types, the worst sort of jackals. Pedro had marked them well during the voyage. When they saw Pedro standing over them, they all shifted their eyes toward Lobo to take their cue from him.

Lobo looked up lazily from under the low, shaggy shelf that served for his forehead. "Well, if it isn't the spoilsport from the ship," he drawled. "Did you want something, *moco*?"

Pedro had made sure his knife was loose in its sheath before approaching the fire. In a thick voice he said, "I want a word with you."

Lobo glanced around at his chums, registering mild astonishment. "He wants a word with me," he said. "Fancy that. Maybe he's changed his mind about having us get him a girl." A laugh went around the circle, and he turned back to Pedro. "You can talk in front of my friends, *moco*. Go ahead, don't be bashful."

"I'll talk to you alone," Pedro said, losing his patience.

Lobo winked. "He's bashful. Maybe he wants me to procure him the dainty little miss he spent the morning dawdling with. Sorry, *moco*, I've reserved that piece for myself. Once I stick it in her, she's mine. Zarco passed a law requiring all rapists to marry their victims—it's very moral."

Pedro's arm shot out, and he grabbed a handful of Lobo's shirt. With a yank of ripping cloth, he hauled him to his feet.

"We'll go off a little way and talk, eh?" Pedro said.

They began a silent, swaying struggle. Lobo was big and he was strong, but he hadn't spent his recent years pulling oars and hoisting spars, as Pedro had, and his belly was lard. One of Lobo's hands was out of sight between their bodies, and Pedro felt a furtive movement down low near his belly. He clamped a hand around the hidden wrist and twisted with all his might. Lobo gave a grunt of pain. A knife clattered to the pebbled beach—a knife that *degredados* weren't supposed to have.

Pedro kicked it away with a bare foot and gave Lobo a shove that sent him staggering backward, off balance. Lobo's companions were starting to get to their feet. Pedro drew his own knife. "Anyone," he said. The *degredados* settled down again.

Pedro picked up the fallen knife. It was a fish knife, about six inches long. A chilly sweat broke out all over him. He'd been right about that flutter of movement. He'd seen men gutted in the Canaries before they realized it was happening. He stuck the knife in his belt but kept his own knife in his hand.

Lobo was spreading his hands, a servile smile spreading over his face. "All right, *moco*, we'll talk if you want to," he said.

Pedro prodded him out of earshot of the others. They stopped at a bend in the beach, where tumbled boulders marked the outlet of the stream that had saved the colony.

"Leave the girl alone," Pedro said.

"Sure. Whatever you say, *capitão*."

Pedro poked him in the chest. "Don't be clever with me. Leave her alone."

Lobo looked murder at him. "All the women will have to choose a man sooner or later," he growled. "Zarco's laid down the law about that. I have a right to try."

"Not with this one you don't."

Lobo's eyes turned sly. "You've spoken for her, have you?"

Pedro's temper boiled over. He gave Lobo another shove in the chest that forced him back a step. "That's none of your business! It's hands off for you, understand?"

He shoved Lobo in the chest again.

Lobo raised his hands to placate him. "All right, all right.

The chit's yours, as long as you feel that way about it. One quiff's the same as another. There's other merchandise around."

The blood began to retreat from Pedro's head. He took a deep breath.

"One more thing. You know I'm sailing with Morales. I won't be gone long. If I find out you've been bothering her when I get back . . ."

"Sure, sure, *chefe,* didn't I say I'd look elsewhere?" The eyes shadowed under the bushy overhang of brow stared back at him calmly.

Pedro's jaw worked, but he couldn't think of anything else to say. "Okay, then," he glowered. His hands unclenched.

Lobo held out his hand. "How about my knife back?"

Pedro took the fish knife out of his belt. He carefully placed the flat side of the blade under the heel of his foot and snapped it off. He handed the broken-off hilt back to Lobo.

"Here, take it," he said.


There was a flap of thunder as the stiff offshore breeze caught the big square mainsail and then filled the foresail as well. Timbers creaked as the broad heavy hull of the *não* began to move on its course. A few feet away, his bow legs planted wide to compensate for the tilt of the half-deck, Morales shouted orders down a companionway to the man below at the tiller, and the ship swung another degree or two closer to the wind.

Pedro, with no urgent duties for the moment, stood at the taffrail for a last look at the island. The tiny figures on the beach were like a peppering of fleas, but he could still make out some distinguishable arms waving at the ship. He wondered if Inês was among those persevering wavers; he was too far away to pick out individuals.

From this distance, Madeira's scars could be seen all too plainly. The smell of burning carried over the water. A smudge of brown smoke rose from the crown of the island into a yellow-streaked sky. Pedro's eyes rose from the broad curved bay up the charred slopes to where a necklace of orange flame was draped around the heights of Pico Ruivo. If the fire had crawled that far inland, then the lovely forests of Madeira must be a thing of the past. Pedro could have wept at the thought of all that wood gone.

"Too bad, eh?" said a voice at his elbow, echoing his thoughts.

It was Morales, picking his teeth with a splinter. He stumped to the rail and stood beside Pedro.

"Yes," Pedro said.

"Masts," Morales said. "Think of all the masts those trees would have made. Masts a hundred feet tall. And planks for the hulls of ships. And house timbers. What a waste."

"Maybe the forests will grow back."

"The forests never grow back. When I was a boy growing up in Seville, there were still forests all around the city where the peasants could gather firewood. Now they've shrunk down to hunting preserves for gentlemen, and the peasants be damned. And we all know how extravagant gentlemen are with their wood." He waved a hand at the smoldering island. "How many hearths would that have warmed."

"Do you think Prince Henry will give Zarco more tools and supplies?"

"It's a foregone conclusion. Look at what he's done for Perestrello and that rabbit-eaten wasteland of his. It's already starting to show a profit as a cattle ranch."

"How . . . how long do you think we'll be at court?"

"Thinking about getting back to that little girl of yours?"

Pedro reddened.

"None of my business," Morales said quickly. He scratched his head. "Gentlemen never do things quickly. They like to spin things out. It goes with an air of importance. This fine delegation of *cavalieros* we've got aboard will want to make a lot of long speeches. If the prince says yes right away, they'll keep right on with their arguments, just as if they hadn't heard him. Convincing the convinced, d'you see? But I'll go on loading anyway while they're spouting off. I'll work things out with the old household constable, Bartolomé. He's a sensible old war-horse with no nonsense about him, and he'll start things moving at the first nod from the infante. As soon as we've got a full cargo, I'll send the *não* back without waiting for the additional ships to be outfitted. I'll have to stay behind to oversee things at the shipyard, but you can return with the *não* to Madeira."

"Me?" Pedro's jaw dropped.

"Yes, why not you? You've made the trip often enough with me while we were ferrying supplies and materials back and forth for that fine country estate of Zarco's that got burnt up in the flames. I've taught you everything I know about navigation. Think you can find your way back across the Green Sea by yourself?"

"Yes, but . . ."

"No buts about it. You're a born pilot."

"But I'm only an ordinary *moco de bordo*. A gromet before that. I come from plain people—fishermen."

"Hombre, where do you think I come from?"

"I . . ."

"In Seville, I was a pig boy, a *mancebo*. When I was lucky I could earn an extra penny helping with the harvests or the threshing. But the seagoing ships came up the river from Sanlúcar de Barrameda at high tide, and I couldn't stay away from them. Finally I signed on. I was about the same age you were when you signed on with Zarco. We were in the wine trade, taking cargo to Bristol and London and bringing back English wool, taking our chances with the Channel pirates. The pilot thought I was a bright lad, and showed me some of the tricks of the trade. He was a tippler, you see, and needed someone to cover for him. He died one night during the long swing around the Bay of Biscay, when we were two hundred miles from land. The crew thought we were lost. They made their last confession. The captain went to pieces—he was a landlubber, a fat merchant from Palos. There was nobody but me. I followed the rhumb lines down to Coruña and hugged the coast from there. I was sixteen at the time. But when I brought her into port at Sanlúcar, I could write my own ticket. I had the old pilot's *portolani*, and I set about making new *portolani* of my own on every voyage. By the time the Moors captured me, I knew the waters from Bruges to Tyre, and all the important open sea crossings too." He grinned with rotten teeth. "That's why Zarco wouldn't let go of me."

"You've got Zarco's respect and Prince Henry's respect too, even though . . ."

Morales spat. "Even though I'm no *fidalgo*?" Those things matter less and less. It's a new world. It's going to belong to those who can do. Do you think that any of those *fidalgos* in the cabin, whose eyes are crossed from looking down their noses, could find their way from Lagos to Portimão on a clear night with the wind blowing east? You'll get your chance, *hijo*, and when it comes it won't matter how many sardine nets there were in your coat of arms."

Pedro fell to silent musing. Glory seemed remote now. He was in his twenty-first year already, and being a member of the crew of the ship in which Zarco had discovered Madeira had been the high point of his life. Zarco had given up on the quest for glory and had settled down to being the captain of half of Madeira, if he could ever get his colony going. Why, Pedro thought glumly, should it be any different for him? Where else could a fisher boy from the Algarve coast hope to become a freeholder subsidized by a prince? He resigned himself to a life of farming, submitted to the fate of becoming prosperous.

He hadn't had much of an opportunity to bid farewell to Inês. There had been a scare during the night. A gusty south wind had blown sparks from the inland heights over the beach, and everyone had rushed into the water. A lean-to had caught fire, and there were a few minor burns from live cinders falling on bare skin. But there was no real danger anymore—the fire could find nothing edible for a quarter-mile north of the beach. Heitor was already planting seeds mentally in the exposed soil, and was infecting others with an eagerness to get started once the relief ships returned.

Pedro had found himself standing knee-deep in the water next to Inês, but with all the excitement, and with everybody staying up the rest of the night, there had been little privacy. Mafalda had come wading over and had taken Inês away to see to Blossom, the cow, and then the officer of the watch had enlisted Pedro and some other sailors in a bucket line to wet down the unaffected lean-tos. By the time Pedro was released, it was an hour into daylight, and the bustle attending the departure of the *não* had taken possession of his time.

Still, he did manage to speak to Inês alone for a few minutes before he had to climb into the ship's boat that would row him and the others out to the anchored *não*. Mafalda had sense enough to keep at a distance. Pedro and Inês had held each other's hands and mumbled a few inanities at each other, but their eyes had said everything that needed to be said. Pedro had wanted to take her into his arms and kiss her, but he did not yet have that right.

He settled for a mute squeeze of her hands in his and a lame *"Adeus."* His eyes traveled reluctantly down the graveled shore to where an impatiently beckoning coxswain stood in the surf by the waiting longboat. Lobo was there, part of the convict labor detail that was loading casks of fresh water into the boat, but he had not once looked in Inês's direction. He had a whipped, sullen appearance, and he was puffing at the exertion. He didn't look like anyone to worry about anymore. Pedro turned back to Inês. Their hands broke contact. "I've got to go now," he said.

Her eyes had gone to Lobo too, and looked quickly away. *"Adeus,"* she said. "Hurry back."

Now, as Pedro stood at the taffrail with Morales, watching the diminishing shore, he felt a stir of resolve. The first thing he would do on returning to Madeira would be to formally declare himself to Inês and go to Zarco for permission to marry. There were worse things to do with one's life than to settle in paradise.

Morales nudged him. "Well, youngster, what do you say? Are you willing to take over as pilot on the trip back to Madeira? You'll have Ruy Paes for a captain, but he knows he's in over his head. I'll have a word with him to see that he doesn't ride you too hard."

"All right," Pedro said. "I'll try."

# CHAPTER 5

"Granted," Prince Henry said.

"You see, Dom Henrique," persisted Ruy Paes, his mustaches twitching, "the reserve supplies which were to have seen the colony through until the first crop are quite gone, but we have every hope that, with the land burned off, we'll have an abundant harvest, and while Madeira may not be quite self-sufficient for a few years more . . ."

"Granted, I said," the prince repeated with a face like stone. He turned to old Bartolomé, who was standing next to the long trestle table on which were spread the sheepskin charts that he had been studying. "You'll see to the acquisition of flour, beans, lentils, oil, wine—all the staples. Put it on the household account."

"It will be done, Dom Henrique," Bartolomé said.

"We'll be scraping the bottom of the barrel this time of year. If you run short of wheat, you can fill in with chestnuts. There's always a surplus in the interior."

"Yes, Dom Henrique."

"And send them shoes, clothing, candles, nails, canvas—anything else you can think of. Dom Ruy can help you make up a list."

Ruy Paes waited out the exchange impatiently, his hand resting on the hilt of his sword. His dignity was affronted by the informality of the audience—being received by the prince in an unfinished lecture hall of the school for navigators that was being used as a workroom, with all sorts of artisans, Moors, Jews, and salty types wandering in and out at will, instead of in the great hall of the Sagres palace. He was further miffed at the idea of being turned over to the old constable, a jumped-up commoner.

"As for the wood," Paes said without waiting for the constable to reply, "it was a tragedy, but perhaps it was a blessing in disguise."

Thunderclouds gathered on Prince Henry's brow. "We are not pleased at the loss of the wood, Dom Ruy," he said. "Lumber's turned out to be one of the most valuable commodities supplied by Porto Santo, and we were hoping to do even better on Madeira. We can only hope that, when the fire dies down, you may find unburned tracts."

"It was an act of God," Paes protested.

"It was an act of stupidity. The colony didn't need all that cleared land all at once for a few hundred people."

Paes sputtered.

"But as we've *got* all that cleared land," the prince went on implacably, "we might as well make use of it. I'm sending a load of sugarcane ratoons with the supplies. You'll see that Zarco plants the burned-over acreage in sugar." He paused. "They burn the cane fields in Sicily and it gives them a better yield. Perhaps it will do the same thing on Madeira."

A small stooped man in the drab robes of a scholar had appeared at Henry's side, holding a pair of dividers and a sheaf of charts, and was waiting with obvious impatience for Henry's attention. The prince broke off, to Paes's annoyance, and conferred with the savant, who spread his charts over one of the sheep-sized parchments and pointed out some detail of interest with the dividers.

At the rear of the hall, where a jumble of raw lumber was still being fashioned into benches and small desks by the carpenters, Morales poked Pedro in the ribs.

"Mestre Jaime," he said. "His credit's even higher with the infante than when you left for the Canaries."

Pedro had no trouble recognizing the famous mapmaker. Jaime of Majorca was dull-looking only at first glance. Then one saw the fire in his eyes, the absolute assurance that showed through despite his bent posture. Of all the Catalan school of Jewish geographers, the son of the great Abraham Cresques was the most eminent, and only the highest salary had lured him to Henry's court.

"One of the charts is mine," Morales confided. "Mestre Jaime had me closeted with him yesterday for hours while he sucked my brains dry. He's interested in my plotting of the current between Madeira and the Canaries. He has some theory about the way it feeds into the Canary current as it flows past Cape Non and seems to speed up there. He thinks it portends some unknown feature of the African coast past Non. He's been agitating for the Prince to send another expedition."

"Where's he going to find a mariner brave enough?" Pedro said. "Goncalo Velho Cabral was the only one willing to try, and now . . ."

He shrugged regretfully.

"Fray Goncalo's here," Morales said. "Prince Henry sent for him."

"Fray Goncalo's in Sagres?" Pedro exclaimed.

"It's the Canary current again. The good friar didn't spend all his time fighting. He logged the currents east of Grand Canary and found them unexpectedly strong. He reported the discovery to Prince Henry, and the prince turned him over to Mestre Jaime. Something's up. The rumor is that Prince Henry's paid off Cabral's debts from the Canary defeat. He's waiting outside now."

At the front of the hall, Paes had succeeded in getting Prince Henry's attention again. "And cattle," he said. "We'll need to restock with cattle. After all, if Perestrello can make a go of it with cattle on Porto Santo, with the rabbits eating everything, we ought to do twice as well."

"Yes, yes," Prince Henry said wearily. "Didn't I say I would send cattle? And sheep and goats, and peacocks, partridges and other fowls? Enough of this. It's done. Madeira's already conquered. We've got to go on to other things."

He made a gesture of dismissal. Dom Bartolomé led Paes away with the utmost deference, nodding respectfully as the disgruntled knight expostulated with him about the grocery list for Madeira. On the way out, the old constable caught sight of Pedro and flashed a warm smile of recognition at him.

Cabral came in a moment later, wearing the rich clothing of a *cavaleiro* instead of his friar's attire. The plain, battered sword at his side, however, was the same one that had seen service with him in the Canaries and before that at

Ceuta—a soldier's workaday implement bearing no orna-
mentation except the cross of the Order of Christ at the hilt.

He advanced to the worktable that was serving Prince
Henry as his dais that day and, with his upper body remaining stiff and proud, gave him the knee.

"Rise, Dom Goncalo," the prince said warmly.

The two began an animated conversation about winds and
currents, and within a minute or two the infante had coaxed
Cabral around to his side of the table where Mestre Jaime
joined in, tracing map outlines with the tips of his dividers
and drawing their attention from one chart to another.

"They're ashamed to mention boiling water and sea monsters now," the prince said. "Now they make other excuses.
They say the current's so swift and the northerlies so strong
that no ship passing Cape Non can ever return but must in-
evitably be drawn south to the bottom of the world, there to
join all the other lost vessels in a ship's graveyard. I've sent
fifteen expeditions south so far, and every one of them lost
its nerve at Cape Non."

"I'm not afraid of winds and currents," Cabral declared.

"That's the spirit," said the Prince. He put his head next
to Mestre Jaime's and they spoke together earnestly for a
few minutes. Jaime gestured. Henry looked up, and his
sharp eyes picked out Morales at the back of the hall.

"Some years ago," the prince said to Goncalo Velho, "Senhor Morales had a theory about an African bight. I remember that conversation well—he never had a chance to test
the theory, but discovered Porto Santo for us instead. But a
bight implies another cape south of Non. Let's have the benefit of Senhor Morales's advice."

He motioned Morales to approach the table.

"Stay here," Morales hissed at Pedro. He made his way
forward under the disapproving stares of all the knights and
squires ranged along the walls, who couldn't understand
why the infante seemed to favor foreigners and Jews over
gentlemen of the realm.

"Mestre Jaime would like to put that second bulge—that
*bojador*—on his world map," the prince said. "But first
someone has to find it. What say you to sailing with Dom
Goncalo?"

The gnarled little Spaniard met Cabral's eye without
flinching at their difference in stations. "Dom Goncalo already has a pilot—De Brito, a good man. He doesn't need

me." His bright, recessed eyes were rueful, ironic. "And at the moment I can't leave my employment with Count Zarco anyway. But I can recommend a bright lad who knows some of my tricks."

Cabral followed his gaze to where Pedro stood. "Young Pedro da Costa?" he said. "He was with me in the Canaries. A brave *moço*. He saved the life of one of my knights at the risk of his own."

"You promised him a berth, didn't you?"

Prince Henry pursed his lips thoughtfully. "He was the lookout in the crow's nest when Madeira was discovered. Perhaps he'll bring you luck, Dom Goncalo."

"Call him here," Cabral said.

Morales signaled to Pedro, who came warily to the work-table, cap in hand. "Here's your chance, *hijo*. Dom Goncalo wants to talk to you."

Cabral looked sternly at Pedro. "You asked to be taken if we ever sailed south to Non, didn't you? You even got Dom Sebastião to speak in your behalf."

Pedro blinked. He hadn't known that the wounded knight had put in a word for him.

"*Sim*, Dom Goncalo," he stammered.

Prince Henry gave a booming laugh. "You'd better take him, Dom Goncalo," he said. "It's not easy to find sailors willing to sail into unknown waters."

"There's just one thing, Your Excellency," Morales put in with a nicely calculated show of reluctance. "I was about to give Pedro here a promotion. I told him I wanted him to pilot the *não* back to Madeira for me."

"You hear that, Dom Goncalo?" the prince said. "You'll have to make him a boatswain's mate, at least."

Cabral looked at Pedro with new interest. "You'd trust him with that?" he said to Morales.

"Yes—he'd be giving up a lot." He nudged Pedro. "Wouldn't you, *hijo*?"

"Senhor Morales," Pedro faltered. "What about the piloting of the *não*?"

"I'd have to take the ships back myself." He looked at Prince Henry inquiringly. "But perhaps I won't have to linger at the Lagos shipyard too long if the infante can divert a ship or two that's already fitted out. And if—with Dom Bartolomé's gift for foraging for supplies—we can start loading without delay."

Pedro's head was in a whirl. An hour ago it hadn't seemed possible that he would be part of the adventure of conquering Africa's final barrier. And now, like a phoenix, the chance had risen out of the ashes of his resignation. He weighed it against the dazzling alternative that Morales had offered him—the chance to earn his spurs as a pilot. But that could wait, couldn't it?

Then, belatedly, he thought of Inês. A flush of shame spread across his face, as if she herself had been standing there and had read his thoughts. Hadn't he as good as promised her to return promptly with the resupply ships? His last image of her flashed through his mind—a small, sunbrowned, vulnerable figure in a patched dress standing in the surf, looking across the water at him as the longboat rowed away.

"Well, speak up, *moco*," Cabral said impatiently. "Do you want to go or don't you?"

It wouldn't take long, Pedro told himself. A thousand miles of sailing, with known winds and currents. And then, what of it if Cabral did sail a few miles beyond Cape Non? He would be back on Madeira in time for a second season of planting. Morales could carry his message back to Inês. It would be a disappointment for her, of course, and he would have to work hard to make it up to her. But there was a whole lifetime in which to settle down. How often did one have a chance to make history?

"I'll go, Dom Goncalo," he said, kneeling.

# CHAPTER 6

"Hurry!" Mafalda said, her dark eyes flashing their excitement. "They've come! The prince sent four ships this time! You can just see their sails past the point!"

Inês put down the crude hoe with which she had been clearing her garden plot and wiped her hands on her apron. She winced; one of the blisters on her palms had opened up.

"Good," she said, trying not to appear overeager. "Just in time to get the seeds in the ground before the weeds take over."

Mafalda studied the plot critically. With the ashes scraped aside, the square of earth showed a rich, moist brown, crumbly smooth and ready for planting. "You've done well," she said. "But the work will go faster with a man to help."

Inês blushed. "You know I don't have a man."

"Nonsense! That seagoing lout of yours is devoted to you, even if he's too dumb to show it. So what's this talk of seeds? There's only one kind of seed that counts—the kind that grows babies."

Inês tried to hide her confusion. "And what about you?" she countered.

"I'm waiting to see what new faces the ships will bring. Only the culls are left here. The good ones are taken."

"But not Heitor," Inês teased.

Mafalda studied her fingernails carelessly. They were rimmed with black dirt from grubbing in her own garden plot. The sequined dancer's gown had long since fallen apart and had been replaced by a patchwork gown that Inês had sewn for her out of odds and ends from the sailors' slop chests brought ashore after the first days of the fire.

"Heitor's slow," Mafalda said. "There are half a dozen women casting eyes at him—they know a dependable stick when they see one—but he hasn't noticed it. What can you do with a man like that? No, I'll find myself a handsome young lad from among the newcomers on those ships."

"You won't be alone. All the women who've been resisting marriage have been put on notice." Inês bit her lip. "Zarco himself came round and chucked me under the chin, and asked why—a pretty thing like me, he said—was still unmarried. He said he couldn't allow any unmarried women on Madeira, for decency's sake." She laughed nervously. "He offered to find a good husband for me himself, if I had trouble making up my mind."

"You have nothing to worry about, *minha*." She glanced toward the ocean horizon. "Your problems will soon be over."

"Like Gabriela?"

Their large, competent friend had turned into a docile lovebird after her marriage by the chaplain to her suitor, a little stringy man named Ximenes, who was about half her weight. The cow, Blossom, had gone with the pair to the little patch that Gabriela was working so hard to turn into a cozy homestead, but Ximenes had acknowledged that Inês and Mafalda had shares in the animal—albeit after anxious hovering by Gabriela—and they had each been promised a calf if the relief ships, as expected, brought a bull with them.

"It's a marriage made in heaven," Mafalda said with a toss of her hair. "He's able to puff out his little narrow chest and strut for the other men, and she has someone to smother. If it doesn't go to his head, so that he thinks he can show off by abusing her as her last husband did, it'll work out all right."

"Oh, you're terrible!"

"I've seen men, *minha*. Come on, let's get to the beach."

Work had stopped in the settlement with the news of the sighting of the sails. A holiday throng was waiting at the water's edge, full of chatter and high spirits, some of them prematurely eager enough to have waded out into the ocean up to their thighs. Even the *donas* were there at the bayfront, standing well back in a tight exclusive group with their children and servants, dressed in the fine clothes that had escaped the fire aboard Teixeira's ship.

The billowing sails with their vivid red crosses moved in stately procession past the distant point of Funchal Bay, the stepped hulls of the ships clearly risen above the horizon. Inês recognized the *não* in which Pedro had sailed by its bright trim and distinctive suit of canvas. He might be at the rail now, staring just as hard as she was!

"Oh, Mafalda!" she said. "Why can't they hurry?"

She was being unfair to the sailing master, she knew. He was doing his best with the prevailing northeasterly that had to drive him west along Funchal Bay. As she watched, the sails spilled their wind in a tacking maneuver and were hauled around to fill again. It had the nice economy of the Morales touch, and she remembered how Pedro had explained it all to her. Pedro greatly admired the Spanish pilot, and she was glad he did; with Morales indentured to Zarco as he was, that made another bond tying Pedro to Madeira.

Mafalda, who knew little about ships, said, "Steady, *minha*, you won't make them come any faster by wishing it."

It was past midday when the ships dropped anchor in the bay and began taking in canvas. They rode tall and at ease only a few hundred yards offshore. A number of the more impatient onlookers swam out to them without waiting for boats to be lowered, and Inês could see them being pulled aboard. Zarco expended some of his hoarded gunpowder in a cannon salute, adding to the festive atmosphere.

As the ships disgorged the first boatloads of men, the welcoming throng on the beach milled about impatiently. Anxious women pressed forward to try to catch sight of sweethearts or new husbands. Others, like Mafalda, strained to see what new faces the ship had brought.

"I don't see Pedro."

"Patience, *minha*," Mafalda said with an understanding smile. "It's only the advance guard."

Soon the beach was filled with embracing couples. Officers shouldered their way through the crowd in search of Zarco. Work parties were being formed from among the *degredados* to begin the job of unloading cargo and animals. More boatloads of men came from the emptying ships, then the ferrying slowed and stopped.

"Perhaps he was detained," Mafalda said without much conviction. "He might still have duties aboard."

But it soon became apparent that no one else was going to come ashore. A cold clamp fastened itself over Inês's heart.

"All the officers are ashore," she said. "There's Morales over there."

Morales was having a conversation with Zarco. They were surrounded by a praetorian group of *fidalgos*. Zarco was clapping Morales on the arm, looking pleased and expansive.

Morales caught sight of Inês and excused himself without waiting to be dismissed. The *fidalgos* turned stiff with disapproval at this breach of etiquette, but it didn't seem to bother Zarco, who turned his attention with equal casualness to a primly poised Ruy Paes.

"He's coming over here!" Mafalda said, fussing at her hair and smoothing out her dress.

Morales headed directly toward Inês, his burl of a face closed tight and his step unwilling, and she knew what he was going to say before he opened his mouth.

Lobo came by that night. All of a sudden there was a face hanging in the entrance to the lean-to, indistinct in the starlight, with a gleam of white teeth showing, and Mafalda scrambled to her feet, a knife in her hand.

He was squatting on his haunches outside the curtained opening. "The little tumbler's quick," he said with a grin, "but not quick enough. Don't you know you should use a knife, not show it? Otherwise someone might take it away from you and use it against you."

"Get out of here," Mafalda said.

"I didn't come to see you, *soldadeira*. Why pay a coin?"

"Don't talk to him," Mafalda said to Inês without taking her eyes off the squatting form.

"You don't have to talk to me," Lobo said. "Just listen."

Inês drew back from the entrance as far as the little hutch allowed. "Go away," she whispered.

"It's not so secure here with that big sow of a husband-poisoner gone, is it?" Lobo said, looking around. "Too bad one can't count on one's friends. And now the rope dancer has her eye on a man, too."

"Shut up," Mafalda said.

Lobo laughed. "And the sailor—after all the fine words he didn't come back, did he?"

"Please," Inês said.

"You try anything and you'll get the knife where it will do the most good," Mafalda said.

"I'm not going to try anything," Lobo said, balanced easily on his heels and knuckles. "Why should I? Everything open and aboveboard—that's the way." His eyes rested on Inês. "Nobody's going to ask for you for a wife, little lady. I've passed the word. All I have to do is go to Zarco tomorrow and ask for your hand."


"*Quem passar o Cabo de Não* . . . who passes Cape Not, returns not."

De Brito, the pilot, derisively quoted the old rhyming proverb, and with a wave of the hand dismissed the sandstone cliff that rose out of the flat sea about a half-mile to port. It hardly merited the name of cape: a blunt reddish prominence that stood out at no great remove from the ocher desert behind it.

Pedro had to agree with his disparaging tone. The fearsome cape didn't look so formidable against the clear blue African sky, with a golden sun like a badge above it and seagulls wheeling peacefully at its brow.

"*Sim*, it's hard to understand why everyone's always been afraid of it. From the look of the water it's deep enough inshore, with no danger of reefs, and you can see it clearly enough from a distance."

De Brito frowned, and Pedro realized that he had assented too readily and made it sound too easy. If there was no danger, there was diminished glory in passing the Cape. De Brito was a touchy one, jealous of Morales's great reputation, and consequently suspicious of Pedro and a little resentful of the way he had been foisted on him.

"But still," Pedro said, hastily mending his fences, "fifteen pilots have turned back at this point, and you're the one who'll go down in history for having the courage to pass it."

Mollified, the pilot preened himself a little. He turned away and pretended to study the sea. De Brito was a thirty-ish man with a ruggedly handsome face and many small vanities. He knew his business, though, and Goncalo Cabral paid him generously.

Pedro turned his attention to the set of the single square sail. The expedition ship was a *barcha* with a crew of sixteen—a comedown after sailing the big *não* with Morales. They had sailed for two weeks to reach this point from Sagres, and things were getting a little cramped and stale aboard. Still, the little ship had good lines and handled well, and Pedro had not forgotten that Porto Santo had been discovered in a *barcha* no bigger than this.

He saw no reason yet to step the smaller mast and rig the secondary fore-and-aft sail whose virtues he had learned from Morales. The northerly wind that drove straight down the coast of Africa, together with the coastal current, was more than adequate for getting them where they were going; it was on the return trip that he would have to sail against the wind.

It seemed to him, though, that the current was beginning to pick up here, and he wondered if that was the first manifestation of Morales's theory of a long, shallow bight between two capes, where the Canary current was compressed and a trapped wind would set up a cross swell.

He studied the water intently and thought he saw the slightest coppery tinge—an irregular, almost invisible stain. Something was stirring up the bottom farther south—the mouth of a river, or shoals turning the unhindered current into a set of claws. It was too early to tell yet, but it would bear watching.

Fray Goncalo came picking his way aft from the prow, where he had been hanging over the shoulder of the leadsman. So far the soundings had shown satisfactory depth despite their closeness to shore.

"Well done!" he boomed to De Brito. Every inch the noble, he stood, hands on hips, and watched Cape Non slip by.

"We could turn back now, Dom Goncalo," De Brito said. "You've done what the infante asked."

"Not yet," said Cabral. "Not with clear sailing ahead as far as the eye can see."

"The men," De Brito said uneasily. "They've gone this far, but they don't like it. They're trotting out the old stories about boiling water and sea monsters, and they're afraid we won't be able to get home again against the northeast wind. They . . ." He hesitated. "They say you're planning to beach the ship and make the trek back overland. They're afraid they'll die in as barren a land as that."

"Nonsense," said Cabral. "Tell them I have no intention of beaching the ship. We'll beat our way back against the wind—there's no great mystery about that anymore since Morales showed how to make enough northing to find a westerly far out to sea. We'll sail around the Canaries and pick up the Madeira homebound route. It's true that for every day we spend questing south now, we'll spend three days returning—but what of it? Look at how easily we're borne along. We have a splendid opportunity to explore further. I'll not turn tail while there's no danger in sight!"

He shared his smile with Pedro, and Pedro took the opportunity to press his suggestion.

"Excuse me, Dom Goncalo, but have you noticed how the current has started to quicken? Perhaps we're being borne along *too* easily. There may be dangers this close to shore. If you remember, Morales thought that south of Non, we ought to stand at least five miles out to sea. . . ."

He had struck the wrong note. De Brito was scowling. Cabral gave him a sternly authoritarian look.

"No, Da Costa, we'll sail along the shore. What's the point of being the first mariners to push past the boundary of Cape Non if we don't bring back a detailed description of what lies beyond?"

Pedro hesitated. Morales's theory had been most convincing. Prince Henry had clearly enunciated it, and Cabral had seemed to understand. But it was hard to get rid of old habits of thinking. Cabral had offered a rationalization for sailing close to shore, but behind it was the same old fear of sailing out of sight of land. Cabral was willing to sail the empty seas between the Canaries and Madeira now that navigating them had become a commonplace. But here, faced with the unknown, he had reverted to the old, comforting ways.

"We'll still be able to follow the outline of the shore," he said. "And from time to time we can come in for a closer look. But sooner or later we're bound to encounter shoals or rocks, and if the crosscurrents force us in where there's heavy surf, we could lose the ship."

"Surf?" Cabral said imperiously. "I see no surf. There's plenty of water under the keel. I'm disappointed in you, Da Costa. I thought you were a man of courage."

Pedro bit back a reply. "As you wish, Dom Goncalo," he said.

In the next two or three days, the water became increasingly choppy as a continuous swell from the northwest fought the swift current. The leadsman reported constantly shifting depths, but Cabral refused to admit he was wrong. The sailors became increasingly restive.

"You're one of us," a sailor said to Pedro one morning, taking advantage of a moment when Pedro was sitting in the shadow of the sail with the off-going watch, having some biscuit and a salted lemon for breakfast. "Can't you talk his friarship into turning back? It's getting hotter every hour. Look and you can see where the water's starting to boil."

"Man, that's not boiling water," Pedro laughed. "That's just whitecaps. Don't be a baby."

There was muttering from the other men. "There's no life here," someone said. "Not a speck of green. We're sailing past hell."

"Just be patient," Pedro told them. "Hasn't Fray Goncalo brought you safely this far? Don't you see him praying night and day? Whose prayers are going to be heeded, if not someone like the friar's?"

He got them pacified, but he didn't like the temper of the crew. If someone refused an order and got flogged—that would be bad. In a ship this size, with a small crew living elbow to elbow, the breakdown of goodwill between master and men could lead to mutiny.

He tried once again to persuade Dom Goncalo to put out farther to sea. "You want to turn back, like the others, don't you?" Cabral accused.

"No," Pedro protested. "I want to go on. These waters are churning because they're getting shallower. All I want to do is to get us farther out to sea."

Grudgingly, Cabral gave permission to run out to a distance of one league from shore. It was not far enough. There came a time when the leadsman reported a depth of not much more than a fathom, despite the fact that they should have been in deep waters. The sailors, unfortunately, had heard the leadsman's call too.

"We're going to rip our bottom out, that's what!" a man cried in a voice tinged with hysteria.

Cabral glowered, his hand on the hilt of his sword. The ride got rougher. The little *barcha* bounced over the corrugated surface of the waves, rattling in every timber. The water had turned a red, muddy color, great billowing clouds of it under the surface.

Twenty miles out to sea, the water was still shallow. "We can't get around it," De Brito said raggedly.

The water was oily, malevolent. The water slapped submerged obstacles, sending great showers of spray into the air. Then the lookout screamed, "Reefs ahead!"

It was the Bulging Cape—Bojador—that Morales had predicted. It was a low-lying arm of red, sandy wasteland, more dangerous than Cape Non because its limits could not easily be seen. As the water lifted and roiled, Pedro could see the long fingers of hidden sandbanks, reefs showing their teeth and then concealing them.

"The water *is* boiling," Cabral said, shaken.

"That's the sea racing at ebb tide over shoals," Pedro said. "We can get around it. All we have to do is put farther out to sea—far enough to make deep water beyond the margins of the bight."

"No, we'll put about and turn back," Cabral said, the steel returning to his voice. "We've sailed two hundred miles beyond Cape Non—no man can say we didn't try. The real barrier is here, at Bojador. This is where the navigable sea stops. We'll have to go back to the Prince and tell him that his dream ends here."

# CHAPTER 7

The tall Venetian in workman's clothes had to stoop to get through the low entrance of the Cabra do Mar. One or two of the regulars glanced up from their drinks, then turned their eyes away, not wanting to be caught staring. "O Fidalgo"—"the Gentleman"—his fellow workers at the docks called him, though he performed the roughest labor for a few soldos a day, like any of them. He was known to have been a prisoner of the Moors, but otherwise he kept his past to himself. Though polite enough, he was not a man to be trifled with. Once he had taught a lesson with his big, scarred fists to a loading boss who was riding him.

He pushed his way through to his accustomed corner and sat down at the rough plank table. A couple of sailors moved aside to make room for him. The Goat was crowded, as usual, smoky with the cheap tallow wicks that lit its cavelike interior, and smelling of stale grease. The normal clientele filled the place—sailors, dockworkers, laborers from the Vila do Infante, the Prince's town, that was fast rising on the cliffs of the Sagres promontory. The fine folk did their drinking elsewhere.

The innkeeper nudged the *tauernera*, the tavern miss, a lively wench named Catalina, making sure to get in a good feel at the same time.

"There's your admirer," he teased her. "O Fidalgo. Play up

to him and maybe you'll get your hands on some of those gold *libras* they say he has salted away."

"He's not my admirer," Catalina said with spirit. "He's not interested in being close with any woman. When he has to, he takes a cheap *meretriz* for the night—and he doesn't do *that* too often. He puts it off as long as possible, and never asks for the same girl twice. That slut, Rosa, at the Two Doves, told me all about it. He's careful with his heart, that one, just as he's tightfisted with his money."

"He doesn't spend as much here as a steady like him ought to, that's for certain," grumbled the tavern keeper, a stout, ruddy man named Vasques who had once had a modest celebrity as a bullfighter. "You're not doing your job, my girl. You let him sit there and nurse a drink for half the night." He slapped her on the rump. "Get going and see what you can do to jolly him along tonight."

She evaded his hand before it could close around her buttock. He removed it with a shrug, showing no resentment. Catalina kept him in his place, proprietor or not. Both of them knew very well that she brought the Goat a good share of its patronage. She was popular with the customers—but more than that, was a hard worker who kept the tavern from falling apart. She wasn't what you'd call beautiful, but she had a strong, vivid face with an easy, generous smile that captivated even the unruly customers.

"He doesn't waste his money here because he's too smart," she returned tartly. "He saves every last *dinheiro* for that hole-in-the-wall ship's chandlery he's running on the side. He only comes here to find out what ships are sailing and to drum up business."

"My goodness, such passion," he gibed. "And you say he's not your *admirador*!"

"Pig! I told you he's not interested. And neither am I. *Diabos,* you twist everything!"

"I'll tell you why he comes here. He's spying on the infante's discoveries for Venice."

"He's no spy," she said scornfully. "He's too poor. Spies are the fine Venetian gentlemen in velvets who bribe our captains for copies of the Prince's secret maps before they go back under lock and key at the school up there on the cliffs."

Vasques pulled at his lip thoughtfully. There had been another spy scare at Sagres only a few weeks ago, when Prince

Henry's police agents had circulated through the waterfront to warn people to be on the lookout for foreigners who might be trying to discover Portugal's secrets for commercial purposes. A Venetian secret agent, it seemed, had paid twelve gold ducats to obtain a fair copy of the official *padron*—the standardized world map on which all new discoveries were now recorded. Fortunately the attempt had been discovered in time. A Moorish draftsman at the School for Navigation had been hanged, and the Venetian in question had barely made it across the border with his skin intact. Feeling had run high in the waterfront community since.

"Spy or not, it doesn't matter to me," he shrugged. "I'll take your O Fidalgo's money the same as anyone else's. Get to work, miss."

He aimed another slap, which missed.

Catalina drew a pot of wine and snake-hipped her way through the jumble of tables and benches. The big Venetian looked up at her without expression.

"Why so glum, senhor?" she said brightly, thumping down the pot and pouring him a cup. "It can't be that bad, whatever it is. Here, this ought to cheer you up."

For an instant his face did lighten, but then drew its previous careful lines again. "Thanks, Catalina," he said in his accented Portuguese. "But I didn't order a whole *jarro*."

"Have pity on my poor tired legs," she said. "You'll save me another trip later."

She did an exaggerated imitation with her face of an old beldame drooping with weariness.

There was the almost-smile again. "To your health, then," he said, raising the cup. He put it down again. "This isn't my usual wine. It tastes like the Malmsey."

"Imagine that," she said without repentance. "I must have drawn it from the wrong barrel. Enjoy it, senhor, it's better than the thin stuff you usually drink. And don't worry about the price. It isn't the Malmsey. It's the export wine from Azoia that tastes almost the same—Vasques got his hands on a couple of kegs before the English wine ships were loaded."

One of the sailors at the table was trying to get her attention. "Hold on a minute," she snapped. "I can't be everywhere at once."

"Who're those fellows over there?" O Fidalgo said with a

nod toward the big center table. "They seem to have started their celebrating early."

"Them? They're our local heroes, if a *moco de bordo* can be a hero along with the gentlemen. Those are some of the sailors that doubled Cape Non with Goncalo Velho Cabral. Everybody's competing to buy them drinks. Don't waste your money—for a cup of wine they'll oblige by telling you all about the sea monsters they fought off. The stories get better every night."

She was used to O Fidalgo's questions. He usually began an evening by sizing up the room, and she was sometimes able to help him by pointing out a ship's master trying to shave the costs of supplies or a *comissário de bordo* with a last-minute order to fill before sailing. She had no qualms about steering customers to him. This big Venetian with the villain's scars had proved to be scrupulously honest in all his dealings and was making a good reputation for himself among the shipmasters. She didn't know why he was still working at the docks—perhaps it was because he was a cautious man, unwilling to leave one foothold before he had another. He had arrived in Sagres two years ago, penniless, with only the rags on his back. But the way his little chandlery business was growing, soon he'd have to devote full time to it.

"Who's that curly-haired fellow in the middle? He looks like one of the *mocos*, but the others seem to defer to him?"

"That's Pedro da Costa. He's not exactly an officer. He lives with the ordinary seamen, but he was a sort of assistant pilot to De Brito."

"He doesn't look very happy. He's hardly saying a word."

"He's pining to get back to Madeira. He has a sweetheart there. He's been waiting two weeks for a ship."

"Madeira, is it?" O Fidalgo's expression grew speculative. "They're loading supplies for Madeira all the time. They were burnt out by the great fire. The infante's trying to get them back on their feet."

"I don't know if he has anything to do with supplies. It might be worth talking to him. He sailed with Zarco, you know, when Madeira was discovered. Someone once said that he attracted the notice of the infante himself, but you know how everyone claims he has some kind of access to an ear at court."

"The infante, eh? Maybe it would be worth buying him a drink later. When things thin out a little."

The sailor who had asked for service got impatient. "What do you have to do to get a drink around here?"

"All right, *moco*, don't get your blood in a boil," Catalina retorted. She swept up his empty cup and those of his companions and sashayed off, hips swaying.

"Man, how would you like to have a piece of that?" the sailor said reverently.

"Don't raise your hopes, Rafo," his friend said. "That one, she's not so easy to grab."

"It's not my hopes I'm raising," Rafo said, and the others laughed.

"No, I mean it," said the friend. "She's choosy. She's not one of those who'll do you for a *soldo*."

"How about him?" Rafo said, jerking a thumb toward the tall foreigner. "Hey, friend, how come she's so friendly with you?"

"Excuse me?" said O Fidalgo.

"What's your secret?"

"No secret, friend. There's nothing here of any interest." Rafo's eyes narrowed. "That's a funny way of talking. Where're you from?"

"Italy," the other said in a level tone. "A long time ago." "Venice?"

O Fidalgo put down his cup and met the sailor's eyes steadily. "What of it?" he said. The others might, at that moment, have noticed the scarred knuckles, the width of shoulder, the amount of meat the stranger carried on his upper body. There was a brief contemplative silence.

At that point, Catalina arrived with the drinks. "What's this?" she frowned as she looked at the tense postures round the table, where one or two of her customers seemed ready to rise to their feet.

"Drinks for my friends," O Fidalgo said with a short powerful sweep of one of his bulging arms. "This round's on me."

The sailors sank back on the bench. Catalina shrugged and said, "It's your money."

One of the sailors who had been silent till now raised his cup embarrassedly and said, "Thank you, senhor. To your health."

"To your health," O Fidalgo said, raising his own cup with

manners as fine as any gentleman's. After a pause the others followed suit, though Rafo continued to look sulky.

Catalina waited while O Fidalgo counted out coins in her palm. "You're a man of tact, senhor," she said.

His face widened in an actual smile, though for all the teeth it showed, there was no humor in it.

"Diplomacy's harder than the other," he said. "But it saves trouble."

She returned with her tray under her arm to the *despensus* behind the counter and added a rattle of coins to Vasques's metal money box.

"What's got into O Fidalgo?" the innkeeper said. "He's being openhanded with his money tonight. First the Malmsey, now this."

Catalina flared at him, "He's a gentleman, that's what. He doesn't believe in making fusses."

The well-wishers had fallen away one by one. There was no one left except an elderly bore who kept repeating, "If I were any younger, I'd go with you boys on your next mission to Non," and telling them over and over again of the great deeds of his own youth—chiefly, it seemed, a voyage on a salt ship to Denmark. The Cape Non mariners, well into their cups by now, reacted with glazed expressions.

Sandro got up, and with a signal to Catalina, went over to their table. "By your leave," he said, sitting down. "I'd be honored to buy you brave men a drink."

Catalina did her part by appearing on the instant with a tray and a fresh pitcher. "The best of the house," she said. She dodged a pinch and wriggled out of an arm that had encircled her waist, but dazzled the itchy-handed ones with a smile that made them feel rewarded all the same.

"Why not?" replied one of the crew. "Have a seat. Where do you hail from, amigo?"

"Venice."

"Venice? They breed good sailors there—best in the world except for us. Are you a mariner?"

"Of sorts." Sandro smiled crookedly. "Though I haven't smelled salt water for a while. But we Venetian paddlers can't match the feat you just accomplished. Put us past the Pillars of Hercules and we're at a loss unless we stick to known waters. My hat's off to you lads. You've shown the world what seamanship means."

The sailors warmed under this professional praise. The elderly bore was forgotten, left to maunder unheeded and finally to fizzle into silence with his mouth working like a mackerel's.

Sandro pressed his advantage.

"Talk about pure seamanship! We Venetians get wherever we want to go by brute muscle-power—our galleys can always get back by rowing against the prevailing wind. But to do it by sails alone—that's an art you Portuguese will soon be teaching to the rest of the world." He looked around at the bleary faces. "What are the winds and currents like, down there past Cape Non?"

They competed in babble, then one of them said, "Better ask Pedro here. He's the one who can tell you."

The other men nodded assent. "He doesn't have his pilot's ticket yet, but I'd rather sail with him than a hundred de Britos with a thousand *portolani*."

Sandro turned his attention to the sailor he had asked Catalina about. He saw a swarthy, well-knit fellow, a few years younger than himself, with an earnest, honest face. Pedro had been sitting quietly, a little withdrawn and doleful, nursing some private concern. But he responded courteously to Sandro's questions.

"We're learning our way around that part of the sea little by little, senhor. Some day, by God's grace, we'll have it all figured out. There's a wind down the face of Portugal that we've long known about. Foreign vessels have always anchored in the roadway off Sagres—past the point of Cape Vincent—to wait for variations that will start them off to where they want to go. It's always been easy to sail southward down the great slab of Africa, but nobody's been willing to go too far because the problem then is to get back. The Canary current picks up there, and the fear has always been that the northerly winds and currents would increase to the point where it would be beyond the power of a vessel to return by any means." He gave Sandro an apologetic half-smile. "Even by your Venetian oars."

"I thought the problem was sea monsters," Sandro said, matching Pedro's smile with a grin of his own.

"I've never seen a sea monster, *senhor*. I've seen treacherous currents, lee shores, shoals, breakers."

"No 'senhor.' Call me Sandro."

For a moment he tried to see himself through Pedro's eyes. Despite their closeness in age, Sandro knew that he must seem much older to the young sailor—his ordeals had cut deep lines in his face and given him that gravity of manner that men acquire when the passage of years brings them closer to a consciousness of the patient omnipresence of death. And then, too, there were his noble manners, never to be unlearned, though they might be silted over. His Portuguese, too, must seem stiff and formal to these men, learned as it was as an acquired language with all the proper grammar.

"He's the one they call O Fidalgo," one of the other sailors supplied helpfully.

"*Muito prazer, Dom Sandro.*" Pedro was a little stilted.

"Just plain Sandro."

They reached across the table to shake hands on it. Pedro broke into a big smile. "*Bom.* It's a bargain."

"So you've never seen any sea monsters? What about boiling water?"

"Breakers and foam. But such waters are dangerous, so of course the story gets started."

Sandro took a sip of his wine. "You say the current picks up between the Canaries and the African coast opposite?"

"That's right. But there are signs that, once through that squeeze, the prevailing winds veer toward the west. You'd have to get well past Bojador to tell for certain, though."

"Cape Bojador. The Bulge."

Pedro nodded. "Already it's replaced Cape Non as the obstacle no one wants to cross. The infante has even worked up a little speech about it, like the speech he used to give about Cape Non. 'If you do nothing more than to pass this cape, I shall be satisfied,' he says. But so far he has no takers."

The look in Pedro's eyes was one of pure hunger. Sandro found himself taking a liking to this serious young man.

"You've been at the court of Prince Henry?" Sandro asked, letting it show that he was impressed.

Pedro lowered his eyes modestly. "*Sim,*" he said. "That's right."

"Let me buy you another drink. Let me buy all of you another drink." He called Catalina over.

Pedro returned to his subject. "I—that is, De Brito, with

my advice—was able to take advantage of the slight change in wind direction, after you get far enough out to sea, to zig-zag our way north again."

"That's a valuable piece of knowledge."

Pedro had something more important to say. "If it's true that the prevailing winds veer further and further to the west past that point, then they must make a great circle somewhere in the Ocean of Darkness and come back as the westerlies that the English and the northmen use in the Iceland trade. And that would mean that no one need be afraid to venture out into the Sea of Darkness, to discover what new lands and islands might be there, because return home would always be assured—you would catch the easterlies at the low latitudes south of the Canaries and let them bear you round and back."

His youthful face was transformed by his vision. It all sounded highly improbable to Sandro. He replied with a cautious "Interesting."

"*Com certeza,*" Pedro said, nodding vigorously. "And if there were only a reliable method of determining latitude while at sea—or at least finding the same latitude twice . . ."

That was more like it. Sandro rummaged around in his head and came up with his knowledge of the *kamal,* the board-and-string device used by Arab mariners, and the Arab astronomical lore that he had learned as secretary to Jaybir al-Sumut while a slave in Damascus. That would be knowledge indeed to bargain with at Sagres. His Venetian merchant's instincts came alive again. The reward would be great for such a prize—if he could reach the right ear.

He had already failed once. When he had first arrived in Portugal he had thought at once of trying to appeal to Ezra Ben Abraham, the Jewish physician and astrologer whose unfortunate servant, Said, had been snatched by the Granadan religious police—the "men of violence"—on the eve of departure. Ezra, Sandro had hoped, would get him an interview with the great Jaime of Majorca, Prince Henry's arbiter in geographical matters. Jaime, in turn, had the power to gain him an audience with the Prince. But with Said dead, Ezra had refused to see Sandro. He was a timid, palsied old man, suspicious of an unannounced stranger from Granada who came to his door claiming to have known the dead man. Sandro had retreated—in danger of being denounced as a secret Moor himself.

Now he looked speculatively at this young sailor who seemed to take it for granted that one walked in and out of the presence of Prince Henry.

"The Arabs have such a method," he said circumspectly. "They sail across open ocean all the way to the spice islands and always make landfall at the latitude they've chosen."

"Is that true?" Pedro said.

"I was a prisoner of the Moors. A sea captain showed me how it's done."

"These astrologers at the court claim to be able to take an altitude with their heathen astrolabes, but they're just about useless on the pitching deck of a ship at sea."

"The Arab method is so simple that any sailor can be taught to use it. The only condition is that he must have been to the place before . . . or at least someone else must have been there before him."

"Watch out, Pedro," one of the sailors called good-naturedly. "It sounds like sorcery."

"No sorcery," Sandro said affably. "It's as easy as looking at the end of your nose, once you've learned the trick of it."

He smiled to himself at how absurdly simple the *kamal* was. A chip of wood and a knotted string you held in your teeth, and you knew at once if you were above or below your target latitude. He had whittled one for himself since landing in Portugal. So far the string had one knot in it—for Sagres, the place where he was now. It was an astonishing thought that, armed with that one knot, he could if he wished sail with Pedro out into the Sea of Darkness beyond the sight of land; that he had only to cast north or south till the north star was perched on the corner of the wood chip, and then sail due east until he unerringly found Sagres again. Perhaps it was a form of sorcery, after all.

"So that one would not have to skirt a dangerous coast in order to find a landmark like Cape Non—or Bojador?" Pedro said, his interest awakened. "Provided one had fixed the latitude once before, one could stand well out to sea and make landfall where the approach was safe."

"Exactly," Sandro said.

A big slow grin spread across Pedro's face. "And one would not have to send an astrologer ashore to take a reading."

His shipmates laughed, and Sandro laughed with them.

"Can you teach me this Arab method?" Pedro asked.

"Gladly. When do you sail for Bojador again?"

Pedro's face clouded. "When some rich gentleman works up the courage. In the meantime, I go back to Madeira."

Sandro saw his entry to the Sagres court evaporating. "You don't have to go back right away, do you?"

For some reason, that was the wrong thing to say. "Why are you asking all these questions?" Pedro said irritably.

A weaving presence loomed over the table, smelling of wine. "I'll tell you why he's asking all those questions. He's a Venetian spy."

Sandro looked up into Rafo's red face and bloodshot eyes. The sailor had been brooding, getting drunker and drunker on the Malmsey Sandro had paid for, working up a fine simmering resentment of the way Sandro's deft courtesy had outmaneuvered him.

"Bugger off," said one of Pedro's companions. "O Fidalgo's a friend of ours, see?"

One of Rafo's friends had appeared behind him to try to get him to come away. "Leave it alone, Rafo," he pleaded. "Don't start any trouble in here."

Rafo shook him off. His hand went to the hilt of his knife. *"Deixe-me!"* he spat. "These foreigners have got to be taught a lesson. The authorities'll thank us."

Sandro did not want to hit the man. He watched the knife warily, waiting for any move. The loud voice had attracted unwelcome attention from the other tables.

"Be sensible, man," he said pleasantly. "I've no quarrel with you. Why don't you go sit down with your friends. I'll buy you all another pitcher of wine."

Rafo's peacemaking friend said apologetically, "He gets like this sometimes. He cut up a Sardinian on our last voyage—accused him of being a Moor. He would've hanged for sure if we hadn't hustled him out of the place." He turned to the swaying Rafo. "Come on, boy. You can sleep it off. You'll feel better in the morning."

He put his hands on the drunken man's shoulders and tried to lead him away. With an animal growl, Rafo took a swipe at him. Unfortunately, the knife was in his fist. The other sailor screamed and lurched backward, holding a hand to an ugly gash that ran down his face and neck. Blood welled up between his fingers.

A couple of sailors at Sandro's table sprang to their feet and grabbed Rafo. One of them got hold of the wrist of the hand that was holding the knife and started wrestling it back and forth. The other took a swing.

"Murderers!" Rafo bellowed. "Spies! Help me, mates!"

Patrons heaved themselves out of their seats, knocking over chairs and benches. Rafo's other companions, seeing only struggles and blood, scrambled to get into the fight. The sailors at Sandro's table jumped up to defend themselves. The Goat's other customers—seamen, dockworkers, and other rough types—chose sides at random, clashing with one another for the pure joy of it. In minutes a huge free-for-all had developed.

Sandro struggled with a burly man who had appeared from nowhere, determined to strangle him. He tore the man's hands from his throat, swung him around in an arc, and smashed him against a wooden pillar. Another man came at him. He parried a blow with a thick forearm and sank a fist into the man's large gut. The man dropped to his knees, wheezing.

Catalina was at his side, urgently trying to make herself heard above the din.

"This way, senhor! You've got to get out of here!"

Sandro agreed. No matter what the outcome of the fracas, if he stayed he was likely to become its focus. He had seen the looks on some of the faces when Rafo had shouted that he was a Venetian spy.

He looked around at the seething interior of the Goat of the Sea. There was no way out through the street door or through the door to the courtyard where customers relieved themselves; both openings were blocked by clots of fighting men, who drew anyone who came close enough into their orbits.

"Hurry! There's no time to stand around."

Catalina was tugging at his shirt. He followed her behind the counter to the cubbyhole where the kegs were kept. Vasques, the innkeeper, was standing there with a club in his hand, defending his stock.

"I'm ruined," he said. "Ruined! They're breaking up the place."

"In the morning we'll set the planks back on the kegs and trestles," she said. "We'll replace any broken planks and get a carpenter to knock together a few benches, and everything will be fine."

"He can't go in there," Vasques said.

"You want him to stay down here and have those crazy *mocos* fired to a pitch? Then they really *will* break things up. There'll be nothing left but a pile of splinters and a puddle of wine. Take it easy. We'll get them calmed down in a while."

Tugging Sandro by the arm, she hauled him through a curtain and pointed out a ladder leading to a loft. "That's where I sleep, senhor. Don't get any ideas. It's just that dead customers are bad for business. Climb up there and pull the ladder up after you. And keep quiet."

She turned on her heel, her long black hair swinging. Sandro watched her push her way out through the counter again, every line of her slim body taut and determined. God help the brawlers, he thought, and climbed up the ladder.

Enough candlelight seeped through cracks in the floor for him to take in his surroundings. There wasn't enough headroom for him to stand upright. There was a pile of straw that evidently served for Catalina's bed, a blanket, an old chest with a broken lid, and a few scattered possessions—a comb, a piece of mirror, a little tin box. He found the stub of a candle, but he had no means of lighting it, and a light would not have been a good idea anyway.

He settled down to wait. The sounds from below reached a peak of violence—thumps, crashes that shook the sagging loft floor, shouts, the sound of breakage. But after a time it seemed to diminish somewhat. The violence was spending itself. More and more participants were out of action. He heard Catalina's voice cut stridently through the noise: "All right, you turnipheads, that's enough! Stop it, d'you hear! Did you come here to drink wine or to behave like a bunch of silly *cabritos* butting one another's foreheads? I won't have it, do you understand me?"

Miraculously, the place quieted down. Catalina did not give them a chance to change their minds. Sandro could picture her striding through the wreckage below, following her progress by the sound of her voice as she alternately scolded, cajoled, ridiculed, flattered, or went into furious tirades, as each case called for.

"You, Juan Roiz, aren't you ashamed of yourself, and after all the credit the Goat's allowed you ... and you, Jorge Pires, you come here to seek our little Luiza's favors, don't you? Well, if you don't sit down this minute and behave, you'll never be allowed in the Goat again.... Hey you, *homenzinho,* yes, I'm talking to you! Don't look away from me! Think you're tough, do you, kicking a man when he's down? I saw you. You weren't even the one who floored him. Antão, Dinis, throw the little bastard out for me! We don't want this sort in here. . . ."

There was a scuffle of compliance, and then cheers and laughter. In a remarkably short time, the familiar buzz of tavern conversation was restored, and Sandro heard the sounds of things being set upright. Catalina had them in the palm of her hand. The groans Sandro heard from time to time were presumably the groans of the more seriously injured being helped home by their friends.

Gradually the place emptied out. The cracks in the floor darkened. There was the muffled voice of Vasques saying, *"Boa noite,"* and the creak of the rear door closing.

Sandro waited. After a while a small candle came closer, casting shadows from below, and Catalina's voice said, "Psst, let the ladder down."

Sandro lowered the crude ladder—two poles with lashed crossbars—and Catalina's tousled hair and chiseled face rose through the opening, illuminated by the candle she was carrying. She handed the candle to Sandro and swung herself over the edge with a supple grace that a cat might have envied.

"Everybody's gone," she said. "But I don't think it's wise for you to leave for a while. Some of Rafo's friends are waiting around outside with knives, just in case O Fidalgo shows up. Don't worry, they don't know you're in here— they think you slipped out when the fighting started. They're riffraff, but you won't have to worry about them after tomorrow. They're shipping out on an olive oil carrier. They won't be back for a long time."

"All right. I don't want any trouble."

"Once it starts with knives . . ." She shrugged. "You look like the kind of man who can handle himself, but if you did one of those puppies in and got hauled before a judge, it would go hard for you, being a foreigner."

"I know. I appreciate what you did for me, Catalina. I didn't have a chance to thank you before."

"It's nothing. I told you, dead customers are bad for business. Whether it's you or one of them."

"It wasn't one of them you took up to your sleeping loft."

"Say, didn't I tell you not to get any ideas?"

"Sorry."

She tossed her dark mop of hair angrily. "Maybe I'm only a *tauernera*, but I don't take customers upstairs for money. You want that kind of funny business, you can try one of the other girls!"

"I don't think that of you, Catalina," he said with grave courtesy. His manners might have been used at court.

She looked at him suspiciously. "All right, then."

"I have the greatest respect for you."

"Are you making fun of me?"

"No."

"I've had two lovers in my life, if you want to know. The first was the *capocho de gado*, the boy who helped with the cattle, on the neighbor's farm where my mother sent me to work when I was big enough. It was over in a minute, and I had to wash my dress afterward. He wanted to try again the next day, but I wouldn't let him."

"And the second?"

"Lost at sea. That was a man, that one. We had some time together, at any rate. Almost two years. We might have gotten married some day."

"I'm sorry."

She sighed. "Life doesn't always go where the heart wills. But you ought to know that. You've had your disappointments, too."

"Yes," he said, more curtly than he had intended.

"You don't have to talk about them," she said acidly. "Don't worry, I won't ask."

"Catalina, I . . ."

"Don't bother," she said. "You don't have to explain anything. I don't care. I take you for what you are. You're bitter about something, that's all I have to know. And you don't want to let yourself in for any more disappointments. That's why you're so closed up."

"You're angry."

"Why should I be angry? Am I angry at a clam for closing its shell?"

"It's my business," he said, beginning to lose his temper himself.

"Didn't I say so?"

"My life is just fine the way it is. Even if it didn't go . . . *onde quer o coração* . . . where the heart willed it. I'm beginning to establish myself here in Portugal. I'm making money. . . ."

"Yes, you can make money. And you can get into fights. You want to kill someone, I think."

He caught his breath. "How could you know something like that?"

"I'm right, then."

"I thought you said you weren't going to pry?"

"I'm not prying. I don't care about the particulars. It's what you are *now*! It's easy to tell when a man's poisoned by hate. And remorse. There's something you blame yourself for, isn't there?"

He stopped her mouth the only way he could think of, short of hitting her. He pulled her to him abruptly by the wrists and planted a harsh, bruising kiss on her lips.

He expected scratches, clawed eyes, a stream of invective—maybe even an attempt with the little knife he had felt under her skirt when he brushed against it. He was tensed to back off, retreat down the ladder to face whatever might be waiting for him in the street outside. But when he released her, there was only a stare from widened eyes, inches from his own, and then their lips were fastened greedily again—he could not have said whether he made the move or she, or whether they both moved at the same time—and her long fingers were woven into his hair to hold his head steady.

"I didn't mean that to happen," he whispered when they stopped for a moment to breathe. "Don't think I planned it."

"What a pity. I hoped you had."

"Catalina . . ."

"*Shhh.*" She pressed a finger against his lips. "When I said I didn't take customers upstairs for money, I didn't include this."

They helped each other out of their clothes. Catalina gasped when she saw the terrible scars on his body. "*Ai*, your poor back! What did they do to you?"

"It's nothing."

She held him for a moment, pressing herself against him. "I know, *meigo*. The worst ones don't show."

He eased them gradually apart, shivering with need. His impatience made him clumsier than he wanted to be. One hand found a breast and closed spasmodically around it, while with the other hand he began to jockey her by degrees into position.

"There's no need to go slow," she said with a shudder. She was breathing as fast as he was. She arranged herself on the straw and reached up to draw him to her. Her cry came almost immediately.

A gray dawn was showing between the cracks when Sandro awoke. Catalina was shaking him. "*Diabo,* you sleep hard! You'll have to go. Vasques will be here soon with the wine crier."

Still half asleep, he reached for her and took her once more before getting up. She stretched and sighed, then brought him his scattered clothes. As he put them on, she said, "What, no flowery speeches? I thought gentlemen were supposed to be *galante* to their ladies."

"Catalina, I . . ."

"I don't expect a declaration of love. But you could at least pay me some compliment."

"What devil's got into you? I thought we understood each other."

"Of course I'm not one of your fine Venetian ladies. Maybe that's it."

Exasperated, he said, "I haven't seen any fine Venetian ladies for some time. And I stopped being a gentleman the day they chained me to a bench."

He smiled a twisted smile as he thought of Giuditta. He wondered what she looked like now. She, at least, had gotten the benefit of his flowery speeches and love songs, when he still had such things in him. But Maffeo had collected the result; and as for love songs, the thickened, callous hands he wore now at the ends of his wrists would never make music on a lute again.

Catalina's eyes narrowed. "Who's Marina?"

"What?"

The name came as a shock. He had never thought to hear it spoken aloud again. He himself only murmured it silently on the rare occasions when he could bear to unwrap the little wooden icon that had been hers. Now, hearing it, a swirl of images roared through his head, Marina's pale oval face mingled with the Byzantine face in the icon.

"You said her name in your sleep."

Sandro's mouth tightened. He said nothing.

"So that's how it is? Well, at least we're getting somewhere."

She had finished getting dressed herself, throwing the coarse woolen dress that was her working garment over her head and smoothing it down at the hips. She came over to him and kissed him lightly on the cheek. "It's all right, *meigo*. I told you I take you for what you are."

"Will I see you tonight?"

"Yes, come around after the customers leave and I'll let you in."

"Catalina, I'm sorry . . ."

"Oh, shut up. Just come."

# CHAPTER 8

Pedro woke to a pounding headache. Cautiously he put a hand to his skull and probed the tender place there, where one of the troublemakers had hit him with a chair leg. His mouth tasted like the bilge of a carrack. He rinsed it out with water from the clay jug lying near his head and spat on the dirt floor of the goat shed.

"Awake finally? I thought you were going to sleep away the morning."

Pedro raised his head incautiously, at the cost of a stab of pain, and focused on the round, honest face of one of his shipmates, Ribiero. Ribiero was munching on bread and sausage, a straw-cradled jug of wine sitting close at hand.

"Where are Marto and Roiz?"

"They went down to the waterfront to ask about a ship again." He took a swig of wine and held out the jug to Pedro. "Here, want some?"

Pedro swallowed a couple of mouthfuls. It seemed to help. He wiped off the neck of the jug and handed it back to Ribiero.

"You'll be the local celebrity when you get back," Ribiero said, then belched comfortably. "Madeira's conquering hero—the man who passed Cape Non and sailed to the edge of the world. Even Zarco didn't have the nerve to do that. You'll have all the girls you can handle."

"There aren't any spare girls on Madeira," Pedro said. "There's five men for every woman."

"That's what I heard." Ribiero took a bite of sausage and chewed it with deliberation. "Otherwise I'd go with you. But I'm enjoying myself too much here. Every tavern miss and baker's lass between Lagos and Cabo de São Vicente has been throwing herself at our heads. And I haven't paid for a drink since we returned from Africa. I tell you seriously, I'm tempted to stay put till my money runs out—even if Marto and Roiz find a berth. I can always get another ship later, with all the activity around here."

"Your money may run out sooner than you think," Pedro said. "They won't be buying you free drinks forever—and when the first crew passes Cape Bojador, you'll be past history. The bloom's off the peach already. Even the *gatuno* who rented us this shed is charging us five dinheiros a day for bare earth and straw, whether we're the conquerers of Non or not." He got up and pissed out the door.

"It's still cheaper than dossing down at a sailors' *albergue* in town. The prices in Sagres have gone sky-high, with all the artisans and shipyard workers flocking here for jobs. We sailors are the cause of the boom, and yet we're at the bottom of the ladder."

"There's going to be a shortage of sailors. Wages will go up."

"I can't wait that long. You sound like a priest. Things will be better in the next world."

"No next world. Sooner or later there'll be an expedition to pass Bojador too. The prince won't rest till it's done. Experienced hands, who sailed with Cabral to Cape Non, will be at a premium."

"No Bojador expedition for me. Once is enough to risk my neck. A nice safe *não* with a cargo of wine, that's for me."

"You're a man of no vision."

"Why don't *you* go? You're the daredevil. You can hang around here and keep me company till your ship comes along. Your pay ought to stretch for a while."

Pedro's expression was troubled. "It will be a while before a ship can be found that will go to Bojador. For now, Cabral is refusing to go back himself, and everybody's listening to his proposition that the navigable sea ends there—though the infante is goading Gil Eanes to make a try." He bit his lip. "I'll have to gamble. I can come back to Sagres with the supply ships from time to time to see what 's going on, but for now, I . . . I have to get back to Madeira."

"To slip it to the little *degredada* you've been mooning over?" Ribiero said with a smirk.

"Shut up."

Pedro stood in the doorway for a moment, looking out over the sparse landscape. He saw a few scrubby olive trees, a grazing goat, a dusty path leading downhill past the stony fields to town. Beyond the tiled rooftops a beryl-green sea lay flat and immense, dotted with anchored ships, both Portuguese and foreign, that were waiting for a favorable breeze to take them past the jutting chin of Sagres Point.

Movement on the path below caught his eye. "Here come Marto and Roiz now. They've got someone with them."

Ribiero got up to see. "It's the Venetian. The one who started the fight last night."

"He didn't start it."

"Well, who was the cause of it, then. It was his fault for asking all those questions about Bojador."

"He's an intelligent man. Not like you."

"Where's it got him? The galleys, from the look of him, and then dock work."

They watched the trio approach. As the tall Venetian caught sight of Pedro, he hurried his step, leaving his two squat escorts to catch up. He shook hands with Pedro. "I was looking all through town for you this morning, and then I saw Marto and Roiz, and recognized them from last night."

Roiz came up behind him. "What luck. He keeps a little shop. He knows the movements of all the ships. He steered us to a berth on a merchantman going to Genoa. There's room for two more."

He looked at them questioningly.

"Not me," Pedro said.

"How about you, Ribiero?"

"I'll think about it. First let's finish off the jug."

Sandro accepted a drink. "I brought you the Arab instrument," he said to Pedro. "It's called a *kamal*." He held out a square of planking with a piece of string threaded through a hole drilled through its center.

"It's only a piece of wood," Pedro said, disappointed. He had visualized some beautiful, intricate, polished brass device, like an astrolabe.

"That's the beauty of it. It's so simple that I can teach you how to use it in a quarter of an hour. But don't be deceived. It's more useful than all the astrological mumbo jumbo that learned men mumble about. Once you get back to Madeira, for example, I'll show you how to fix the latitude there with a knot. Then on future trips, once you strike that latitude, all you'll have to do is make landfall is steer due west. No worry about looking for a line of mist on the horizon, or watching the flight of seabirds. Same business when you return to Portugal. You can land on any stretch of coast you want, without overshooting the mark and losing days of sailing. If we could somehow bring this to the attention of Prince Henry or one of his geographers . . ."

"He knows of a ship to Madeira, Pedro," Marto broke in. "I told him how anxious you were to return, and it turned out that his chandler's shop is supplying some of the rope and wax that's being sent. It sails this afternoon, and they can use a few more hands. If you hurry . . ."

"Is this true?" Pedro asked Sandro.

"Yes, but there's no hurry. I can put you on another ship to Madeira in a few days."

"No," Pedro said. "I've been gone too long."


"You can't wait any longer," Mafalda said. "Lobo's going around boasting. He's saying you're already his. He's been drinking. He's working himself up to raping you, I tell you! And then he'll go to Zarco and offer to make it 'right.'" She laughed bitterly. "That's the way of it, like it or not, *cara*. It's the men who arrange things in this world."

"I'll keep away from him," Inês said. "I'll stay where there are other people around. . . ."

"Listen to me," Mafalda said slowly, drawing her shawl around her as if it were cold, instead of hot enough to make the sweat trickle down her forehead, "maybe you can evade him for tonight. I'll sit up with you, and I'll get Heitor to come and sit with you, too. Maybe you can evade him for another day or even two. But sooner or later he'll catch you unaware. On the way to the stream to fill a bucket. Or in the high weeds where you've gone to relieve yourself. Or in your own shelter when there's no one around. And then he'll knock you down and put a hand over your mouth or put a knife at your throat to keep you from screaming, and he'll force your legs apart and rape you. That's what he was sent to prison for—he killed the woman's husband, too, but they didn't hang him for it because he said it was self-defense—and since we landed on Madeira he's raped two other women, but they were afraid to complain. And then, *cara*, you'll belong to him, like a little whipped dog who cringes at the sound of the master's boots."

Inês shuddered, as if she, too, were cold. "In a day . . . two days . . . Pedro might be back. If I can hold out till then . . ."

"No, he won't be back in time. If he comes back at all. That one, he had faraway places in his eyes. You've got to face it, *cara*. You know what sailors are."

"Who'd dare to have me? You said yourself that Lobo's intimidated all the men."

"Not all the men, *cara*." Mafalda gave her a peculiar look.

"Who?"

"Heitor."

Inês stared at her in disbelief. "Heitor? You must be mistaken."

"Haven't you noticed the way he looks at you? He worships you. But he thinks you're so far above him that he might as well hope for a star."

Her tone was perfectly matter-of-fact. She continued to look at Inês with the friendliness she had always shown.

"No . . . I couldn't . . ."

"He's a decent man. He's good and he's honest and he's gentle. He's not the cleverest man in the world, but you'd be his life. He's hardworking and he's steady as a rock and you can depend on him absolutely. Maybe you don't love him, but you can respect him and feel affection for him, and after a while you could learn to accept a life with him."

Inês felt a hot, deep flush rising in her face. "But . . . but Mafalda . . . I thought that you and Heitor . . ."

Mafalda said breezily, "That's all right, *santa*. I can take care of myself."

"I couldn't . . ."

"Didn't I say love's not important? And what I feel for Heitor isn't love anyway. He's just a good choice, that's all." The smile on her face was the bright, professional smile she wore when rope dancing. "I'll get along. One of the sergeants has an eye on me. Good catch, eh? His name's Juan."

"Mafalda, you mustn't . . ."

"I may even try for Morales. He's getting to a point where his guard's lowered. An old man needs his comforts."

Inês burst into tears.

Mafalda put an arm around her. The bright smile broke down, to be replaced by concern. "There, there, *coitada*, you'll get used to the idea. You just have to make up your mind to it. The important thing is to see that you're safe from that animal. It wouldn't have worked with me and Heitor anyway. How do you think I'd feel through the years, knowing he was pining after you?"

"I never . . . I never . . ."

Mafalda stood up. "I'll tell him he can come around."

Heitor shuffled his feet. "I went to Zarco," he said. "He said Lobo had already been there. I told him you didn't want to marry Lobo—that you'd said yes to me. He said all right—that it didn't matter one way or the other as long as you got married without delay. 'Why not let the woman have her choice,' he said. I've spoken to the priest. He'll be ready for us in about an hour."

Inês gave him a wan smile. "You've taken care of everything, senhor. You didn't waste any time."

She had been surprised at Heitor's calm resolution and the way he had immediately taken charge. She had always taken his oxlike stoicism for passivity, and she was impressed by the initiative he had shown.

"Zarco gave me a ring for the ceremony," he said shyly. "Dona Constanca donated it from her jewel box. He gives his blessing as governor—he'll be there."

He extracted the ring from a knot he had tied in the tail of his shirt and showed it to her. It was thin, scratched, and bent a little out of shape, but it was gold.

She faced him, the tears starting to come again, and tried to smile. "I'll be a good wife to you, Heitor," she promised.

He had not yet touched her, and he didn't touch her now. She could see him swallowing hard. "*Bom*," he said. "I'll come back for you in an hour. But first there's something I have to do."

"You're taking secondhand goods," Lobo sneered. "The sailor's had the first dip and left you his scrapings."

Heitor stood planted in front of him, stubborn and immovable. "There's nothing you can do," he said. "Zarco gave his permission, and he'll be there on the beach when the priest says the words, for the whole colony to see."

Lobo, sitting on a fire-blackened log, continued to whittle at a piece of seal meat with his knife. How he had gotten it, Heitor didn't know. Such fare, the bounty of the official hunting parties that Zarco sent to the Cave of the Wolves, were supposed to go into the common store.

"You shouldn't have gone against me, farmer," he said.

Heitor said nothing.

"Tell me, farmer, have you ever killed a man?"

Puzzled, Heitor said, "No."

"Do you think you could kill me over the woman?"

Heitor refused to be drawn. "I tell you, it's settled."

Lobo tore at the seal meat with his teeth and, hardly bothering to chew, swallowed it whole. He looked up at Heitor.

"Go ahead, farmer," he said. "I'll bide my time."

After all this time, Madeira was still burning. As he waded ashore, Pedro could see the thick column of smoke rising from inland, making an umbrella high in a lucid blue sky. But the blackened waste that edged the shore like a funeral border showed shoots of green poking through. And some permanent houses had been built on the cleared land while he was gone—neat, whitewashed cottages with red roofs.

The wide, pebbled beach was an anthill of activity as the island's inhabitants came out to meet the ship's boats and help them unload. They looked better dressed, better fed, and happier than when Pedro had left. Stockpiles of supplies, still undistributed, lay about. The prince's response had been generous.

Perhaps, Pedro thought, there would be a crop before the year's end after all. "The fire's gone underground," a sailor on the ship had told him. "It will take years to burn itself out there in the interior. But it's leaving good farmland behind as it goes."

Pedro stopped the first person he met, a man in a peasant's rough tunic with a hoe over his shoulder. He didn't recognize the man's face; more shiploads of settlers must have come over while he was away.

"Pardon me, friend. Can you tell me where I can find Inês from Faro?" He described Inês.

The man looked blank.

Pedro tried again. "She speaks like . . . like a gentlewoman. She shared a lean-to with a rope dancer, a girl named Mafalda. The lean-to used to be right over there, at the edge of the beach, but it's gone now."

"Oh, that one," the man said, comprehension dawning. "She isn't living with the rope dancer any more. You'll find her in that cottage up there."

He pointed up the slope. Pedro saw one of the new cottages, tiny but trim and well made. The land around it had been cleared for planting, with furrows of freshly turned brown earth striping the carbonized stubble, and there was an animal shed with a thatched roof.

Pedro thanked the man and hurried up the steep hillside. He passed other cottages, other gardens, where a tender dusting of green promised an early vegetable crop.

He saw Inês in the dooryard, scattering grain from her apron to a flock of jostling chickens. He hurried forward.

"Pedro . . ."

She stared at him with widened eyes, the feeding chore forgotten. A handful of grain slipped between her fingers and fell to the ground.

He opened his mouth to speak to her, unburden himself, shower her with apologies for his delay. The ring he had purchased in Lagos was in the pouch of his belt, with the pair of gloves that a virgin bride needed to wear. Before he could speak, Heitor came around the corner of the house with a mattock in his hand, his arms black with dirt up to the elbows.

"See, it's Pedro," Inês said quickly.

Heitor shambled forward with a smile of genuine pleasure on his bluff face. He wiped a hand on his leggings and held it out in welcome. "*Como vai, Pedro?*" he said. "It's good to see you."

". . . Heitor and I were married two weeks ago," Inês was saying through a numbness that seemed to have taken possession of his head. He had to put the individual words together to make sense out of them.

"We were afraid we might have trouble from Lobo—you know, that bad actor who hangs about with the rest of the *malandros*," Heitor filled in, "but he hasn't bothered us. I guess with the governor's seal of approval on the marriage, he decided to give up."

"We're . . . we're very happy," Inês said, her face aflame.

Heitor's expression was sheepish. "I don't deserve her," he said.

Pedro made himself say all the right things. *"Felicidades."* He looked around. "You've made a good start. Did you build the house yourself?"

Heitor beamed. "No, everybody helps, one house at a time. We can put up the walls and roof in a day. There's still plenty of lumber north of Pico Ruivo, believe it or not. We bring it around by ship from the north coast. If the fire stops there, we'll have a surplus for the infante."

"But we've got to get a crop in first," Inês said. "Other than garden vegetables." She darted a brief look at Heitor, to defer to him, but as he made no move to claim his right to speak for them both, she went on: "Heitor's been given millet seed—Zarco's constructing a grain mill—and so we'll show a profit for the first season. But in the long run, we think the grapes will do better—we've been promised some of the cuttings from Cyprus."

She stopped, out of breath. Her eyes were trying to tell him to understand. Pedro turned away.

"It's good that you're here," Heitor said. "You'll stay for dinner. We're still existing mostly on the relief grain and sea rations sent by the prince, but there's plenty of it, and we'll kill a chicken in your honor."

Pedro cast about desperately for a way out. "I . . . I can't. I've got to see Morales. We've got business to discuss."

Word that Cape Non had been passed had not yet reached Madeira, but now, with the arrival of the ship that had brought Pedro and the mingling of the crew and passengers with the colonists, it would spread very quickly. Pedro's refusal would seem very natural in retrospect to Heitor and Inês.

"Will you stay here on Madeira now, Pedro?" Heitor asked. The question brought a look of alarm to Inês's face that he didn't notice.

"No," Pedro said. He admired how calm his voice was. "I'll go back to sea. Prince Henry will be sending out more expeditions. He'll need experienced seamen."

     •    •    •    •

"So you passed Cape Non?" Morales said.

He sat back comfortably in his chair, a real chair of carved wood that he must have brought back from Portugal with him on his last voyage. There was regret in his face, a kind of wistful longing. Pedro noticed how he had aged.

"Yes," Pedro said. "And we would have passed Bojador too, if Cabral had listened to me."

"The gentlemen never listen," Morales said. "They know everything."

"Don't exercise yourself," Mafalda said from behind his chair. "You know it's bad for your digestion. Let me get you another glass of wine."

Morales reached up absently and patted the hand that was resting on his shoulder. "I don't know what I'd do without you, *crianca*," he said.

Pedro looked around at the little house that Zarco had allotted to Morales. It was snug, shipshape, with Morales's sea chest and other belongings arranged in neat, geometric order against the whitewashed walls. Morales seemed to be accumulating possessions—a Moorish wall hanging, a set of cups, a ship model. Too many things for a seafaring man— they could only tie him to land.

"Your theory of a bight between Non and another cape was true," Pedro said. "I kept telling them that."

"So now they've got a new bugaboo," Morales sighed.

"It's the shoals. They stretch so far out to sea in a long sweep that it's easy to imagine that the line of white spray marks the margin of boiling water. It's hot there, too, I can tell you that. The men imagine that if they go on, they'll turn black, like the natives the slave caravans bring back."

Morales sipped at his wine. "Prince Henry will goad his captains to go on. It will be just like Cape Non. They'll go down and nibble at it, and come back and tell him it can't be done, and make a raid or two on the Moors on the way back in order to justify the trip, and sooner or later they'll realize it's a coast like any other."

"Cabral doesn't want to go back. The ocean stops there, he says."

"Then someone else will do it." Morales's inky eyes took on a long focus that must have made a blur of everything in the room. "You're lucky to be young at such a time, Pedrozinho. I envy you."

"You're still the best navigator in the realm," Pedro protested.

Morales shook his head. "Zarco will never release me. Maybe he's afraid I'll discover another island for somebody else. He's jealous of his reputation. Take a lesson from me, Pedrozinho. Don't get trapped."

Mafalda, puttering around in the background, said, "Oh, he's come back to Madeira to put down roots." She shot a challenging look at Pedro. "Wasn't that the idea?"

There was an edge of hostility in her voice that shocked Pedro. He had always gotten along well enough with Mafalda. Morales, nodding to himself, didn't seem to notice.

"No," Pedro said. "I'm going back to sea. I'll return to Portugal as soon as I can. There'll be other expeditions from Sagres. I'm going to sign on with the first one that will have me."

Morales asked, *"Certo?"*

"Yes."

"You can take the supply ship back for me, then. After it unloads. Save me a trip. The pilot decided to stay behind on Madeira. Good lad—I trained him myself. I thought I'd have to take his place for the return." He shifted his weight in the chair to make himself more comfortable. "I'll be glad to skip a voyage."

"All right."

"So you want to sign on for another voyage of exploration?" Morales said approvingly. "Who do you think is going to make the next attempt on Bojador? Gil Eanes?"

"Maybe. But that won't be for a while. He'll take some persuasion. Anybody will, after the stories Cabral's crew is spreading. But for now, the infante has a new bee in his bonnet."

Morales looked at him with interest. "What's that?"

"He's been going through the old maps and charts that are piling up in his school for navigation. He came across a map from Majorca that shows the islands of Saint Brendan only a few hundred miles to the west."

"The Irish monk who was supposed to have sailed to the Land of the Saints?"

"Yes."

Morales spat on the dirt floor. "Brasile. Antilia. The Crystal Island. They're only myths. The mapmaker, whoever he was, was only filling in empty places on his parchment, the way mapmakers like to do."

"Like the Fortunate Islands? But Prince Henry sent you and Zarco to look for Machin's island in case it had something to do with the Fortunate Islands, and you discovered Madeira."

A grin split Morales's creased face. "True."

"Then why shouldn't there be other islands out there in the Sea of Darkness—and even a Land of the Saints farther west?"

Morales thought it over. "If there are, they'll be discovered by accident sooner or later, provided the prince keeps pushing past Bojador. Because the ships that return from the southern latitudes of Africa will have to beat against the northeast winds and take a roundabout course to the west of the Canaries and Madeira, as you did on your way home. And eventually some storm will blow a ship farther west than its captain wants it to be."

"That may be. But the prince wants to take a more direct approach. Porto Santo and Madeira only whetted his appetite. He's sure there are more islands out there to discover."

"Would Cabral be game enough to make the attempt?"

Pedro was startled by the question. After a moment's reflection he said, "Perhaps. He's not afraid to sail a few hundred miles out into the open sea, now that he's been shown how. It's only the end of the world that he's afraid of."

Morales leaned forward. He seemed to have come to life. "Don't forget that Velho Cabral was the one who charted the Canaries currents. He's shrewd. He'll have thought it over. Maybe he won't attempt Bojador, but he's a good seaman, and he was the one who was bold enough to pass Cape Non, after all. Listen, Pedrozinho, I know you're disappointed, but my advice to you is to sign on with Cabral again when you get back to Sagres." He pondered a moment. "You'll be able to show him a thing or two about those winds and currents to the west of Madeira. I'll help you. We'll go over the charts together before you leave."

For a moment Pedro thought of mentioning the Arab navigation secret that the Venetian, Sandro—O Fidalgo—had told him about, but he decided against it. It would seem primitive to a man like Morales, who knew how to use the cross-staff, and besides, the Arab trick with the chip of wood only helped you fix your latitude, not your longitude. It wouldn't be important if he wasn't going to voyage south. Of course, he thought, he could test it out on the voyage home by fixing the latitude of Sagres before he left. That way he could at least tell if it was a fraud, in which case he certainly wasn't going to mention it to Morales, Jaime of Majorca, or anybody else.

"It would be a miracle to find land in so vast a sea," he said.

"Miracles can be helped along, Pedrozinho. Land is like a perfumed lady. It sends out its signals far beyond itself. Birds, currents, clouds, the color of the sea."

He called to Mafalda. "Bring me the locked box, *crianca*. The one with my charts and *portolani* in it."

Soon they were down on their hands and knees, with all the bits and pieces of Morales's existence spread around them. No landsman could have made sense of the feathery sketches with their spiderwebs of ruled lines. To Morales it was an interlocking universe, with no distinction between air, water, and solid ground. Pedro lost himself in the wonder of them. This must be, it occurred to him, what written poetry is to a learned man, or what written music is to a minstrel.

"Trust your nose, Pedrozinho," Morales said at the last, as he folded up the charts and put them away. "Your nose will lead you to land."

Mafalda saw Pedro to the door. After a glance over her shoulder, she slipped outside with him.

"You're an idiot," she told him. "You lost four lives. Yes, go! Sail to the edge of the world. Don't come back. Leave her alone now."


"It's like magic," Catalina said.

She leaned over Sandro's shoulder as he wrote in the leather-bound ledger. He could feel her breasts pressing against his shoulder blades, and he wanted her. He thought of taking her into the little room in the back where he slept, but he was expecting a customer, a ship owner named Cutilero, at almost any moment. It would have to wait for tonight.

"Not magic, just the Venetian method of keeping accounts," Sandro said. "It's called double entry. You enter all the debits on *verso* and all the credits on *recto*. You can strike a balance, a *conto saldo*, at any time. It will always balance perfectly."

"*Ai*, those little Arabic numbers make me dizzy," she said. She straightened up and made an admiring inspection of the piles of goods that crammed the narrow shop—coils of rope, candles, crates of Venetian sandglasses, kegs of tar, canvas, and other ship's stores. She sighed. "Vasques, at the tavern, writes all the money owed to him on a slate. He carries it in his head till he gets around to it. He's always forgetting. I have to keep reminding him, or the tavern would go to ruin. Maybe you should give him lessons. Is this why Venice is so wealthy?"

"Venice leads the world in bookkeeping, as it leads in sea power," Sandro said dryly. "It's these little columns of figures that give us our strength, not ships or cannon."

"It's beyond me," she said. "A coin I can feel in the hand—that's money."

"I learned how to do this as a boy."

He fell silent, and Catalina did not press the conversation any further in that direction. Sandro had come out of his shell enough to share neutral memories but not personal ones. She had no picture of his life beyond a bare and hollow outline.

"So many things a ship needs!" she said in her most cheerful voice, pirouetting for another quick scan of Sandro's inventory. "And a penny to be made on each one! Even this double book of yours soon won't be able to keep up with it, the way things are going."

He managed a smile for her. "The business is growing," he admitted. "I'm only working at the docks one or two days a week now. And that's mostly for the information I can pick up there."

"You need more light and air in here," she said critically. "You'll ruin your eyes." She flounced over to the shop's lone window, where a thin sheet of parchment let in only a fraction of the bright sunlight outside, and flung it open. "You have a visitor," she said. "He's crossing the street to come here."

"Is it my customer?"

"No, it's the sailor from Madeira—the one who was fretting over some woman he left there."

"Pedro?" Sandro put down his pen and slammed the book shut. He was on his feet when Pedro came through the door.

*"Entre,"* Sandro said. *"Como está?* How long have you been back in Portugal? I thought you were going to stay on Madeira for a while."

Pedro seemed flustered at the greeting. He looked around. *"Bom dia, senhora,"* he said to Catalina.

"I'm glad to see your head healed," she said.

"Thank you," he replied. He turned to Sandro. "No, I changed my mind. I'm going to ship out with Cabral again."

Sandro raised an eyebrow. "I hadn't heard that he was putting out to sea. Has he decided to try to round Bojador after all?"

"No, he's going to venture west to look for more islands. The Prince is convinced the ocean is filled with them."

"What a thought!" Sandro exclaimed, his eyes glinting with excitement. "This prince of yours is going to shake up the world!"

Catalina broke in. "I can't stay any longer. Vasques is probably having fits by now. Come to the tavern when you're finished here."

"Yes, yes," Sandro said absently. He turned back to Pedro. "Have you thought over what I told you about the *kamal?*"

Catalina shrugged. *"Adeus, o senhores,"* she said. "Don't get carried away with your imaginary islands." She gathered up her skirts and left.

"I've thought some about it," Pedro replied to Sandro. "A marvelous thing, if it works as you say."

"If we could bring it to the attention of the prince's geographers . . ."

"I'm only a sailor, *amigo.* I don't have much to do with the rare gentlemen who influence the prince."

"You could ask for a hearing with Jaime of Majorca. After all, you were with the ship that sailed past Cape Non to the Bulging Cape. He'll want details of the contour of the bight for his new maps. . . ."

"De Brito has that all sewed up. I'd just be seen as another upstart petty officer, inserting myself to claim a share of the credit. I tell you, I'd be blocked."

"But you were the one who brought the ship back. Without the knowledge you brought them from the Madeira voyages, they'd never have dared to leave sight of land and beat their way north against the wind."

"The glory goes to Cabral. And maybe some rubs off on De Brito."

"Cabral knows what you did."

Pedro's mouth twisted into a line of good-humored resignation. "I think maybe he's forgotten that."

"You could speak directly to the prince," Sandro said impatiently. You'll have plenty of chances. He likes to poke around the ships while preparations are being made."

Sandro himself had tried once or twice to approach Prince Henry personally, but hadn't been able to get past the great swarm of courtiers. There was always some officious popinjay to ask him his business, and when he said chandler, to direct him to some minor functionary.

"You said yourself," Sandro added lamely, "that he likes to talk to the common mariners."

"With Cabral and De Brito around? I couldn't open my mouth to the prince in front of them. I'd be swatted down like a mosquito."

Sandro fought a mounting sense of frustration. "But I'm offering a gift beyond price. Can you imagine the riches the prince would heap on us if we could present him with this Arab secret and convince him that it works?"

"People are always trying to sell him secrets—maps that show the location of the kingdom of Prester John, incantations that whistle up the wind, instruments for telling time at sea by peering through the navel of a painted man on a disc and turning a pointer."

"I tell you, this is no humbug!"

Pedro thought it over. "I'll do one thing for you," he said finally. "You'll have to trust me with your secret. Teach me how to take these sightings and tie these knots you speak of, and I'll test it out on the voyage to discover the isles of Saint Brendan."


"He'll do it," Sandro said.

Catalina turned on the bed of straw to face him and propped herself up on one elbow. "A secret's only valuable when no one knows it," she said.

"I'll have to take a chance on him. I think he's honest and uncomplicated."

"Honest, maybe. Uncomplicated, I don't think so."

"He's the son of a fisherman, trying to get ahead in the world. He knows the value of a secret."

Catalina plucked at a straw that was poking through the

rough blanket and scratching her. In the darkness of the loft, Sandro could see the outline of her naked body—the fine shoulders, the deep breasts, the splendid curve of hip—and he couldn't help thinking how magnificent she would look in expensive clothes, how much better than some dumpy *dona* who could afford the trappings of gentility.

"If he cared about wealth, he'd keep your secret," she said. "But he's driven by something else. If he can get it by betraying your secret, he'll do that instead."

Sandro said, with a trace of uneasiness, "What would he get by doing that?"

"A way to take him to far places, places nobody's been before. Like these imaginary islands to the west. Or the boiling lands to the south. He'll do anything to get there—even if it means hurting other people, hurting himself."

"You're talking nonsense."

"He's as crazy as the infante. If you can't see it in his eyes, you can at least hear it in his talk. Couldn't you tell, after sitting with him all that time on the night of the fight?"

"He's not crazy. A man isn't crazy if he wants to do things."

"He is if he gives up too much for it. He gave something up on Madeira. That's why he came back so soon. And it's eating away at him."

Sandro tried to make light of it. "You can tell all that by looking at a man's eyes?" he teased.

"I've had practice," she said.

"I see no islands," Cabral said. "Only a line of rocks."

He stood at the gunwale, shouting to make himself heard above the crash of waves. Pedro, drenched by spray, stood beside him, looking out across the roiling sea at the line of white froth and the black, slick humps of the rocks that broke through the oily surface.

"There must be islands beyond, senhor," he shouted back. "These are only their outposts. Think—how would these rocks raise themselves above the surface of the water in the middle of the ocean, seven hundred miles from land, if they were not the spine of some sort of ridge?"

"We've taken soundings," Cabral said with a determined shake of his head. "It's deep ocean here."

Pedro tried to choose his words. At least the friar was ar-

guing with him, not imperiously and abruptly cutting him
short. De Brito, aware of his limitations and leery of the
open sea, had refused to sign on for the westward voyage of
discovery, and Cabral had enlisted another pilot of reputation, Diego de Silves, to take his place. But De Silves too
had overreached himself, and now sat huddled in the waist
of the *barcha*, paralyzed by indecision. Cabral had tacitly
promoted Pedro to the job of pilot, without admitting it
aloud.

"It's deep because of the steepness of the slopes as they
fall away down to the ocean floor. But there'll be other peaks
that have thrust themselves higher, making bigger islands—
islands that a ship can land on. We'll find them a little farther to the west—I'm sure of it. Look at those cloud
formations.

Cabral squinted into a steel sky. At last he turned to look
at Pedro, pursing his lips.

"The men won't stand for it. De Silves reckons that we're
a thousand miles from Portugal, not seven hundred. The
isles of Saint Brendan are supposed to be much closer. Our
stores are running short—we miscalculated. Besides, that
freak east wind that brought us most of the way is shifting.
We'll make no headway now. We'll have to turn back."

Pedro clenched his fists in frustration. How could he
make Cabral see? His eyes ran unhappily over the *barcha*'s
two conventional square sails, now beginning to flap and sag
as the east wind that had filled them all these days continued to veer toward the northeast. Cabral had refused to let
him rig a fore-and-aft sail, saying the ship could run well
enough with the wind on one quarter or another.

"We can forereach a few more degrees," Pedro said, beg-
ging now. He began to improvise wildly in his head. "And
we can lie closer to the wind, even with the sails we have
now, if you'll let me rehang the main yard off-center—all we
have to do is lower it a few feet so as to let out the starboard
lift to support the heavier side and run a stay from the short
side and lash it to the gunwale."

Cabral was a good enough seaman to take in the import
of what Pedro was saying, but he shook his head. "I won't
risk the main yard a thousand miles out to sea. If she tried
to jibe, the stay would snap like a thread, and we could lose
everything."

"Just a few more days of weathering as best we can,

then," Pedro pleaded. "You can't go back and tell the infante you got this far and turned around."

He had gone too far. He saw Cabral's thin aristocratic nose turn white and the penetrating eyes hood themselves.

"We've done what we can. The infante knows we did not flinch at Cape Non. Perhaps we'll come back next year and search these seas again for islands."

He collared a passing gromet. "Ask Senhor de Silves to come aft for a moment," he said. "Tell him we're preparing to come about."

The gromet scurried off. Pedro watched him with despair. He cursed himself for having offended Fray Goncalo. He turned again to watch the tantalizing rocks, set in crowns of fanning spray from the waves that slapped at their flanks.

His eyes traced the imaginary spine that he could see underwater, and turned westward. He raised his vision to the sky, a hard gray bright sky with streaks of pale blue showing through, and saw a black speck hovering there. His breath stopped.

After a moment he saw a second speck, wheeling and dipping in great circles. He watched for a moment to be sure.

"*Azores!*" he said. "Hawks!"

Cabral turned to look too. De Silves, coming over to join them, lost his hangdog expression and followed the circling motes with professional interest.

"There must be solid land there," Pedro said unnecessarily.

Cabral turned to him with a grim unforgiving look on his face. But the words he said were, "All right, rehang the main yard as you suggested. We'll sail a little farther west and look for these islands of the *azores*."

# CHAPTER 9

The assembled fleet filled the sea for miles, paving it over with a parquetry of wooden hulls and thrusting a scratchy forest of masts and spars and reefed bamboo sails into a pale yellow sky.

Tom Giles stood on the broad temple terrace overlooking the Yangtze estuary, savoring the fantastic sight. He tried to pick out the Treasure Ship on which he'd be sailing; it was one of the nine-masted leviathans—floating villages with two-acre decks and herds of pigs and farms of wooden tubs growing vegetables.

As Tom stood there, looking out over the fleet, his mind harkened back ten years and thousands of miles—back to 1420, when he was a youth of fifteen skulking around the Bristol docks, seeking a means of escaping his drudge existence. Tom smiled to himself. Never could he have dreamed just how well he would succeed.

From the time he was around ten, Tom had liked to sneak down to the waterfront whenever he could to look at the ships, then creep around to the taverns and, if he had not been thrown out, to eavesdrop on the fantastic tales told by sailors—tales of sea monsters and pirates and strange ports and people. He could not have counted the times he had been dragged back to Master Philpot's and given a sound beating for deserting his chores.

He had been only eight years old when Master Philpot, a

wealthy wool merchant, had come to the weaver's cottage
near Bristol and offered to take Tom, the baby of the family,
off his father's hands. Though his mother had wept when
she gave him over, too many mouths in Jack Giles's home
had made it necessary for Tom to be bound over for service.
But the promised vista of a proper apprenticeship had never
opened before him, and it eventually became apparent to
Tom that he was nothing but a slavey.

Finally, after some seven years, Tom, small and wiry and
as agile as an eel, had decided to run away from his life of
servitude and headed for the docks, stowing away on a ship
bound for Calais. From there he had made his way on foot
to Bruges, where he had been befriended by a Flemish
spinster, but after killing a brutish, corrupt guild master who
had been about to steal everything Tom's benefactress had
owned, he had soon been on the run again.

He had made his way—again on foot—to Venice, where
he had found a Greek ship short a hand and worked the rest
of the way to Constantinople. In that Byzantine capital he
had met a Venetian traveller named Conti, who had spun
tales of the splendor and riches to be found in Vijayanagar,
a Hindu kingdom in southern India. Determined to get to
the fabled land, Tom had once again set out on foot, crossing
the Turkish lands and eventually reaching Trebizond, where
he had been hired as a camel driver on a caravan headed for
Baghdad. Signing on from there as a hand on an Arab ship
bound for Calicut, he had landed in that port city in southwest India some seven years before. Because of his mysterious, blue-eyed-blond appearance, he had soon found himself
living in splendid luxury in the Zamorin's palace like some
exotic pet.

Though his new surroundings had been strange and won-
drous, Tom had quickly found himself growing restless.
Then a mysterious fleet had arrived—scores of gigantic
ships carrying twenty or thirty thousand yellow-skinned
crewmen and soldiers and led by a moonfaced eunuch
named Cheng Ho bearing gifts from the Ming emperor of
Cathay for the Zamorin. Searching for a gift with which to
reciprocate, the Zamorin's eye had fallen on Tom. Tom had
been abruptly deemed the good-luck charm of the mighty
voyager Cheng Ho, commander of the emperor's fleet, and
so the poor weaver's son from Bristol had found himself
dubbed Chin Mao—"Yellow Hair"— and, after a four-month

voyage, during which time he had become almost glib in his new benefactor's singsong language, living in grandeur in the Forbidden City.

But even that incredible adventure had become humdrum, and when Cheng Ho had announced that he would be undertaking another expedition, aiming to go farther than he had ever gone before—around the triangle of the Dark Land of Africa and into the western seas up to Europe—Tom's imagination had caught fire. He had pictured the immense fleet of gigantic Treasure Ships, each inconceivably huge to an English eye, sailing up Bristol Channel. What, he had wondered, would the good people of Avon and Gloucestershire make of Cheng Ho's fantastic armada of ships that hardly resembled ships at all and with thousands of strange yellow faces at the rails?

"Would you like to come with us?" Cheng Ho had asked. Tom's heart had banged in his chest. "Would I!"

And now that day had finally arrived.

"We sail with the morning tide," Cheng Ho said. "The soothsayers have been bribed to proclaim tomorrow a lucky day. We have to be in Fujian province in time to leave with the northeast monsoon for Java. We'll load more supplies at Foochow in the meantime." He turned his moon face from the rows of ships to look at Tom. "You had better say your good-byes tonight."

The serenity of the Temple of the Celestial Spouse was being disturbed by the swarming activity below. Tom could hear the shouts of foremen, the creak of oxcarts together with the curses of the cartmen, the harsh voice of a Captain of a Thousand screaming at his men, the whinnying of horses being ferried out to the troop ships. Tom didn't see how the loading could possibly be finished by morning, even if they worked through the night with torches. Then he reflected that this was the Middle Kingdom, with unlimited numbers of sweating, straining men and animals available to get the job done.

"Sixty-three Treasure Ships and more than a hundred ships of the other types," Cheng Ho mused. "Thirty thousand men. It's even bigger than the expedition that found you, Chin Mao. Do you think your English king will be impressed?"

Tom wondered if Cheng Ho realized he was being facetious. England's largest oceangoing ship could have fit on the poop deck of one of the Treasure Ships, with room to spare.

"I'm sure he will be pleased by the gifts of the Hsuan-te Emperor," Tom said judiciously.

Cheng Ho laughed. "You are getting to be Chinese, Chin Mao. Tell me again, how is the name of your king pronounced?"

"*Henry*—if he's still alive, that is. I left England more than ten years ago. But when I was in Constantinople, I heard that he'd sired a son, whom he also named Henry. So one way or another, there'll be a King Henry on the throne."

"What a curious custom."

Tom wet his lips. "Do you really expect to get as far as England?"

Cheng Ho grew serious. "If there is a way around the southern tip of the Dark Land, the land you call Africa, then there is nothing to stop us from reaching the kingdoms of Europe this time."

"Your map?"

Cheng Ho nodded. "The world map of Chu Tsi-ben. It's over a hundred years old. It shows that Africa does not extend indefinitely, creating an impassable barrier between the eastern and western seas, as European and Arab maps picture it, but comes to an end at a southern cape. How Chu Tsi-ben learned this, we cannot know. But recently there came into my possession a Korean map that shows the same thing. There is a western bulge of immense size, but it can be rounded. The map shows the way. This time I will not turn back."

Tom's blood stirred at the thought of seeing England again. The quiet force in Cheng Ho's high-pitched voice had convinced him as nothing else could have; until now there had been an element of make-believe in the frenetic preparations of the last year and a half, in the long duel Cheng Ho had waged at court with the Anti-Maritime Party for the heart of the Hsuan-te Emperor, who at last allowed Yung Lo's dream of voyage and discovery to be revived.

Cheng Ho saw his excitement and cautioned him: "The wise rooster doesn't crow till he can see the sun. Wait till we're out to sea before rejoicing. Even now we could be ordered not to sail."

Tom said in disbelief, "You can't mean that!"

Cheng Ho did not answer immediately. He brooded for a

while at the vast assemblage of vessels in the estuary, then said, "Our enemies are still strong at court, Chin Mao. They're like the cur who waits till you pass him before he bites. That's why I'm sailing with the second winter moon instead of waiting. I'm determined that their teeth will close on empty air."

"Is that why you bribed the geomancers to hurry things up?"

"One may not disobey an imperial command. One may only not be there to hear it."

Tom stole a look at the incredible fleet spread out below. Whole forests had been cut down to build it, whole populations moved from province to province. The riches of the soil had been plundered to provision it, and an army five times larger than the one that had defeated the French at Agincourt had been mustered to sail with it. It was impossible to believe that this great solid material thing had less reality than a single word uttered by a middle-aged man in Peking.

"I'm sure you have nothing to worry about, San-pao T'ai-chien," Tom said, respectfully using the court title that extolled Cheng Ho as a Three-Jewel Eunuch. "You've outfoxed your enemies all the way. There isn't time for them to do anything now."

"All the same, be on your guard till we sail, Chin Mao," Cheng Ho said. "They'll try any petty trick to harass me. They know I put a value on you, though they don't quite grasp why—these Confucian bookworms couldn't understand the practical use I hope to make of you once we reach the western ocean. Do you know that for a while I didn't think I'd be allowed to take you with me? They tried to persuade the emperor that the luck of the Auspicious Barbarian ought to remain at court, along with the giraffe. This, from the same people who tried so hard to belittle you in the first place! I had to work on the emperor a long time to get him to change his mind."

That shook Tom. It was the first inkling he'd had that his presence on the expedition had ever been in doubt.

"Thank you, San-pao T'ai-chien," Tom said. He struggled for honesty. "I guess I shouldn't have bragged so much about going on the seventh voyage with you."

"No one listens to what a barbarian actually says," Cheng

Ho laughed. "They're too amazed at hearing the sounds of language coming out of his mouth."

Tom took the gibe in good part. He was proud of the role Cheng Ho was allowing him to play. He was no longer a pet with an allowance out of Cheng Ho's pocket. He had been given a stipend as an official translator for the fleet, the same pay as faithful old Ma Huan.

A bell rang within the temple. Cheng Ho raised his head with an alacrity that showed Tom that he had been trying to suppress his impatience.

"Come, Chin Mao. The soothsayers have finished. It's time to receive the blessing of the Temple of the Celestial Spouse."

"Old Mrs. Wind is with you," the Taoist priest said. "The goddess Feng-p'o-p'o. And K'uei-hsing, the god of the four stars of the Big Basket in the north, will guide you. Is there anything else?"

Tom jumped as a firecracker went off. Guiltily, he realized that he had dozed off while standing and almost dropped the joss stick given to him by one of the young monks.

Cheng Ho scratched his head. "How about the Princess of Streaked Clouds and her husband, the Son of the Western Sea? He's not included among the tutelary sea gods."

"An oversight, San-pao T'ai-chien," the priest apologized. "Excuse me. Hand me that joss paper you're holding, and I'll burn it at the altar for you."

It was all very businesslike, and Tom had been bored stiff for an hour. This haggling over divine commodities was nothing like the beauty and order of an English service, with its central mystery. The way the Chinese mixed their religions together astounded Tom. The bewildering array of gods and goddesses seemed to have little to do with what Tom understood of the teachings of the lord Buddha, or the austere Confucianism professed at court, as laid down by the Ministry of Rites. The Taoists believed in magic, immortality potions, divination—though otherwise they seemed like imitation Buddhists, with priests called Tao-shih instead of Bonzes. It was to them, evidently, that one went when one needed the services of geomancers and soothsayers.

Cheng Ho was handing over a heavy string of cash coins. "And this is for joss sticks to petition the Celestial Administrators to mention us in their monthly reports to the August Personage at the top of Heaven."

Tom yawned. His attention strayed to the miniature panels depicting the thirty-three heavens and the eighteen hells. The tortures in the various hells were very colorful—better than the torments you could see in some of the panels in Christian churches. The heavens, too, were more interesting, offering more specific pleasures than the vapors and angels of Christian salvation; Tom peered more closely at one of the miniatures to see if the salvatee depicted there was really doing what Tom thought he was.

In the background the priest continued to drone on. Now he was dedicating the stone that Cheng Ho was leaving at the temple and reading from the inscription, with much bobbing by him and his monks, and swinging of censers of incense.

". . . the countries beyond the horizon and at the ends of the earth have become the subjects of the Ming, and however far they may be, the distances are calculated. Thus the barbarians from beyond the seas, despite the vastnesses of the distances and despite the double translation that is required, have come to audience, bearing precious gifts. . . ."

Tom had seen some of the ambassadors, from places with names like Java and Ceylon, Hormuz and Aden. The zamorin of Calicut had sent an ambassador, a little nervous, scrawny man in a loincloth, and there were even black men, dressed in animal skins, from the Dark Land itself.

Whether the rulers who had sent them realized that the Ming emperor regarded them as his subjects was another matter. The diplomats of the Starry Raft would likely skirt that touchy interpretation as best they could. Tom smiled to himself at the thought of what England's proud King Henry might say if one of Cheng Ho's envoys were foolhardy enough to translate that part of the tablet for him.

". . . the emperor, approving of their loyalty," the priest was intoning, "has ordered his Grand Eunuch of the Three Jewels of Pious Ejaculation, Cheng Ho, at the head of several tens of thousands of officers and flag troops to embark on more than a hundred large ships to go and confer presents on them, in order to demonstrate the power and virtue of the Dragon Throne, and to treat distant people with kindness. . . . We have traversed more than one hundred thousand li of immense waterspaces and have beheld in the ocean huge waves like mountains rising sky high, and we have set eyes on barbarian regions far away, hidden in a blue transparency of light vapors, while our sails, loftily un-furled like clouds, day and night continued their course as steadily as the wheeling stars, traversing those savage waves as if we were treading a public thoroughfare. Truly this is due to the majesty of the emperor and the protecting virtue of the Celestial Spouse...."

There was a final explosion of firecrackers and a fuss with gongs and clappers. Cheng Ho came briskly away from the altar with the vice admiral at his side and his eunuch entou-rage swirling around him. He stopped to speak to Tom and motioned the others to go ahead without him.

"Well, that's over," he said. "Now perhaps I can go aboard the flagship and attend to some practical matters."

"Will you need me?" Tom asked.

"No, you can say good-bye to your Lan-ying," Cheng Ho said indulgently. "You won't see her for two years."

"Thank you, San-pao T'ai-chien," Tom said.

He kept his thoughts to himself. It had occurred to him that his future was tied to Cheng Ho, and Cheng Ho was not all that young any more. He had already tasted the best that the Middle Kingdom had to offer. He could set himself up as a great man in England with what he had. But what would England be like after all these years?

He'd have to wait and see.

Did Cheng Ho sense his mental reservations? The eu-nuch admiral peered at him searchingly.

"You really ought to sleep on board tonight, Chin Mao," he said. "Just see that you're aboard before first light if you don't want to be left behind."


"The sky's getting light," Tom said. "I'd better go."

Lan-ying clung to him. He could feel the wiry strength in her small, slender body. "There's time yet, lord," she said.

He disengaged himself as gently as he could, but had to pry her loose two or three times before she gave up. "I can't stay, little blossom," he said. "You know that."

She sat up on the silken mat, her long hair falling in straight lines to her small, nubby breasts. She had removed all the pins and combs for him this one night and combed it out—a tremendous concession. After their first few couplings he had fallen asleep, and when he had floundered awake an hour later, he had felt around on the mat for her, expecting to find her gone. But she was still there, wide awake, watching him by the light of the small lamp they had left burning. He had been immensely touched—it was the first time she had broken her own rule about not staying the night in order not to disturb the harmony of the household by making the other concubines jealous of her special status.

"You'll forget me," she said.

"I'll never forget you, precious jade." He forced a confident smile. "Anyway, it's only two years."

"You won't come back."

"Don't be stupid," he said harshly, pretending that she had meant that the voyage would be dangerous. "The Star Raft is as safe as a city. The ships are big enough to ride out the worst storms. It carries so many troops that no one would dare to attack it. And Cheng Ho's navigators know the art of finding their way home through all the seas of the world. . . ."

She began to weep.

Tom took a deep breath. He knelt on the mat, facing her, and took her by the shoulders. "Listen, Lan-ying," he said, looking directly into her eyes, "the Yellow Gate will take care of you while I'm away. They'll keep the household intact. You'll have Wo and the other servants to watch over you, and the other concubines for company. Everything will be fine."

Her lips gave him a tremulous smile. "You are right, Chin Mao. Forgive me."

He was relieved to see that she had composed herself. "There's nothing to forgive."

"There is something I was not going to tell you yet. But I had not expected the Star Raft to depart so soon."

"What is it? You mustn't keep anything from me."

She hesitated, her eyes fixed anxiously on his face. "A son will be waiting for you when you return," she said.

Tom hid his consternation. "That's . . . fine, Lan-ying." He took refuge in heartiness. "How could you know it will be a son?"

"I know."

Her steady gaze unnerved him. "But how?"

"I went to a soothsayer. But I knew before."

Suddenly it sank in. Tom gave a whoop of joy and lifted

her in the air. Tiny though she was, her compactness made her heavier than she looked, and he had to set her down after whirling her around twice. She giggled and fell against him, and her naked body tempted him, but the sky was growing lighter.

He found his clothes and was starting to get into them when the screen slid back and Wo entered without so much as a discreet cough, bearing a heavy tray. He and half the household staff must have been listening outside, waiting for the first permissible moment for him to intrude; privacy was only an illusion in the Middle Kingdom.

"Breakfast, master," Wo said, putting down the tray and setting out dishes with a brisk professional disinterest in the two naked bodies. It was the breakfast for two that he had been restrained from serving all these years by Lan-ying's insistence on evaporating from Tom's room in the middle of the night, and Tom was moved by the gesture.

"What are you doing here?" he scolded in the expected manner. "It is not yet morning. And you know that I take the *tsao ts'an* alone."

Wo protested peevishly, also as expected. "The master is abandoning us, to travel to barbarian lands. What are we to do? We'll have to beg in the streets. And yet, to show our devotion, we slave until our fingers are worn away, that the master may leave with good cheer and a full stomach."

Tom looked at the incredible feast that was being spread out. The number two and number three boys had entered with more trays. There was peach flour rice with a sauce of fermented fish, jasmine cakes, crossing-the-bridge soup with noodles, and eggs with oysters and soy sprouts. But the dish that touched him beyond words was a plate bearing a small pile of thick chops—real meat that a man could sink his teeth into; meat that had not been reduced to little cubes or shredded, minced, marinated, or pickled; the barbarian slabs of meat that Wo had steadfastly refused to serve to Tom before.

"I can't stay to eat this," Tom said. "There's no time. You'll have to feed it to the carp. Leave me now, so I can say goodbye to the lady Lan-ying."

He knew the food would not be thrown to the fish but would provide a banquet for the servants. The meat would be diced and would eventually make an appearance in a more acceptable incarnation. And it would be duly noted, down to the last mote, what morsels, if any, Tom had sampled before leaving.

Wo and his assistants backed out, bowing. Tom turned to Lan-ying.

"I'll have to hurry now," he apologized. Somewhere outside, in one of the courtyards of the city, a rooster crowed. The light coming through the oiled paper of the windows was luminous enough to overpower the feeble glow of the lamp. Tom finished dressing—silk robe, winter cloak, jade-buckled girdle with a purse dangling from it, silk cap topped by a button—and thought how much more practical for shipboard were the trousers worn by the soldiers and common sailors. He had nothing to pack—a chest of clothing and personal items had been taken aboard for him the previous day, and the well-stocked commissaries on the Star Raft could supply any conceivable need.

His eye roved to the heavy carved chest standing against the wall. It contained a king's ransom by now—all useless because there was no way to spend it; the Yellow Gate took care of everything. Lan-ying watched him silently as he unlocked the lid.

It had been a long time since he had bothered to gaze at the treasures inside—gems, objects of gold, exquisite porcelains, jade—but their power to dazzle had not diminished. He picked up a gold bracelet and examined it. Gold was always valuable, wherever you went, but it was heavy. You could carry only so much of it on your person. He selected some articles—chains, brooches, rings—and stuffed them into a sack. The porcelains were out of the question; they were breathtaking pieces and of incalculable value here in the Middle Kingdom, but they would not travel well. The jade was another story. He made a selection of carved pieces and added them to the sack.

He opened the coffer of jewels given him long ago by the Yung Lo Emperor and sifted the loose gems between his fingers. There were emeralds, rubies, sapphires, fire opals, garnets, chrysoberyl. He didn't bother making a selection. He was on the point of emptying the coffer into his sack when he saw Lan-ying staring at him.

She didn't say anything, but he knew what she was thinking. Cursing himself for a fool, he took less than half of the trove and put the rest back so that she wouldn't think he was clearing out for good.

"Here's something to remind you of me while I'm away," he said carelessly. "No, take it. I don't want any arguments this time."

He held out the huge emerald he had tried once before to give to her, the time she had refused to marry him. He had had it set in a ring anyway, hoping to give it to her later, and it had stayed in the coffer ever since.

"Chin Mao, no," she said, blushing.

"Go on," he said. "I want you to have it."

He took her hand and pushed the ring onto her finger while they met each other's eyes. There was no way he could transfer ownership of the remainder of the coffer to her; if he failed to return and claim it, it would become the property of the Yellow Gate. But a trinket or two could be overlooked. The emerald was worth a fortune. It would keep her in her old age, if need be.

He thought of his son. "Here," he said, rummaging in the chest. "Here's a gold chain to go with it. And a bracelet."

"No," she protested. "They will say I stole them."

"No, they won't," he said. "Not if you're wearing them when you see me to the door." He remembered all the other gifts he had given her through the years and felt easier. If the Yellow Gate did not reassign her, she could retire in comfort.

"When I return," he said, the words coming easily, "I'll be covered with glory. The Emperor will heap honors on me, and I'll shower you with riches!"

The total attention she always gave to anything he said seemed to have wandered. "He will have yellow hair," she whispered.

"What?"

She gave him a remote look. "The soothsayer said our son will have yellow hair."


The black ship appeared on the tenth day out from Fujian, as the Star Raft ploughed through the Formosa Strait on its way to the South China Sea. Tom was resting in his cabin—one of a hundred or so cabins on the second deck assigned to the middle and minor ranks, but incomparably more spacious and comfortable than the cramped cubbyhole reserved for the captain on most European ships. He had been dicing and drinking the night before with some of the

Treasure Ship's marine guard, and needed a little extra
sleep. There was a knock on the door, and Tom roared,
"*Djin-lai*—come in, damn it!"

Ma Huan shuffled in and clucked reproachfully at him.
"Cheng Ho asks that you come topside," the old scholar
said. "He wants to talk to you."

"All right," Tom said, wincing as he got up.

He followed Ma Huan aft, to the enclosed deck where the
gang of helmsmen managed the huge rudder, and climbed
with him to the massive poop, where there was a deckhouse
for the navigator. Above it was a platform called the "pheasant's roost," where a sailing master could have a better vantage point for ordering the manipulation of the sheets
according to the wind.

He paused for a moment when he reached the topmost
level of the poop to look forward along the broad, tremendous sweep of deck, dwindling toward a squared-off prow.
The nine immense masts rose like an avenue of mighty
trees, bearing acres of stiff rectangular sails and multiplying
webs of lines. The lookout's nest at the crown of the tallest
was a distant bower of bamboo, with the faces of the men
peeping over the edges reduced to specks.

Hundreds of sailors went about their tasks on that wide
expanse of sun-bleached wood. Children played in the odd
corners—some of the sailors had brought their families. A
squad of marines in leather corselets drilled in a cleared
area amidships. Farmers tended plot-sized tubs of cabbages
and beans, and a swineherd was chasing an evasive pig that
had gotten out of its pen.

Tom looked out across the sea at the rest of the fleet,
stretching from horizon to horizon in loose formation. There
were more than sixty great Treasure Ships like the one he
was riding, horse ships, troop ships, supply ships, armored
Turtle Ships.

Ma Huan hurried him along. "He's in a conversational
mood this morning," he confided. "He sent for me early to
keep him company. He seems restless. Then, to settle some
point, he asked for you."

Cheng Ho was standing by the taffrail, talking to a sailor.
The ship's astronomer and some of the other officers of the
bridge stood at a distance, not participating in the exchange.
The sailor was gesturing sternward, to the north. Cheng Ho
said something succinct. The sailor nodded and sprang to

the pheasant's roost, where he chose a route in the highway of ratlines and began clambering aloft.

Cheng Ho saw Tom and Ma Huan and motioned them genially over. "Something's worrying him," Ma Huan said to Tom in an undertone, "but he won't say what it is."

"Ah, Chin Mao," Cheng Ho said in his high, clear voice. "Time must be weighing heavily at this stage of the voyage, with nothing much to do. Would you like to have a look at the ship's shrine?"

"Very much, San-pao T'ai-chien," Tom said.

Cheng Ho led the way to a cabin off the corridor in the poop's upper level. It was bright and spacious inside, with sunlight streaming through windows of thin scraped parchment and making yellow bars on the floor. A statue of the lord Buddha was there, with shrines to the sea goddess and other deities. The compass stood on a pedestal in front of one of the shrines, a bowl of water in which floated a thin leaf of iron in the shape of a fish, its edges upturned to make it into a little boat. There was a chart table with a map spread across it and boards hung with various navigational instruments made of ivory, metal, or ebony.

The smell of incense was heavy in the air, and Tom saw a row of joss sticks in graduated sizes burning in a holder in front of the sea goddess. A shaven-headed sailor with the bare feet and wide pantaloons of the ordinary seaman was standing at the shrine, staring with single-minded intensity at the joss sticks, and at first Tom thought he was praying. Then Cheng Ho spoke, saying, "Are we into the second *gen* of this *keng* yet?" and the man, with his eyes still fixed on the joss sticks, answered, "I just changed the stick a moment ago, master."

*Keng* was the Chinese term for a shipboard watch—somewhat longer than a watch on a European ship—and a *gen* was the measure of time used, ten *gen* for a twenty-four hour day.

Cheng Ho removed the shortest incense stick at the end of the row from its holder and inspected it. "Do your western ships use a similar method for measuring the passage of time, Chin Mao?" he asked.

"No," Tom said. "We turn a glass every half-hour."

It was the first duty he'd been given as a ship's boy aboard the wool ship from Bristol, and he had been cuffed when he had failed to be prompt enough. He explained to

Cheng Ho about the little sandglasses that came from Venice; how they were so fragile that a prudent captain carried a large number of spares.

"That seems very primitive," Cheng Ho said. "We use the same principle in our large astronomical clocks, but we've added a mechanical escapement to it to smooth out errors that would be caused by variations in the flow of sand alone. I've often thought it would be nice if we could take a clock aboard—it would make it possible to measure longitude, *ching tu,* as well as latitude. But a clock tower's much too big, even for a Treasure Ship, and besides, even if we could shrink it, a mechanism based on the running of sand or water would not be reliable in a heavy sea."

Tom did not reply. He had only the vaguest notion of what Cheng Ho was talking about.

Cheng Ho replaced the joss stick and picked up one of the instruments. It was a beautifully made device of ebony plates, in graduated sizes, that slid along a brass rod. There was a second sliding arrangement of a small ivory tablet with clipped corners, which could be turned in various directions and used in conjunction with the ebony plates.

"This is the *ch'hien hsing pan*—the guiding-star stretchboards," Cheng Ho said. "This is one of the ways we measure latitude. Do your western navigators use anything like this?"

Tom searched his mind. Neither the English wool ship nor the ships he had worked in the Mediterranean had used anything other than the compass or the greasy parchment portolans that were so jealously guarded by the pilots, as far as he could remember.

"No," he said.

Cheng Ho raised the contraption to one eye and sighted experimentally along the rod. He twiddled the ivory tablet, making some small adjustment. He sighed and put it down.

"With it you can measure the altitude of the north star, the *pei chi hsing,* and thus know your latitude," Cheng Ho said. "Of course it can't be used below the Belt of the World, but we've developed other methods for that. The Arabs employ the same principle in a crude device they call the *kamal.* It has only one wooden rectangle and a knotted string instead of the twelve sliding boards, but they get surprisingly accurate results with it."

Tom knew about the *kamal*. He had seen it used every night aboard the Omani ship that had taken him to Calicut.

"The Middle Kingdom leads the world in all things," he said politely.

Cheng Ho laughed. "I'll teach you a little navigation to while away the time, Chin Mao. By the time we reach England, you'll be able to use the stretch-boards as well as anyone."

"I don't have the head for it," Tom said.

"Nonsense. There's nothing to it."

Tom foresaw long, boring sessions ahead of him at the hands of some dried-up old pedant on Cheng Ho's staff. He squirmed at the thought. Never mind, he'd find some way to wriggle out of it!

A eunuch petty officer entered the cabin and whispered to Cheng Ho. Cheng Ho became quiet and thoughtful.

"We'd better go out on deck," he said.

A Malay vessel had sailed into the midst of the fleet, a rakish craft with a gaudily painted stern and a tripod mast carrying a wide rectangular sail laced to a yard. A couple of sailors, lean wiry men in sarongs, were standing in front of the thatched dockhouses to stare at the giant ships. One of them waved.

Cheng Ho visibly relaxed. The Malay ship slipped past and shrank from sight. Tom wondered what the fuss had been about.

But it had not been the Malay ship that had brought Cheng Ho out on deck. He continued to stare sternward at the horzion long after the craft had disappeared. Twice the lookout's relay climbed down from the pheasant's roost to report quietly to Cheng Ho. Tom caught the words *hei ch'uan*—black ship.

Whatever the lookout was tracking, it was just over the horizon, where it could not be seen from the deck. Tom stayed topside through the remainder of the morning, entertaining himself by watching the pilot and the sailing master as they kept the fleet on course, but Cheng Ho seemed to have forgotten him.

About noon, as the astronomer took the altitude of the sun with one of the ivory instruments from the ship's shrine, the lookout's relay again descended from his perch and spoke diffidently to Cheng Ho. This time Cheng Ho became more attentive. He went to the admiral's verandah built out over the stern, ignoring an officer who attempted to intercept him, and stood in chilly solitude at the rail, staring back along the wake. Nobody dared to join him on the verandah without invitation, and this time he obviously wanted to be alone. The officers of the bridge looked at one another questioningly, but no one had anything to say.

"What's going on, Ma Huan?" Tom asked.

"If the Admiral of the Triple Treasure wished us to know, he would tell us," the elderly scholar replied imperturbably. He plunked himself down on a bench and raised his parasol over his head.

Tom went to the nearer rail and scanned the horizon that Cheng Ho was searching so intently. The sea, ruffled by the northeast monsoon, marched away in white ridges toward the unseen Malay coast. After a while Tom thought he saw a speck. A little while later he was sure. Though it was no larger than a grain of rice, it was unmistakably a ship—a ship with the tall narrow sails of the Middle Kingdom. It wasn't black, though, or even particularly dark—the other meaning of *hei ch'uan*. In the copper sunlight of noon, it appeared to have the same amber sails as any ship in the Treasure Fleet.

He lost it, and then after a time he found it again. In the next hour it dropped below the horizon three or four times, then reappeared, neither falling behind nor overtaking them. Tom thought irrevelantly of a lone wolf stalking a herd of deer—but that was ridiculous. The vast fleet with its crossbows and cannon, its thirty thousand soldiers and marines, its escort of Tower Ships and Turtle Ships, had nothing to fear from anyone. The ship on the horizon couldn't possibly be shadowing them for any sinister purpose; surely it was only some random mechantman of the Middle Kingdom, keeping its fellow countrymen in sight for comfort in those trackless southern seas. But Cheng Ho never took his eyes off it.

At last Cheng Ho roused himself. He called to the flagship's captain to join him on the verandah and conferred lengthily with him. The captain began to give orders. Signal flags went up, and cannon boomed from ship to ship.

Sailors swarmed aloft like brown ants on a cake and began manhandling the gigantic rigs. It was not easy for Tom to follow what they were doing at first. Running before the northeast monsoon as it was, the fleet, with its tall rectangular sails set almost flat, was already making the most efficient use of the wind, or so Tom thought.

But now he saw that the massive yards were being jockied farther to one side of the masts, to unbalance the sails somewhat and marginally reduce the sail area on the luff. This was very dangerous for the men; on a Treasure Ship to starboard, a small flailing figure plummeted downward to splatter on the deck.

No one paused to take note of the tragedy. Next the struggling sailors, hauling on a complicated system of lifts, drew the slats on the leading edges of the sails closer together, further reducing the luff and fanning the sails to coax every last bit of push out of the wind. Tom could tell it was an unorthodox maneuver by the way the petty officers in charge of each work party had to keep sending men to claw at the battens, lashing them together if need be with improvised lines. The cost and risk of the effort hardly seemed worth it, just to gain another degree or two of reach from a fine following wind that already had had the sails drawing nicely.

But little by little, with a creaking of readjusting timbers and a whitening of the wake, the tremendous ship seemed to respond.

"See what we've gained," Tom heard Cheng Ho say to the pilot.

The pilot sent a runner to the bow. Straining his eyes, Tom saw the tiny distant figure drop a piece of wood into the water and then begin walking rapidly toward the stern. People got out of his way so as not to impede his progress. The pilot, leaning out over the rail to watch for the arrival of the piece of wood at the stern, announced, "*Shang gen,*" long before the walker made it back, but Cheng Ho still wasn't satisfied. He had runners repeat the process at intervals, until at last the pilot, with a big smile on his face, proclaimed, "*Guo gen!*" before the runner had reached the fourth mast.

The black ship, if that's what it was, dropped behind and disappeared from view. It did not reappear again that day or the next. By the third day Tom decided it would not be seen again.

"We've outrun it," he said to Ma Huan.

"Outrun what?" Ma Huan said blandly, and that was all Tom could get out of him.

Cheng Ho had become affable again and invited Tom to

dine with him, but he kept his own counsel. "We'll stop at Java to exchange ambassadors, Chin Mao, and then it's through the Strait of Malacca to the Indian Ocean," he said. "I'll show you a marvelous land called Serendip, and then we'll go on to Calicut to see your old friend, the zamorin."

His words were jocund, but Tom could sense an underlying tenseness. He had the feeling that Cheng Ho would not relax until the fleet was safely through the Strait of Malacca.

# CHAPTER 10

There was an eclipse of the sun the day the king died. It had put Lisbon in an uneasy mood. The coincidence was too strange. There had been an eclipse eighteen years earlier, on the day the queen, Philippa of pious memory, had died. On her deathbed, she had sent her sons to conquer Ceuta for Portugal and Christ. What this new omen foretold, no one knew.

Hemmed in by the tremendous crowd that filled the Terreiro do Paco, Pedro sweated in his white mourning cloak and hood of coarse wool. The restless sea of white homespun was punctuated here and there by those of the poor who kept no mourning garment at home, and who had to settle for wearing their clothes inside out. On the fringes of the square and on the facade of the great palace opposite, banners and draperies fluttered in the bright morning sunlight. Knights in glittering armor sat atop caparisoned horses at the rear of the crowd, keeping order.

Pedro had a good vantage point. Thanks to a word from Afonso Baldaia, Prince Henry's young cupbearer, he was standing with the privileged commoners in a section just behind the waist-high wooden barricades that set off the cleared area in the center of the square. Ordinarily the barriers were used for the bullfights that were staged here, but for this occasion they had been decked at intervals with pennants of the House of Avis.

Within, a royal dais had been set up. There was a throne, on which Prince Duarte would take his seat after the proclamation of his kingship, and places for the bishop, the other princes, and the great of the realm. Several of the lords, in their white garments of mourning, were standing around, chatting to one another, but the bishop and the royal family still had not arrived.

Pedro saw Baldaia coming toward him. With a nod to the pikeman standing guard here, the cupbearer slipped through the barricades and stood next to Pedro.

"What's holding things up?" Pedro asked.

Baldaia gave a frown. "The infante Duarte was in a bad way last night when he and the other princes were supposed to carry the coffin to the cathedral," he said, leaning confidentially toward Pedro. "He could do nothing but cover his face with his hands and weep. His confessor, Fray Gil, finally had to shake him by the shoulder and say several times, 'Wake up, Sire. Wake up to your royal office.' Prince Henry spoke to him, brother to brother, and finally got him to move."

Pedro nodded soberly. Baldaia was a good fellow to have come to keep him company when he might have been standing on the other side of the barrier with the rest of Prince Henry's entourage from Sagres. Though of noble blood, he never put on airs. He had interested himself in the ongoing effort to explore the Azores—had become something of a buff, in fact. After the last two voyages that had discovered more islands, he had sought Pedro out and plied him with questions. Intelligent questions. Pedro counted him a friend and ally.

"Yes, I saw Dom Duarte stumble during the procession," Pedro said. "He seemed like a sleepwalker."

"Now Prince Henry and Prince Fernando are in with him. There's some problem about the astrologers."

"Has the infante Dom Pedro arrived?"

"He arrived this morning. They sent for him to Coimbra when King John began to fail, but by the time he reached Leira, the news caught up with him that his father had died. So he broke his journey there to don mourning and to write Dom Duarte a long letter full of high moral sentiments and political advice." His mouth twisted wryly. "The letter got here before he did. They're a letter-writing family, these children of King John and the good Philippa."

A portly, well-to-do tradesman standing next to Pedro overheard the last words and turned to offer comment. Seeing that Baldaia, despite the prescribed homespun cloak, was gentry, he addressed himself to him, ignoring Pedro. "Dom Duarte will be a high-minded monarch, no doubt about it," he said sententiously. "But nobody will ever take the place of King John. Without him we'd be under the yoke of Castile. The fifty years of his reign were a golden age."

"Quite so," Baldaia said politely.

A grimy little man with a tear-streaked face and the inky fingertips of a notary joined the exchange. "He'll be made a saint," he said. "Have you heard about the miracle at the cathedral last night? They started out with two hundred and sixty-four pounds of wax. And after all those candles were consumed in the services, they had two hundred and sixty-four and a half pounds of wax."

"He called for a barber to shave him before allowing himself to be confessed," a third man put in eagerly. "He said he didn't want to look hideous in death and frighten the people. Then he sent for Prince Henry and laid some charge on him."

The tradesman asserted his authority. "King John was too indulgent of Prince Henry's fancies," he said. "Dom Duarte will be a stern but loving brother. He'll listen to the sensible men around him and put a stop to all this foolish and expensive exploration."

Across the square at the palace entrance, some new activity was taking place, with a lot of horse and men milling around, and the tradesman stopped talking to crane his neck for a look. Pedro and Baldaia exchanged a glance.

"What about it?" Pedro said. "After two more failures to pass Bojador, there's a lot of opposition."

"Dom Duarte listens to everyone and lets them make up his mind for him," Baldaia said, biting his lip. "He's too bookish. Worse, he doesn't just read books—he's always writing them. Handbooks on the art of riding. Manuals of fencing. Tracts on healthful dining. Treatises on proper filial behavior. He'd rather write a book than take action in real life. Everybody's at him already with their advice, and he hasn't even been crowned yet. Prince Henry lost his temper when Dom Pedro's letter arrived from Leira, and Duarte started agonizing again about this and that. '*Res, non verba!*' he told him. 'The thing, not the word! Cease your clerking if you would be king!' I think the fire in Prince Henry frightens him. Prince Henry's dreams and plans are too large, and he feels threatened by them. And there are those around him, like Dom Pedro, who encourage this distrust of what they call useless exploration."

"Madeira wasn't a useless endeavor," Pedro said. "And neither were the Azores. There'll be discoveries to be made south of Cape Bojador, if we ever can pass it."

Baldaia scowled. "We'll never pass Bojador as long as there are captains who piss in their hose every time they see a little white water. Prince Henry thought that Gil Eanes was going to be different. But it was the same old story. He sailed thirty miles beyond Cape Non, the sailors started to come to him with tales of sea serpents, so he got sidetracked to the Canaries, took a few slaves, indulged in a little piracy, and went sailing home with a sheepish expression on his face. Prince Henry was not amused this time. I've never seen him in such a rage."

"What . . . what did he say to the squire?" Pedro asked, horrified but fascinated.

"You know the infante. When he's too angry to trust himself to talk, he becomes all icy politeness and dismisses people, saying that he doesn't want to intrude any further on their time. I can assure you that Gil Eanes felt it more keenly than if he had been called a coward to his face."

Pedro shook his head. "He's not a coward. He's bold enough in a fight, or where he knows what he's about, and he's good at getting men to follow him. It's just that he—"

"That he's not exactly a deep thinker?" Baldaia suggested.

"I didn't say that," Pedro protested.

"Let's face it," Baldaia said. "The man's impressive. He looks like a bull—and he's just about as brainy."

"If only I'd been on that expedition," Pedro brooded. "I might have persuaded him to go on."

Pedro had been torn. Prince Henry himself had suggested to Gil Eanes that he take Pedro as his pilot, since Pedro had been a member of the expedition that had first passed Cape Non, and Gil Eanes had been amenable. But Cabral was about to sail back to the Azores for the fourth time, and he had first call on Pedro's services. Pedro's fellow pilots envied him because the fourth expedition had discovered three new islands of the Azores group, which had since been named São Jorge, Graciosa, and Pico. But Pedro had been thrown into a sense of helpless, fist-clenching frustration when he had returned to Sagres and learned that Gil Eanes had turned aside from his quest without even venturing as far as Cabral and De Brito had gone originally.

"Before"—Baldaia glanced past the teeming square toward the cathedral, where King John's body lay in a sealed lead coffin before the altar of Saint Vincent—"before this happened, the old king suggested to Henry that if he sent Gil Eanes back to Bojador, he send me along with him to help stiffen his spine."

"King John said that?"

"He started out a skeptic, but he couldn't ignore the benefit to Portugal of Madeira and then the Azores. That's why he gave Prince Henry the soap revenues and the other monopolies to finance his work. Now"—his gaze went to the empty throne on the dais in the square—"it's all in the balance again."

"Duarte wouldn't forbid the prince . . ."

"No, but without the active support of the crown, it would be immensely more difficult."

They both turned their attention to the palace entrance, where a few lackeys in livery stood around aimlessly, waiting for their masters. The flurry of activity that had drawn the spectators' attention a few minutes previously had only been the late arrival of some provincial nobleman with his retinue. There was still no sign of the bishop or the royal party.

Baldaia sucked in his breath. "What are they *doing* in there?" he said.


"I beg you, Sire," the astrologer wept, throwing himself on his knees before Duarte. "Postpone the coronation until this afternoon!"

Duarte looked helplessly at his brothers for support. His weak, handsome face was bloodless above the white garment of mourning he still wore. The black cloak that had been brought out for him lay neglected across a bench; only a king could wear black, and he was not yet a king.

"We've already been through this," Prince Henry said. There was no help in his stony expression. "The decision is yours to make."

Duarte turned back to the old man. Mestre Guedelha had served as a court physician and astrologer to his father for as long as his childhood memories went back. It was hard to go against him.

He bit his lip. "Mestre Guedelha," he said, "I know that you are moved only by love for me and by your loyalty to the family. I don't doubt that astrology is a true science and that the stars may reveal hidden things to us. But I have greater faith in God, and I know that my fate is in His hands alone."

"There's danger, Sire," the astrologer insisted. "Jupiter is retrogressing. The sun is shadowed. What harm would it do to put off the ceremony for a few hours?"

"No," Duarte said. He cleared his throat. "I won't do that. It would appear as if I had no faith in God." He pulled the old man gently to his feet.

Mestre Guedelha shuffled off, shaking his head. "I asked only a small thing," he mumbled. "The stars are unfavorable. If you go ahead now, you'll reign only a few years, and those will be weighed down by cares and anxieties. . . ."

The five brothers stood in embarrassed silence. The two youngest, João and Fernando, couldn't help stealing a glance at Dom Pedro, the second oldest. He had been next in line for the throne after Duarte, until Duarte had married the lively and beautiful Leonor of Aragon at the age of forty and assured the succession by siring two sons in quick succession. Henry, bound for life by his vow of celibacy, had promptly made the oldest boy his heir. Pedro had put a lid on his ambitions and behaved with the utmost discretion, but that hadn't helped him with Leonor. She had never warmed to him as she had warmed to Henry. Perhaps she saw Pedro as some sort of long-range threat to her children, or perhaps she had become uneasy when Pedro, following Duarte's example, had married another Aragonese, Isabel of Urgel, whose father once had been a rival of her own father for the throne of Aragon. Duarte, his head in the clouds, was oblivious of his wife's distrust of Pedro; there had been a special bond between him and Pedro since childhood, and they were always writing long, excessively serious letters to each other, some of which had been duly copied and bound into books for the edification of the world.

Dom Pedro broke the silence. "Well said, brother," he approved. "The stars may rule us, but it is God who rules the stars. Be not put off by what Mestre Guedelha said, but assume this new duty humbly, and pray to God to help you govern wisely and well."

Duarte seemed to have grown paler. He swayed, and Prince Henry stepped forward to steady him.

Duarte said in a parched, distant voice, "What did our father say to you on his deathbed?"

Henry replied unhesitatingly, "He made me promise never to forget my duty to defend Christendom against the infidel and to go forward with my explorations into Africa."

Duarte managed a smile. A little color seemed to return to his face. "So be it," he said in a firmer tone. "We have always been obedient sons, and death has not relieved us of that obligation to obedience. You'll have my support in your endeavors, brother."


"Here they come now," Baldaia said, sounding relieved. The acres of crowd stirred as the bishop and his train filed through the gate of the old palace, splendid in their ecclesiastical vestments. The bishop held his staff aloft, striking a flash of gold out of the bright August sunlight, and his miter glistened with pearls. The brilliant brocades, the rippling cloth of gold, were a vivid contrast to the sea of white wool through which he strode, and the spectators sighed their appreciation of the pageantry. The nobles who came next—the constable of Portugal, the count of Viana and other greats— made a somber contrast in their plain white garments of mourning, but that was only to be expected when the entire realm had covered itself with hood and wool overnight. But there was a murmur of disappointment when Dom Duarte and his queen-to-be made their appearance in the same cloaking of homespun. Few now alive had ever seen a coronation, but there was a sense that there ought to be ermine and kingly robes.

The brothers followed closely, tall and fair like their English mother, though Henry was noticeably darker from the baking he got from the Algarve sun and built more powerfully than the others—a contrast that could be seen despite the enveloping white cloaks.

"It lacks only the princess Isabel to make a complete family," Baldaia commented.

Isabel, the only surviving girl, had married Philip the Good of Burgundy three years earlier and now dwelt in

Flanders. Philip had taken the precaution of sending the painter Van Eyck to Portugal to paint Isabel's portrait, and he had been so pleased by it that he had promptly proposed. She now presided over his court at Bruges and had not seen her brothers since.

"You're leaving out the count of Barcelos," Pedro said.

"He does well to stay away," Baldaia growled. "Prince Pedro is too thick with him. He should remember from the example of his own father that bastard half-brothers are a danger to the throne."

Afonso, the count of Barcelos, had been an error of King John's youth, before he had married Philippa of Lancaster. Philippa, when she had taken charge of John, had banished Afonso's mother to a convent but permitted the boy to be raised at court. By the time his half-brothers were out of the nursery, Afonso had married the richest heiress in the land. He now brooded on his estates in the north and made mischief whenever he could.

"Still," Pedro demurred, "he fought shoulder to shoulder with the infantes at Ceuta."

"That was a long time ago," Baldaia said. Seeing that his cynicism had shocked Pedro, he added, "He paid himself well for his help against the Moors. For his share of the plunder he took more than six hundred columns of alabaster and marble from the palace of Sala ben-Sala and an entire vaulted roof of giltwork from a city square that he used later to construct his palace at Barcelos."

Pedro contented himself with looking stubborn. It was no part of his business to contradict a member of Henry's household on a family matter.

By now Dom Duarte had taken his seat on the raised chair that would become his throne, and Dona Leonor and her attendants were arranging themselves in their places below it, but the interminable procession of bareheaded nobles and officials continued, finally diminishing in rank to the minor *cavalieros-fidalgos* who had earned a place in the pageant. At last came another splash of color—the mounted trumpeters and drummers and the heralds in bright tabards emblazoned with the coat of arms of the House of Avis.

Pedro shifted his feet as the bishop droned on for the next hour. The sun climbed higher in a shimmering blue sky, and around him was the smell of thousands of onlookers sweltering in their woolen shrouds. People in the square were fainting by now, but no one carried them away. The weak-minded were doing strange things—butting their heads against walls, lacerating their cheeks with their fingernails, kicking out with their feet at their neighbors. One man, making unseemly, piercing shrieks, had to be dragged away by the knights to calm down elsewhere.

The bishop was anointing Duarte now. The constable brought him the crown on a cushion, and he placed it on Duarte's bowed head. A royal robe was brought to Duarte, but he refused it. Around Pedro, people muttered their bewilderment.

There was a brief conference on the dais, and the count of Viana stepped forward with a furled banner in his hand. A vast rumble of approval rose from the crowd. The old soldier was greatly admired. He had held Ceuta for Prince Henry for almost twenty years against an encircling tide of Moors. The bishop made an impatient gesture, and the heralds ordered the people to silence. Then as the trumpets and kettledrums sounded, the count unfurled the banner, revealing it to be the royal standard. *"Real! Real! Real!"* he cried, in a voice that could be heard to the farthest ends of the square.

The nobles around the throne took up the shout; then it caught on in the crowd, and in moments a thunder of *"Real! Real! Real!"* filled the square and began to spread through the streets beyond.

On the dais, King Duarte stood up. He took off the white cloak and handed it to a page. Another page brought him a black cloak and he put it on.

Later it was reported by those close enough to be within earshot that Duarte turned to the bishop and said, "Wouldn't it be a good idea to burn some tow before me at the end of the ceremony as a reminder that the pomp and glory of this world are brief and transient?"

"I'm inclined to think, Sire," the Bishop retorted, "that by making such a request you've shown you don't need that kind of reminder."

The ceremony ended on that inconclusive note. The royal party retired to the palace, causing a scramble of lords and lordlings to follow them. The count of Viana rode off with his knights to plant the royal standard on the highest hill they could find, while the heralds scattered through the town, and from there through the kingdom, to spread the proclamation.

"It's done," Baldaia sighed. "Now it remains to be seen how much Prince Henry can make him catch fire with his dream."

"I don't care," Pedro said. "As long as the infante can give Gil Eanes a little more backbone."


"I'm amazed that you take these stories seriously," Prince Henry glowered, pacing back and forth with the hood of his mourning cloak thrown back and his hands clasped behind his back. "If there were the slightest authority for these old wives' tales they tell, I wouldn't blame you. But you come to me with the opinions of a few sailors who are familiar only with the Flanders trade or other well-known routes, and who know nothing of the needle or sailing chart."

Gil Eanes sweated in his heavy mantle. It was close in the small chapel off the public hall where the prince had taken him, and his tight golden curls were plastered against his wide forehead by perspiration. He was a broad-chested, thick-necked man with frank gray eyes in an uncomplicated face.

"I swear to you that I'm not afraid, Dom Henrique," he said, throwing his hands wide.

Prince Henry's manner changed. He stopped in front of Gil Eanes and put his hands on his shoulders, looking him in the eye. "I know it's not from cowardice or lack of goodwill, but from the newness of the thing," he said. "Hear me, Dom Gil. I raised you from a small boy, and I have confidence in you. That's why I chose you to be captain of the *barcha*, and that's why I'm going to send you out again. But this time I want you to strain every nerve. I ask only that you pass Cape Bojador. If you do that, I promise you every honor and reward."

"I'll do it for you, Dom Henrique," Eanes said fervently. "I swear to you that I won't return without success!"

Prince Henry released him. "Go on your voyage, then, with the grace of God," he said with an abrupt nod. "Don't delay. Return to Sagres immediately and begin making preparations. A *barcha* will be waiting for you when you're ready."

"I'll leave in the morning," the squire said, moving toward the door.

Prince Henry was staring toward the small altar, where a rank of candles burned for his father, his shoulders hunched and his head down. "I desire you to take Pedro da Costa with you as pilot," he said without turning around. "Cabral won't need him now. He'll serve you well. He knows the waters around Cape Bojador as well as any man alive."

It was warm in the dream. The sky over Madeira was a clear blue, unsullied by the haze of smoke he remembered. The sun was a golden seal pasted against the sky, a seal with a sawtoothed edge and a round smiling face, like the suns that sometimes decorated maps. Inês was coming down the wide curving beach toward him, and she was smiling at him, too.

"Wake up, senhor," a boy's voice said. The soft hand of a gentleman's son shook him.

Pedro opened his eyes and saw a page in the livery of Prince Henry's household. His first thought was that Baldaia had sent for him.

"You're to come with me, senhor," the boy said.

Pedro's bedmates, a sailor and a traveling friar, stirred and grumbled in their sleep. Pedro did his best to climb over them without waking them. The friar scratched his fleas and went back to snoring.

Pedro shouldered his sea chest and followed the page downstairs in the silver half-light of the hour before dawn. The innkeeper, already awake, was waiting for him with the reckoning. His manner had been improved by the sight of the infante's livery, but unfortunately so had the size of the bill. Pedro paid what the innkeeper asked, though he was leaving without the breakfast he'd been promised. He hoisted his sea chest to his shoulder once more and asked the page, "Where are we going?"

"I have horses waiting, senhor," the page said. "I'm to take you to Dom Henrique's *escudiero*, Gil Eanes. You'll ride with him to Sagres."

Pedro's heart lifted. After Baldaia's gloomy assessment he hardly dared hope that this was what he thought it was. "Is he going to sea?" he asked.

The page hesitated. Probably he was wondering why he had been sent to fetch a simple sailor.

"Come, you can tell me," Pedro said.

The page's face shone with hero worship for the doughty Gil Eanes. Like all of Prince Henry's household, he was infected with the excitement of the sea.

"*Sim, senhor,*" he said self-importantly. "He's taken it upon himself to pass the bulge of Africa."

Heitor came through the kitchen door, carrying one of the hundred-pound baskets of grapes as easily as if it had been a laundry hamper. His face lit up when he saw the baby, little Amélia, sitting on the floor playing with her doll, and he set the basket down with a thump and swung her into the air, to her squeals of delight.

Inês was sitting at the table with the five-year-old, Beatriz, sewing a tablecloth, while Beatriz, with intense concentration, sewed large practice stitches on a piece of cloth she had been given. Inês looked up with a smile and put her sewing down.

"Sit down," she said. "I've kept your dinner warm for you. You shouldn't work past noon like that without stopping."

Heitor set the little girl down carefully. She resumed playing with the doll he had carved for her and that her mother had supplied with a miniature dress.

"Look!" Heitor cried joyfully.

He went to the basket and held up an enormous bunch of grapes more than two feet long. "Just look at this! They're all like this," he said. "There are almost more bunches than leaves. We're going to have a bumper crop."

He popped a grape into the mouth of the baby, and then gave one to the older girl.

"*Maravilhoso!*" Inês said warmly. "The wine lodge ought to give us a good price this year. I'll go down to Funchal tomorrow and bargain with them. I can arrange for Granny Elizabete to stay with the children." She glanced at the embroidery that was spread across the table. "Dona Constanca's tablecloth can wait a day."

A concerned expression passed across Heitor's bluff face. "You work too hard. The kitchen garden. The animals. The house. The children. Keeping the accounts. And then sewing for the wives of the *fidalgos* on top of everything else."

"I enjoy sewing. And the money comes in handy. Zarco's organizing a company to export Madeira lace off the island, and the prices ought to be even better then. You're the one who works too hard. In the fields from light to light with only Alonso and Escobar to help you—when they feel like it. And then pitching in at planting and harvest to help others with *their* crops. You work beyond your strength!"

He grinned. "I'm the happiest man in the world. Just think—a blockhead like me, the master of a prosperous *fazenda* like this. But I couldn't have built it without you. If only I could read, at least I could take the accounts off your hands."

"Enough! Sit down before your dinner gets cold, after all the trouble I took to preserve it!"

After he had finished, when she had cleared away the dishes and he was sitting back with his belt loosened and a contented expression on his face, she brought him a glass of wine.

"Here, try this, Heitor."

"What, more wine? I've had enough. I've got to get back to work."

She was waiting with an odd expression, almost of expectation, on her face. "Just have a taste."

He took a sip, and his eyebrows lifted. He took another sip and held it in his mouth, savoring it.

"What's this? It's not our Malmsey."

"Do you like it?"

"It's marvelous! I've never tasted anything like it."

"It's our last year's vintage, from the little cask I put aside and kept heated behind the stove all winter. I've been letting it cool off slowly these last few months."

"Your little experiment?"

"Don't laugh. I thought it was worth trying. After that shipload of wine that wasn't sold came back—the one that was impounded by the Tunisians and kept sitting in port for a year before the bey released it. Everybody thought the wine would be ruined, after cooking below decks in that climate for so long. But it tasted better! I thought I could try the same thing here. I added a little brandy to it first, to keep it from getting out of hand."

He shook his head. "Whoever thought of such a thing?"

"It will be even better if it's aged for a few years. I'm sure of it."

"Have you told them about it at the wine lodge?"

"No. We'll keep it a secret for a while. Some day everybody on the island will be doing the same thing, but I want for us to have the benefit of one or two vintages first—at a good price. Then we'll tell them how it's done—if somebody else hasn't figured it out first."

"You don't mean that you intend to make more wine than just for our own use?" he said uneasily. "The lodge won't like that. It's only Zarco's licensees who have the privilege of selling abroad."

"I only want you to hold back a small part of the grape harvest this year and next—enough for a few dozen barrels. We'll have to build a heating shed, like a smokehouse. We don't have to tell them anything about it till the wine's at its best. Then they can buy it from us for marketing. They won't complain. They can make a big profit on it in England."

He scratched his head. "You think ahead," he said admiringly. "All right, I'll trust your judgment. You're smarter than I am. I'm a lucky man. I don't know why you agreed to have me." For a moment his eyes avoided hers. "Do you have any regrets?"

"No," she said. "No regrets."

He looked into his wine for a while, then tossed it off. He set down the glass and got to his feet. "I'd better get going," he said. I've got to mend the fence around the wheat plot. Lobo's cow got into it again."

"Again?" Her eyes flashed angrily. "Heitor, he does it on purpose. He breaks down the fences of his neighbors to let his animals fatten on their crops, then blames it on the animals."

"I know. But nobody can prove it."

"Where's the cow now?"

"I tied it up in the shed." He shrugged. "He can come get it if he wants."

"We should keep it till he pays for the wheat. He lives off the labor of others. He keeps a few miserable animals and makes a show of planting, so as not to attract Zarco's attention, but he doesn't tend his fields. He gets along by stealing and extortion, by selling contraband, and by renting out the services of that slut who lives with him."

"Some day Zarco will catch on to him," Heitor said uncomfortably. "It's not our affair."

"I know, you don't want trouble." She pressed his hand and saw him to the door. Before he could go outside, little Beatriz ran to him with the cloth she had been sewing."

"Look, Papai, look what I did."

He inspected the crude stitches gravely. "Very pretty," he said. "Some day you'll be as good a seamstress as your mother."

"She will," Inês smiled. "She already shows talent for her age, and she has an eye for good work."

"She has you to take after. And she has the name for it, if what you told me about her grandmother's sewing is true." He broke off as he saw the expression on Inês's face. "I'm sorry, I didn't mean to distress you."

"It's all right," Inês said.

"Some day you'll see her again," he said awkwardly.

"I don't even know if she's alive." She gave his hand another squeeze. "Come, I'll walk you to the gate."

They emerged into hot sunlight. The air was heavy with perfume and buzzing with bees. Inês looked down the tilting landscape at a green mosaic of neatly fenced fields and vineyards. It always reminded her of a stained-glass window. Down below, near the turquoise curve of the bay, a church steeple poked up at the sky. The air was fresh and clean. The great fire had finally burned itself out after seven years, and Madeira no longer smelled of ashes.

"Speak of the devil," Heitor muttered.

Lobo was coming up the roadway toward them, a shaggy bareheaded figure in a loose tunic and seedy two-color hose. He stopped at the gate and looked Inês over in a way that made her seethe, then turned a mocking gaze toward Heitor.

"I hear you've stolen my cow," he said.

"Watch how you talk," Heitor said. "I've got her tied in the shed. You can come around with me and take her."

Lobo picked at his teeth lazily with a straw. "This is the second time in a week," he said. "You entice her so that you can steal the milk. You owe me for that."

"*Ladrão!*" Inês burst out. "You should pay us for the crops she devoured!"

Lobo ran his eyes without haste over her body. "The better-off never change," he said. "They squeeze a dinhiero better than the poor." His gaze traveled to the well-kept house with its painted shutters, the thatched outbuildings that Heitor had constructed, the poultry in the yard, the flourishing vegetable garden, and the lush vineyard within its palisade. "With all you've got, you shouldn't begrudge the less fortunate a few handfuls of grain."

"You could be prosperous, too, if you worked at it as hard as Heitor does," Inês told him. "Everybody here was given the same start."

His mouth opened in a wide smile. "I'm a poor man without a wife to help me," he said. "If I had a woman like you, I'd prosper. Some men have all the luck." He gave a sham sigh. "What I wouldn't give to trade places."

He shifted his stance as if by accident so that his short tunic lifted and she could see the way his codpiece was standing out.

She flushed with anger. "Take your cow and be off!"

"Yes," Heitor said. "You'd better go now."

Lobo laughed. "Take me to your shed."

She watched as Heitor led Lobo off to the cowshed, a vague misgiving taking shape inside her. She didn't like having Lobo inside her property where he could notice things. When he saw something that caught his fancy, he was apt to take it, if he thought he could get away with it. There had been a number of small robberies in the district recently— chickens, a hay rake, some baskets waiting to be sold, a ham taken from a larder. Nobody had caught Lobo at it. But she had seen the way his head had darted back and forth, like an animal sniffing out scents, as he had climbed the lane, looking at people's dooryards to see if anything valuable had been left lying around. She would tell Heitor to put things away more carefully and keep small items inside the house. At this moment Lobo was probably coveting old Blossom in the cowshed, but there was no danger of Blossom being stolen; a cow was too conspicuous a commodity in this small community, where everybody knew everybody else's business. But she would see that the chickens were locked up tonight.

She took a deep breath of the sweet air, determined not to let Lobo spoil the day for her. She looked out over the harbor. Three ships were anchored there, all Portuguese— Portugal held her navigation secrets closely, and other nations had not yet developed the confidence to stop at Madeira's harbors. No doubt that would change some day.

The sight of the ships made her think of Pedro da Costa. He had never come back again with the supply ships after that last time, when he had returned to find her married to Heitor. "Good thing, too!" Mafalda had told her. "You're better off never to see him again." Mafalda was angry at Pedro, seeing him as a thief of happiness, a threat. But Inês didn't feel that way. What was done was done, and what she had felt for Pedro was locked away in her heart for good. Heitor was a good man, and she had made her bargain.

Her eyes lifted from the ships to the horizon, where a heartbreakingly blue sea met a still bluer sky. Pedro was out there somewhere doing great things. She had found out on the day he left Madeira that he had sailed with the ship that had passed Cape Non, and now Prince Henry's mariners were discovering one island after another in the group called the Azores. Pedro would be older; he must have a wife and children of his own by now.

She made an effort not to think about him. Here, on this island where God had placed her, she would be looking at the sea every day of her life. It would not be a good idea to turn the ocean into a reminder of Pedro.

# CHAPTER 11

It was hard not to feel fear, even though he had been told what to expect. Tom lowered the nested set of ebony and ivory star sighting boards and turned a baffled face to Cheng Ho.

"The north star's gone. It's disappeared."

"Yes, Chin Mao, it has," the eunuch admiral said gravely. "It's been swallowed by the belly of the world."

Tom suspected that he was being teased. But he responded with equal gravity, "Then how will we know where we are?"

Around him, on an immense dark sea, the fanlike sails of the fleet were scratched in by starlight. The stars had rearranged themselves into unfamiliar groupings. Gone was the comforting oblong of Charles's Wain, the constellation the Chinese called the Big Basket. There was a hole in the Milky Way, and next to it were four bright stars that made the shape of a cross. The cross must have been placed there as a sign, because though it lay on its side when it first rose in the evening, it gradually righted itself until, at the moment of meridian transit, it pointed almost due south.

The north star, though, had been sinking night by night ever since the Treasure Fleet had left the Red Sea and begun sailing down the coast of Africa. Tom had not worried at first, because the same thing had happened when the fleet had sailed southward along the coasts of the Middle Kingdom and Vietnam, but then the star had begun gaining altitude again as soon as they rounded the Malay peninsula and came safely through the Malaccan strait.

But by last night, only a few days' sail out of the great port city the Africans hereabouts called Mogadishu, the star had sunk so low that the pilot could no longer measure its height even by the smallest ebony plate, the one-*ch'ih* plate, which was only one finger's width in size. Shaking his head with misgiving, he had taken his reading with only the small ivory plate, which could measure fractions or a *ch'ih,* and then turned to Cheng Ho and said something that Tom didn't understand about right-angle triangle calculations and the "Arithmetical Classic of the Gnomon and the Circular Paths of Heaven."

Now Cheng Ho turned a broad, amused face to Tom and replied, "There are other means of navigation we can switch to, Chin Mao. For a time we can make calculations by the Hua-kai constellation, which is still eight *ch'ih* above the horizon. The fish-compass still works below the waist of the world—though of course it can only give us our bearing— and for latitude we'll depend more and more on the chip-and-walking man method and other forms of dead reckoning. But even when the Hua-kai begins to sink below a *ch'ih*'s breadth, we can rely for many li to come on the star maps of the southern skies which our astronomers made on previous voyages."

"And then?"

Cheng Ho shrugged. "And then we will make new maps of the stars and pray to the sea goddess."

Tom repressed a shudder. He handed the star-sighting contraption back to the pilot and went through an elaborate ritual of thanks in the style of the Middle Kingdom before turning back to Cheng Ho.

"What are they like, these lands below the equator, honorable one?"

"We've already mapped the coast about three thousand li beyond Zanzibar, as far as a rich kingdom called Mozambique. The shores are mostly as you see them now—low-lying, skirted by shallows, sandbars, and low islands. We'll pass through a strait between Mozambique and a large island called Madagascar. The current runs more swiftly there, and it can be dangerous. There's a cape just opposite the southern tip of Madagascar where the current, for no apparent reason, sets directly on shore, and when we pass the Cape of the Currents, we'll stay well out of sea to avoid the danger of shipwreck—"

He broke off as he saw Tom's impatient fidgeting.

"What is it, Chin Mao?" he said kindly.

"I meant . . . I meant . . . what kind of *people* will we find there?"

Cheng Ho lifted a wry eyebrow. "Ah, your insatiable barbarian curiosity about human beings. We'll never make a proper Confucian bureaucrat out of you, Chin Mao. You don't have a decent regard for abstractions."

"You're curious yourself. You know you are."

Cheng Ho rested his hands on the rail and settled his bulk into a more comfortable position. "The next city we will visit is Mombasa. It's a large and prosperous port, not unlike Mogadishu. The inhabitants follow the teachings of the Prophet, of whom they've heard through visiting Arab traders. They wear rich clothes, build handsome mosques, and live well. They're lighter in color than the people of the interior, whom they avoid, but not so light as the people farther north. . . . Is this what you wish to hear, Chin Mao?"

"Yes, please."

"The influence of the Prophet wanes as one travels farther and farther south. In Mozambique the people speak the language of the region, Swahili, among themselves, but Arabic in the public places and so are still able to converse with the Arab traders who come calling. They're a brown-skinned and well-formed people, they wear fine clothes in stripes of many colors, and every man wears a cap embroidered with gold thread. Beyond the island port of Mozambique the trading cities become scarcer, and they are like circles of light in a surrounding darkness. There are wilder places along that coast as well, and in the interior things are very different. There you will find tall men who dress in lion skins and wear lions' manes, who do not eat any of the five grains but eat only meat. They drink blood drawn from the veins of their cattle, mixed with milk. There are rumors of lost cities in the interior, the ruins of great civilizations, but I don't know. I've never seen them."

"Lost cities?" Tom cried excitedly. "What do you mean?"

Cheng Ho hesitated. His face grew solemn, and finally he said, "I'll tell you because you're a barbarian and it doesn't matter. At the farthest extent of our last voyage, at a place called Beira on the lower Mozambique coast, we kept hearing stories about a fabulous city named Zimbabwe—only a few hundred li inland. The stories more or less agreed on its wonders, which such tales rarely do—an enclosure as large as the Forbidden City, with walls more than a *chang* thick and three *chang* high. Towers, temples and tombs, conduits to bring water, a hidden treasure of gold. I did a foolish thing. I sent a detachment of marines, a thousand men, to investigate. I believed such a show of force, with disciplined men in armor and with steel weapons, would be sufficient to impress any of the primitive tribesmen they were likely to encounter. But the people of the forest flit through the trees like shadows. Little men, no larger than children, so they said, began to pick them off with poisoned arrows, and there was no way to fight them. They marched three hundred li, and Zimbabwe was just as far away as it had been before. The marine commander very sensibly turned back, over the objections of the scholar who had been sent with them. Fewer than six hundred returned. None of this, naturally, was reported to the emperor or to the civil service, and the surviving marines were dispersed through the Treasure Fleet so their numbers could not be counted. In an expedition this size the deaths of a few hundred men are scarcely worth mentioning in themselves. But the manner of their death, at the hands of the Zanj, would be seized on with glee by my enemies."

"The Zanj?"

"Yes, Chin Mao. There are many kinds of Zanj, each with their own customs, and once you have broken through Africa's crust, the land belongs entirely to them. Beyond these lands of which I've told you, we don't know what exists. We can only hope that the great southern cape which we expect to find will not extend more than a few thousand li past the shores of Mozambique."

There was a bay with a river flowing into it, white sands, tumbled rocks, a flat expanse of scrub vegetation interspersed with isolated trees of twisted shape, a background of low mountains. A settlement of conical huts could be seen in the distance, and men tending cattle.

"We'll anchor here," Cheng Ho decided, "and wait out this storm that's brewing."

Tom stood on the poop deck, trying to keep out of the way. The ships carried a minimum of sail because of the difficult and contrary winds of the last few days, and these were the heavy mat sails that could stand up to bad weather; as the breeze stiffened, swarming gangs of men labored to get the remaining expanse reefed.

The great fleet dotted the water for some miles. Now it was condensing, drawing closer, as the ships on the outer flanks began to catch up with those that had already taken in sail and dropped anchor.

Cheng Ho was busy giving orders. A stream of officers dispersed to various parts of the ship; signals went out to the fleet. The astronomer was packing up instruments to take ashore, and an artist was sitting by the rail, sketching the shape of the coastline.

Ma Huan appeared on deck and joined Tom at his corner of the poop. "I'm to go ashore with the advance party," he said, sitting down on the little bench in the angle of the taffrail and fanning himself. "There's not likely to be much use for an Arabic translator—we haven't heard any Arabic for three thousand li. We haven't even heard any Swahili. But Cheng Ho asked me to go along anyway."

He fanned himself more vigorously. "We must be very foolhardy, Chin Mao. The Arab ships are afraid to venture past the northern Mozambique ports. They're afraid of the way the current speeds up in the passage between the Mozambique coast and the big island, Madagascar. They call it the Channel of No Return, and they've invented all sorts of superstitious tales about sea monsters the size of islands and giant birds that carry off ships." His old eyes came to a watery focus on Tom. "Perhaps those Arab ships that failed to return simply ran afoul of the Zulu. Those fierce men don't like strangers taking their water. I believe they might have attacked our shore parties, in spite of our numbers, if Cheng Ho had not exercised the utmost diplomacy."

Tom squinted at the distant herdsmen. The appearance of the ships seemed to have caused great consternation, and the tiny figures were running about, rounding up the cattle and driving them into an enclosure circled by the beehive huts.

"Those look like more Hottentots," Tom said. "I can't tell what the huts are made of from here, but they might be animal hides."

The Hottentots had been friendlier than the Zulus. They too had been sensitive about water rights, and they didn't like strangers approaching their huts or corrals too closely, but they had shown a willingness to barter fresh meat for clothing and trinkets and in the end had made no difficulty about the ships refilling water casks at the mouths of their streams. Tom, mingling with the parties of curious warriors who came to look at the Chinese encampment, had picked up a few useful words of their odd language—enough to be able to communicate with them in a rough-and-ready fashion, the way he had always managed to get by in other lands during his travels. The Hottentot language had nothing to do with Swahili or even the Zulu tongue, which at least bore some resemblance to other Bantu dialects. Hottentot was full of peculiar clicking sounds, and, as in Chinese, a change in pitch of a single syllable could change the meaning of a word drastically. Tom, with his freewheeling approach, had shown more aptitude for it than some of the fleet's official "Zanj" translators, a fact that made him none too popular with them.

Ma Huan brightened at Tom's words. "Would you like to come along?"

Tom jumped at the chance. "*Shir-shir!* Very much. If it's all right with Fei Hsin."

Fei Hsin was the petty officer who had been in charge of the advance landing parties. He was a Confucian scholar who, improbably, had found himself conscripted into military service in order to expiate some petty crime. He spent a great deal of time in his cabin, writing a book he called *The Triumphant Visions of the Starry Raft,* by which he hoped to get back into the good graces of the emperor and win his freedom.

Ma Huan snorted. "Who's Fei Hsin? A ticket-of-leave man! *I* say it's all right."

"Well . . ."

"Here comes Cheng Ho. We'll put it up to him."

Cheng Ho stopped in front of them, large and imposing, his cloak thrown wide and ruffling a little in the increasing breeze. There was a muted air of exhilaration about him that was at odds with the hitch in his plans that the worsening weather had caused, as though he was looking beyond the immediate problems to something else.

"We'll probably have four or five hours before the storm

strikes," he said, "but you never can be sure. I've instructed Fei Hsin not to proceed too far inland. In any case, I don't intend to set up an encampment here. We'll be on our way again as soon as the weather improves—I hope that won't be more than a few days."

Ma Huan cleared his throat. "I was thinking that it might be a good idea to take Chin Mao with us. He has a way with languages, and we've come so far into unknown territory that there's no such thing as an expert. If you remember, he got along with the large-buttocked Zanj very well at our last landfall. Perhaps it takes a barbarian to communicate with barbarians."

"I was just telling Ma Huan that those people over there on shore look like Hottentot, too," Tom contributed.

"Yes, yes," Cheng Ho said. "That will be fine." He gave Tom a crisp nod. "I don't know how you got us out of our difficulties with that last lot, but you had them smiling and eating out of our hands."

"It wasn't me," Tom said. "They worship the powers in nature that cause rain. They don't really have a god, but they believe in a ruler of all things who came out of the East—I guess because that's where the rain winds come from." He lowered his eyes. "So when they saw the Treasure Fleet come sailing from the east, they just naturally thought that its admiral had something to do with that."

Cheng Ho laughed uproariously. Then he stopped, and with mock severity said, "That was wicked of you Chin Mao. You should not have imputed divinity to me. The emperor is the only person with links to heaven. As an emissary of the Raft of Stars, it's your duty to inform these backward people that it's the Hsuan-te emperor on the Throne at the Center of the World who rules over all."

"Yes, San-pao T'ai-chien," Tom said meekly. "I tried, but it's hard to get across an idea like that with only a few words."

"You do very well with your 'few words,' Chin Mao. Perhaps there's something in what Ma Huan says about barbarians communicating. You aren't afraid to lose your dignity by gesturing and capering." He pondered a moment. "I don't want you to get in the way of the official interpreters in Fei Hsin's shore party. But see what you can find out on your own."

"Yes, firstborn, anything you say."

Cheng Ho gazed speculatively to the west. The graying of the sky had cut visibility and made a mist of the horizon. But it was still possible to follow the line of the coast for some distance, and it was not hard to see that it was turning slightly to the south again.

Tom knew what was on Cheng Ho's mind, and he felt sorry for him. Because if it was true, it meant a brutal end to all Cheng Ho's dreams and ambitions.

"Ask the Zanj," the eunuch admiral said, "what they know of the land to the west. The information may not be reliable—these tribes think their own small territory is the entire world—but they may have gained an impression of the shape of the coast from their contact with neighboring tribes."

"You think," Tom said hesitantly, "that the coast is beginning to run south, and that there isn't any bottom to Africa after all? That there's no way to pass from the eastern seas to the western seas?"

Cheng Ho's smooth face tightened under the stress of emotion. He shook his head with great firmness. "No, Chin Mao. I haven't come this far to be thwarted. We've been trending west for more than fifteen hundred li. If it were a fluke, we'd know it by now. I'm convinced that this is the bottom of Africa. This deviation to the south will turn out to be another cape, like the ones we've already passed. We have only to keep following the coast and eventually we'll find the ultimate cape. And then we'll turn north toward the seas of Europe."

Tom would not have dared to contradict him. He bowed. "Yes, San-pao T'ai-chien."

"Go, Chin Mao. It may be that this is the ultimate cape before us now."

Tom followed Ma Huan to the waiting tender. It was crammed to the gunwales with officials in court robes with plaques of rank. The claque of scholars around Fei Hsin looked at Tom with disdain as he clambered down the wooden gangplank. Tom had adopted sailors' dress for practicality—wide drawers with plenty of room in the seat, a short shirt belted at the waist. It gave him more freedom of movement than the long robes with the drooping sleeves that he had kept tripping over. The only concession he made when going ashore was sandals instead of bare feet. Africa was full of thorns and sharp stones.

Tom found a place forward, among the marine guards. They squeezed their ranks a little to make room for him. They were good fellows, most of them, and several of his dice companions were in this shore detail. They'd been togged out impressively for first contact; they wore short robes and trousers tucked into boots, with cuirasses and helmets, and they carried long pole-swords and twelve-foot lances decorated with ceremonial standards. Despite their sharp appearance when viewed at a slight remove, when you got in among them they smelled powerfully of garlic, sweat, and leather.

Fei Hsin was holding forth to his little group. Several of them were in the same shoes as he—technically, criminals serving out a sentence—and they held themselves superior to the personnel of the Yellow Gate. Fei Hsin had shown enough ability and capacity for action for Cheng Ho to entrust him with command responsibilities, but some of the others were hopeless except for pushing brushes around on paper. At the moment Fei Hsin seemed to be treating them to one of the poems with which he liberally dotted his travelogue.

> "Wherever one looks,
> One meets only sighs and sulky glances.
> Desolation.
> The hills are uncultivated,
> And the land is wide...."

He broke off as Ma Huan pushed his way in among them. It was well known that Ma Huan was writing a book too. His book had almost the same title as Fei Hsin's— *Triumphant Visions of the Ocean Shores*.

"I'm too old for this," he grumbled. "My bones are stiff with damp. When is one of these savages going to offer us a cup of tea, tell me that?"

The coxswain cast off and the sailors pulled for shore. The swells were deepening, and one of the sailors lost his footing and almost drowned in the surf when they hauled the boat up on the beach. But with the marines to help, they got the boat far enough out of the water so the scholars could climb to the sands without getting the hems of their robes wet.

Tom hung back, away from the shore party. They were busy setting up tables on which small gifts were displayed, and the marines were disposing themselves nearby, where they could come to the aid of the diplomatic party if necessary. The sailors stayed near the boat, under the watchful eye of the coxswain. Fei Hsin wanted no incidents. A sailor had been stoned during a previous shore encounter, when he had approached a native village too closely, looking for women; he would have been left for dead, except that it would have been bad policy to let the Zanj think the Treasure Fleet did not value its own, and a squad of marines had chased his assailants away and carried him back to the boat.

The natives had not yet worked up enough courage to come down to the beach, but some of the curious were edging closer. Tom could see that they were indeed Hottentots as he had surmised—smallish men whose skin was yellow, not black or brown, wearing little but sheaths to cover their private parts. The near-naked women who were crowding behind them had the same unusual buttocks that Tom had seen before, almost like camels' humps. Fei Hsin was making encouraging gestures, holding up some of the trinkets he had brought.

With no one paying attention to him, Tom slipped away, skirting the impending encounter. He climbed the thorny slope and sat down on a knoll to watch from a distance.

After a while a Hottentot came along the beach path, saw him, took a startled step back, then came forward a few steps, holding his spear in front of him.

Tom called to him, dipping into his meager store of Hottentot words and taking care to get the peculiar clicks right, but he did not get up from his seat. After a while the man came closer.

Tom grinned insanely at him and spoke volubly, using nonsense words interspersed at random with the rest of his Hottentot vocabulary. He was careful not to make his gestures too large or do anything to startle the man. Eventually the Hottentot lowered his spear and began speaking back to him with equal incomprehensibility.

In no time he was the center of attention of a half-dozen Hottentot warriors and a somewhat larger number of women. They marveled at his yellow hair and pale skin; he had to show them, by the vigorous rubbing of a forearm, that he was not painted. One of the young men produced a carved flute and demonstrated it with a complicated melody full of trills and bird calls. He responded by dancing a jig for them, then an English hornpipe. They laughed with pleasure and clapped their hands. More flutes appeared. Presently one of the women slipped away to the village and came back with a cup of milk, which she presented to him. He drank the warm stuff, miming pleasure by rubbing his belly, and reciprocated by distributing some small Chinese sweetmeats that he had foresightedly brought with him, wrapped in oiled paper. There was a bad moment when the first man to try one spat it out in surprise, but Tom reassured them by chewing one himself with an exaggerated smacking of lips, and the others condescended to sample the confections.

Down on the beach the Hottentots were at last mingling with Fei's group, but Tom could not tell what was going on. Other boats had landed by now, and small exploratory parties were pushing their way into the bush, taking care after the lesson learned from the stoned sailor to keep well away from the Hottentot village.

Tom progressed to inquiries. With sweeping gestures at the coast and sketches in the air accompanied by interrogative clicks, he gave them to understand that he wanted to know what lay to the west.

He got a torrent of conflicting babble and accompanying pantomime in return. Tom could not pin any of it down. He learned that there were cliffs, mountains, and high country. Equally, he learned that there were islets, reefs, and tumultuous seas. He tried scratching an outline in the dirt with a stick, but this abstraction was beyond their powers.

He was at the point of despair when the jabbering died down and the crowd fell apart. A Hottentot personage of some distinction came striding into the gap. In addition to the sheath for his member, he wore a cape made of the skin of some spotted beast and a necklace of claws. There were copper ornaments in his ears—the first metal Tom had seen—and ivory bracelets on his upper arms.

He barked questions, stopped them from talking all at once, and got respectful answers. When he was satisfied, he turned to Tom and commenced the business of communicating.

A half hour later, Tom had his answers. The southerly turn of land did not go on forever, but came to an end within the ability of a man to walk. No man of the tribe now alive had ever walked that far, but within the memory of the grandfathers of the oldest, their ancestors had made a trek that followed the curve of the shore. Tom's informant illustrated the concept of generations by dragging forth a woman with a baby, poking first at one and then the other while supplying a word to indicate their relationship and repeating it three times.

Tom had no idea how long such a migration might take—the Hottentot language had a flexible concept of time—but he could guess that, what with cattle to drive, children being born, and the necessity to gather food and hunt as they went, they could not have averaged more than a few li a day. But even if the journey had taken some months on foot, Cheng Ho would be able to sail it in days.

The important thing was that the shoreline not only turned west again, it kept turning until it trended north. This, surely, was the meaning of the Hottentot chieftain's insistence that there was "only water" around the bend. Those expansive arm gestures clearly meant that there was another bay there, a false bay, and a final cape to round—a dangerous rocky cape guarded on either side by mountains of peculiar formation. There, the spirits of the waters were always angry, stirring up turbulent rollers, swift currents, and waves as high as hilltops—high enough to swallow even the mighty "floating huts" that were tethered offshore. Tom put it down to exaggeration.

He smiled warmly at the chief and felt in his pockets. The copper ear ornaments had shown him that the Hottentots prized the metal. He dug into his pockets and came up with a few Chinese cash coins—small discs of copper with a square hole in the center for stringing them together into higher denominations. The Hottentot seemed delighted to get them. His knobby cheeks widened in an impossibly broad smile, and he took off one of his ivory bangles and pressed it on Tom.

The chief departed, and the bevy around Tom lost its temporary shyness. The flutes started up again, and Tom recited a bawdy song he had learned from the apprentices at Master Philpot's. The Hottentots couldn't understand a word of it, but Tom bawled it out with great energy, and they seemed to enjoy the rhymes and all the "fa fa lillies" and "too a tee tallies."

They moved in closer, and took turns touching the ivory bracelet on his arm. They seemed more impressed by it than by the power and strangeness of the fleet in the bay. Several of them began to make gestures, urging him to his feet. Tom waited for something more definite, but he believed he was on the verge of being invited to the village.

A Hottentot maiden giggled shyly at him and peeped at him from between her fingers, but Tom was not willing to take that kind of chance among strange people of uncertain temper. He wondered if they brewed anything worth drinking. They lived on milk, meat, and blood, like Mongols. The Mongols fermented a drink out of mare's milk, but it was hard to take unless you were used to it. The Zulu and some of the Bantu folk farther east, however, had made a sort of beer.

"Lion water?" he inquired, putting together two of the Hottentot words he was sure of and hoping for the best. He made a quaffing motion, then went through a dumb show of staggering in a circle.

They took up his phrase immediately, regarding it as a great joke. "Lion water," they took turns repeating, and one of the young men mimicked Tom's stagger. There was more laughter. They let him know through gestures that help was at hand. Tom smiled benignly at his new friends.

A cannon boomed. Tom almost jumped out of his skin. The fleecy heads around him jerked up.

He looked out at the fleet and saw smoke curling up from the deck of Cheng Ho's flagship. There was another flash and roar and then another, as more cannon went off on other ships, and then the air was split by the bright notes of a bugle calling retreat.

The Hottentots disappeared like a flock of startled birds. One of them hurled a spear at Tom as an afterthought, but he wasn't really aiming and it tumbled harmlessly past.

Down on the beach was a swirl of confusion that resolved itself into Hottentots running away and Fei Hsin's people dashing about to fold up the tables and get to the boats. Sailors were heaving at yokes to drag the tenders toward the surf without waiting for the more finicky scholars to climb aboard first. Tom watched, openmouthed, until it came to him that he was about to be stranded here.

He plunged down the slope, slipping and sliding, scrambling to his feet when he fell, and made it to Fei Hsin's boat just as the last sailor was hopping aboard. He floundered in the breakers, choking on salt water, and a marine pulled him up over the gunwale.

When he had finished coughing up brine, he looked out at the Treasure Fleet again. The huge windlasses were drawing up anchor, and the mat sails were being raised again. Tom could not understand the reason for it. To the southeast one could already make out the dark mass of the advancing storm, blotting out the gray horizon and veined with lightning flashes. This was no time to be putting out to sea.

"What happened?" he asked the marine commander. "Why are we being recalled?"

The commander, a tough, scarred veteran of the war in Vietnam, whose name was Li Loy, scratched his head.

"I don't know. The storm's not here yet. We could have stayed another two hours, maybe three."

"They're weighing anchor!"

"Looks like it."

The maneuver was hasty enough to pose dangers. It wasn't like Cheng Ho at all. Waves slapped at the flanks of the tender as it drew up against the wallowing bulk of the Treasure Ship. Without the anchors to hold them, the broad-beamed leviathans were drifting leeward. The tender was hoisted with difficulty. As the last frightened scholars scuttled up the swaying gangplank, a hundred groaning men pulled at the eight-foot spokes of the windlasses, winding rope as thick as house rafters around the tremendous drums. The boat banged against the hull of the ship with each heave of the waves, and at one point a windlass got away from the sailors. A spinning spoke caught a sailor in the ribs and hurled his broken body twenty feet across the deck. One end of the tender slipped and dropped almost to the vertical; if people had still been in it, it would have spilled them into the sea. Finally the tender was righted again and hauled up the rest of the way.

Tom found Cheng Ho on the poop deck, surrounded by people who were waiting for his orders. Fei Hsin had swept on ahead with his bevy of translators and pushed his way into the circle.

Tom hung back as Cheng Ho questioned them with growing impatience. Ma Huan was standing to one side, and when he saw Tom he gave him an ironic shrug.

Cheng Ho spotted Tom and motioned him over.

"Well, Chin Mao," he said with heavy sarcasm, "I've been informed that our scholars are making substantial progress with this clicking language. It has genders, for example, just like some of your European languages. With a few more productive encounters like this one, we may actually begin to parley with them, just as if they spoke the Ki-Swahili trade tongue." He gave Fei Hsin's interpreters a disgusted look and turned on Tom again. "Have you found out anything?"

"Yes, Admiral of the Triple Treasure," Tom said carefully. "There's one more cape ahead—a dangerous one. This is the bottom of Africa as you believed. The shoreline turns north again after this, probably within a few hundred li. Then, once you get past a final obstruction, it's clear sailing to the waters of the western world."

Cheng Ho sucked in his breath. "You're sure?"

"The Zanj I spoke to walked around it within living memory." Tom remembered the Hottentot warning of treacherous shores and angry waters, and all at once it became more real to him. "But, firstborn, we shouldn't try to sail around it in a storm."

"Some dangers are greater than others," Cheng Ho said, and walked away.

Slowly, ponderously, in the teeth of a wind that was trying to drive it ashore, the enormous ship shuddered and moved toward the darkness of the storm. Tom could feel the first chilly hint of advancing scud on his face. It was madness.

Ma Huan was standing beside him. "What's it about, Ma Huan?" Tom said. "Why is he doing this?"

"Have you not yet seen, young scholar?" Ma Huan said. "Look there, toward the east."

Tom followed the pointing finger. It was a speck in the gloom, wearing the storm clouds like a canopy, limping along under tattered sails.

"It's found us again," Ma Huan said. "The black ship."

The wave was tremendous, higher than the tallest masts of the fleet. Tom watched in disbelief as it rolled toward them out of a gray wall of fog, lifting the gigantic vessels like so many corks.

He grabbed for a stanchion as a trough opened up to meet the onrushing mountain of water, and the great ship slid down the green slope. The acres of decks tilted at an impossible angle. Everything broke loose. Tom hung onto his stanchion for dear life. A garden tub the size of an oxcart came tumbling toward him, barely missing him, and smashed through the rail into the surging sea below. Overhead, spars as thick as tree trunks whipped around the masts, sending down showers of slats and bamboo splinters.

The towering wave slammed into the ship. The prow buried itself to the mainmast. Somehow the remaining scrap of foresail had managed to keep the bows to the sea; otherwise the ship would have gone under. Tom felt the deck lift under him, a giddying sensation. The upper works of the ship shed torrents of water, tons of it. A chest-high flood raced along the deck, filled with struggling men who had been swept off their feet. Tom saw a dozen sailors washed overboard; others fetched up against obstacles or managed to get hold of something solid. Long minutes later the ship righted itself, shook itself off, and was riding the swells again.

A bruised sailor was hugging the same stanchion. He hadn't been there a moment ago. "Big!" he shouted to make himself heard above the screaming wind. "I've never seen one so big!"

Tom surveyed the fogged-in sea. Rain and flying spray obscured the air. He could see less than a half mile in any direction, and he could not tell from the ghostly outlines around him if any more ships were missing. He himself had seen a heavily armored Turtle Ship break apart on the rocks of the false bay and sink like a stone, and he knew from the cannon signals he could hear that the fleet had lost at least three more.

The sailor showed no inclination to leave the safety of the stanchion. Tom found one of the lifelines that had been stretched across the deck and hauled himself along it. He found himself alternately climbing up a steep hill, then skidding down a slippery slope with the rope burning his hands, as the ship tossed and pitched its way through an undulating universe. It was a sobering experience. He had gotten used to thinking of this enormous floating ark as a solid platform, not subject to the toying of the elements.

Thrown off his feet a half dozen times, he climbed to the tall poop. Even here, a hundred feet above the water, the effects of the wave had been felt. Tom saw snapped lines, overturned benches, and soggy joss sticks and prayer papers that had been washed out of the shrine.

"What are you doing here, Chin Mao?" Cheng Ho yelled above the wind. "You should be in your cabin!"

"What, and miss this?" Tom yelled back.

Cheng Ho grinned damply at him. He'd lost his pillbox hat, and his hair stood out in sopping-wet tufts. The pilot stood next to him, gripping the signal lines that ran to the lower deck where a gang of men operated the rudder tiller; Tom saw that he was continually yanking one line or the other to make the exquisite adjustments that kept the ship alive. Above, lashed to the partridge's nest, the assistant pilot kept an eye on the few sections of bamboo sail that had been left aloft. It was astonishing that Cheng Ho dared to maintain even this small amount of windage in this shrieking gale, but it had been explained to Tom that he was sailing fast to escape the trap of an embayed shore.

"Look, Chin Mao, there it is," Cheng Ho said, pointing. "What we've come so far to conquer."

A long narrow cape thrust itself out of the darkness at them, its reach falling short. From this new, foreshortened perspective, Tom's perceptions did a flip-flop, and he could see that the white line of crashing breakers was the perilous shore along which the fleet had been sailing. It was an awesome sight, an extended arm of rocky crags, with a flat-topped mountain like a table behind it. The vertical peak described by the Hottentot chief was visible too. A lion's head, he'd called it.

"Now we may begin to hope," Cheng Ho said, and Tom realized that he was no longer shouting. The howling wind seemed to be dying down. Visibility must have been getting rapidly better, too; otherwise Tom could never have seen all the way back to the table mountain.

In the next hour or two the sea became blue again, and a yellow sun forced its way through the thinning clouds. The flat waters were littered with the debris of the fleet—floating tubs and chicken coops, broken spars, a litter of bamboo battens like scattered straws.

There would be bodies out there, too, Tom thought grimly—bodies that eventually would be washed up on the African shore to become a cause of wonder to the Zanj.

But the fleet was mostly intact by the look of it. The losses could not have been as heavy as Cheng Ho had feared. These stout ships, with their triple planking and the ingenious watertight compartments that would have been a puzzlement to European shipbuilders, had come through in triumph.

The black ship had not. They were rid of its unwanted company for good. The last view Tom had had of it had shown it battered, low in the water, a section of its hull stove in. By now it must be at the bottom of the false bay.

He took a look at the empty horizon to the south to reassure himself. He knew better than to bring up the subject of the black ship to Cheng Ho, but he was certain that he was thinking the same thoughts. It was impossible that a ship in that condition could have survived the passage around the cape, but even if it could—Tom smiled at the absurdity of it—its mysterious captain would not have known, as Tom had known from what the Hottentots had told him, that the way north was at hand.

Cheng Ho's good humor had returned. "You should resume your stargazing lessons, Chin Mao," the Grand Admiral of the Triple Treasure said genially. "I'll speak to the astronomer. You're on your way home. Soon you will see the north star again."

# CHAPTER 12

Beatriz was a responsible little girl, old enough for tasks. Heitor lifted his head and saw her coming up the hillside road toward the vineyard, struggling with an enormous basket that was covered with a white cloth, setting it down every few steps to rest.

He put down his pruning knife and hurried over to help her. "Eh, what's this, little cricket? That's too heavy for you."

She didn't want to let go of it. "I can do it, Papai. Mamãe said she'd let me if I was sure I could carry it all the way."

He squatted down on his heels and lifted the corner of the white cloth. "What have we got here, eh? It's a feast! Chicken, fresh-baked bread, peppers in oil, sausage and white beans, honey cakes, a bottle of wine. I can't eat all this, little one. I'll be too heavy to finish my work."

"Mamãe says you've got to eat," Beatriz said in a piping imitation of adult severity. "She says you can't work without your dinner."

Heitor gazed at his daughter with unabashed adoration. She was a perfect miniature of Inês—the same delicate features, huge eyes, raven's-wing hair. Life had been good to him—given him more than his portion. He cut off that line of thought. It was tempting fate to dwell on your luck.

"I'll tell you what, *menina*." He picked up the basket and started to carry it back to the vine he had been working on. "I can't take the time right now, but I'll save it for later."

"No," she said, running ahead of him and standing in his path. "Mamãe said to eat it while it's still hot."

"She did, did she?"

"She told me to stay here till you finish it."

He laughed. "What can I do? Come on, let's take it over there. You can watch me eat it, and you can go back and tell your mother."

He sat down on the ground and spread the cloth. She sat cross-legged opposite and smoothed out her dress and apron.

"Papai?"

"Eh? What is it?"

"Why don't you like to stop working?"

"I've got to get these new vines in shape before they get ahead of me. They're the ones I grew from the shipment of roots that Prince Henry sent last year. By next year they'll be ready to bear fruit like our other vines."

"If you want them to grow grapes, why are you cutting off all the little branches?"

"So the others will be strong and make better grapes."

He settled back comfortably and poured himself a glass of wine. While Beatriz watched him gravely, he worked his way through the chicken and the hard-cooked eggs that went with it, then started in on the sausage dish.

"Papai?"

"Umm ... what is it, *menina*?" he said with his mouth full.

"Can I help you prune the grapevines?"

"Bless you, no. That's a man's work. You help your mother, and learn your embroidery."

"Mamãe works in the vineyards sometimes."

"That was only at harvest time, when I couldn't get enough help. And even then, she filled the baskets, she didn't carry them. That's too hard for a woman."

"Can I help you and Mamãe stamp on the grapes next time to make *mosto*?"

"Why not?" he laughed. "Even a little pair of feet like yours can make a contribution. We'll have the neighbors in, and get someone to pipe us tunes on a shawm while we dance on the grapes, and have a real party."

She laughed and clapped her hands. "Can Mamãe sing songs?"

"If she likes."

"She sings songs to me sometimes. They're very pretty. They're about knights and ladies and things. She said she learned them from a *cancioneiro* she had when she was a girl."

"Your mamãe has a very pretty voice," he agreed. "Not that a simple chap like me understands these high-flown *cantigas*."

"If I can't help in the vineyard, is it all right if I help Mamãe in the *estufa*?"

"The hothouse I built for that special batch of fortified wine she's developing? What could you do there?"

"I could fetch twigs for the stove. And help with the rinsing of the butts."

"You're a good little girl to think of it. Your mother gives herself too much to do."

"Papai, why did she want an *estufa*?"

"She has the idea that she can make a better kind of wine, and that we'll be rich some day."

"Rich like Senhor Zarco?"

He laughed. "Bless you, no. Senhor Zarco's a great gentleman. *Um poderoso*. I mean rich for people like us."

"Don't you want to be a *cavaleiro* some day?"

He wiped his mouth with the napkin. "That can never be. There, I'm finished. You can run along now and take the basket back to Mamãe." He rummaged through the uneaten sweets. "Here, you can have a honey cake for being such a good girl."

"Mamãe and I already ate our dinner. She says I can't have any more sweets till after supper."

"You can have just one. Otherwise you'll be too thin and no man will marry you."

After some deliberation, she took the cake. Heitor watched with satisfaction as she ate it—fastidiously, a broken-off fragment at a time, not cramming it all into her mouth at once as some children would have done.

"Your mother's made a real little lady out of you," he said with approval. "Run along now. I've got to do the rest of these vines."

He worked steadily through the rest of the morning and early afternoon, cutting back all but the strongest shoots and retying vines to their supports where necessary. There was a steady traffic up and down the steep roadway that went past the vineyard, and Heitor waved to those he knew, but he did not break off his work to chat.

As the bells of Zarco's church in Funchal finished ringing none, he heard someone come in through the trellised gate by the road—a careless someone who did not bother closing it behind him. He did not immediately turn his head to see who it was; he was down on his hands and knees with his back to the road, trimming off root suckers. He hoped it wouldn't turn out to be someone garrulous.

Footsteps came closer, stopped behind him, and a taunting voice said, "Still grubbing in the earth, farmer? There are easier ways to make a living."

Heitor twisted his neck around and saw a pair of legs in shapeless hose, a hand resting on a poniard, grinning yellow teeth, and hair like a rough pelt.

"It's you, is it, Lobo?" he said. "What do you want this time?"

"Aren't you going to at least offer me a glass of wine? I was admiring your vineyard earlier and saw your little girl coming up the slope with a basket from your woman."

"You spend too much time envying other people's property and not tending to your own."

He turned away to sever a last shoot growing up from the root stock.

"Pretty little girl. She's going to grow up into someone's juicy morsel. How did an ox like you manage to sire such a doll? Or maybe you didn't, heh?"

Heitor got to his feet, clenching the pruning knife in his hand. "Leave my family out of it. Get to it. What do you want?"

"What do I want? That's a good one. I want my cow back."

"I haven't got your cow."

"Nevertheless, I want her back."

"You're talking riddles, man. I'm busy." Heitor started to turn away.

Lobo touched his shoulder to stop him. Heitor looked down at Lobo's hand, and Lobo took it away.

"She wandered off yesterday," Lobo said somewhat sulkily. "She fell off the mountainside and broke her neck, and now I'm out a cow."

"What have I got to do with it?" Heitor said. A slow furrow started on his forehead. "Nobody lets their cows roam

free except the people who graze them on the Ilhas
Desertas. These steep slopes are too dangerous. You keep
your cow in a shed, bring it fodder, and when it needs exercise you walk it on a leash, like a dog. We all learned that
the hard way."

"It's your fault. My cow was always over here. If you'd
tied her up and kept her until I could collect her, it wouldn't
have happened."

Heitor shook his head like a bull trying to get rid of flies.
He tried to speak reasonably to the smaller man. "Your cow
was attracted to my wheat patch, that's true. And when I
found her there, I rounded her up and put her in my cowshed. I even brought her fodder. The poor thing broke loose
all those times because she was hungry when you didn't
feed her. But she didn't come here yesterday. If she had, I
would have tied her up the way I always do."

"You stole her milk," Lobo accused.

Heitor took a deep breath and said impatiently, "Inês had
to milk her sometimes. When the poor animal was in agony
because her udder was bursting. Everybody knows you're a
lazy man. People talk about passing your place late in the
morning, long after the milking hour, and hearing a cow bellowing. I always kept the milk for you and offered it to you,
but you never wanted to be bothered. It was too much trouble for you to make the extra trips with the buckets."

The quarrel had attracted onlookers. People passing by in
the roadway had been attracted by the raised voices and
stopped to see what Lobo was up to this time. Heitor was
half aware of his long-winded neighbor, Jorge Paula, loafing
by the gate with a loaded donkey and of some men carrying
willow rods for baskets.

"It's your fault," Lobo repeated stubbornly. "And you owe
me your cow to make it up to me." Despite the words themselves and the deliberate raising of his voice, Lobo sounded
curiously indifferent, as if he were going through the quarrel
by rote.

"What? Give you a cow?" Heitor said in amazement.
"You're crazy, man."

"You can afford it. You've got a fine property here, with
the best vineyard on the island. You don't deserve it." His
dark lips twisted in some private amusement. "You don't
know how to enjoy it."

Heitor's face had gone brick-red with exasperation. With

enormous self-control, he said, "That's my business. I don't want to hear any more. You can take yourself away from here right this minute and stop concerning yourself with my affairs."

Lobo nodded to himself for no apparent reason. He said silkily, "If a property like this should fall into my hands, *I'd* know what to do with it."

"I'm busy. I haven't time for this," Heitor said and turned away.

"Look at me when I talk to you," Lobo said softly. He reached for Heitor's shoulder and spun him around. Heitor opened his mouth to speak, but before he could say anything, Lobo's hand moved like a flash. Somehow the poniard was in it. He made a quick slice across Heitor's belly and stepped back immediately. Heitor staggered backward, his jaw hanging open. The pruning knife dropped from his fingers. His intestines were spilling out of the gash in his abdomen. He put a hand down to himself to hold them in. He sank to his knees, his mouth moving as if he were trying to talk. Then, the blood gushing down over his thighs, he fell over sideways.

There were gasps of shock from the gate, but nobody there moved. Lobo turned toward the startled faces.

"He had a knife in his hand," he said. "You all saw it."


The hearing was held in the large hall of Zarco's town house in Funchal. Its rather barren, slate-floored interior had been furnished for the occasion with benches borrowed from anywhere convenient—mostly the houses of his neighbors and his rebuilt church, Our Lady of the Flints, in the bay. Additional benches had been improvised from planks and dining trestles and set along the whitewashed walls, and there was seating—albeit somewhat crowded—for about two hundred people.

Teixeira had sailed from his domain on the north half of the island to lend Zarco his support as Madeira's cocaptain in whatever legalities might come up. If a sentence of death or mutilation were to result, the case would have to be referred to Portugal; otherwise Zarco had a free hand. Looking prosperous and a little heavier than he had in the days of exploration, Teixeira sat with Zarco behind the long table in one of the two high-backed chairs with canopies, the *cathe-*

*dras*. The other chairs were occupied by the three *cavaleiros* Zarco had chosen to assist him, and the pastor of Saint Catherine's, the church founded by Zarco's wife, Dona Constanca. The fact that the court's spiritual advisor was to be his wife's priest, not his own, was widely interpreted as evidence of Zarco's predisposition to leniency.

"They were quarreling, that's all I can tell you," said Jorge Paula, the dead man's neighbor. "From where I was standing, I couldn't hear everything they said."

"But the defunct one, this Heitor, had a knife in his hand throughout, isn't that so?" Zarco prompted.

"Yes." Jorge nodded his head vigorously, pleased to be able to give details. "It was a pruning knife. Heitor was pruning his vines that day."

"Did you see a knife in the hand of the other one, Lobo?"

Jorge screwed up his florid features. "I don't remember seeing one. Except at the end, *naturalmente*."

"When he was defending himself, you mean?"

Jorge became flustered. "I couldn't say, Your Excellency. Heitor was a peaceable man. Everything happened so fast."

One of the *cavaleiros* leaned over and whispered in Zarco's ear. Zarco sighed. "You said you couldn't hear every word," he said. "But it was something about a cow, wasn't it?"

"Yes," said Jorge. "Lobo's cow was always getting loose and ending up in Heitor's crops. Mine, too."

The *cavaleiro* whispered again.

"You don't like Lobo very much, do you?" Zarco said.

Jorge Paula shuffled his feet. He stole a glance at Lobo, who was sitting on a front-row bench, then jerked his eyes away when he found Lobo's gaze meeting his own.

"He ... he doesn't have the best reputation," he said weakly.

"His reputation has nothing to do with these proceedings," Zarco said severely. "We're only interested in the facts of what happened. You understand that, don't you?"

"I'm sorry, Your Excellency." Jorge's florid face became redder.

"Didn't you say a moment ago that you have a grievance against Lobo because of his cow getting into your garden?"

Jorge risked another glance at Lobo, who was lounging back on the bench as if he didn't have a care in the world.

"I wouldn't exactly say I have a grievance against him, Your Excellency," he mumbled.

The priest cleared his throat and spoke in a soft voice directed at Zarco. "The widow's waiting outside with some of her friends, Dom João. We could bring her in and ask her about this dispute over the cow between her husband and the Lobo fellow."

There was an interval of whispering as those in the front rows relayed the gist of this suggestion to those farther back. It was an unusual idea. There were no women in the room, not even a small reserved section for those socially overweening wives of *fidalgos* who might have been expected to nag their husbands to attend, the subject of the proceedings being deemed not fit for feminine ears.

Zarco clasped his hands magisterially on the table before him, making a fine display of glittering jeweled rings. "I don't think we have to bother her," he said. "There's no need to distress the poor woman any further. We know there was bad blood between the two men over the cow. It was simply a case of self-defense."

Teixeira concurred. "It's nothing we have to bother Prince Henry about. We can count ourselves lucky that we didn't have to get approval for a hanging. We don't want Sagres to think we can't manage our own affairs."

There was a ripple of approval in the room at how well the thing had gone. Lobo wore a wide grin. Some of his cronies tried to catch his eye to grin with him.

Teixeira said to Zarco, "What about the property, Dom João? I've been told it's one of the more prosperous spreads on the south slope. Now the *casado* of record is dead. It can't be left without a man to guide it."

"We can give the widow time to recover," he said magnanimously. "She won't lack for suitors. Then, if she doesn't remarry in good time, we can take a hand in choosing a new husband for her."

For miles out to sea the water tasted fresh, and the ocean was brown from the enormous volume of mud the great river brought from the interior. The Treasure Fleet lay comfortably at anchor well within the fine, spacious harbor made by the river mouth. The water casks could be filled simply by lowering them over the side, and an encampment was being set up on one of the riverbanks where several acres of jungle had been cleared away.

"Mbanza Kongo, the city of the king of the Congo, lies about two hundred li inland. It is not possible to sail any farther than that as the river there is broken by impassable falls."

The interpreter paused to wipe his forehead. The almost vertical sun beat down on the high deck as though a brass furnace hung suspended overhead. The sailors worked stripped, but Cheng Ho still maintained the dignity of silk robes, and appeared not to notice the streams of perspiration that ran down his face.

The black man who was being questioned waited with an amiable smile on his face to be asked more. He was a smoothly muscled man with skin the color of dark-lacquered wood, wearing a skirt of palm cloth and an ivory necklace.

Tom idled by the taffrail, dressed only in a loincloth and fanning himself with a palm leaf. He was listening with half an ear. It was hard not to be distracted by the exotic birdcalls and the cries of strange animals coming from beyond the green walls of the riverbanks. Somewhere nearby there was the sound of a very large beast crashing through vegetation, a snuffling snort, and then a mighty splash. The ocean was not visible from here and seemed very far away. It was the brown stain far out on the ocean that had alerted Cheng Ho to the fact that some immense river must have its outlet on this part of the coast, and he had diverted a squadron of smaller ships to find it. It was his belief that where there was a large river emptying into the sea, you would also find a settled human population, and he had been correct. The thatch-roofed villages were thick along the banks here. Tom could see one on the shore opposite—the village that their current visitor had come from.

"Is this Mani of Mbanza Kongo truly a king?" Cheng Ho asked. "Or is he merely another tribal chieftain, more powerful than most?"

The interpreter put the question in his halting Ngala dialect. It wasn't the villager's own dialect, but he seemed to understand it well enough; it had a surprising number of words in common with some of the Bantu variants the Treasure Fleet had already encountered thousands of li away.

"Yes, the Mani is a true king," he reported. "He sits on a throne of ivory, raised on a high platform so that he can be seen from four sides. He rules six provinces through governors who pay tribute to him, and he also receives tribute from tribes and states to the east and south."

"And to the north?"

The villager spoke reluctantly—the first reticence he had shown. He seemed distressed by the question.

"There are many kingdoms to the north, but the greatest of them is called Benin," the interpreter relayed.

"Why doesn't he like it?"

The villager became more voluble. Benin was an evil place, lately come to great power and always at war with its neighbors, though it was too far away to be an enemy of the kingdom of the Congo. Tom got the impression that the villager's distaste stemmed from something about the character of the place itself. He caught the phrase "city of blood" and heard many repetitions of the word for sacrifice. He had the feeling that the interpreter wasn't getting the half of it.

"He says it's unlucky, a place of death," the interpreter summed up for Cheng Ho.

Cheng Ho smiled in understanding. "I can see why it might have made a bad impression on the kingdoms around it. Young, aggressive nations can be brutal—as the Mongols were brutal when they conquered the Middle Kingdom. Ask him what else he knows."

Under prodding, the villager supplied additional details, all of them clearly hearsay. The people of Benin lived in big houses set close together on wide streets. The king dwelt in a palace of wood with a tall tower, and he was attended by many nobles called Ukoba, or the "King's Boys," who were required to go about naked until such time as the king gave them a wife and clothing. The king himself was called Oba. His power in Benin was absolute, but he himself was beholden to a monarch named Ogané, who lived at an immense distance inland—a march of "twenty moons." Each new Oba of Great Benin had to be confirmed by this Ogané, who then sent him a crown, a scepter and a brass cross in token of his legitimacy. The ambassadors of Benin never saw the face of Ogané. He sat concealed behind a curtain and only put out his foot to be kissed.

Cheng Ho became excited at that. "We must find out more about this Ogané when we reach Benin. There may be a great empire in the interior that stands in the same relationship to Benin and the kingdom of the Congo as

Vijayanagar does to Calicut. And if its emperor is so unapproachable as to conduct his business from behind a curtain, then we may at last have found a suzerain who, if not on an equal footing with the Son of Heaven who sits on the Dragon Throne, is at least worthy to pay obeisance to him."

The villager didn't understand what Cheng Ho was saying, but he smiled to be sociable.

"But for now," Cheng Ho went on, "our business is with the Mani, the king of the Congo." He rearranged his silk robe, taking the opportunity, Tom noticed, to peel it away from the wet surface of his body. "We'll see about sending a Treasure Ship and a suitable escort upriver to Mbanza Kongo. Ask him about the navigability of the river close to the falls, and if we'll have to go any great distance overland with the horses."

The visitor realized what Cheng Ho's intention was from the questions, and he grinned broadly. He started explaining something to the translator.

"He says that the king of the Congo already knows of our presence here," the translator summarized. "There is a means of sending word quickly through the bush. Ambassadors from Mbanza Kongo are already on the way, bearing gifts."


It was marvelous how clean and dry it was in the hold of a Chinese ship, compared to the stinking bilges Tom had seen in England and the Mediterranean. The treasure chambers occupied eight of the fifteen watertight compartments, and you could pass from one to the other only by undogging the stout dual doors between them, each set on either side in closely fitted and rabbeted frames and opening in opposite directions.

The treasure chamber that Tom was in now was piled high with bales of silk, crates of porcelain in straw, shelf after shelf of exquisite bronzes, chests of gold and gems, sealed jars of perfumed oil, jeweled tapestries, incense burners, statues of the Buddha, and barrels of coins. In the flickering light of the oil lamp all seemed dreamlike.

Tom swallowed hard. He thought that he had become inured to wealth. It had no meaning when you had no way to spend it. But this tremendous hoard slammed you across the eyes and forced attention. The thought of what just one cor-

ner of this storehouse would mean in a place like England
was staggering. Barons had gone to war over less.

He stole a glance at the single guard whom Cheng Ho
had brought in here with him. He was just there for form's
sake; there wouldn't have been room for him to swing his
pole-sword even if the occasion came up. A determined man
with a small knife could easily step in close and gut him
while he was trying to bring his clumsy weapon to bear.
There was another marine guard waiting outside the end-
most of the treasure compartments, also with a lamp and a
pole-sword. He wouldn't stay there after the place was
locked up again. Tom was always amazed at how lightly
guarded this treasure trove was. But then, no one would
have dared to steal from the emperor, and even if someone
had, there was nothing he could do with his loot on a ship
on the open sea, whole worlds away from the Middle Kingdom.

"What do you say, Chin Mao?" Cheng Ho inquired.
"What gifts will impress the ambassadors of the Mani of the
Congo?"

"It's ridiculous," said Ma Huan. "They're trying to outdo
*us*. I say let them."

Tom thought about it. "Gold doesn't impress them," he
said. "They've got plenty of it themselves. I say silks. That
will be a luxury beyond price here. And Ming porcelain.
Anyone can look at it and understand that it's fit for a king.
And you should include some bronzes. They'll recognize the
quality of the metalwork, even if they don't know the art of
casting themselves."

"You have a good brain under that yellow thatch, Chin
Mao," Cheng Ho said approvingly. "Your points are well
taken."

"Don't neglect jade carvings, Grand One," Ma Huan said
grumpily. "The one area in which these Zanj craftsmen ex-
cell is their ivory carvings. We mustn't let them think that
Ming civilization is in any way inferior to theirs."

"You shall help me choose the jade, old friend," Cheng
Ho said. "Now we'd better get some porters in here. We
want to be topside in time to greet our guests."

The ambassadors from Mbanza Kongo were an impressive
lot—tall, dignified man in long flounced skirts of palm cloth

draped below the knee, short capes of leopard skin, intricate headgear, and many ornaments of gold or ivory. There were eight of them, and each came equipped with two attendants who fanned away the flies and performed other small services.

Cheng Ho received them with due pomp on the raised poop, surrounding himself with high-ranking eunuchs in gorgeous silks. Long speeches were made on either side, though they went untranslated and could not have been taken for anything but ceremonial necessities. They were followed by more serious attempts at communication, involving the Chinese interpreters and some of the river people who had been visiting the ships and had acquired some sort of rapport with members of the translating staff. The locals were awed by the dignitaries from Mbanza Kongo, and it took some little time to get them over their shyness. But it was soon established that the emissaries of one great king were parleying with the emissaries of another, and the exchange of gifts began.

Tom, rigged out for the occasion in his best robes, jumped into the exchange to settle a point or two, to the annoyance of the translators but with Cheng Ho's blessing. He had gone fishing the day before with one of the villagers who was now being drawn on as an intermediary—a bright lad named Mbuji—and they had developed an argot of their own.

"Lion Hair" was the name the delegation gave to Tom, but otherwise they didn't seem to make any distinction between him and the Chinese. They had never seen men with light skin before, and to them, Tom was just another one of the inexplicable *msungu*—"colorless men"—who had appeared in the river in floating palaces. They seemed more intrigued by the high voices of the eunuchs.

"Mtom," said Mjubi, "they want to know why your chief and his nobles speak with the voices of birds."

Tom relayed the comment to Cheng Ho, who seemed amused by it and set out to answer the question himself. The Congo kingdom did not seem to have the custom of manufacturing eunuchs, as did the Arabs, the Chinese, and the Byzantines, and Tom did not want to give them any ideas that would reflect on Cheng Ho's status. After a little thought, Cheng Ho said, "As you know, it is the manly parts that give one a deep voice. Women do not have deep voices, nor do boys have deep voices before their parts develop. The kingdom of the Son of Heaven, whom we serve, is very far away, and we must be gone for some years. So they must leave their manly parts behind in order to keep peace in their households and so that their parts may continue to sire sons in their absence."

The ambassadors absorbed this with great solemnity and after some deliberation asked through Mjubi, "Why then does Lion Hair not leave his manly parts at home? Does he not have wives?"

"Tell them," Tom said, "that I am very young and have been given only one wife." Unexpectedly, an image of Lanying sprang into his head, and he had to shake it off before continuing. "And since she is with child, it was not thought worth the trouble of making the powerful jujus that are needed."

They nodded in understanding. The extravagant compliments went on, and the piles of gifts grew. Tom could see that the representatives of the Mani were becoming nonplused at the sheer quantity of the goods that Cheng Ho was heaping up on the deck. They had come prepared for contingencies but not this aggressive generosity, and it was moot as to how long they would be able to keep up with him.

Now it was the bolts of silk that were stacking higher. Twice the coolies had returned to the treasure hold and brought up additional loads, and the Mani's delegation had called down to the dugouts that were bobbing thickly around the Treasure Ship's vast hull. Both times several dugouts had gone darting back to the village on the far shore and returned with new bales of animal skins—magnificent skins that were speckled, striped, parti-colored with the markings of rare and wonderful creatures that had never been seen in the Middle Kingdom. A third batch had the ambassadors conferring with one another. Once again they sent to the village. This time the dugouts returned with a collection of skins that were of lower quality than the ones the ambassadors had brought with them from Mbanza Kongo, and it was plain that the villagers were being taxed to uphold the honor of the Mani.

Cheng Ho smiled and desisted. He had made his point. No nation on earth could match the wealth of the Middle Kingdom. The lesson would be repeated on a greater scale in a few days, when the treasure flotilla he intended to send upriver arrived at the stronghold of the Mani.

Jade had been answered with ivory; silk with skins; coins with cowries. The porcelain was a demonstration of the Dragon Throne's largess that could not be matched. Finally the bronzes that Tom had suggested were brought out. A splendid assortment was soon arranged on deck, and the smaller pieces were passed reverentially along, one by one, for the inspection of the ambassadors. There were incense burners from the Emperor's own foundry, cast bronze bowls and basins in fantastic animal shapes, dragons, gods, votive items. The ambassadors' eyes widened at the sight of a massive altarpiece depicting the Buddha surrounded by his attendants, and they held another of their whispered conferences.

Another dugout was dispatched to the village. Cheng Ho waited indulgently to see what it would come back with. "One canoe," he said to Tom and Ma Huan. "I wonder what they held in reserve."

"These Zanj can do fine work in metal," Ma Huan admitted grudgingly, "but it's generally forged, not cast. I don't believe they've discovered how to make clay molds."

The canoe returned with not more than a dozen metal sculptures, some of them heavy enough to require two men to move them. They were astonishing, every one of them. There were bronze heads showing strange headdresses in marvelous detail and wearing gorgets that came up over the chins. There was a startlingly lifelike bronze horseman wearing intricate armor and carrying a broad-bladed weapon. There was a plaque representing a royal personage riding sidesaddle on a horse and supported by two walking attendants on either side. There was another bronze relief showing a seated king wearing helmet and gorget, with two kneeling retainers to support the weight of his arms for him. There was a bronze cock with exceedingly detailed feathers, and a leopard whose spots were painstakingly rendered as raised rings. There was a group of female figures with gourds, surrounding a giant head, and another group apparently representing cretinous dwarfs who might have been court jesters. But perhaps the most astonishing bronze of all showed an entire rite of some kind—a very large group of men wearing hats resembling bishops' miters and carrying ceremonial objects, all standing in array on a raised rectangular platform.

"These are not forged," Ma Huan breathed. "They are cast—and cast by some method that the Middle Kingdom does not possess."

Cheng Ho fingered one of the plaques. "These head-dresses don't look anything like the ones our visitors are wearing. Ask them if these bronzes represent their own king."

The answer came after much hedging and diplomatic beating about the bush.

"No—these are highly valued objects that come from trade. They are the possessions of the Mani, and he wishes to give them as an expression of his goodwill."

"Where do they come from?"

Tom waited along with Cheng Ho and Ma Huan, but he thought he already knew the answer.

"Great Benin."

Cheng Ho was ecstatic. "Remarkable! To think that we never suspected the existence of this great empire. Tell me, Chin Mao, have Europeans heard of this Benin?"

"No," Tom told him.

Cheng Ho raised his eyebrows. "That's surprising. Benin must be at least as close to you as Trebizond and some of the other places that Europeans visit. And it's on the west coast of Africa, so that your ships don't have to find a way around the tip of the continent, as we did. But I forgot. Your ships don't venture south. You're afraid of the equator."

Tom's mouth went dry at this reminder that the Star Raft was on its final approach to Europe. "How . . . how far?"

"Haven't you been paying attention to your astronomy lessons? Here in the Congo, we're only a few hundred li below the equator—at about the same latitude as Zanzibar on the east coast. The star maps we made while sailing south tell us that—the Southern Cross is at almost exactly the same height in the sky, when you measure it with the star stretch-boards. Benin cannot be more than another few hundred li above the equator—perhaps at the latitude of Somalia. And from there, by piecing together the Arab estimates of the distances *they* travel south from Arabia on their East African excursions, and from what you've told us of your own travels, I'd judge that it cannot be more than a few thousand li north of Benin to this seafaring kingdom of Portugal that you've told me about."

He fixed Tom with an owlish eye. "That ought to be an

easy sail for a European," he said. "It's a fraction of the distance the Star Raft has traveled to get this far."

Tom felt obliged to defend his fellow westerners. "We don't have ships the size of yours, San-pao T'ai-chien," he said in his humblest Middle Kingdom fashion. "But we will."

Cheng Ho let out a laugh. He got true conversation from only a few of his subordinates, and he never minded being on the receiving end of a sting.

"Europe will have to wait a little while longer, Chin Mao," he said. "And so will Great Benin." He returned his attention to the politely waiting ambassadors. "Tomorrow we sail upriver to call on the king of the Congo."

Something woke Tom in the dark. He lay on his mat, straining to listen, and at first heard nothing but the creak of the ship's timbers and the lapping of water against the sides. It was too early for the shrieking racket of monkeys and birds that usually woke him at the first blush of daylight; the square of oiled paper at his port showed only the faintest hint of the gray light that preceded dawn.

After a while he became aware of footsteps passing overhead and an occasional sound of muffled voices. A halyard squealed through a pulley block, and from somewhere forward came the brief rattle of a chain.

Tom sat up. It was too early for the *tsao keng*, the morning watch, to be moving about. The breakfast fires were not even lit. Cheng Ho could not possibly be preparing to raise anchor before daylight.

He didn't want to miss what was going on. He dashed water in his face from the ewer, used the chamber pot, and put on his drawers. He heard voices in the corridor. He shut his cabin door behind him and felt his way down the long passage to the companionway.

The sky showed a streak of plum-colored light to the east. The dark silhouettes of treetops bulked against the stars. The light was enough for him to see that there were more sailors on deck than there ought to have been at this hour; most of them were standing around doing nothing.

He raised his eyes to the poop deck and saw Cheng Ho standing there with a number of his officers. The admiral's bulky form was unmistakable. They all seemed to be staring downriver, toward the west.

Tom looked out over the broad waterway, past the forest of bare masts that surrounded the flagships. The sky was getting brighter by the minute, the first daytime chirps and croaks were coming from the jungle, and he could see a ship sitting in the channel that hadn't been there the night before.

As its outlines grew clearer in the spreading dawn, he discerned the boxy shape of an oceangoing ship of the Middle Kingdom. It wasn't as big as one of Cheng Ho's Treasure Ships, but it would have made a toy out of any European vessel. Even if Tom hadn't recognized it from the near encounter at the southern cape, it could only have been the *hei ch'uan*—the black ship.

It must have come limping in during the night and dropped anchor in pitch blackness. Tom could make out mitelike figures moving about on its deck. Two of its five masts were broken-off stubs, and there was a great irregular patch in one side where the gaping hole Tom had last seen must have been mended with native timber sawn into planks.

It had the Treasure Fleet bottled up in the river. There was no way to evade it this time.

"Its captain must be a demon, sent by the demon king," said Ma Huan's voice behind him. "To have risen from the bottom of the sea and pursued us for six thousand li."

The old scholar was still struggling into his clothing. He was too arthritic to reach around and fasten the loops on his right side, and Tom helped him.

"It rode out the storm somehow," Tom said. "Enough of its watertight compartments must have stayed intact to keep it afloat. Then they would have had to have stayed in the harbor of the Hottentots for several months, making repairs. In that time they'd have learned from the Hottentots of the false bay and the final cape that forms the southwest corner of Africa. They must have lost those masts again in another storm while trying to round the cape, but they made it. Then all they had to do was to hug the coast, asking after us wherever they saw people—the Star Raft must make quite a sight sailing past—and putting in at every river mouth. I don't know if their skipper's a demon, but he's tenacious."

"This is an unlucky day, Chin Mao."

Tom let his exasperation show. "What's this all about, Ma Huan? Surely you can tell me now."

"It means that Cheng Ho's enemies in the Anti-Maritime Party have won out, of course! They must have won out shortly after we set sail. We've been sailing all this while on borrowed time."

"What can one ship do against the Star Raft? Can't Cheng Ho just sink it?"

Ma Huan was horrified. "You're a barbarian, Chin Mao," he said. "Sinking the black ship—what an idea!"

On reflection, Tom could see why sinking the black ship was not a good idea. There would be thirty thousand witnesses.

"Well, then," he said, "why can't he just go on ignoring it?"

"You don't understand, Chin Mao. The ship will be bearing a contingency message from the emperor himself. Or at least written in his name."

After ten years in the Middle Kingdom, Tom had some idea of the way the Chinese mind worked. "You mean that as long as Cheng Ho could pretend not to see the black ship, he could go on sailing?"

The language of the Middle Kingdom made it easy not to give a direct yes or no if you didn't want to, but Ma Huan vaguely indicated the general correctness of Tom's statement with a reluctant "*Shir.*"

"But that's crazy," Tom said. "The black ship *knew* that Cheng Ho saw it."

"No. Now that he can't evade it any longer, Cheng Ho will receive its captain with all honors."

"Well, they're too late anyway," Tom said. "We've rounded Africa—proved it can be done. You can't put *that* piece of knowledge back in the box. And we've reached the Kingdom of the Congo—we'll be at its capital in a few days. And . . . and Great Benin isn't far from here, and Europe itself is beyond that! We've opened it all up for the Middle Kingdom! When we get back to Peking, the Anti-Maritimes will just have to crawl back to their hole."

He looked up at the poop deck and saw Cheng Ho and his officers standing like statues. He took a step in their direction.

Ma Huan stopped him with a hand on his arm. "Where are you going, Chin Mao?"

"I'm going aft. I want to see how Cheng Ho handles this."

Ma Huan's fragile fingers gripped his arm with surprising strength. "Stay here, Chin Mao. This is no time to bother him."

"His name is Wang Chen," Ma Huan said. "He's a very ambitious eunuch. He was the childhood playmate of the crown prince, Ying-tsung, and he's made himself agreeable to the Emperor's mother, the grand dowager empress Chang. He'd be in a position of great power if the emperor were to die and the dowager became regent for her grandson. Already, there are many court officials who are pinning their careers on this presumptuous fellow. They think that one day he might become Chief Eunuch of the Yellow Gate."

They were sitting on the deserted poop deck, listening to the sounds of festivity coming from the admiral's verandah one level below. Cheng Ho had provided musicians for the entertainment of his guest, and the entire verandah and what could be seen of the admiral's cabin that led off from it were hung about with paper lanterns.

"But Cheng Ho's the Three-Jewel Eunuch. *He* rules the Yellow Gate. Doesn't he exercise authority over this . . . Wang Chen?"

"The root of power can grow many stems, Chin Mao."

"The Anti-Maritime Party, you mean?"

Ma Huan did not find it necessary to reply. He sniffed the night air. A delicious smell of roast pork was coming from below.

"A eunuch who allies himself with the Anti-Maritime Party!" Tom said in disgust. "Doesn't he realize that Confucian officials like Hsia Yuan-chi are his natural enemies?"

"People like Wang Chen and Hsia Yuan-chi use each other to gain their immediate ends, like vines twining together for mutual support. In the end, one will strangle the other."

"Maybe he's riding high at the moment," Tom said angrily. "But when Cheng Ho gets back to the Forbidden City and takes hold of things again, it'll be a different story." A thought struck him. "How did Wang Chen usurp so much power at the Yellow Gate anyway? He'd have had to get past

Yuan-chi and his faction. And they've always thrown their support behind Cheng Ho."

"Ah, of course you don't know yet, Chin Mao."

"Know what?"

"I only found out myself this afternoon when I struck up a conversation with one of the rather overbearing attendants in Wang Chen's train."

"God's blude, speke playne!" Tom exploded in English. "Found out what?"

"Yuan-chi and ten eunuchs close to him were executed shortly after the Star Raft sailed from Fujian. A charge of corrupt activities was brought against them by the Office of Scrutiny. The Yellow Gate's been reshuffled."

"But . . ." Tom was stunned. ". . . but the emperor hates to execute anybody."

Ma Huan nodded. "That will work in Cheng Ho's favor when we return."

"What are you saying?"

"That he'll likely be facing charges himself."

"But that's monstrous!"

"Be tranquil, young scholar. Cheng Ho himself is taking it with the greatest equanimity. He's very resourceful. He'll probably end up with a small pension and some minor post."

The African sky above them was deep, and brilliant with stars. Tom located the Southern Cross and the Triangle, and the curious constellation that looked like a crow—old friends by now—and stared at them for a while. When he felt able to speak again, he said, "What happens to the Treasure Fleet now?"

"We must return immediately. We are not allowed to go even one li farther."

"So we won't sail up the Congo after all? We'll never see Mbanza Kongo, or meet the Mani."

"*Bu-shir*," Ma Huan said. "Not-be." It was the closest you could get in the Middle Kingdom's language to a no. "The ambassadors will be sent on their way tomorrow, laden with more gifts. Doubtless a legend will grow over the years of the great floating city, inhabited by bleached men, that appeared in the river one day and then vanished again."

"The Star Raft will return here," Tom said from between clenched teeth. "One day it'll all blow over—your Ming intrigues and your fear of the outside world—and some other admiral will sail west again."

"Chin Mao," the old man said gently, forgetting to be his usual crotchety self, "Wang Chen is here tonight to demand Cheng Ho's sailing charts and the star maps the expedition's astronomers made, so that no one will be able to sail here again."

"What? He can't!"

Ma Huan nodded sadly. "All records of the voyage will be suppressed so that no one in the future will be infected by Cheng Ho's dream of discovery. It's intended that the edict that was published after the death of the Yung Lo emperor—the one that made it a crime to build oceangoing ships—will be reinstated."

Tom felt sick. He huddled miserably on the bench, listening to the sounds of festivity coming from the deck below. The twang of an orchestra mixed with the clashing sounds of dishes and trays from the lavish banquet being served by Cheng Ho to the silken nemesis that had overtaken him. There was a burst of laughter from those assembled—someone was telling jokes to the company.

"Wang Chen's orders were to shadow us at a distance," Ma Huan went on. "He wasn't to stop us as long as we ventured no farther than our previous trading stops—but Cheng Ho's enemies were all too aware of his propensity to always want to go a little farther, of his itch to see what lay beyond each new horizon." He gave a dry little laugh. "It was beyond their bureaucratic minds, though, to imagine that he'd actually find a way to sail clear around Africa. That was a dangerous dream indeed—so dangerous that no one really believed it."

He paused to clear his dusty throat. "It must have been a great shock to poor Wang Chen," he cackled gleefully, "to find himself chasing the Star Raft into another world. Perhaps we should give him credit for finding the courage and seamanship in spite of himself. Where vision first finds a path, blindness can follow."

The dry laugh developed into a hacking cough. Ma Huan wheezed and choked; finally, with the tears running from his eyes, he got it under control.

Tom sat in silence. There was nothing left to say.

Ma Huan leaned out over the rail to see what was happening below. "They're carrying in another course—it must be a hundred-course feast at least. Cheng Ho is sparing no effort. I've counted twenty courses so far, and they've barely got started. Just smell that cooking—there'll be a lot of Yunnan specialties if I know Cheng Ho. There'll be a place for me—it would be a pity to miss it."

His face lit with anticipation, he rose creakily to his feet and shuffled with ill-disguised eagerness to the companionway, leaving Tom to himself.

Tom listened to the sounds of the feast for a while. The river insects kept flying into the paper lanterns, making a sound like a continuous rattle of rain. At intervals a toast would be proposed in a high eunuch voice, but he could not distinguish the words. The jangling music began to get on his nerves.

He was alone on the poop deck. All the senior officers were at the banquet. Tom felt small under the large African night. He got up and went to the shrine. No one was there, although a rack of joss sticks was burning. The coastal charts and star maps that were to be confiscated lay scattered about, some spread out on chart tables, some rolled up in waterproof silk and piled on shelves. He stuffed as many as he could into his shirt.

He met no one while going down to his cabin except for the few sailors about their chores. He let himself into the tiny cubicle and closed the door behind him. The jewels and gold he'd taken with him from the Middle Kingdom were hidden at the bottom of his sea chest, divided into small parcels that could be spread out flat under a layer of clothes and toiletry items. He distributed as many of these about his person as he could and made a bundle of the rest. He was wearing a seaman's smocklike shirt and wide baggy trousers; he bulged a little here and there, but not enough to look especially unusual.

After some thought, he discarded his sandals for a pair of the leather shoes the Chinese called "oiled footwear" and then took a spare pair as well. For weapons he had his knife and a three-pronged hand spear, short enough to be concealed down the leg of his trousers, that he'd won at dice from a marine. He also had the little Venetian folding knife that he'd killed Mijnheer van den Vondel with.

He descended three more decks to the level that opened onto the floating gangplank. On impulse he stuck his head down a hatch that led to the treasure hold. A ladder had been left in place, and he could see no guard's lamp down there.

After a quick look around he scooted down the ladder. The massive bulkhead leading to the series of treasure rooms was secured by an iron bolt and a padlock. Tom had a long acquaintance with locks, beginning with his apprenticeship at Master Philpot's, where pantry and brewery were kept under ward and key. He had never seen a lock he couldn't open, not even the tricky Venetian kind. The lock for the treasure room was extremely large and imposing, but that only made its components easier to manipulate. He had noticed when he was helping Cheng Ho and Ma Huan in the removal of some of the choicer items for the Mbanza Kongo ambassadors that the lock had a tendency to get stuck. You sometimes had to rap it sharply to get the talon to fall back in place, and once the porter in charge had even had to wiggle a stick around inside to release the spring. He wondered if anyone had been careless on the last visit.

He found the guard's lamp and lit it with the flint and steel that had been left behind. Getting down on his knees, careful not to touch the lock for fear that jarring it might make the talon snap back in position, he put his eye to the thumb-size keyhole.

Sure enough, the ratchet was jammed just a hairsbreadth from being properly engaged. He felt for the little Venetian knife with its thin blade and, holding the padlock carefully to keep it from moving, he worked the point of the blade into the tiny crack. Gingerly he levered the catch a fraction of an inch by rotating the blade and heard it snap to an open position.

He let himself inside with the lamp and, working quickly, stuffed the rest of the sack he carried with jewels and small items that were at least equal in value to the hoard he was already carrying. He chose only the most costly examples— jade, diamonds, emeralds, rubies. He had no qualms about stealing from Cheng Ho; the treasures of the Star Raft would never be distributed now. They would only go back to the Middle Kingdom to finance canals and other public works projects.

Besides, Tom thought with a quick predatory grin, weren't some of these royal treasures meant for England anyway? He was the only Englishman for thousands of miles.

He locked the treasure room carefully behind him and made it back to the deck without incident. Dozens of boats, large and small, were tied up at the foot of the floating gangplank. Cheng Ho was breaking camp in the jungle, and the traffic would be heavy all night.

Wang Chen's gilded barge was moored there, its thwarts now occupied only by his oarsmen, a dozen wiry coolies who were passing the time while waiting by gambling. Beyond it, a work gang of marines was unloading a boatload of prefabricated ramparts from the jungle camp. Tom was afraid that he might be stopped for conversation by one of his drinking companions, but they were all too busy to notice him.

He found a small skiff that didn't seem to be in use, and, throwing his sack in the stern sheets, he cast off. He rowed directly for the shore opposite. The idea of traveling by water was tempting, but he would have had to row for a couple of miles upriver in order to get past all the anchored ships of the Treasure Fleet, and he would have been sure to have been noticed by some officious lookout who would wonder why he was leaving the fleet's anchorage. The idea of being brought back under guard with his loot to face Cheng Ho did not appeal to him.

He tied the skiff up at the landing that served the Treasure Fleet's encampment. Traffic was heavy here, and no one paid any attention to him.

He walked with his sack of jewels along the roadway that had been hacked out of the jungle. Hurrying porters, preoccupied army engineers, and mounted marine pickets jostled him. The camp was still far from being dismantled. Up ahead he could see the drum towers, stretches of portable stockading, and some folding warehouses and granaries still standing. There were temporary depots along the road where laboring coolies had trampled rough paths. At the first opportunity he took one of these and slipped into the jungle.

He headed in a direction that paralleled the riverbank, walking warily and using his fork spear to push aside vegetation. For some distance he could still hear the night patrol with their bells and clappers, but he didn't meet anybody.

After some hours, slapping at insects and pausing frequently to listen for sounds of any large beasts, he struck out for the riverbank. He stumbled onto a path made by natives and followed it until he came to a place where the vegetation thinned out enough to allow a view of the river.

The Star Raft was still visible from here, sparkling with

the light of thousands of lanterns that cast their reflections in the dark water. Tomorrow it would vanish as though it had never been. Tom stood there for a while, brooding on Cheng Ho's lost dream.

He sighed and trudged on. It was a long walk to England. But at least he'd get to see Great Benin along the way.

# CHAPTER 13

The sea had been a red, muddy color north of Cape Non, but now it turned to a dark bottle-green. Pedro pointed out the change to Gil Eanes.

"These are the waters of the bight between Non and Bojador, senhor," he said. "I noted it before. It comes from a black sand on the ocean floor that you don't find elsewhere. We got a sample of the bottom when the leadsman took soundings. It ought to be safe to tack toward the coast for a while."

Eanes stood balanced with one foot on the rail, holding on to the stays for support as the *barcha* swayed in the easy swells. For the sailors he must have made a commanding figure, with the sun in his golden curls, his thighs and arms bulging with muscle, his barrellike chest bared by an unlaced doublet and open shirt.

"I don't know, Pedro," he said doubtfully. "The current was carrying us in toward the shoals before. I don't want to take any chances with the ship."

"There won't be any danger for a hundred miles, I promise you. We ought to take observations of the shoreline for the infante while we have the chance."

Eanes had learned his lesson too well. Pedro had struggled to make the stiff-necked Velho Cabral understand that it was not necessarily safer to keep land in sight; now Gil Eanes was carrying caution in the opposite direction.

"We were doing so well," Eanes said wistfully. "The sea's as easy to sail in here as the waters back home."

"We'll have plenty of warning, senhor. The sea changes color again."

Reluctantly, Eanes gave the orders. The *barcha*'s single square sail canted conservatively to put the vessel on a long shallow tack that would bring it in without the necessity of wearing ship; the helmsman fought the tiller. Gradually the coast came into view.

"Sand, nothing but sand," Eanes said, shaking his head. "There's no profit in such a wasteland."

"We don't know what's beyond," Pedro said. "There may be green lands, as fertile as any we know."

"The River of Gold, that's what I'd like to find," Eanes said. "The place where the gold that reaches the Moors' caravans is said to come from."

"First we've got to find people," Pedro said. "Then we can ask."

"Slaves," Eanes said. "At least there'd be a profit in slaves."

Pedro knew that Eanes was thinking of the Canary Islands, less than a day's sail to the west at this latitude. That was always the big temptation for the captains Prince Henry sent questing southward; Eanes himself had succumbed on his last voyage. Pedro was determined not to let him get diverted again.

"Patience, senhor," he said. "At this point, Cape Bojador is closer to us than Grand Canary. Who knows what lies beyond it?"

"How can you be so sure?" Eanes said, shaking his golden head. "These modern methods of navigation are beyond me. Those Jewish astrologers and Moorish mathematicians have bewitched Dom Henrique. Give me the old days, when you sailed by what you could see with your own eyes."

"It's still guesswork, senhor. But the more we learn, the easier we can make it for those who come after us."

He had been practicing with the wood chip—the *kamal*—that the Venetian, Sandro, had given him. He had tied a knot in the string for Cape Non late the other night when everyone was nodding, and he planned to tie one for Cape Bojador and for whatever point farther south they reached after that. Perhaps the Venetian could make something of it when he got back home.

"*Diabo*, it's hot!" Eanes said, wiping his forehead with his sleeve. "The pitch bubbles in the seams."

To demonstrate, he thrust a finger into the crack between two planks of the decking and withdrew it with a gob of the tacky black stuff stuck to it. He gave Pedro a reproachful look before wiping it off.

Pedro turned to his duties. It was pointless to reply to what Eanes would not state openly. The old superstitions died hard, despite Prince Henry's rational approach. Eanes—though he knew very well that Cabral had already traveled this far south—could not quite get it out of his head that farther on lay a mythical zone of boiling water. Pedro himself had to admit to a certain residual unease. But logic told him that, whatever the untested dangers of Bojador, the Bulging Cape, the ship still had a long way to go before it reached the world's equator. He'd have to tie many more knots in the string of the *kamal* before the polestar disappeared.

The ship fled south, driven by the same strong wind that had hurried them from Sagres only fifteen days ago. The wind had veered a little toward the west, but not enough to make it necessary to hoist the small fore-and-aft sail that all of Prince Henry's *barchas* now carried as standard equipment; they were still running free with the wind on the port quarter. A dolphin had decided to escort them, its sleek black form leaping ahead of the bow, and Eanes had forbidden the crossbowman to shoot it. The crew sucked lemons to ward off thirst, and as the fresh fruit they had brought with them from Portugal began to go bad, Eanes saw that they had plenty of wine to keep them happy.

Once they had a scare. A huge patch of ocean ahead of them suddenly turned silver, and the water seethed with a hiss like steam. Cries of panic came from the sailors crowded forward. Pedro sprang to the shrouds and shouted frantically, "It's only sardines! A tremendous school of sardines suddenly rising! They can extend for miles! I've seen it before along this coast!"

The sailors calmed down. There were a few sheepish laughs. The fishermen among them got to work, and as the *barcha* ploughed through the school, dragged nets through it and got a catch of fresh fish for their supper.

On the morning of the next day the water began to grow choppy, and its color changed to a gray-blue. Pedro climbed the mast and studied the shore ahead. He had a good memory and the *portolano* sketches he had drawn on the Cabral voyage.

"Bojador lies ahead," he told Gil Eanes.

Eanes, who was a brave man in spite of everything, held his course until the long, low spit of land came into view. The day was deceptively calm—a clear, blue-skied day with a few puffy clouds. Bojador loomed closer. At the foot of the red sandstone cliffs was a skirt of white, like lace.

"That's where the danger is, senhor," Pedro said. "Breakers and foam, nothing more. But the shoals run shallow, well out past the tip of the cape."

Eanes nodded. Now that everything was plain to him, his natural animal confidence asserted itself. "God's wounds, Pedro!" he said joyfully. "Here's where we show Prince Henry what men are made of!"

He veered far out to sea, getting away from any peril of reef or shallows. He sailed on for the rest of the day, out of sight of land, bearing due south by the stars, and Pedro appreciated his prudence. At nightfall he took in all but a scrap of sail, and let the current bear the ship along. Nobody slept very much. When morning came, he gave the crew time for a good breakfast of biscuit, cheese, and olives, then ran the *barcha* in toward shore.

It was the same sandy waste they'd seen before, shimmering in the heat. But this time it ran unbroken to the south. Pedro turned his eyes north and saw Cape Bojador behind them, a low ridge of red rising out of white water.

"*Por Deus*, we've done it!" roared Gil Eanes. He hugged Pedro in a mighty grip, then turned to hug the helmsman and any sailor within reach.

The *barcha* continued to lean in toward shore. The water was a fine clear blue. The sailors forgot their chores and lined up along the rail in high spirits.

"There was nothing to be afraid of after all," Eanes said to Pedro as if he had invented the idea. "We've passed the cape. We'll never have to be afraid of it again. The way is clear."

"We could sail on a few hundred leagues south," suggested Pedro. "Perhaps we'll find your River of Gold. Or some great African kingdom whose existence we could report to Prince Henry."

Eanes lost some of his high excitement. He became

brusque. "We've done what Dom Henrique asked. That's enough for now. We'll put in to shore here and see if we can find something to show for it—some token for the prince."

There was nothing but sand when they waded ashore from the ship's boat that rowed them in. Pedro's eyes searched the barren landscape and found no sign of people, animals—not even plants. He wondered what Eanes would bring back to Sagres. It would have to be a bucket of sand. He turned and looked at the shoreline with a sailor's eye. At least there was no violent surf on this side of the cape. Once you passed Bojador, there was sheltered anchorage. The soundings while coming in had shown a comfortable margin of about nine fathoms. That ought to be worth something to the next explorers. If only Eanes wasn't so bullheaded! There might be a river just a little farther south—a place where ships could take on water. Or signs of people. Anything to encourage the doubters around Prince Henry.

Gil Eanes was tramping over the sand with a couple of sailors at his back. Pedro could tell that he was getting disgruntled. Eanes topped a ridge and stopped.

"Pedro, come here!" he cried jubilantly.

Pedro hurried to him, wondering what he had found. He saw Eanes staring down at some beach roses, the same kind that grew in Portugal. People called them Saint Mary's Roses.

"Get a barrel," Eanes told one of the sailors. "We'll dig them up and take them back to Sagres with us."

He turned a sunburned face to Pedro. "Here's our token for Dom Henrique," he said. "Roses for the prince."

The reliable northeast wind bore them far out to sea and let them escape the swift current that would have carried them south along the African coast. Pedro began the long and difficult task of tacking to the north again, until he could pick up a westerly between Madeira and the Azores that would take them home.

"We'll put in at Madeira for water and provisions and to hear mass," Gil Eanes decreed. "Then we can go on the rest of the way to Sagres well refreshed."

To Pedro, the order was a thunderbolt. He had not been back to Madeira for seven years—had tried every day of his life since then to avoid thinking about what he had lost there.

"It will take us out of our way, senhor," he protested. "On our present course we'll skirt Madeira by a wide margin. We'll do just as well to go on as we are."

"No," Eanes said. "We've been at sea too long. The men need a few days ashore."

By which he meant himself. Eanes knew very well—at least intellectually—of the great ellipses of wind and current that were gradually being mapped at Sagres, but he had reached the limit of his tolerance for the open sea. Pedro thought Eanes had done very well, considering, for someone who had been brought up on the old-fashioned ideas, but he knew it was no use trying to press him any further.

"All right, senhor," he said. "I'll try to bring us in at Madeira."

It took all his skill. At this season he had to overshoot—almost all the way to the Azores, and come in due south of Santa Maria—then sail almost four hundred miles with the wind very nearly abeam. By the time the western shore of Madeira came into view, they might have been at Sagres.

In the barrel that was lashed to the mast under the shade of the sail, the transplanted Saint Mary's Roses withered and died.


Mafalda met him at the door. "It's you, is it?" she said. "What are you doing here?"

Seven years had not taken away her sharp edges; Mafalda would never be called plump. The lean gypsy features still peered out of a somewhat smoother face; her body still had its wiry grace under its masquerade of housewife's kirtle and apron. The tangle of black hair was the same. Pedro could still imagine her dancing on her rope.

"I had to come—not my choice," he said. "How's Morales?"

"How should he be? He's getting old. He forgets. What do you expect? Still, he gave me a baby." She bit her lip. "All right, come in."

Morales was sitting over a low chest on which a set of Italian pasteboards had been spread, playing a game of cards against himself. A small curly-headed boy was crawling about at his feet.

"Pedrozinho!" The walnut face lit up.

"We passed Bojador," Pedro said without preamble.

"You did? It took long enough. What now?"

Mafalda scooped up the little boy and took him with her to the kitchen. Morales did not notice her go.

Pedro pulled a stool over next to Morales. "Gil Eanes was the captain. He wouldn't go any farther than the anchorage in the lee of the cape. There's nothing there but sand. He found some beach roses. He dug them up and put them in a barrel to prove to the Prince that he'd been there."

"Inch by inch," Morales said in disgust. "That's how Prince Henry's captains discover the world for him. Where's the man who'll go all the way?"

"Eanes needs stiffening," Pedro agreed. "Prince Henry's cupbearer, Baldaia, told me he'd never seen the Prince in such a temper as when Eanes returned the last time after sailing only thirty miles beyond Cape Non. It was Baldaia who suggested to the Prince that he order Eanes to take me along as navigator on the next try. He thought it might give Eanes some resolve, knowing that he had someone aboard who'd been as far as the north side of Cape Bojador."

"Cupbearer, eh? Maybe the infante ought to send his cupbearer out on a return trip."

"He'd go," Pedro said seriously. "He's an *aficionado*. He wasn't cut out to be a court popinjay. I think he'd acquit himself well if the Prince gave him his chance. I'll tell you this—if he'd been along with us on this voyage, he'd have goaded Gil Eanes to venture another hundred leagues farther south. As a gentleman of Prince Henry's household, his word would have carried more weight than mine."

Morales put a hand on Pedro's shoulder. "I know you're disappointed, Pedrozinho. But take the long view. The world's changed now, once and for all. Bojador's finally behind us. That barrel of roses you brought back proved it wasn't the gate of hell, but a place on earth, touched by the finger of God. Now the fear will be gone. There's nothing to hold the infante's ships back any more."

Pedro shook his head. "We've got to find something more than sand and a few beach roses if the Prince is to be encouraged to keep pouring money into this quest of his."

"Oh, we'll find something, Pedrozinho. Who knows? Maybe gold. An island as rich as Madeira. The kingdom of Prester John that good Christian monarchs have been searching for these many years. Some great river that connects with the Nile and would let us sail clear across Africa. Maybe even an ocean passage at the bottom of Africa that would let us trade with the East without being stopped by the cursed Moors."

"You think Africa has a bottom?"

"Why not? It has a top."

Pedro stayed talking until Morales showed signs of growing tired. He excused himself by saying he had to see to ship's stores and some small repairs. Morales invited him to stay for dinner, while Mafalda looked daggers at him, but Pedro begged off. "Come back and see me before you leave," Morales said, and Pedro assured him that he would. "Bring your *portolano* notes for Bojador," Morales said. "I want to add them to the grand *compasso da navigare* I'm compiling." He bared blackened gums in a smile. "I'm willing it to you."

To Pedro's surprise, Mafalda intercepted him on the way out. "Are you going to see Inês?" she asked.

He was mildly astonished to hear himself reply in a normal tone of voice. "I thought you wanted me to stay away from her. Besides"—he was equally surprised to hear an edge of malice creep into his voice—"I don't think Heitor would appreciate my coming around."

That was wildly unfair. But he felt he would not have been able to endure Heitor's bumbling friendship.

"Haven't you heard?"

"Heard what?"

"Heitor's dead."

The room reeled. For a moment, shamefully, all he could think was: now the way's free. Then the rush of emotion passed and decency returned.

"How . . . what happened?"

"Lobo murdered him. He picked a fight and killed him."

It was too much to digest all at once. "Then Lobo's dead, too? Or maybe he hasn't been hanged yet?"

"Hanged?" The black eyes flashed. "He's paying court to her."

"But that's diabolical!"

"Oh, he's very contrite," she said bitingly. "He's impressed Zarco and his little council of *fidalgos* with how contrite he is. He even forgives Heitor for attacking him. He should have seen where the quarrel was going, he says. He only wants to make it up to Inês now. She's been left a widow, unprotected. She's liable to lose everything she has, if a man doesn't take charge of things for her. He's willing to take on the task. Out of contrition. It would be a great relief to Zarco. It would solve the problem of what to do about Inês. Under the terms of the royal charter a widow's equity in a grant is renewed for three lives. Lobo's willing to respect that. He'll raise the two little girls as if they were his own."

Pedro swallowed. "There are two little girls?"

"You wouldn't know about that either, would you?" she said scathingly. "You've been away too long."

"For God's love, Mafalda, what do you want of me . . ." he began angrily.

"Go to her now," she said. "She needs you."


He let himself in through the little gate that hadn't been there the last time. A few people standing about in other dooryards along the steep mountain road stared at him with open curiosity. The house was larger than he remembered it. Heitor must have built additions. The vineyard climbing the mountain slope beyond it was new too. When he'd been here before there was only half-cleared land broken by stands of wheat that Heitor had put in.

As he followed the path to the house, he couldn't help noticing how trim and neat everything was. Heitor must have been a hard worker, and Inês just as unresting to have kept things up.

He knocked on a freshly painted door that was bracketed by potted geraniums. After an interval it was opened by an elfin child dressed like a doll in a flawlessly starched and pleated kirtle and miniature apron tied with a big bow.

"Hello," he said. "What's your name?"

"Beatriz," she piped at him. "What's yours?"

"Pedro," he said gravely. "Is your mother home?"

She ran off into the interior of the house, calling, "Mamãe! Come to the door! Someone's here!"

Inês appeared, a wooden spatula in her hand and her hair tied up in a cloth. She was as trim and finely chiseled as before, but the indefiniteness of youth had gone. Pedro found himself looking at a mature woman of thirty with purpose in her face. He thought she was more beautiful than before.

She put a hand to her breast. "Pedro, is it you?"

"Can I come in?"

She looked past him at her neighbors across the road. She hesitated a moment, then said firmly, "*Seguro*. Of course."

She stepped aside to let him enter, and he followed her through the house to the kitchen. She had been working there, making bread, and her hands and the trestle table were white with flour. A toddler was sitting on the floor, playing with dough. Beatriz was making a proprietary fuss over her. "This is Amélia," she informed Pedro. "She's my sister."

"They get along well," Inês said. "Beatriz is like a little mother. Sit down. Would you like a glass of wine?"

He was going to refuse, but she had already turned aside to fill a goblet at a small cask resting on a support. Pedro guessed that she was a little flustered and needed a moment to compose herself. He was glad of the moment himself. He found a bench and sank down on it.

"We . . ." She flushed. "That is, I make this myself. From the grapes in the vineyard."

He tasted it. It was sweet, with a deep flavor. "It's very good," he said.

"It needs to be older," she said. "It's only been aged a year . . . after six months being warmed in the *estufa*—" She stopped abruptly and looked down at her hands.

"I heard about Heitor," he said. "Mafalda told me."

"Oh," she said. She realized she was looking at her hands, and tucked them into her apron. She sat down on her kitchen stool. "Mafalda's been a good friend. Her . . . her tongue's sharp sometimes. She doesn't mean anything by it. She learned in a harsh school. She . . . she didn't . . ."

"No," he lied. "Don't think of it. She wasn't sharp with me."

"The girls miss Heitor," she said. "But they've been very good."

Beatriz broke in. "Mamãe, Amélia's getting flour on her new smock."

"That's all right, *querida*. We'll wash it later. Let her play for now."

She turned back to Pedro. She smiled at him, and it took away the awkwardness. "You're looking well," she said. "You've grown older."

He gave a start at that. He had never thought of himself

changing. He felt the same as always. "I've been at sea most of the time these last years. . . ."

"Yes," she said a little too quickly. "We heard here that you'd been with Cabral on the voyages that discovered the islands of the Azores. Even here, the word gets back. It was a great thing. A special mass was celebrated at Our Lady of the Flints. The *fidalgos* were green with envy when it came out that Cabral had been given the rank of captain donatary for two islands, when Zarco and Teixeira share the captaincy of Madeira. There was . . . a lot of talk about you. Morales told anyone who would listen that you should have gotten the credit as pilot instead of Diego de Silves. Zarco kept reminding everyone that you got your start with him, on the first Madeira voyages. He"—she flushed—"he said that he thought Cabral had treated you shamefully—that you should have been given a share equal to the grants given to the men of rank he brought along later as colonists—or at least a pension, like the one he gave to Morales."

"I was well paid," he said uncomfortably. "He doubled my wages on the following voyages to pilot's scale."

"He should have done it sooner," she said indignantly. "Morales says that if it hadn't been for you, he never would have passed Cape Non. I remember the day—"

She stopped abruptly. Pedro remembered the day, too. It must have been when he left Madeira for what he thought would be the last time. Morales would have spread the word, and it would have been on everybody's lips.

"We've gone past Cape Bojador now," he said to change the subject. "That's why I'm here now. I sailed with Gil Eanes. He's a gentleman of Prince Henry's household. He swore on his honor that he'd round Bojador for the prince, and he did. We're on our way back to Sagres now, on the western tack."

"Oh." Her face fell. Then she realized that a more appropriate response to one of the great accomplishments of the age was called for. She whipped up enthusiasm. "But that's wonderful, Pedro! You'll be famous. They'll have to give you some recognition now."

"There'll be a purse from the prince. That's what Gil Eanes says," he said uneasily.

She waited a moment, then said tentatively, "I suppose you'll go back to sea again?'"

"Yes . . . the Prince will want to send out more expeditions, now that we've got a foothold past the Bulge. . . ." He cleared his throat. "But I could settle on Madeira," he said, looking directly at her. Now that he had said it, the idea excited him. "I'd have no trouble finding regular work, now that there's steady commercial traffic between Madeira and the mainland. And I'd be in a position to sign on with the Prince whenever there was a new voyage south. But I'd make my home here."

"Oh, Pedro, that would be wonderful!" She lowered her head, then raised it with a defiant blush showing. "We'd be neighbors."

"Yes."

Pedro longed to declare himself formally, but he fought the impulse. It was too soon after Heitor's death. It would not have been right. Neither of them could say too much. This would have to do for now. But he could be explicit about his plans. Give Inês something to count on.

She took a breath. "Zarco would do much to have you become one of his citizens. All you'd have to do would be to apply for a land grant—the same one that's already owed to you. After all, you worked alongside the rest of us in the days of the fire—you came over with the first shipload—"

She stopped. The word *degredados* hung between them. Neither of them wanted to get any closer to it.

"I'd have to have someone to look after things when I was gone," he said, plunging on. "I'd be absent six or eight times a year—sometimes for weeks. It would have to be someone reliable."

"You . . . you could make an arrangement with a neighbor," she said. "That's often done. They were very helpful to me when . . . when . . ."

He rescued her by saying, "You're handling things very well. The place looks very well run."

"It's a lot of hard work. I pay a hired man when I can afford it these days . . . one of two men who used to work sometimes for Heitor when he was shorthanded. There's not much silver on Madeira, and a little goes a long way. They're glad to get it. I earn a few soldos with my embroidery, and by selling baskets for the mainland. But it's the grapes that are going to be my main source of income. I expect to do very well with the wine lodge this year."

There was pride in her voice. Pedro felt a little discomfited. He had come here expecting, after Mafalda's carryings-on, to find Inês in desperate straits—in need of instant rescue. Instead, he had found a determined and confident woman of property who, once her present difficulties were behind her, clearly expected to make her way in the world. All of a sudden he was aware of how little he had to offer. He had never managed to save much, and he owned nothing beyond his precious *portolani* and the knowledge in his head. On top of everything, he knew little of farming—his people had been fisherfolk. What could he do for Inês except consume her substance?

"At least I could pay a hired man, then," he said. "I'd be earning silver. Sometimes"—he could not help adding the small brag—"we're even paid in gold coin."

Much to his relief, she gave him a delighted smile. "Then on Madeira you'll be a real *poderoso*," she said. "Even some of the *fidalgos* that Zarco brought out with him hardly see a minted gold piece from one month to the next."

"Mamãe," Beatriz said, "can Pedro fix dolls the way Pai did? The head came off Amélia's doll, and there's no one to put it back."

"Don't bother Pedro," Inês said.

"It's all right," Pedro said. "Bring it to me, little one. I'll see what I can do."

She ran and got the broken doll. It was only a wooden peg that had come loose. Pedro carved a new one from a piece of firewood with his sheath knife. He handed the doll back to Beatriz.

"Here you are, *menina*. As good as new."

"What do you say?" Inês prompted.

"*Muita obrigada, Pedro*," Beatriz said.

"*De nada*," Pedro said. "You're very welcome."

"Mamãe?"

"What is it?"

"Can Pedro come and live with us?"

Inês colored. "What a thing to ask! Run along and play now." She turned to Pedro. "You'll have to excuse her. She misses Heitor."

"I understand," Pedro said. He jumped up. "Why am I sitting here talking? As long as I'm here, there must be something I can do. Have you any heavy chores you've been putting off?"

"I couldn't take advantage—"

"Think nothing of it. I insist."

In the end she admitted that there were a number of tasks that the handyman had sloughed off that were too difficult for her to manage herself. Pedro spent the next hour digging post holes and setting some heavy posts for the livestock pen to replace those that had rotted away. Then he levered a weighty block of stone into place for her to be used as the base for a stove in the hothouse where she was—inexplicably to Pedro—heating casks of wine. Finally he attacked the woodpile with gusto, splitting kindling for the hothouse.

"You don't have to do that," she protested. "I can split it a little at a time, at my leisure."

"You don't have any leisure, that I can see," he replied. "You need to get a little bit ahead on your firewood. That pile ought to last you a month or two."

When he finished, she asked, "You'll eat with us?"

"No, no, I couldn't," he said.

"Please," she said. "The children will be disappointed."

It was an early supper because of the children's bedtime. Pedro thought Inês was going to more trouble than she ordinarily would have; they must have had their dinner that morning, like most people, but instead of a light supper, Inês served a full meal of three courses, with soup and side dishes. There was a roast, a chicken fricassee with hard-boiled eggs, a dish of lamprey sautéed with parsley and onion, and at the end a milk pudding. The children were well-behaved, picking out things they liked, and Beatriz helped feed the baby, cutting her meat into fragments. Inês plied Pedro with wine—two varieties that tasted like normal table wine, and, after the pudding, another glass of the sweet hothouse wine that she said she had invented. When he finished, he felt full to bursting. "No," he said, pushing away the lettuce preserves she tried to offer him, "I couldn't eat another bite."

She put the children to bed, then returned to share a glass of wine with him. "When will you sail?" she asked.

"Tomorrow morning, after mass. There's to be a sung mass for the crew at Our Lady of the Flints, and then we'll sail on the tide. The water casks have been refilled, and Eanes has already taken on a load of firewood."

"I wish you could stay longer."

"So do I. But I'll be back."

She gave him a clear, bright, brave, understanding smile. "When do you think?" she asked matter-of-factly.

"It might be some time. If Prince Henry is impatient and wants to send another expedition past Cape Bojador right away, I might not be able to return for a few months."

"I'll pray you a safe voyage," she said. "The children will be glad to see you again. They took a liking to you."

"I'll be glad to see *them* again," he said, and that was as close as he came to saying what they both knew he meant to say.

She accompanied him to the door. Outside, there was still an hour of summer daylight left. The warm air was filled with the smell of the island's flowers. Gulls circled inland in a late search for food.

"We were young," Inês said. "We didn't know what life had in store for us."

Pedro knew she was talking about their first meeting on the prison ship that had taken them both to Madeira. "Yes," he said.

"There was a song in a *cancioneiro* I had when I was a girl. It said that life was like walking through a fog—that good things came out of the fog toward you, and bad things, but that you could never tell what was going to come next, and that you could only keep walking."

"Your two little girls are good things," he said.

"Yes."

"Sometimes you let the good things go past and disappear into the fog behind you, and you can never go back for them. But what if one of them comes out of the fog again toward you?"

He could see that she was affected by the thought. "That wasn't in the song," she said. "But it ought to have been."

She waited for him to answer himself.

"This time," he said, "you don't let it go past you."

"*Ai*, Pedro," she said, closing her eyes at the pain of whatever memory he had called up. "You can't take away a whole past, and you wouldn't want to. Everything's so mixed."

He could see her lip trembling. At that moment he would have taken her in his arms and kissed her, if one of her neighbors hadn't gone by on the mountain road just then, leading a cow on a rope like a dog.

"*Dona Inês, boa noite,*" the neighbor called, peering into the dooryard.

*"Boa noite, Senhor Vicente,"* she responded.

She smiled up at Pedro, but the moment was gone. "I'd better go," he said. "Perhaps I'll have a chance to see you tomorrow before we lift anchor, if I can get away for a few minutes."

"I'll come down to the beach with the children to see you off," she said.

*"Bom,"* he said. Their hands touched and withdrew as if burned. He turned quickly and let himself out the dooryard gate.

Lobo was waiting just out of sight down the road. He materialized from between two hedges and waited for Pedro to approach him. Pedro knew him at once, in spite of the years that had passed. He was more unkempt than ever in a grimy jerkin and hose that sagged at the thighs, his black hair coarse and matted. He looked like a poor man, and one could almost feel sorry for him.

"So the sailor's come back from the sea, has he?" he said in a raspy voice.

"Get out of my way," Pedro said. He took a step forward, prepared to seize Lobo by the throat if necessary. Lobo was thicker in the body and looked strong, but Pedro had the advantage of height.

"Take it easy," Lobo said. "There's no need for that."

"What are you doing, skulking around the senhora's place? Stay away from her, do you understand?"

"I live on this hillside," Lobo said in an aggrieved tone. "I'm the *proprietário* of a farm."

"I don't want you bothering her," Pedro growled.

"What have you got to say about it—you who've been away for seven years?" Lobo hissed at him. He took a step backward, cringing, as Pedro raised a hand. "Easy, now, easy! Is it bothering the senhora to make her an offer? I just want to set things right."

"Set things right?" Pedro burst out in amazement. "You killed her man!"

"That's past," Lobo said. "Now I'm trying to make up for it. Everybody knows I was only trying to defend myself."

"You murdered him," Pedro said. "You picked a fight and you murdered him."

"You've been talking to the rope dancer, the old pilot's

doxy. She hates me." He added thoughtfully, "She hates you, too."

Pedro winced. "She's the senhora's friend. She looks out for her."

"She's a carnival girl and a *meretriz* who looks out for herself." He paused and said carefully, "Did you ask the senhora what happened?"

"What are you talking about?"

"What did the dona say?"

"She didn't say anything. She doesn't discuss filth like you."

Lobo didn't seem to mind being insulted. In fact, he acted pleased at what he had heard. "She's too good to be concerned with the likes of me, is that what you think?" he said.

Pedro exploded violently, "Yes!"

Hastily, Lobo said, "She *is* too good. That's why she wouldn't let on what she suffered."

Pedro itched to get a handful of Lobo's jacket in his fist, but he controlled himself with an effort. "Enough! I won't have a jackal like you discussing the dona. Get out of here before I knock out your teeth."

Lobo stood his ground. "She'd have been ashamed to admit it to you, naturally, but your friend Heitor abused her—beat her and worse. He was an ugly one when he got drunk." At Pedro's sudden movement he raised an arm to ward off a blow, but Pedro kept his fists by his sides. "You can ask anybody. Why do you think I was acquitted. Do you think murderers are let go? He came after me with a pruning knife, and I had to stab him to save myself."

"You're a liar. I knew Heitor. He wouldn't have hurt a fly. He worshiped . . . the dona. He thought she was too good for him."

Lobo nodded sagely. "*Sim*, that was the problem. He knew how far above him she was, and it ate at him. He knew he was too dumb for her. He resented owing everything he had to her. He turned into a different man than the one you remember. He drank all the time, and it turned him mean. He used to have the senhora send one of the little girls to him with baskets of wine while he worked. By the middle of the day he was a raging bull if anybody crossed his path. She had to go out to see him that day, and he started a quarrel with her. He knocked her down—even then kept hitting her with those ham hands of his. I happened to be passing by. I called to him to stop—"

"You?" Pedro exclaimed in disbelief.

"Yes, why not me? Anybody would have said something. How was I to know he'd rush at me with a pruning knife in his hand? The dona's lucky I was there—he might have used it on her."

"I don't believe you."

Lobo shrugged. "Suit yourself. You see for yourself that I'm walking around free. There were witnesses, a *julgamento*. If you don't believe that's how it happened, go back and ask the senhora."

The man's confidence shook Pedro. "Still . . . to offer to marry her . . . the widow . . ."

"Maybe she's forgiven me. Maybe she realizes that I might have saved her life. That's her business, isn't it? Or maybe you think it's yours!"

Lobo was cringing no longer. It was a convincing display of anger. Pedro became further confused.

"Oh, I didn't ask her at once," Lobo went on. "No matter what you think of me, even I wouldn't do that. But I was there with the other neighbors when she needed help with the harvest. I lent her my milk cow when she needed milk for the children—that old cow of hers has gone dry. I did what I could. I was here, while you were off in the four corners of the earth! She's a good woman. After a while she started talking to me. I know that a lowlife like me isn't worthy of someone like her. But who else was there around here for her. Another *degredado*? Don't forget that Zarco had to empty the prisons to start this colony going, and Heitor was no better than me. But I'm a *proprietário* now, and if she joined her farm to mine, at least she'd be sure of providing for her children. After what she's been through, maybe that's good enough."

"No," Pedro said. "Shut up."

"You can hit me if you want, but she agreed."

This time Pedro's temper gave way. He grabbed the front of Lobo's jacket. "You're a liar!"

"Easy, man, easy." Pedro released him, and he dusted himself off with dignity. "Maybe you don't like it, but that's what happened."

Pedro gave a bellow of pain. "We talked . . . she said nothing . . ."

"Do you think she'd tell *you*? You're getting back on your ship tomorrow, aren't you? Are you going to be gone for another seven years? Maybe she had feelings for you once, but that's all she can count on now. That's what she must have been thinking."

"No . . ." Pedro said. "We discussed it. . . ."

"Listen to me, da Costa," Lobo said, his voice turned candid and amicable. "Maybe your intentions are good. Maybe you could get her to go back on her word. But can she really trust you? Can you trust yourself? You're only a vagabond sailor. Can you be sure you'll give her and her children the life they need?" A whining tone came into his voice. "You're trying to steal my woman, that's the size of it. I don't doubt you can do it if you really want to. You come here after seven years and confuse her, just as she's decided what to do about her life. But if you care for her, and not yourself, why don't you do the right thing by her? Get on your ship and go, and don't torment her any more. Maybe I'm not much to look at, but I'll be good to her, I promise. . . ."

"No," Pedro said, fighting his anguish. "That's not the way it is. We talked it over. She's going to come down to the beach tomorrow with the children to see me off. I have another voyage that I've got to sign up for. She knows that. I'll be back when it's finished. . . ."

He stopped and shook his head from side to side. There was a buzzing in it, as if a bee had gotten inside.

"All right," Lobo said. "You get on board your ship in the morning. You look for her there. See if she really meant to be there."

He backed away a step, and when he was out of reach of Pedro's arms, he turned on his heel and walked away.

She couldn't place the ragged man who appeared at her door at daybreak, leading a spavined old horse. He was a grimy, shambling individual who appeared to be put together out of slats and tatters, one of those types who lived on the beach and scratched out a subsistence by doing this and that. "He's waiting at Machicho, at the house of the pilot, Morales," he repeated in exactly the same words he had used before. "The lady, Mafalda, said to tell you that he decided not to sail after all—that he's staying. They want you to come at once." He furrowed his brow, as if trying to remember something. "There's a priest with them."

He smiled then, a display of mottled gums from which a few yellow teeth hung like pegs.

"But Machico ... that's so far. I have the children ..."

"That's why they sent me with the horse."

Inês's heart fluttered wildly. What could it mean? She looked past the man's shoulder, out at the bay, where Gil Eanes's ship rode at anchor. A small bobbing boat was tied up alongside it, and tiny figures were passing up cargo.

"Wait here," she said. "I'll get them ready. It won't take long."

She got a sleepy Beatriz dressed, then got the baby ready with the little girl's eager help. She packed a basket with food to eat on the way, then remembered to go to the shed to milk old Blossom, so she wouldn't be uncomfortable. She brought the jug of milk back to the kitchen and poured a glass for each of the children, to have with a bit of bread for their breakfast.

The ragged apparition outside rose silently from his haunches when she emerged, and made clasped hands to help her to the saddle. After a moment's hesitation she mounted astride under full skirts, like any peasant woman on a mule, with the baby propped in front of her and little Beatriz riding behind, holding onto her waist. The man walked off, leading the old horse at a snail's pace.

He followed the path around the mountain, avoiding the road that would have led them down to the beach. When Inês asked him why he was taking the slower and more difficult route, he only grunted. She looked down the steep slope toward Funchal Bay and saw half the population of the town gathered along the water's edge to see the Gil Eanes expedition off. Perhaps that was why her tatterdemalion escort was taking the mountain road; he wanted to avoid the crowds. It was a good thing he had come for her early. She would have been on the beach herself in another hour, and would have missed getting his message.

It was twelve miles to Machico, where Morales had built his house near the site of what had been Machin's cross before the fire. After the first couple of miles, she dismounted to spare the horse. By this time her guide had descended to the coastal road, where it was flat and easy going. She walked alongside the broken-down animal, keeping one hand on the baby, though Beatriz had her sister in a clutch that even a pry bar could not have dislodged.

It was high noon by the time they got there; it had taken almost six hours of plodding progress, counting the short stop to eat. The man had eagerly accepted the bread and cold meats she had offered him—leftovers from the supper she had made for Pedro—and had wolfed the food down as if he were starved.

Quite a little settlement had grown up around Machin's Bay—it was the capital for Teixeira's half of the island, and the grant of land for Morales had had to come from Teixeira, though the old pilot was technically Zarco's pensioner. There had been no difficulties; both men were conscious of their debt to Morales. As Inês rounded the bend in the shore path, she saw at least twenty houses sprawled around the shorefront or peeping through the greenery farther back. There was a church, too, though not so grand as either of the two churches in Funchal.

Morales's small, sturdy house faced the sea, looking northeast toward Europe. A round-bottomed boat rested upside down on the beach in front of it, though from what Mafalda had told Inês, Morales never went out in it. The land behind the house was not cultivated; Morales was not interested in such things. He bought what he needed from his neighbors, though Mafalda kept a few chickens and a milk goat. She wasn't much of a gardener either.

"Mamãe, is this where Tia Mafalda lives?" shrilled Beatriz. She had never been here, though Mafalda came once in a while to visit and stay a night or two.

"Yes, *preciosa*, it is."

She took the baby from the saddle. With a squeal of delight, Beatriz slid down from the horse and ran toward the dwelling's door.

Mafalda was coming out of the house and met her halfway. She stopped to give the little girl a hug and a kiss, then dragged her by the hand to where Inês was advancing with the baby.

"*Que surpresa!*" Mafalda said. "What are you doing here? Why aren't you saying good-bye to Pedro? Is everything all right?"

"*Como?*" Inês wrinkled her brow. "Pedro sent this man with his horse to bring us here."

She turned around, but the man with the horse was walking swiftly in the opposite direction.

"Pedro's not here," Mafalda said, puzzled. "Morales is disappointed—Pedro was going to drop by one more time with some maps." She looked at the tattered man's retreating back. "Hey you!" When she got no response, she ran after him and grabbed him by the sleeve, turning him around. "Who sent you to this lady, heh?"

The man said in a mechanical voice, as though repeating a lesson, "The sailor. Pedro da Costa. He paid me."

"You weren't paid by any sailor. Who was it?"

"The sailor. Pedro da Costa . . ." the man repeated.

Mafalda tossed her hair impatiently. "How much did Lobo pay you?"

"A silver soldo, senhora," the man said, smiling with his few teeth.

"*Ai de mim!*" Inês exclaimed. "Why would he do such a thing?"

"Did Pedro come to see you yesterday?" Mafalda asked.

"Yes," Inês said. "I gave him supper. He's going to settle on Madeira. He has another voyage to go on first. It may take some months. I was going to meet him on the beach this morning to say good-bye."

"It's clear. Lobo wanted to prevent it."

Inês's face had a stricken look. She turned her head toward the retreating man and the horse. "Mafalda! Will you watch the children? I'll be back for them tonight!" She ran after the man who had brought her. "Wait! Take me back with you!"

Mafalda snared her by the arm. "It's too late," she said. "Look."

Inês followed her gaze out to sea. A ship could be seen there rounding the Prainha point, a *barcha* whose billowing square sail carried the red Jerusalem cross of the Order of Christ.

Inês sagged, and Mafalda caught her. "It's all right," she said. "You say he's coming back? We'll straighten it out then."

The news had preceded them. They climbed the path to the prince's cliffside retreat to the pealing of churchbells from Sagres and nearby Raposeira, and with a large, noisy procession of townspeople and fisherfolk following behind them. Within an hour of their landing at Lagos, fifteen miles down the coast, not a shop had remained open, not a net was tended, not a field looked after.

Pedro walked a little behind Gil Eanes and the Prince's chamberlain, who had come down to meet them. Close on his heels, a sweating sailor pulled at the bridle of a donkey whose wooden panniers were somewhat overbalanced on one side by the barrel of sand containing the transplanted Roses of Santa Maria. Eanes might just as well have carried the dessicated weeds in his hand, but he was bent on presenting them to the infante, barrel and all.

"What kind of temper is Dom Henrique in?" Eanes asked.

"He's delighted, of course," replied the chamberlain. "He's readying a fast messenger to carry the news to King Duarte, but first he wants to hear the details from you. He intends to ask the King to proclaim a day of thanksgiving throughout the land, and there's no doubt that it will be done."

They had reached the flat, rocky top of the promontory. Eanes looked across at the barren surface, thinly covered by lichen and weeds, and surrounded on three sides by a heaving green ocean. The scattered buildings of the Vila do Infante, the prince's town, lay about like dice on a baize tabletop.

"You've made a lot of progress, just in the short time we've been away," Eanes remarked.

"We've got a new pilot's station going up," the chamberlain said, "and there's been more work done on Saint Catherine's. The prince is establishing a cemetery behind it for the foreign sailors who get washed up on the rocks."

"The foreigners toss their dead into the water off the cape like dogs," Eanes said with a grimace of distaste. "Every country in the world comes through the Strait of Gibraltar, and when they meet an unfavorable Atlantic wind, they lay offshore for days—sometimes weeks. It's decent of the prince to want to give them a Christian burial."

"The Genoese have got wind of all the new construction going up here," the chamberlain said. "They know that something's up. You know how they always keep an eye open for profit. They've offered to buy the whole Vila do Infante."

Eanes laughed. "They'll wait a long time. Can you see Dom Henrique agreeing to sell the Sacred Cape to a bunch of foreigners?"

"He told them he'll lease them anchorage rights—for a tidy sum. We'll soon be in a position to service some of the traffic that gets stalled here. It ought to help finance the prince's program of exploration."

A questioning glance went with the last remark. Eanes, conscious of the barrel of dead plants that constituted his only offering to the prince, flushed a sullen red.

Pedro helped the sailor with the donkey over a final rise by giving a push. He could see the prince's gray eyrie ahead, perched on a final outthrusting spit of land—the rocky point, marking the place where Europe ended, that Henry had claimed for his own. The immense compass rose he had laid out before it served as a plaza, surrounded by the long low buildings of the school of navigation. It was from these radiating paving stones that pilots whose ships were anchored in the roadway below could take a heading.

People were pouring out of the houses and workshops to greet the returning explorer. Eanes waved and smiled with great style. The Vila do Infante residents merged with the trailing villagers from Sagres and Raposeira to form a joyous, celebrating throng. Quite a few were already drunk.

As Pedro passed one of the new buildings he saw Jaime of Majorca standing in a doorway, his face unreadable. He was not about to join the throng. In his black robe and tall conical hat, the old mapmaker looked for all the world like some sorcerer about to cast a spell.

The crowd broke like surf against the boundary of the prince's courtyard, and Gil Eanes's party was hustled inside. Two huffing sailors unloaded the donkey and carried the barrel in between them. Pedro expected that they were going to be conducted to the audience room, but Prince Henry met them halfway and took them with him to the antechamber. A few privileged noblemen were waiting there on business, and they looked up with interest as the Eanes entourage entered.

Prince Henry seated himself in the high-backed cathedra, and Gil Eanes dropped to one knee in front of him, sweeping off his cartwheel hat in a broad gesture.

"I have fulfilled my sacred vow to you, Dom Henrique,"

he said in a voice that carried to everyone in the chamber. "I have passed Cape Bojador. The last barrier is gone."

Pedro's eyes, wandering around the room, landed on the face of Afonso Baldaia, the Prince's cupbearer. Baldaia had been trying to meet his gaze, and raised his eyebrows in some question. Pedro shrugged. He didn't know what questions Baldaia had in mind, but he'd get his answers soon enough.

Prince Henry responded in his deep public voice, giving Eanes his moment of glory. "We are pleased, Dom Gil," he said. "You have done what no man has done before. Your name will ring throughout history."

That was about as much formality as he had patience for. He leaned forward with lively curiosity and said in a practical voice, "Did you find men, houses?"

"No, nothing, *Vossa Excelência,*" Eanes replied. "Sand, desert, the sky. There was just one sign of life."

He motioned the sailors forward with a theatrical gesture. They rolled the barrel toward the prince.

"It seemed to me that I ought to bring you some emblem as proof of my landing," Eanes declared, "and God placed just such a sign at my feet." He uprooted the dried plants from the barrel and presented them to the Prince. "Saint Mary's Roses, Vossa Excelência," he said, "the same kind that grow on Portugal's beaches."

If Prince Henry was disappointed, he didn't show it. He took the brittle stalks graciously from Gil Eanes and said, "They are a sign indeed. If flowers can grow in a desert, then men can flourish too. We have only to search them out." He gave Eanes a keen look of appraisal. "You say, Dom Gil, that you found these flowers at your feet. How far south did you proceed?"

Eanes looked like a schoolboy caught making excuses. But he drew himself up and made a creditable recovery. "We only rounded the cape and anchored in the bay we found there, Dom Henrique. We left further exploration for later expeditions. It seemed to me that I ought to hurry back to you without delay to inform you that the great feat of passing the Bulging Cape had finally been accomplished."

Baldaia caught Pedro's eye again. This time there was a sardonic smile on his face.

"Your zeal is appreciated, Dom Gil," the prince said with all solemnity. "We mustn't let your accomplishment be dissipated. I'm going to send you back immediately, so that you may go farther this time." His voice took on an edge. "Another fifty leagues farther, at least."

"Yes, Dom Henrique," Eanes said manfully.

"At least," the prince repeated with emphasis. "And so that there need be no worries about my receiving the news quickly, I'll send my cupbearer with you in a second ship— something faster, a *barinel*."

His eye singled out Baldaia, who stepped forward. A stir of interest went through the chamber. Baldaia knelt and bowed his head.

"Well, Dom Afonso, do you want to go?" the infante asked.

"I desire nothing more, Dom Henrique," Baldaia said. "I would make a request."

"Speak, Dom Afonso."

"Ships can become separated. Since Dom Gil is a seasoned seaman who has passed Cape Non more than once and who now knows the way past Bojador as well, I'd like to borrow Pedro da Costa as my own pilot."

"What say you, Dom Gil?" Prince Henry inquired.

There was no way Eanes could refuse. Pedro expected bluster, and then he realized that Eanes, caught up in his own accomplishment, had summoned up his usual overweening self-confidence and actually welcomed the chance to be rid of him.

"I have no objection, Dom Henrique," Eanes said magnanimously.

Henry beckoned Pedro forward. The thought flashed through Pedro's mind that it wasn't every day that one had the ear of a prince—that he ought to use the opportunity to tell the infante about the *kamal*. But his nerve failed him; he was not yet ready to stick his neck out for the Venetian. He had previously tied knots in the string to mark the latitudes of Sagres, Madeira, and Cape Non. On the last voyage he had added a knot for Cape Bojador. Before telling anyone, he should test it—see if it brought him to safe anchorage again.

Prince Henry was regarding him with lofty benevolence. "You've earned your reward many times over, Pedro da Costa. I have a purse of gold for you. It's well deserved. You've been on loan first to Velho Cabral, then to Dom Gil, and you haven't disappointed me. You're free, of course, to go back to Zarco and claim your piece of Madeira. Perhaps you're anxious to quit the sea and settle down. But Dom Afonso thinks highly of your talents. What say you to sailing with him? Are there any impediments?"

"No, *senhor*," Pedro said, his mouth dry. "No impediments."

# CHAPTER 14

From outside there was a great roar of people. Lan-ying hurried to the window and saw the crowds rushing by like leaves in a windstorm. The servants had stopped their work to gawk, and the other concubines were twittering like birds.

"What is it?" she asked Wo.

He put aside the tallies he had been sorting and started for the door. "I'll find out," he said.

He came back a few minutes later, his clothing disheveled. He must have been buffeted by the running hordes before he could stop someone to ask. Lan-ying could tell that the information was benign; he wasn't exactly smiling, but he was having trouble maintaining his usual glum expression.

"The Star Raft has returned," he announced. "It's been sighted sailing up the Dragon River. The first ships should be dropping anchor within the hour."

A shriek went up from the concubines. "Chin Mao is back!" There was much fluttering about and attention to costume. Small Enclosed Pearl came mincing over to Lan-ying and said, "He'll be pleased to find he has a son. You'll be elevated to greater heights in this household than before. You won't let him neglect the rest of us, will you?"

Lan-ying smiled to reassure her, then Wo was shooing all the women away from the windows. "Behave yourselves," he reprimanded them. "Behave decorously or the master will have you beaten with rods!"

Lan-ying returned to her quarters. Little Golden Bird was there with the wet nurse, sitting on the floor and playing with one of his toys—a porcelain bird on a stick that opened its beak and chirped when a string was pulled. He had more toys than Lan-ying knew what to do with—paper puppets, clay animals, miniature ships with paper sails for his bath, even a little man who swiveled on his heel to always point north. The doting personnel of the Department of Eunuchs delighted in spoiling him.

She took him from the wet nurse and lifted him up. He made a gurgle of pleasure. "Chin-niao," she told him softly, "your father is home."

He was a large, sturdy child, not yet two years old. As the soothsayer had predicted, he had yellow hair, and so she had named him Hsiao Chin-niao, Little Golden Bird. It would do for his baby name, though it would have to be changed to something more propitious when he was older. She wondered what that name would be; on the first anniversary of his birth, when various objects had been placed around him, he had reached unhesitatingly for a toy ship. Once—when the short-lived Hung-hsi Emperor had decreed death for those attempting to go to sea—that would have been an unlucky choice, but since Cheng Ho had triumphed again, it bespoke a brilliant future.

The wet nurse looked up at her. She was a good-natured country girl from Hochou whom the Yellow Gate had found for Chin-niao. "Is it true, my lady?" she asked. "That the bones-outside who rules this house has returned from the western seas?"

"You must not call him a bones-outside," Lan-ying said severely. "I won't hear that superstitious nonsense. He's a foreigner, it's true, but his name is Golden Hair, and that's what he is to be called. You need have no fear of him—he's a very lenient master."

"When will he arrive, mistress?" the woman said, chastened.

"Soon," Lan-ying said. "Very soon. He'll be kept very busy for the rest of this day, and perhaps, if there's a banquet, he won't be able to return tonight. But he'll come as soon as he can, and if he's going to be delayed, he'll send word."

But the days passed and Chin Mao did not appear, nor did he send word. The household grew restive, and Wo looked unhappy. There were whispers among those servants who did the marketing and other outside chores of a strange mood in the city; a damper seemed to have fallen on the celebration that might have been expected at the return of the Treasure Fleet. The self-appointed eunuch godfathers from the Yellow Gate who had been smothering Little Golden Bird with their visits failed to appear.

"Where is Chin Mao?" she asked Wo. "Is something wrong?"

"I don't know, Lady," he said. "The auditor who comes from the Department of Eunuchs to go over the accounts sent an assistant instead this week. Everyone's very skittish over there. Rumors are going around. They say a new eunuch, Wang Chen, who's a favorite of the Dowager, is to be appointed head of the Yellow Gate."

On the tenth day, Ma Huan paid a visit. The old gentleman showed up at the Moon Gate without fanfare and slipped past the demon screen almost before the doorman knew he was there. He spent a quarter hour whispering with Wo behind drawn panels, then came to see Lan-ying.

Little Golden Bird's face lit up when he saw him. "Uncle," he crowed, waving his chubby arms, *"po fu."* He had never seen a man, except for the servants, and perhaps had mistaken him for a eunuch.

Ma Huan patted him on the head and gave him a curious doll carved out of ivory, a grotesque figurine representing a man with fish legs. "It comes from the land of the Zanj, Chin-niao," the old scholar told him. "See, your *po fu* remembered you, even though he just learned of your existence this morning."

Lan-ying summoned all her training and, putting a composed expression on her face and using a cultivated voice, offered Ma Huan refreshments.

"I'm too old and sour and worn-out to worry about good manners, so I'll refuse," he said. "I've come to tell you about Chin Mao."

"Where is he?" she said in a whisper.

"Chin Mao did not return with us," he said. "We left him in the land of the Zanj."

She felt her face grow as cold as porcelain. She had

known it all along but had thrust the knowledge aside with joss sticks and prayers for his return.

Ma Huan gave her time to recover, then said, "We were still ten thousand *li* from Chin Mao's country, by the astronomer's estimate, when he ran away, but he must have known that was as close as we ever would get. He absconded with some jewels and maps. Cheng Ho doesn't begrudge him the jewels, and as for the maps, perhaps he's glad that Chin Mao took them. They only would have been burned."

"Thank you, First Born, for coming to tell me," she said formally.

He wagged a finger at her. "You can't count on the protection of the Yellow Gate. Things are changing. In fact, it might be a good idea to find a quiet place in the countryside, where Chin Mao's son will be beyond the attention of those who are now rising to the top. Cheng Ho told me to tell you that no inventory will be taken of the jewels Chin Mao left behind with you. It's the only thing he can do for you."

"What . . . what will happen to Cheng Ho?"

"He's being taken to Peking under guard. He'll have to answer to the Emperor."

"Oh!" This time her training failed her.

Ma Huan's wrinkled old face remained calm. "Don't worry about Cheng Ho. He'll land on his feet—if only he can get to the Emperor while the Emperor's still alive."

"Still alive . . ." she said, stunned at the blasphemy.

"I mustn't say any more," he said. He rose to go. Before leaving, he paused to chuck Little Golden Bird under the chin. "Good-bye, little yellow-hair," he said. "When you grow up, stay away from the sea. It won't be healthy."

A few days after that, Wo gathered the concubines and servants together to tell them that the household would be dissolved. Its goods would be returned to inventory. It had been officially ordered that Chin Mao was to be forgotten. The Auspicious Barbarian, it seemed, was no longer auspicious.

Two grinning Ukoba, the King's Boys, appeared at Tom's hut to tell him that the king had sent for him. "He wishes to make you a Big Man," one of them said, nudging the other slyly. "He will give you a coral necklace."

Tom's heart sank, but he smiled back at them. The Big Men were not allowed to leave the city under pain of death, and even the lower classes of nobility needed special permission. As for the coral necklace, it was an ambiguous honor. There was a death penalty for losing it or having it stolen from you. Nobody who was awarded a necklace ever dared to take it off, night or day.

"I'll be right along," Tom stalled, trying to find out if this were a legitimate summons or an attempt at extortion. The King's Boys held the city in terror. One of their favorite tricks was to deliver a sick goat to a householder and tell him that the king wanted him to take care of it for him. When the goat died, they could milk the chosen victim dry for life—the fiction being that they would intercede for him in return for money and gifts. The King's Boys also served on the official murder parties sent into the streets at night to kill anyone they met, whenever the king felt the need to augment the daily human sacrifices. On those occasions, they were not allowed to return to the palace until they had done in fourteen victims, and they sometimes filled their quota by invading the homes of people they had a quarrel with.

The two King's Boys grinned more broadly at him, seeing through the ploy. They were big strapping men in their thirties, stark naked except for their coral necklaces and the bangles on their ankles. Tom had hoped to outbluff them, seeing that they had been forbidden to wear clothes and were of low degree despite their years. They were only one-string Boys, who had not yet been given a wife and a piece of cloth to cover themselves by the king.

"*Egu atuwo,*" one of them said, shaking his head. In the dialect of Benin, the dread phrase meant only something like, "The king sends you his compliments," but it was calculated to strike terror in the hearts of those who heard it.

"All right," Tom said.

He took a last look around the house he had been given to make sure that his belongings were well hidden. The house had formerly belonged to a sacrifice victim, and it had already been well-looted, so he didn't think the two Ukoba would bother to come back while he was gone. There was only a couch and stool, both made of clay, and a grisly collection of human and animal skulls in wall alcoves and atop the juju altar. Tom had excavated a small hole under the al-

tar and deposited his jewels and maps there, then replaced
the juju fetish, a clay cone set with teeth and bones.

The house itself was built on the usual Benin plan—
separate rooms set around a central courtyard. The walls
were built up of long courses of red clay, ribbed to resemble
brickwork and topped by tall pyramidal thatched roofs supported by wooden beams. For interior decoration the previous occupant had covered the walls with handprints of
blood and lime.

Tom followed the two Ukoba into the street. The door
closed itself behind him—front doors in Benin were fitted
with an ingenious hanging weight suspended from the lintel
that closed them automatically. Tom thought the idea might
be worth bringing back to England. He didn't bother locking the door behind him. Door keys in Benin were iron
rods, bent in a zigzag to engage the peg in a bolt on the
other side, and they tended to be interchangeable.

The main avenue was broad and straight—broader than
any street Tom had seen in England—and enclosed along
much of its length by high walls that formed the sides of
compounds and were shared by many houses in common.
Great Benin was a huge city; when Tom looked down the
side streets he could not see the ends of them.

The people Tom saw strolling about looked happy and
prosperous. They seemed entirely unintimidated by the
daily horrors of this bloody place. He saw substantial
middle-aged men so wound round with lengths of cloth below the waist that they resembled hand bells; women wearing long blue skirts and bare above the waist except for a
multitude of brass and copper ornaments; men in grass kilts
and conical hats made of beads. Large numbers of people
were entirely naked. Youths and maidens customarily wore
no garments of any kind, and no woman of any age was allowed to wear clothing until it had been given to her by her
husband. Many of them made up for it with extravagant jew-
elry and complicated hairstyles: one popular hair fashion
was a braided wreath sitting on top of the head like a crown,
with one half dyed black and the other half dyed red.

The inhabitants of Benin were a tall, handsome people
who carried themselves well. Their skin color ranged from a
light olive to jet black. For Tom, their fine appearance was
marred by the ornamental scars that everybody seemed to
have. Both men and women were marked by a chevron of

three stripes on each cheek, and some had added the three-
stripe motif to the breast or stomach. Many of the women,
in addition, had adorned themselves with beauty buttons—
little raised excrescences of scar tissue. Both sexes wore the
same cosmetic—iron on the eyebrows, a distinguishing mark
of the citizens of Benin that Tom had encountered nowhere
else on his thousand-mile trek north from the kingdom of
the Congo.

Once Tom and his guards had to step aside for a
nobleman—a Big Man—and his attendants. He was a big,
powerful man in a skirt with many flounces, the lower part
of his face completely hidden by a high collar composed of
circlets of coral beads piled on top of one another. On his
head he wore a tall beaded helmet with earflaps, and he was
liberally festooned with armlets, anklets, and necklaces. The
two attendants at either side holding shields over his head
must have been nobles of lower degree because they were
attired in a similar getup, but the other attendants, fanning
him and leading the way, were naked slaves.

"Is he an albino?" the Big Man inquired.

Tom knew the word for albino, and he shuddered. Albinos
were especially prized as sacrifices. He'd seen several of
them around the city, waiting to be called for their turn.

"No," one of the King's Boys answered respectfully. "He's
some kind of a foreigner from the south. If you look closely,
you can see that his eyes aren't pink."

The Big Man moved on, with two attendants hastening to
support his elbows and take some of the weight off his feet.

One of the King's Boy's prodded Tom, and they resumed
walking. As they came closer to the district where the king's
palace was situated, the horrors began. Tom spied a headless
corpse propped on a rooftop, being picked at by birds, then
a couple of seated crucifixions by the roadside, the necks
tied to stakes behind the stools. A little farther on, a rotting
corpse was spread-eagled between two trees; it had been
disemboweled, to judge by the blackened heap of offal lying
on the ground in front of it.

As they walked on, such sights became more frequent.
When they reached a marketplace at a crossroads, the
ground was littered with human remains in every stage of
decomposition. Vultures were fighting over the choicer morsels. The passersby seemed indifferent to this open-air char-
nel house except to hold their noses against the stench.

Another mile of walking brought them to the palace. The first thing visible from the distance were the crucifixion trees, turned into what looked like giant's ladders by crosspieces nailed between them. Tom counted five bodies hung for display, but he knew that any number of headless and eviscerated cadavers lay about at the bases of the trees.

Tom had tried to get used to such sights in the short time he'd been here, but as they entered the courtyard of the palace, he found that he was badly shaken. Bodies were kept on display in every civilized country—he'd seen them in front of the doge's palace in Venice, in the market squares of the German towns he'd walked through on his way south from Bruges, in Constantinople, in Trebizond. Even in England the approaches to London Bridge, so he had heard, were decorated with the heads of traitors. But he had never seen carnage on such a scale as in Great Benin.

Urged on by the King's Boys, he passed through a gate framed by elephants' tusks and found himself inside a second court, big enough to hold several thousand people. It was bordered on one side by a long gallery decorated by a row of outsize brass heads, each one supporting an ivory tusk in a socket on the top. On the other side was a row of juju altars, raised clay platforms each bearing a crude mace for killing the victims. Tom tried not to look at the bodies that had been left lying about. The entire compound reeked of human blood.

He looked up at the main tower of the palace. It was about seventy feet high, with a sharp metal roof, and at its peak was the brass sculpture of a serpent, gazing downward at the Golgotha beneath. Tom's guards propelled him quickly through a brass door into a spacious audience hall. The far end of the hall was empty, except for an ivory couch that evidently served as a throne. Several hundred people, the majority of them nude, milled about in the other half of the chamber.

A naked man armed with a spatulate sword whose blade was riddled with holes, like a colander, came over to confer with the King's Boys about Tom's status. Tom, though he was able to communicate face to face in a rude fashion, still found it difficult to follow third-party conversations, but he gathered that as a first-time visitor to the court, who had not yet received the king's largesse, he was not permitted to wear clothes, even though he was technically a foreigner who had arrived in Benin already clad.

He shrugged and handed over his shirt, then stepped out of his trousers. It was no great loss; after a thousand miles of travel through the African jungle on foot and by canoe, the Chinese garments were falling apart. Then, at the armed man's insistence, he surrendered his loincloth, too. The clothes were borne off. Tom shifted his feet. It occurred to him that he'd had dreams like this.

After a long wait, a door at the far end of the hall opened and about thirty enormous King's Boys filed in, all of them unclothed. The one at the front carried a huge curved sword in a ritual position—held straight up in the right hand while the left hand supported the right elbow. Having made a fine entrance, the assembly spoiled the effect by crowding in a disorganized fashion into a space at the right of the throne. The bearer of the official cutlass took his place nearest to the throne.

Next came a parade of ten old men, bare above the waist but wearing bell-like skirts and stiffened petticoats below. These must all have been Big Men, because they wore high collars of coral, composed of many strands of beads. They placed themselves in an ascending array along the left-hand ramp leading to the dais.

A ripple of laughter went through the waiting crowd when the door opened again. Out came a random collection of dwarfs of varying types and deformities, two men leading leopards on chains, and finally a couple of bewildered-looking men who had no entertainment value that Tom could discern.

He nudged one of his guards. "Who are those last?"

The reply was a word he didn't know, so he asked again and this time got a pantomime of deafness. "The king likes to keep people like that around," he was told.

The ragtag troupe of court jesters took up a position in front of the throne and to one side, where the king could see them, and the eyes of the crowd fixed expectantly on the door.

The king—*Oba,* as he was styled in Benin—now made his appearance, supported on either side as if he were an invalid, though he was a powerful-looking man in his forties. For a crown he wore a large loaflike hat janglingly festooned with coral and gold ornaments. Like his nobles, he was bare to the waist, but he wore more bracelets and necklaces than anybody.

His attendants guided him solicitously to the ivory couch and seated him under its silk canopy. They fussed over his skirts until every drape and pleat was in place, then stepped back. The court ceremonies began.

Tom watched attentively, to be sure that he would do everything right when his time came. He was interested to discover that those who approached the king were expected to cover their faces and peep through their fingers, just as in the court of the Zamorin of Calicut. But where the Zamorin had not much stood on ceremony after that, petitioners of the *Oba* had to creep forward and grovel, touching their foreheads to the ground—though only once, not nine times as in the Ming court.

The first few interviews went very well. They were all naked men who, on arising, were given coral beads and anklets, and in the case of one who was awarded a three-strand necklace, a piece of cloth he was allowed to wrap around his waist on the spot.

But after these preliminary knightings, the throne was approached by a nervous man who had bad luck written all over him. When he raised his head, the king asked him a few questions in a benign voice. Tom thought he must have misheard. The only sense he could make out of it was that the king wanted to send him with a message to his father.

"Are you ready to go?" the king asked.

The man's face had a trapped expression. He rolled his eyes around and began to babble something or other.

The king cut him off. "Are you ready to go?" he repeated sternly.

The man's body sagged. "Yes, *Oba*," he said.

A member of the king's guard came forward with a peculiar instrument. Tom craned to see. The device looked like a brass tube with a metal knob sticking out of one end. The guard worked the knob back and forth a few times to make sure it was loose, and Tom saw a thick spike emerge from the other end of the tube. The guard put the tube on the kneeling man's head and struck the knob sharply with his fist. There was a sound like that of a nut being cracked, and the kneeling man keeled over sideways.

The king laughed uproariously. Two Ukoba dragged the

body to a juju altar at the side of the audience hall and dumped it unceremoniously there.

It went like that for the next hour—an alternation of honor awards and summary executions of unfortunate "messengers." The bodies piled up at the side of the hall, and an official gathered cupfuls of blood to sprinkle over the pile of coral necklaces the king was awarding. Evidently it was considered a form of good luck to do so.

When it was Tom's turn, he stepped forward without showing any hesitation. He sensed that it would be dangerous to seem unsure of himself. He covered his face with his fingers, as required, but he decided not to grovel. He stopped at the regulation distance from the throne and dipped one knee in a curtsy, as gentlemen did in Europe.

A gasp was heard from the courtiers, and the guards stirred uneasily, but the king took it in good humor. Someone whispered in the king's ear. "You are not an albino?" he asked.

"No," Tom said. "I am from a country in the north, where everyone is this color."

The king frowned in puzzlement, and again the attendant whispered in his ear. "To the north is the kingdom of Mali, and I have heard that the people of Mali are a normal color, like us. Are you a Malian?"

"No, Your Majesty, I come from a kingdom still farther north."

After another whisper, the king said, "It is told that a lighter-skinned people sometimes come to the kingdom of Mali in caravans of humped animals to buy slaves. Are you one of those?"

"No," Tom said. "Those sound like Arabs. They are the bitter enemies of my people, and we sometimes have wars with them."

"Too bad," said the king. "My *Ojomo* here has just suggested that if these slave-buying people ever decided to come this far south, we could make a nice profit selling people to them. What is your kingdom called?"

Tom drew a deep breath. "It's called Bristol, Your Majesty. It's extremely large and powerful, and it takes a thousand days to walk from one end of it to the other. I'll be glad to carry word of your friendship back with me."

"Hmmm," the king said. "Well, you belong to me now, so you'll have to stay here. I'm going to make you a two-string noble of the second class for the time being. When next I send for you, I'll give you clothes and a wife."

He beckoned with his finger and someone handed him a triple strand of coral beads. "More blood," the king said, and an attendant hurried forth with a cup and sprinkled a few drops over the necklace. Tom bowed his head, and the king pulled the necklace down over his ears, while two husky men fitted him out with coral bead anklets, lifting each leg in turn as if shoeing a horse.

Tom thanked the king and backed away in approved fashion, holding his hands over his face. He looked around for his warders but didn't see them. A new round of executions was starting at the other end of the hall, and he didn't feel like staying to watch. Nobody seemed to be paying special attention to him, and people were coming in and going out, so he drifted gradually to the entrance door, and the next time everybody was diverted by a skull cracking he departed.

He was congratulating himself as he reached the broad main avenue without company, but at that moment one of the pair of King's Boys appeared from nowhere and fell in step beside him.

"The *Oba* say I walk along with you so you don't get lost," said his unwelcome companion with a grin.

The trip back to his house through the thronged streets was the longest walk Tom had ever taken, and it was not because of his nudity. He kept thinking of the executioner with his brass punch and remembering what the king had said about sending for him again. He resisted the impulse to finger his tight collar of beads. He was a noble of Benin, it seemed, but that was no guarantee of anything. He had seen how easily nobles were dispatched. He grinned sourly to himself. Even if he got through the next summons without a hole in his skull, the alternative prospect was not terribly enticing—to be given a decoratively scarred local maiden for a wife and to be forbidden to leave this city of blood for the rest of his life.

He was passing one of Benin's horrors now, a corpse sitting in the neatly swept street with its hands tied to its ankles to keep it in an upright posture. He shuddered and walked faster.

To his relief, the King's Boy showed no inclination to hang around outside his door once he had delivered him.

Tom made a meal of some starchy stuff left over from the potful he had bought in the market the previous day and some warm millet beer. He managed to get it down—he could not have eaten meat even if he had been able to make himself go out into the street to buy some.

He waited until dark. The sounds of the city gradually subsided. The streets were pretty well deserted at night—people didn't like to go out for fear of meeting one of the roaming killing parties. That suited Tom fine. It would make things easier for him.

He thought over what the king had said about Arab slave traders farther north. Where there were Arab caravans, civilization was within eventual reach. He had been a caravan boy once—he could be one again.

How far could this kingdom of Mali be? A thousand miles? He had already come a thousand miles from the kingdom of the Congo, and he had discovered that there were people everywhere. You could usually get along with them, one way or another. They'd always feed you and help you on your way.

He stuck his head outside the door and found the north star, low on the horizon. It was a comfort to be able to see it again after its long disappearance. All he had to do was follow it to Europe.

He moved the conical juju fetish aside and dug up his possessions. The bag of gold and jewels was still there, undisturbed, along with the silk-wrapped maps. There was the spare pair of shoes for walking, but as for clothing, there was not even a loincloth. The handle of the three-pronged Chinese spear had broken off the last time he had hunted with it, but he could find a straight branch and whittle a new one later.

He stuffed everything into the sack along with the jewels. After some hesitation he added the little Venetian knife, though he didn't have a spare hand to carry a knife around and no clothing to tuck it into, and if he encountered an armed party from the palace, a little knife wasn't going to do him much good anyway.

He slung the sack over his shoulder and went out into the dark streets. He avoided the main avenue as much as possible and threaded his way through the side streets, staying close to the high clay walls. Once or twice he encountered other people at some distance, but they ran away from the sound of his footsteps.

At the outskirts of town he had to reenter the main thoroughfare. It was the only approach to the bridge across the stream that delineated the town's borders. He stopped at the corner and looked out both ways from behind the shelter of a wall. No one was in sight. His skin prickled. He thought he heard a sound behind him and looked around quickly, but he saw no one following him.

The horrors came thicker at the entrances to the city. Tom could smell death all around him, but a merciful darkness shrouded the details of the headless and rotting forms staked out beside the road. He made his way toward the bridge, hurrying his steps.

Too late he heard the running footsteps. He turned his head and saw the swift agile figure angling across the avenue to intercept him. Someone had been following him after all.

He made a dash for it, but his pursuer was there at the bridge ahead of him, blocking the way. Tom flailed to a wild stop, fighting for balance. He had time to see that it was the King's Boy who had been assigned to him, brandishing one of the perforated cutlasses.

"I saw you," the King's Boy grunted. "You were not supposed to leave the city."

His eye was on the sack Tom carried. He was probably counting up his loot, and that was what saved Tom. The riddled blade whistled down, its aim a little off. Tom ducked and got inside the swing. His hands, windmilling to keep him on his feet, encountered his assailant's coral necklace. Tom closed his fingers around it and yanked.

The string broke and beads scattered everywhere. Tom flung the rest of the necklace into the river.

He waited for the swing of the blade that would kill him, but it never came. The King's Boy's whole frame slumped in disgrace and despair, the sword hanging forgotten at his side.

"I am dead," he said simply.

Tom walked past him, across the bridge toward the jungle beyond. When he reached the other side he looked back. The man was still there, a statue of grief.

The constellation that the Middle Kingdom called the Big Basket pointed the way to England. Tom turned his back on Great Benin and followed the star north.

# CHAPTER 15

At first Inês thought she was still dreaming. A hand was moving on her breast and a body was pressed against hers. "Heitor," she murmured, and the hand closed roughly, hurting her in a way that Heitor never had.

Her eyes flew open and she saw the dark figure squatting over her, silhouetted against the bright square of moonlight coming through the open window. A curtain fluttered in the warm night breeze.

"Don't fight," a voice said, "or I'll kill you."

With the sudden strength of panic, she pushed the body away from her and rolled quickly off the bed. She scrambled to her feet and backed away, edging toward the door.

The intruder cursed gutterally and came after her. She saw that it was Lobo, naked below the waist. He seized her by the hair and put a knife to her throat. Inês made an involuntary gasp of terror. "Be quiet," Lobo said. "You don't want to wake your children, do you?" He grinned evilly. "Or maybe we should have them in to watch, to show them who their new *papai* is."

Inês went rigid at that, and Lobo said, "Very good. I'll be able to tell them you cooperated. I'll stay till noon and walk out picking my teeth. I'll say you cooked me a meal."

"Please, senhor," Inês said in a choked voice. "Leave here now. I'll give you everything I have."

"I'll have it all tomorrow anyway," he said. "When you report the rape, I'll be forced to marry you. Zarco's a stickler for justice. By vespers tomorrow we'll be husband and wife."

Despair washed over Inês like an icy flood. She was not too paralyzed by fear to recognize the truth of what Lobo was saying. She had seen it happen too many times before. Usually the woman herself, with no other recourse open to her, accepted the marriage—even insisted on it, but it was a recognized way for a man to get hold of a woman's property. There had been an awful case the year before. A widow who was eight months pregnant with the child of her late husband had been raped by a suitor who, with the help of armed friends, had broken into the house where she lived with her sister and brother-in-law's family. They had carried her off and returned her a few days later. She had lost the baby as a result of the rape, but the ipso facto marriage had been deemed legitimate. A woman, perhaps, had a slim chance of getting a rapist punished as a criminal if she were immediately to run naked into the street, screaming, and there were witnesses to go back into the house with her. But if she delayed as much as a half hour, she was judged to have been willing.

Through tears of rage and shame, she said, "Then I won't report it."

He only laughed at that. "It makes no difference. I'll spread it all over Funchal anyway. I'll say you squealed with pleasure once I got started. The neighbors will testify that I stayed all night."

He took the knife away from her throat and began to lift the light chemise she slept in. Inês kicked out at his ankle with her bare foot, and with a sob, tried to twist out of his grasp.

He cursed and hit her with his fist. She could taste salty blood filling her mouth. He cuffed her a couple of more times, then, holding her head up by the hair, drew the knife blade lightly across her throat. She could feel it cut, a thin burning line.

"Bitch," he said. "Hold still."

He stuck the knife in the belt he still was wearing and that had now slipped down over his hips, and, still holding her by the hair, ripped her chemise down the front. Backing her against the wall, he began the job of forcing her legs apart.

"Mamãe, I woke up."

The small voice made Lobo pause in his assault and turn his head. Inês froze. Beatriz was standing in the doorway. She was crying.

"Mamãe, I'm scared," Beatriz quavered. "I had a bad dream. Will you come and stay with me?"

Still locked upright with Lobo, his knee between her thighs, Inês forced her voice to absolute calmness. "Go back to your bed, *menina*. Stay with your sister. Mamãe will be there in a little while."

The little girl rubbed at her eyes with her fist. "All right, Mamãe," she said.

When she was gone, Lobo said, "Better and better. I'll tell them how you put the children to bed first."

He ripped the chemise entirely off her and tossed it away. He hit her again to stop her squirming and brought his face next to hers. She could smell rotten teeth and garlic. His knees still prying at her thighs, he rubbed himself against her. Something hard was digging into her abdomen—the handle of his knife.

She pushed at him with all her strength and snatched the knife from his belt. With a cry of anguish she plunged it into his naked belly once, twice.

He backed away from her with disbelief on his face. He was holding his hand over his belly. She saw a glistening loop of something try to ooze through his fingers.

"Bitch," he said hoarsely, and tumbled to the floor. Inês backed away, the knife still in her hand.

"Mamãe," came Beatriz's voice from the other room, "I'm scared."

Inês dropped the knife. Blindly, she groped for something to wipe her hands with. "Mamãe's coming," she said. "I'll be right there."


"Bring the murderess in now," Zarco said.

The faces of the members of the court turned toward the door. There were not many people present. Zarco had excluded the public because of the inflammatory nature of the case, and was holding the trial in a smaller chamber of his house. Still, there were a couple of dozen members of the higher *fidalguia* present who ought not, strictly speaking, to have been there, but who had wangled their way in because of their position.

Teixeira was not there to share the judges' dais this time. He had sent word back by the fast, twelve-oar longboat that Zarco had dispatched for him that he was unable to leave on such short notice because of some pressing business or other that had come up. But Zarco suspected that he simply wanted to avoid dealing with a touchy matter that hadn't, after all, taken place in his jurisdiction.

But he had Ruy Paes and Gonzalo Ayres Ferreira sitting with him, two worthy *fidalgos* from the first wave of colonization, and their presence would add sufficient weight to his decision. For spiritual guidance he had Father Jaime of his own church, Our Lady of the Flints, a lean, fierce young man of some style. There had been some who had argued for the pastor of his wife's church, Saint Catherine's, as a symbol of womanly mercy, but a murder that involved rape or an attempted rape was a serious matter—man's business.

Two armed squires brought the woman in between them. Zarco searched his memory. He had not seen her at the inquiry that had looked into the death of her husband a short time previously—her presence had not been thought necessary at the time—but he had noticed her often enough around Funchal in the past. She was a handsome woman, young to be a widow, with huge dark eyes in a face that had gone as white as flour. Her pallor showed ugly purple bruises on her cheek and a lower lip that was split and swollen. She had made an effort to dress neatly and comb her hair.

Zarco glanced down at the paper in front of him, the summary by his secretary. Her husband's name had been Honorato—Heitor Honorato. Her given name was Inês, but there was no record of a maiden name. She had been a prisoner in the first shipment of *degredados*. A bad one, evidently—the offense had been thievery. Good looks and presentability were no indication—you never could tell about these women.

"You may sit down," Zarco said.

He motioned to the squires, and they led the woman to the small bench that had been placed in front of the dais. Zarco noted with approval her fine trim figure. She sat with her spine stiff and her chin up, apprehensive but not cowed.

"You've been accused of killing the man, Lobo. You've admitted it, is that true?"

"Yes, Vossa Excelência," she said.

He was startled to hear the genteel accent; now he vaguely remembered the young girl at whose marriage he had officiated, and before that the frightened child he had interviewed in prison and for whom he had made an exception to his rule against thieves—clearly a mistake. Her accent had taken him by surprise then, too. He shifted uncomfortably in his high-backed chair. He had been prepared to be lenient with a cheap woman of the town or a peasant who knew no better, but now he became more stern.

"You don't deny that you stabbed him, and more than once?"

"No," she said in a whisper.

"Speak louder."

"No, Vossa Excelência."

Zarco nodded. "We've heard from your neighbor. You went to him with your children and asked him to take care of them. His wife took them into the house. He and some others who'd been awakened went back to your house with you and found the cadaver on the floor. There was a knife and some bloody garments you'd wiped your hands on. Do you confirm this?"

"Yes, Vossa Excelência."

Zarco saw the priest trying to catch his eye. He made his voice hard.

"You're aware, aren't you, that to kill someone is a mortal sin?"

"Yes," she said. A tear ran a path down the bruised cheek, but she made no effort to wipe it away.

Father Jaime leaned forward with the dark intensity that enlivened his sermons. "Did the man die with Christ's word on his lips?"

If anything, the woman's drained face became paler. "No, Padre," she said.

"Then you've done worse than commit murder, haven't you? You've condemned a soul to hell."

The woman's lip trembled. "Please, Padre . . . I'll pray for him. . . ."

"What was the last word you heard him utter?"

"I don't like to say," she said.

"Tell us!" the priest thundered, pleased with his effect.
She lowered her eyes. *"Cadela,"* she said.

A stir of disapproval went through the assembled gentlemen at hearing such language from a woman. It confirmed Zarco in his inclination to be severe.

"Why did you do it?" he said. "Was it revenge for the fact that Lobo killed your husband in a fight?"

"No!" she cried. "He broke in . . . he had a knife at my throat . . . he was trying to rape me . . . I was afraid . . . and then . . . and then I was afraid for my children. . . ."

It was Ferreira's turn to say something. He raised an eyebrow. "Perhaps," he drawled, "the fellow was just trying to claim his conjugal rights."

There was laughter from the *fidalgos,* and Ferreira went on with a smile, "A bit prematurely, I admit. But many fine marriages have been made that way."

Zarco, frowning at the levity, said, "That's a point. Wasn't Lobo a suitor of yours?"

"No," Inês said. "I told him to stop bothering me."

"You didn't encourage him?" Zarco said. "Lure him to your house?"

"No," Inês said. "I swear it."

Zarco spoke to the others. "This Lobo came to me and asked for permission to marry her. He said he wanted to make it up to her for killing her husband. I told him I had no objection, as long as he obtained her consent. And then I heard no more about it until today."

Ruy Paes said, "It's beginning to look more and more like a case of cold-blooded revenge." He turned a cold eye on Inês and bore down hard on her. "You say you were afraid. And yet you didn't scream, did you?"

"He . . . he had a knife at my throat. . . ." Her hand flew of its own accord to her neck.

"So you say. The fact remains that you didn't scream. The neighbors testified to that. No screams were heard. You don't deny it, do you?"

"No, senhor."

"And you took the trouble to wash and dress, and then to dress the children, before you went for help, didn't you? You thought it all out."

"No . . . yes . . ." She was confused. "I didn't want the children to be frightened . . . there was blood on me . . . and

I thought, if I had to go away and leave them with Senhora Paula across the road, I wanted them to look their best. . . ."

Paes sat back, satisfied. "It's clear that she was a cool one," he said to the others.

Zarco brooded over what he had heard. He had noticed the thin red line on the woman's neck before she covered it up. Of course, it didn't necessarily mean anything. She might have been scratched by a fingernail. There were no actual wounds. There were the bruises on her face—bad ones, admittedly—and the cut lip, but lots of women got knocked around by men, and took it. It didn't justify murder.

On the other hand, the woman seemed to have been a good wife and mother all these years. There had never been a hint of trouble until the fight between Lobo and her husband, and she had not been involved in that. Since the death of her husband, she had worked hard, building up the property. Through the wine lodge, she had helped bring income to the struggling colony.

He thought back to the frightened girl he had taken out of the prison in Lisbon. She had been petrified of him—he hadn't understood why. One of the hard cases, a gypsy *soldadeira*, had intervened in her behalf. The gypsy had become Morales's woman. She seemed to keep the old man happy. She was waiting outside now—the servants had told him she had made a fuss the previous night about taking food to the cowshed where the prisoner had been locked up. Zarco hadn't understood how she had gotten here from Machico so quickly, until someone told him that she had forced her way into the longboat he had sent for Teixeira.

His secretary was standing at his elbow with a paper. "Excuse me, Dom João," he said. "Here's the form of the petition to Lisbon that you asked for. There's no precedent for hanging a woman, but I suppose we could use the form for men."

His secretary was a canny one. He was reminding Zarco of what a mess it would be to turn this into a capital case. On the other hand, Lobo was already dead. A fine for attempted rape could easily be collected from his pitiful estate. It would be no trick at all; from all reports, Lobo had been a thoroughly bad actor, and it was on record that he had been a rapist and murderer in Portugal.

He studied the straight, slim figure before him, her hands folded in her lap, sitting with quiet dignity despite the ugly bruises and the badgering she had taken from Paes. Though she had lived the life of a peasant all these years, she had been born to the middle nobility at least—probably to an older family than his own.

On impulse he leaned forward and asked, "What was your family name?"

The question threw her into confusion. She stammered and hesitated, and finally said, *"Perdão, Vossa Excelência?"*

Zarco's secretary bent toward him again. "I found her marriage record, Dom João. She went by the name do Faro."

Zarco waved a hand impatiently. "Yes, yes, we're up to our ears with do Faros and de Taviras and de Sintras and Lisboas. The last place half of our *degredados* slept became their names. So you come from the vicinity of Faro, do you? What was your father's name?"

Her face turned a bright red, submerging the purple bruises. "Alves," she said.

"Alves," he mused. "One of the fine old names of the district. Was he any relation to Dom Martim Alves e de Aragão?"

She seemed ready to faint. "He was my father."

Zarco sat motionless. He remembered the glimpse of Dom Martim's family he'd had that time he had put in at Faro when they'd hunted bandits in the hills together; of his admiration for the qualities of the older man that had led to his enlisting him as *dispensero*. Until now he hadn't connected the woman in front of him with the bright and earnest little girl he'd teased in the orchard until the servant woman had called her away. Now he could see something of Dom Martim's features in the bruised and puffed face before him, sense something of Dom Martim's iron pride in her bearing.

"What is it, Dom João?" Ferreira said beside him.

Zarco brushed him off. "Dom Martim, my old shipmate?" he asked incredulously. "Who sailed with me to discover Porto Santo and Madeira?"

"Yes," she said.

The flush was fading, and she was regaining control of herself again.

Paes looked down his long nose at Zarco. "Oh, *that* Alves?"

"You should have told me," Zarco said.

She lowered her head. "I couldn't, senhor."

Father Jaime seemed about to say something, but a dangerous look from Zarco forestalled him. "Teixeira should be here now," Zarco said. "Alves would have been entitled to the same share as everyone else. He deserved it, after being cheated once, in the business of the rabbits. But he died too soon. The shares were redistributed."

"You can't undo that, Dom João," Paes said with a frown. "You were generous to the widow. Obtained her a pension."

Zarco said gently to Inês, "Is your mother still alive?"

"I don't know, senhor," she said.

"Just one thing. Did you take that handkerchief?"

She met his eyes steadily. "No, senhor. Not that it matters anymore."

Zarco turned to his colleagues. "It's clear that the woman was defending herself against an attack. She stabbed him with his own knife. We can see the marks on her face for ourselves. He came through the window in the middle of the night, after all. It's not as if he were invited. Don't you agree?"

Paes said to him, "What about the *fazenda*? That's a rich property to leave in the hands of a woman. We can see the trouble it caused. She should be married off."

"No one will bother her now," Zarco said. "We'll see to that. She's done very well with the property since her husband died. Let's give her a chance. She deserves to be left alone."


"A little better than beach roses this time, eh?" Baldaia said with a broad grin. He dropped to one knee in the sand to examine the tracks more closely.

The men from the shore party straggled to a halt, bunching up around him. They were all lightly armed as a precaution. Pedro had a sword that Baldaia had loaned him.

"Camel tracks," said one of the mates, an old soldier named Pinto who was a veteran of Prince Henry's Moorish campaigns. "Lots of them. And fresh. A large caravan passed by here not too long ago."

Involuntarily, some of the men scanned the horizon and toyed with the hilts of their swords.

"So," Baldaia said, getting up and dusting off his hose,

"the Moors come this far south. And what they trade for is farther south still."

"Slaves," Pinto suggested. "The black slaves that are seen in the Tunis markets."

"Or gold," Baldaia said. "The Moors have plenty of it."

Pedro bent for a better look and saw human footprints mixed with the camel tracks. Some were barefoot, some were shod.

"We might find a settlement of some sort within one or two days' sail south from here," he said. "People and fresh water can't be too far away, or it wouldn't have been possible for the makers of these tracks to exist in this hell. The distance we can cover in a few days by sea could take months on foot, and they couldn't carry so much water so far."

He looked back over his shoulder at the shallow cove where the ships were anchored. They'd named it the Angro dos Ruivos because of the fine catch of red mullet they'd had for breakfast. Baldaia's swift, tall-masted *barinel* was bigger than Eanes's *barcha*—Eanes was touchy about that, because his was supposed to be the flagship—though still not too large for rowing when it was in a tight spot. It was a fine ship to go exploring in. Pedro itched to be in it once more, running south, the red cross of Christ borne before him in the billowing canvas. They had come fifty leagues beyond Cape Bojador this time, and Eanes was getting fidgety. Pedro saw no point in being satisfied with more desert, camel tracks or not, and he knew Baldaia felt the same way.

Some distance away, Eanes had intersected the tracks with a party of his own men, and he followed the line of churned-up sand until he reached Baldaia. He took off his broad-brimmed hat and fanned himself with it; under this scorching sun, even he was not willing to cook his brains in a steel helmet.

"Too bad we missed them, Dom Afonso," he said heartily. "A little skirmish would have been good exercise, and perhaps we might have captured one or two to take back to Prince Henry for questioning."

"By the look of it, they outnumbered us many times over, so perhaps it's just as well," Baldaia said dryly. "As for captives, I don't doubt we'll have another chance farther south."

Eanes shifted his feet like a large boy. "We've fulfilled Dom Henrique's commission—we've gone another fifty leagues and seen what lies beyond Bojador. We ought to get the news to the infante without delay, not go on wild goose chases. Who knows how far this cursed sand extends? It may go on forever."

"It would be a pity to turn back so soon," Baldaia said, "when we may be on the verge of discovering some inhabited region."

"That's why the infante sent along a *barinel*," Eanes insisted stubbornly. "To get word back fast."

Pedro listened with dismay. It was not going as planned. Baldaia had been sent to stiffen Eanes, to make sure he didn't get cold feet. Both Baldaia and Eanes knew that it was a sop to Eanes's pride to say that Baldaia was there as a messenger, and it rankled. But if Eanes chose to dig in his heels, there was nothing Baldaia could do except to hope that Eanes might go on a little way by himself after all.

"What will you take the infante this time, Dom Gil?" Baldaia joked. "It's a little hard to pack up a footprint in a barrel. Perhaps a sample of camel dung might do."

He had gone too far. Eanes was not the brainiest of men, but he knew when he was being made fun of. His sunburned face got redder and his fingers twitched in the vicinity of the handle of his big battle sword. Baldaia was in a cold fury himself, though he had tried not to show it. He met Eanes's glare with a steady, narrow gaze, his own hand hovering close to the hilt of his weapon.

The men of the two parties looked on without saying anything. Sailors learned to keep their mouths shut. They were all plain men. They'd been getting along together all right.

Pedro stepped between the two captains. A fight between *fidalgos* was the last thing the expedition needed. "*Cavaleiros,*" he said, "perhaps one ship could lay over here a day or two while the other sniffs out the coast for a few leagues more. Then, if the second ship is delayed getting back, the first ship can make all haste to Sagres."

The ship that went on, he hoped, would be the *barinel*. Once out of Eanes's sight, Baldaia would easily be persuaded to take another large bite out of the world.

But Eanes was not deceived. Whatever one thought of his intelligence, he was shrewd enough to see what Pedro was trying to do. He was not about to allow Baldaia to steal a march on him and negate the clear claim he had to another fifty leagues of achievement.

"No," he said. "We've done well, by God. Dom Afonso,

get ready to hoist sail. I'll follow you north as closely as I can. We'll proceed by the *volto do mar*, with a long tack to the northwest, and if I lose sight of you, we can meet in Madeira for the final leg home."

Baldaia shrugged gracefully. "Just as you say, Dom Gil."

The tension went out of the watching men. Nobody was going to have to take sides after all.

Pedro's mouth was set in a grim line. Eanes's pilot was fairly good, and understood the *volto do mar* maneuver of proceeding north by long boards in alternate directions, but with the *barinel's* superior speed, Pedro could easily contrive to lose him some dark night. Let Gil Eanes find his own way home. There was nothing in the world that would ever make him set foot on Madeira again.

The *Cog Anne* out of Bristol looked out of place in the Algerian harbor amidst all the Moorish ships, the long low Genoese galleys tied up beside it, and the great Venetian merchantmen from the Galley of Barbary. But its captain had been greatly daring.

Having called at the ports of Lisbon, Huelva, and Cadiz with a cargo of tin, hides, and good English dyed cloth, and taken on a cargo of Spanish wine, he still had space in his hold. He had decided to risk a dash through the Strait of Gibraltar, despite the standing threat of the Genoese to sink any English ship they found in the Mediterranean and the equal danger of attack from Moorish corsairs or Venetian galleys. Moorish leather brought a fine price in England, and he had thought at first only to obtain what he could at the Granadan port of Almeria.

But then the Moorish traders at Almeria had told him about the caravans that now came into the Algerian port of Oran, a bare day's sail across the narrow part of the Mediterranean if you had a good wind behind you. Ever since the fanatical Portuguese Prince Henry and his brothers had captured the rich prize of Ceuta some twenty years before and turned it into a Christian city, the caravans from the south that once had made Ceuta their terminus now ended their journey at Oran or Tangier. These were caravans of Berbers and other half-civilized men of the *bled es siba*, the lawless lands, a talkative Granadan merchant explained, but they regularly braved the fearful Sahara and brought back

spices, gold, ivory, and slaves from the fringes of the unknown land beyond.

It was a tempting thought to the *Cog Anne*'s captain—a
cargo of spices or other precious merchandise without having to go through a middleman and pay through the nose.
The Genoese and Venetians wanted to keep it all to themselves, but by the rood, an Englishman had the right to sail
anywhere on God's oceans!

The *Cog Anne*'s mate was nervous. He didn't like it at all,
being hemmed in here in an alien harbor, surrounded by enemy races and, still worse, men who called themselves
Christians but who preyed on their fellow believers. The
Moorish authorities didn't allow Christian feuds in their own
territory—otherwise the Genoese and Venetians would be at
each other's throats. But once outside Algerian territorial
waters, the *Cog Anne* would be fair game—if they caught up
with her.

They would slip out after dark. The tide turned at matins,
and they could float out on the ebb without alerting anybody by raising sail. Once clear, the longboat, with muffled
oars, could kedge her into the roadstead.

The *Cog Anne* had loaded up on pepper, oil, ivory, and
silk, though not without difficulty. The Venetians were having a price war with Barbary, and though the price of pepper had plummeted for them, the Oran authorities were
inventive in the matter of fees, duties, and other charges for
everybody else. Every thief, confidence man, and shady op-
erator in Oran had approached the anchored ship with their
deals and bargains, most of them illegal. The captain had reacted with extreme caution; he'd seen the human skins
hanging from the city walls as a warning. And so he was especially leary of those who purported to deal directly with
caravan masters without first going through customs.

A caravan was going past on the quayside now. It was an
exotic sight—the huge snorting beasts with stilt legs and
necks like snakes, the swathed men leading them, the bundles of elephant tusks lashed to humps, the lines of black
slaves roped together.

One of the robed Arabs had stopped to study the English
ship. It must have been an unusual sight to him, with its
high curving bow and stern like a crescent moon, towering
over the other ships tied up to the quay, even the much
larger but lower Venetian great galleys.

The caravan was passing him by; the fellow would have to run to catch up to his place in it. But he didn't. Instead he hitched up his robes and headed purposefully toward the ship.

The mate became wary. He had learned to be mistrustful of the natives who came poking and sneaking around the *Cog Anne*. They always meant trouble. They either had some dubious deal to offer, or they claimed to be some sort of official and demanded a bribe, or they just wanted to get aboard the ship to look for something loose to steal. The captain had caught a thief red-handed only that morning, but instead of giving him a drubbing and throwing him overboard, he had simply chased him away. A Christian had to tread lightly in a Saracen port; even a thief could appeal to the authorities against infidels.

"See what he wants, Master William," the captain said.

The mate planted himself at the head of the gangplank and watched the Arab as he approached. He little liked what he saw and liked it less when the whoreson stopped at the bottom of the gangplank, and he saw him close up.

The mate looked him over. He was the scruffiest sort of Saracen knave—with tattered, grease-stained robes, a face mottled with the ingrained dirt of ages, his eyebrows blackened by the soot of a thousand camel-dung campfires.

And then the mate got a surprise as the fellow lifted his shrouded head and stared him full in the face out of a pair of bright-blue eyes. Just as the mate was reminding himself that many Saracens, particularly the kind called Berbers, had blue eyes and blond hair, the scurvy apparition spoke.

"What ship is this?" he said in accents of purest Wessex.

The mate clamped his jaw shut with an effort. "The *Cog Anne* out of Bristol," he said before he could think.

"Then you won't have any objection to my coming aboard," the fellow said. "I'm from Bristol myself."

He pushed his way past the mate, who was too surprised to block his way. He seemed anxious to be out of sight of the passing caravan.

"What's this, Master William?" the captain said, coming around from the other side.

"He says he's an Englishman, Captain," the mate replied.

"Tom o' Bristol," the man in nomad's robes put in. "God's blood, it's good to hear English spoken! I haven't seen an English face for yfere these fifteen years."

"Tom o' Bristol, is it?" the captain said sourly. "You look like a gynne rascal to me. What are you doing among the Moors?"

"I've been to Cathay and back," the visitor said. "I've sailed, ridden, and walked for nigh two years to get this far."

"A lying babelavaunte as well as a renegade," the captain said. "Well, what do you want here, Tom o' Bristol, if that's your name?"

"Why soth," the fellow said, as bold as a lord, "I want you to take me back to England with you."

"Do you now?" the captain said with scornful amusement. "We have all the hands we need, in case you were planning to work your way back. And our paying passengers, when we take them, pay mekyl wele for the privilege. So why should we take a lowe gadling like you?"

"I'll pay for it."

The captain looked him up and down, saw the tattered castoff of a robe, the grimy face. All the possessions he had in the world were probably in the gunnysack he had tied to his waist cord.

"You? How?"

"With this."

From under the greasy robes he extracted a ruby the size of a thumb joint. The captain was no expert, but even he could see that it was worth the passage price of an entire shipload of spring pilgrims, twice over.

"All right, Tom o' Bristol," he sighed. "To Bristol ye go."


"We lost him somewhere west of the Canaries," Baldaia said with a sidelong glance at Pedro. "He's probably laying over at Madeira for a few days. I imagine he'll arrive here at Sagres before too long."

They were closeted with Prince Henry in his private chamber. When the infante had heard of their arrival, he had sent his secretary to conduct them there to wait for him rather than receiving them in the public audience hall. He wanted them to himself before he gave the news to the world.

"Sim, sim," Prince Henry said distractedly. His tone suggested that he wasn't much interested in the present whereabouts of Gil Eanes. "When he arrives in port, we'll receive him with all honors."

He returned to the subject at hand. "You say the foot-prints were both of men shod and unshod?"

"And camels," Baldaia amplified.

"Two kinds of men, then?" the prince mused.

"It's possible," Baldaia said.

"But many men and animals—not just a few who mayhap stopped for the night and trod the area around?"

"No," Baldaia said after some thought. "In that case we might have found traces of a campfire, trash left behind—even if only a few poor scraps and leavings. The footprints didn't mill around. They were going somewhere.

The familiar gleam of intellectual excitement lit the infante's eyes. He clasped his hands behind his back and began to pace.

"It's apparent that some populated region cannot be far from there," he said with mounting zest. "It may be that they were men on their way to some seaport with goods to trade—a seaport where we ourselves might anchor safely. . . ."

While Prince Henry paced, Pedro unabashedly let his gaze wander around the sanctum. Its clutter was at odds with Henry's austere habits. It was a rat's nest of things that had caught his fancy and then had been left lying around in no particular order. There were maps, Moorish astrolabes, an armillary sphere, odd instruments that no doubt had been fashioned for him by Jaime of Majorca. There were many religious articles as well—reliquaries, a worn Psalter, a plain crucifix carved of wood, the blood-encrusted scourge that had so frightened Pedro as a boy. The famous sword that Prince Henry's mother had given him with her death-bed command to conquer Ceuta was enshrined in a wall niche.

But what caught Pedro's eye was a wooden ship model ly-ing on a trestle table in the midst of an untidy jumble of working sketches and carved templates. The model was un-finished and bore chalk lines where Henry had tried to show the shipwrights how he wanted the hull shape modi-fied. It was something like a *não* but with cleaner lines and without the pronounced upward curve at the bow. After a moment Pedro could see why. The mainmast was stepped far forward and was raked in a manner that could only mean that it was intended to carry the oversize spar of a lateen rig, like an Arab dhow. The unobstructed bow would allow the heel of the spar to swing at a slant.

Pedro admired the idea. It was a new kind of ship—one that combined the characteristics of the kind of European ships that sailed the open ocean and the Arab vessels that were so well adapted to coasting. It would make the perfect ship to go exploring in.

Prince Henry was finished with his pacing. He turned to face Pedro and Baldaia, the long jaw he had inherited from his Lancastrian grandfather set in a resolute line.

"There are still some months for sailing left in the year. Therefore I'll send you back again as soon as a ship can be outfitted. You'll take horses with you this time. Make the farthest advance you can and try to bring me news of these people whose footprints you saw. Capture one of them if you can. It would be no small thing to me to have some man to tell me of this land."

Baldaia exchanged a glance of triumph with Pedro. "Shall we wait for Gil Eanes, Dom Henrique?" he asked.

The infante's tone was dry. "Dom Gil has earned his reward. I'll see that he's not disappointed. Yours can be richer still."

# CHAPTER 16

Walversham Manor loomed up ahead of him like a male-
diction in stone. Tom reined in his horse and sighed. He had
no stomach for the piece of business ahead of him, but it
had to be done. He gave the horse a slap on the rump and
rode on.

The day was gray with a hint of rain still in it. Tom drew
his cloak more closely against the damp. He could smell salt
in the air. It would be time for high tide about now at
Avonmouth, where the waters of Bristol Channel invaded
the river twice a day. The seagulls had come far inland in
search of food. Tom could see a noisy flock of them in a
stubbled field, fighting over something they had found.

The demense had shrunk considerably since Tom was a
boy. Sir Eustace still ploughed a few acres around the
manorhouse to keep up appearances, but now he had to pay
for the labor. The villeins who had once been bound to such
service had fled to seek employment in the cloth trade or to
begin life anew as copyholders of some scrap of land in a
place where no one knew their past, and where they were
out of Sir Eustace's grasp. A score of sorry strip-holdings
were still tilled by a shabby collection of money-rent tenants, but Sir Eustace made a poor landlord, squeezing them
so hard for all sorts of questionable servile dues that they
could not prosper and neither could he prosper with them.
As he had ridden toward the demense, Tom had seen the re-

sults in the form of hundreds of acres returning to tangle or wood.

The ugly gray jumble of stone that was the manorhouse had been partially rebuilt in the new style with chimneys and family apartments and glass windows facing outward in place of arrow slits. It could never have been defended.

Tom rattled over a drawbridge that had rusted in place and that never would be raised again. Vines grew along the chains, and the drained moat was overgrown with grass.

"My lord is out," said the warder at the gate. "He said you was to wait for him in the great hall."

Tom found his own way there. Sir Eustace kept a mean household with few servants. A slovenly churl took his horse from him at the courtyard trance, and Tom showed himself inside.

No fire had been laid in the great hall, and no one came to see to his comfort. Sir Eustace was not missing the opportunity to put Tom in his place.

The hall was a bleak and cheerless expanse with little to relieve its bareness but its wainscotting and the heavy oak trestle tables that were now pushed against the walls. Underfoot, half hidden by scattered straw, were a number of threadbare carpets that had once been part of someone's plunder from France. Tom sat down on a bench. A lethargic old hound with its ribs showing was his only company.

He had been left sitting in the great hall for no more than five minutes before Margery's tirewoman, a pinchfaced spinster named Edilda, appeared. Obviously it had all been arranged.

"My mistress would speak to you," she said with a sniff of disapproval.

"Then I nedes must obey," he said gallantly, and rose to his feet.

She sniffed once more at him and turned to lead the way. Tom was sorely tempted to give her a surprise and pinch the spare buttocks, but that would never do. He composed himself to a proper solemnity and followed.

Margery was sitting by one of the diamond-paned windows that passed a weak light into the family rooms above the hall. She raised her face at his footstep. The tip of her long nose was red. Walversham Manor was drafty. Tom had never seen her when she didn't have the sniffles.

"Master Giles!" she cried in assumed consternation, as if

she herself had not sent for him. Her rather large hands fluttered with their usual awkwardness. "My father is not here."

The tirewoman, in the meantime, had ostentatiously plunked herself down on a stool across the room and taken up her sewing. She would not be pried away from it until he left, he knew.

"I'm early," Tom said with a smile. "I could not think of a fairer way to spend the time but with you."

He made a leg and swept off his hat. He cut a gaudy figure in his new doublet and parti-colored hose. He knew it wasn't what a sober country gentleman should wear, but he was never able to resist indulging himself. He told himself that he would tone it down when he had settled himself in his fine new house.

"I saw you riding up," she said guilelessly, becoming flustered as she realized she had punctured her little charade of surprise.

Tom rescued her with blandness. "It's a pretty enough day for riding, as long as the rain holds off," he said. " 'Tis scathe I didn't meet my lord on the way. Does he ryden ferre to-day?"

"He's gone with the reeve and bailiff to collect heriot. One of his tenants died yestreen, and he had to make haste to get there before the widow hid the best beasts."

"Oh," Tom said noncommittally. Sir Eustace, strictly speaking, was not entitled to claim his manorial prerogatives from his money-rent tenants. "I suppose he moot watch the villeins closely."

"Father says the tenants are a wicked lot," she responded earnestly. "They're always trying to conceal a part of their harvest, or gather firewood where they're not supposed to, or avoid paying the marriage fine. He says the world turneth on its head when folk like that eat wheaten bread and wish to dress like their betters."

She blushed as she suddenly remembered that Tom was a weaver's son, as no doubt her father reminded her daily.

"In Cathay," he said, "the peasants eat wheaten flour every day, though as bread is not known to them, they eat it in the form of long ribbons called *mein-tyow*, which they lift to the mouth with a pair of wooden sticks. As for clothing, even the greatest lords must wear robes of a particular color that is prescribed for them and embroidered with particular designs."

Margery's eyes shone as he talked. Tom was gratified in spite of himself. No one else in Bristol or its environs believed that he had been to far Cathay, despite his great wealth. It was indisputable that he had been *somewhere* in the East; his Chinese jewels were proof enough of that. But at best people were willing to credit him with having reached Antioch or Jerusalem and having stolen or traded for his baubles there.

Warmed by her rapt attention, Tom spun out his eastern tales at length. He told her of the splendors of the Forbidden City, the grandeur of the Dragon Throne, the immense size of the Middle Kingdom and the numbers of its people. Margery pressed him for details about the women—what they looked like, how they dressed, the lives they led.

"The ladies of rank adorn themselves much with combs and head ornaments, and lacquer their hair into fantastical shapes," he said, obliging her. "They pencil their eyebrows and paint their faces and their fingernails, and they wear the finest silks. Their robes are like the robes of men, except that they are fastened on the left instead of the right. They may not lift a finger but spend their time on parlor games and amusements."

Margery was entranced, but Tom grew depressed as he spoke. The talk of the Ming realm's ladies reminded him of Lan-ying. His mouth went dry with a sudden sense of loss. There would be a child by now—perhaps a son, as she had so confidently expected. Tom thought of her fragile beauty, her luminous complexion like a fine porcelain teacup with the light shining through it, her total devotion to pleasing him, her skills on the mat. He could not help contrasting her and his other concubines with poor, clumsy Margery with her large hands and feet, her winter-chapped face and reddened nose. Margery would be worth a tumble, he guessed—despite her priggish upbringing, there was an eagerness of the flesh beyond her awkwardness. She was, Tom thought, as ready for release as a drawn bow.

He could have her any time he wanted, he knew. He had only to bear her away whenever he was willing to face the consequences. Sir Eustace, whatever noise he would make about it, would be glad to get rid of her without having to pay a dowry—and to have a rich son-in-law whose coffers he could tap. Tom could have the piece of property he had come here today to buy and pass it on to a son complete with manorial rights that would come through Margery.

But the price was too high. She would cling, he guessed, and eventually try to domineer. Her father's Norman strain was too strong in her. It would be better to buy the property for money and allow Sir Eustace to cheat him.

"My lord cometh," the tirewoman said without stirring from her spot. Margery flushed and became all hands. Tom went to the window and peered past her. Three horsemen were coming over the drawbridge at a walking pace, leading a cow. Tom recognized Sir Eustace's bony form sitting stiff and straight in the saddle. The other two were Black Rob, the bailiff, and Hodge Parys, the reeve. They'd collected the death duty, and a poor enough animal it looked.

"I'll take me down to the great hall," Tom said. He smiled again at Margery. "Until eft," he said.

"Until eft," she said weakly.

Tom made his way down the stone stairs and was waiting on his same bench when Sir Eustace and his men jangled in. Sir Eustace shouted, "A posset, a posset!" at the walls and sprawled in the hall's only chair with his legs stretched out. He gave Tom an indifferent glance and shouted again, "God's wounds, where's my posset?"

A lackey came running in from the undercroft and knelt in front of the chair to help Sir Eustace off with his boots. The first boot got momentarily stuck while he was pulling it off, and Sir Eustace took a swipe at his servant's head, but the lackey dodged it and got the boot off all the way. There must already have been ale and milk heating in the kitchens because it was only a few minutes later when another servant shuffled in with a tray. There was a steaming posset for Sir Eustace and mugs of ale for Black Rob and the reeve, but Sir Eustace did not offer Tom any refreshment.

"Well, sir teller of tales, what have you come for this time?" Sir Eustace rasped.

Tom refused to be baited. "If you remember, my lord," he said, "we agreed to discuss your selling of the Perry Hill field that abuts the land at Crocken on which my house stands."

"Agreed?" roared Sir Eustace. "Lythe to the impudent fellawe! I agreed to nothing!"

Black Rob and Hodge added their own fierce glares to that of their master. Tom smiled pleasantly back at them.

"The land's worthless to you, my lord," Tom said, "bounded as it is by common lands and the freeholds of franklins. It's gone back to tangle, and no tenant will ever be found to farm it. The peasants take firewood from it as they please, and it is too far from your other properties for Hodge Parys to keep an eye on it for you. Yet it would round off my property nicely and bring my land to the king's road, and for that I would pay a good price."

Hodge Parys growled, "Don't listen to the lesynge carl, my lord. I ride out to the Perry Hill field three times a week at the least."

"And neglect my lord's other properties while you're doing it," Tom said.

Hodge Parys half rose from his bench, his hand tightening around the hilt of his dagger, but a negligent wave of Sir Eustace's hand sat him down again.

"So," Sir Eustace said with an unpleasant smile, "the cackling vavasor wishes to set himself up as a gentleman, and sit in that heap of brick he's built for himself as if he were a parfit gentil lordling? Next you'll want a lady and an heir. But ye're a weaver's get, Tom o' the loom, and nane but a weaver's get will ever issue from the shriveled coillons that swing between thy legs."

Tom held his hot anger in check. Sir Eustace's day was passing, and that made his contempt easier to bear.

"Think on it, my lord," he said. "The land is not worth a penny a year to you in livelode. And yet if you were to sell it, it would yield the value of twenty years' rents to you at once."

Sir Eustace scowled from the soreness of the nerve that Tom had touched. He sorely needed ready cash; he was deep in debt to Italian moneylenders, and he had already diminished his estates by several hundred acres by selling choice income-producing land to wealthy Bristol merchants who also wanted country houses.

He leaned forward in his chair, his greasy locks dangling, and almost spat the words:

"I'll have eight hundred marks for it."

It was five times what the property was worth. Tom smiled thinly and rose to his feet. "I'll think on it," he said.

As he rode out across the rotting drawbridge there was a sour taste in his mouth. The fury was a cold indigestible lump within him. He would have the land, and he would have Margery too, he decided.

He would come back on the morrow and give himself the satisfaction of paying Sir Eustace his eight hundred marks, without attempting to bargain him down. He'd let Sir Eustace gloat about that—and welcome to it. Sooner or later Sir Eustace would need money again, and the way the manor was falling apart, it would be sooner.

And that was when, Tom thought, he'd take Margery—not run off with her to mumble a few words in front of a hedge-priest and force Sir Eustace to swallow it later. He'd have her to wife at Saint Mary Redcliffe for all Bristol to see, let Sir Eustace grind his teeth as he may. And he'd force the settlement of a fine piece of property on Margery, jointure with inheritable privileges of livelode. And then, to all intents and purposes, Tom would be a gentleman.

He had what he had always dreamed about when he was a ragged starveling lad under the thumb of Master Philpot. He wondered why he didn't feel good about it.


Two hours at an easy gait brought him to his new-bought manor across the Avon above Redcliffe. It was not of brick, as Sir Eustace had alleged, but was timber-framed, though Tom was adding a wing in brick, still unfinished. He had chosen the site because he could look out over the Frome and the Avon, see the masts of the ships anchored amid the spires of Bristol, and watch downriver to see the approach of ships coming from foreign parts.

It was drafty and uncomfortable, and there were too many servants running about the place, but that didn't matter. Here, gentleman or not, he lived like an esquire and had all that his money would buy him.

He might have had a town house in Bristol, too, and perhaps some day he would, but for now he preferred not to be confronted by daily reminders of his boyhood servitude. He had found, when he returned to Bristol, that Master Philpot had been dead these ten years or more. The old charges against Tom were forgotten, and Mistress Eglantine would not have wished to revive them. She would not want to set tongues wagging in Bristol again about her involvement with a scullery lad. There had been enough gossip about journeymen and apprentices since Master Philpot had died.

Mistress Eglantine had married one of the apprentices who used to sleep under the roof, a silly fode named Snayth with a horse's face and pintle to match, whom Tom remembered well. Tom had seen him since around the streets of Bristol, giving himself airs. Mistress Eglantine gave him money for his fripperies and amusements, but otherwise she held the reins closely. Tom had seen her in Bristol as well. She had grown fat, with a great overflowing bosom spilling from the square neck of her gown, but she had dyed her hair and colored her cheeks to make herself look like a young girl, and she was dressed like a duchess, with a train and overlong sleeves and a steeple tottering on her head. She had given him a sidelong look in his own finery, and Tom thought she knew who he was. She would have heard that he was back in Bristol, of course, and the stories of his wealth.

Tom's father and mother were both dead; he had missed seeing them by only a year or two. A minor outbreak of the plague had carried Jack Giles off two summers since. There had been plague in London that year, and it was thought that it had been brought to Bristol by a traveling wool merchant. Tom's mother had not survived the bitterly cold winter that had followed, a hard freeze that had begun in early December and caused many in Bristol and Redcliffe to die. Tom's one regret was that he had not been able to return in time to elevate them to a life of comfort. He had searched out what brothers and sisters of his still remained in the vicinity of Bristol or Redcliffe. The four oldest brothers who had been well apprenticed were now prosperous and did not need him; they had been embarrassed by what they viewed as his pretensions, and they avoided him now. Of the other brothers—those who had not died or run off to sea—there were only two, both doing poorly as day laborers hired at the market cross. Tom had set Geoffrey up in a small freehold of his own, and he was on his way to being a successful member of the yeomanry. It was no use buying a farm for poor Hal, though—he could never have managed it. Tom had instructed his steward, Hugh, to pay out regularly the small sums that would keep Hal comfortably in the cottage of an elderly couple who would look after his needs. The sums were kept small enough so that Hal would not be taken advantage of but large enough so that he would never want for anything. Three of Tom's four sisters were married. One was the wife of a rich franklin who did not want anything to do with Tom. Tom had helped the husbands of the other two out; they were overawed by him, and he did not impose on them by visits. For his fourth sister, Alice, Tom provided a dowry for Christ and saw her settled with the good nuns of Wrington. For better or for worse, Jack Giles's brood was taken care of, and if Tom thought of it at all, he thought that perhaps now his mother could rest in peace.

A fire was waiting for him, but Hugh, his steward, did not give him much time to enjoy it. "If it please you, sir, the Flemish masons come tomorrow and await your instructions. And in the matter of the north acres, I have a yeoman of the neighborhood who will plough and sow them with his oxen, but thinking you rich and careless of money, he asks too much. I ask your leave to put him off till he thinks better of it. And the accounts—they must be gone over tomorrow at the latest. I've had them ready for you these fele days."

"Do what you will, Hugh," Tom said. "You know you will anyway, and a better job of it you'll make than I would."

"Yes, sir. And the servants—are they to have new vestments at Michaelmas, when you gave them each a shilling at last quarter day? I fear you are too generous, right worshipful sir."

Tom looked at Hugh's attentive, hovering face and said peevishly, "The devil take it, you do what you think best. How did I ever get so many servants anyway?"

"You do not have too many, your mastership. My last gentleman had half the hyne again as you, and yet his house was no meete to yours." He began ticking off a list on his fingers. "You must have a sewer to see to your dishes, a panter to manage the trenchers and bread, a butler for your ale, a wardrober for your clothes. You must have a bailiff, grooms, groundsmen. You must have a cook, a confectioner, scullions. . . ."

"All right, all right!" Tom said. Then, defiantly, "They shall have their vestments at Michaelmas and a shilling, too!"

"Just as you say, master," Hugh said reproachfully. "Will you have your dinner now? There's a gilded fish, venison, boar's meat with mustard, and a subtlety in the shape of a shepherdess leading a lamb."

He beamed at Tom.

"I won't sit at table and have a parade march round me," Tom said. "Bring me a joint, a loaf, and a mug of ale here by the fire."

"I'll tell them in the kitchen," Hugh said in a voice that was stiff with disapproval. He walked away with his nose in the air.

The food was brought, and Tom sat by the fire and gnawed at the meat and bread without appetite. He called for more ale. He could not understand why this black pall of dissatisfaction had settled over him. He had the piece of land he had set out this morning to acquire—or would have it on the morrow. The daughter of a knight was his for the taking. He had a house worthy of an esquire, an army of servants at his beck, and the wealth of a duke's ransom safely salted away among the Italian bankers in London. Why was he not happier?

He got up and walked over to the window. The panes were of clear glass such as was beginning to be used in the mansions of great merchants and Bristol's new aristocracy of Merchant Adventurers; it was still rare enough so that those who had both town and country houses often took the windows with them when they moved their households.

Tom looked through the clear pane at the Avon. He could make out the sail of a ship threading its way up the river. It was either an English ship or a Portuguese; the cross of Saint George was the same as the cross of the Order of Christ. The sight of it gave him a thirst for foreign parts. These days he could only satisfy it by frequenting waterfront taverns and listening to the talk of sailors.

He tried to shake off the feeling. It made no sense. He had traveled farther than any mariner to be found in the dives of Bristol town—farther than any man in England, even if no one believed him. He might very well be the only European to have reached far Cathay since the days of Marco Polo—unless Conti had gotten there after all—and he was the only man alive to know the true shape of Africa.

It was daft to be restless again. He had done his traveling—more even than he could have imagined as a skinny boy haunting the Bristol docks. Now he was home from the sea, to travel no more. It was his time to settle, to grow his roots.

He resisted as long as he could, then got his cloak from the hook by the fire. Hugh gave him a morose look, knowing his habits but not daring to ask where he was going, and at last contented himself with saying, "The accounts, Master Tom."

"The accounts be damned," Tom said. "Is my money to own me, then?"

The day had cleared after all, and Tom felt better. He had the groom saddle the palfrey for him again. There was plenty of money in his purse; he would sup in Bristol if he felt like it, and let Hugh cluck about the low company he kept.

The Dolphin, on Saint Nicholas's Back at the corner opposite the loading crane, was warm, full of people, and noisy, as usual. Tom was conscious of a general scrutiny as he pushed his way through the door from Crane Lane. The regulars knew he was always good for a drink.

"What will it be, squire?" asked Joseph, the host, hurrying to him at once.

"Don't call me squire," Tom said. "I'm no more a squire than you're a saint."

"Just as you say, Master Tom," said the tavernkeeper, continuing to fawn.

"The devil take it," Tom said. "Bring me a tankard of ale. What ships are in today?"

"There's a Janney galley with a cargo of green ginger, sulphur, and sugar candy." The tavernkeeper indicated a table where a half-dozen Genoese sailors in striped smocks sat over cups of the Dolphin's cheap red wine. "There was a bit of excitement this morning. One of the Turks they keep chained to the oars broke loose and got all the way to the Frome Bridge before they caught him. They dragged him back to their stinking ship for a flogging. You could hear him bellowing for near a half hour before the sounds stopped." He cocked his head in inquiry. "You might want to talk to them—you understand their jabber, don't you?"

Tom would have been interested in talking to the Turk—he might have had a tale to tell—but the Janney sailors would have nothing to offer but boring accounts of their coastwise stops and the profits they made at each. They would be vying with one another to sell him trinkets from their personal trading chests, and they would whine at him until he bought something.

"Maybe later," he said.

"There was an Icelander here, smelling of dried fish," the landlord said doubtfully. "He came in with some sailors from the *Mary and John*—begged passage because he said he always wanted to see this place called Bristol where the English fish traders came from. Biggest man I ever saw."

That was more like it. Iceland was a place at the edge of the world—an isolated, backward land about which little was known except that it provided most of the salted stockfish that was a staple of the English diet at Lent. Tom had often wished to hear more about it, but the English sailors who went there had little to say and little interest in it except for the enormously profitable cargos of fish they brought back. The Bristol men stayed there for months on end, used the land as their own, helped themselves to the local women, and had been known to kill or hold for ransom any ill-advised Danish governors who tried to stop them.

"Where is he?" Tom asked.

"We had to throw him out. He not only smelled like a fish, but he drank like one, too. Trouble was, he was one of those fighting drunks—got worse and worse, and finally he broke the heads of two stout lads who thought they could get him under control. It took four men to hold him down long enough for me to give him a tap on his thick skull with the cudgel I keep behind the bar."

"Oh." Tom was disappointed. "I'll sit down over there," he said, pointing to an empty table. "You can have the fair Alice bring me my drink."

The landlord winked. "That I will, and a good swippyng may you get out of it." He started away, then turned and said, "There's a Portuguese wine ship docking. Maybe we'll get some trade from them later."

"They're wrthe fellows, right enough. Almost as sturdy sailors as our Bristol lads." As a boy, Tom had spent many happy hours loitering around the Portuguese wine ships tied up at the quay and had picked up a fair smattering of their oddly accented language with its traces of Latin and Spanish—as much of a smattering as the sailors on the regular wine run had picked up of port English. "Send them over if they come in—I'll buy them a drink."

"Perhaps they'll have a tale for you," the landlord said, nodding. "I wot that prince of theirs, Henry, they call him, the Navigator, senden forth ships from his duchy like honeybees from a hive. Many's the island they've discovered where no dry land was known. 'Twas only yestreen when some Portuguese captain made it past the spit of Africa that they call Cape Not because ships that went beyond it re-

turned not. Now their captains have found a new barrier—
they call it Cape Boojums or somesuch—where 'tis said the
water boils. It may be that by now there's more news of
that."

Tom smiled to himself at that. He could tell the Portuguese a thing or two about what lay south of this impassable
cape of theirs. If the Portuguese captains had persevered
and fared a bit farther, they might have met Cheng Ho's
mighty fleet at the mouth of the river of the kingdom of the
Congo.

"I yeue no tale of boiling water," he said, "but I'd lythe
most gladly to what they have to say about these voyages of
theirs."

"They're not supposed to talk about them to foreigners,"
the landlord said with a wink, "but they're simple fellows,
and a few friendly drinks is a wonderful loosener of
tongues."

Tom seated himself at the still-empty table and stretched
out his legs. Alice, the tappestere, brought him his tankard,
and he paid her with a silver penny.

She was a saucy baggage with a broad Saxon face and a
knowing smile. She thanked him by leaning over the table
to give him a view of her pillowy breasts. "That's hende of
you, Master Tom," she said.

He took her by the wrist and said, "Are you be-hyth tonight, mistress?"

"Why don't you wait until all depart and see?" She walked
off, hips swinging. Tom raised the tankard to his lips and
over its brim watched her depart.

He was not alone at his table long. One of the Dolphin's
regulars, a journeyman webster whose name, Tom thought,
was Aston, wandered over as if by chance and sat down on
the bench opposite, his fist around a half-full mug of ale that
he must have been nursing for some time.

"Even to you, squire," he said. "I've not seen you here for
some time."

"I've been busy," Tom said and instantly felt embarrassed
by his words. He had little to do with his time but amuse
himself, while swinkeres like Aston were hard put to earn
enough to put meat in their mouths and a sloppe upon their
backs.

"Aye, aye," said Aston, taking a carefully measured sip
from his mug. "Whether we be moche or lyte, there's always

mekyl to take away our time. I suppose a place like the Dolphin has small attraction for a man of your quality."

Aston was a secret Lollard, Tom was sure. At least the opinions he was wont to let slip sounded as if he harbored the dangerous notions of human equality that had gotten John Ball drawn and quartered and his followers hanged by the thousands. Some day Aston would drop one hint too many, and the authorities would catch up with him, too.

"I was born a weaver's son," Tom said defensively. "I know what it is to go hungry and to shiver through a long winter."

"You've come up in the world, though," Aston said. "Where was it you made your fortune? Some land to the east, beyond Tartary, did you say?"

"In far Cathay," Tom said unwillingly and hoped the matter would drop there. He did not want to get trapped into a discussion of his travels that would, as always, end with him looking foolish and people laughing at him behind his back. These days when people asked him where he had been, he merely said "the East," and hoped they would be content with that. But he had been incautious on his first arrival, and the memories of the hangers-on at the Dolphin were long.

Aston collared a bleary-eyed fellow passing by. "Will, my friend, have a seat. The squire here's just been telling me about Cathay."

The newcomer sat with a thump and mumbled a greeting. He turned out to be a hedge-priest—an itinerant preacher without church or benefice, who delivered his unauthorized and probably inflammatory sermons at market crosses and worked in the intervals as a weaver to hold body and soul together—and that served to confirm Tom's opinion of Aston.

"Cathay, you say? That's beyond the Holy Land."

He was drunk as a piper. If he'd ever had a post, that explained why he'd lost it.

"Beyond Tartary," Aston amplified, coaching him.

The hedge-priest managed to focus a foggy eye on Tom. "Now, how would you get to such a place?"

"Well," Tom said helplessly, "I sailed in a ship of that land from the port of Calicut."

"Calicut?" The other dragged himself bit by bit to a semblance of sobriety. His next remark showed that he was not unlettered. "No Christian's ever been to Calicut. How did you get there?"

Tom breathed a sigh of resignation. He called Alice over to fill their mugs. "Well, you see," he said, "I rode with a caravan to Baghdad, then sailed with a Saracen ship from there. . . ."

Soon enough he was surrounded by the usual collection of sots, idlers, and sponges, some of whom were there only to bait him. But after a few more drinks he didn't care. He stopped noticing the nods and nudges. He got carried away by his memories, as always, and the blurred circle of faces around him became fine fellows. He drew laughter and cat-calls when he told them about the temple girls of Calicut, then launched into an account of the eunuch delegation of Cheng Ho and the gigantic ships of the Star Raft.

"Ships as wide in the beam as a Bristol cog is long?" said a merchant named Clement Bagot, with a broad wink at the others. He was co-owner of a leaky tub named the *Trinity*, a stingy man who was glad to have a drink at someone else's expense, but who thought himself a gentleman of the county. "And sailed by a gelded admiral! The rudders must have bit deep indeed to maintain way for a ship of such dimensions!"

A king's customs collector named Pynke, a scoundrel with eyes so weak that they could be made blind by a shilling, took up the refrain. "It may be that removing a man's coillons and pintle improve his qualities of seamanship. Perhaps it might do the same for Master Hugh Russell."

There was an outburst of raucous laughter. Hugh Russell was the master of the *Trinity* and had recently made himself the butt of the Bristol waterfront by getting lost in a fog for three days off Calais and having his unlicensed cargo seized by agents of the Staple.

"Or it might be that we ought to perform the same operation on some of our lords and improve the governance of England," said Aston.

Bagot, already stung by the gibe at his captain's expense, glowered and said, "And perhaps you'd like to repeat that treasonous remark in front of a magistrate, fellawe."

"Come, gentlemen, be merry," Tom said expansively.

He called for another round of ale for the table. As he paid, he noticed a number of greedy eyes on his purse and congratulated himself on his cleverness. He never carried more than a mark or two worth of coins in his visible purse when he had been drinking. The rest of his money he kept concealed in a flat gypser under his padded doublet, as careful travelers did, and transferred it a little at a time, as need be. He also kept a handful of jewels, sewn into a small pouch, hidden on his person at all times; old habits died hard, and he could never shake the feeling that all his good fortune might vanish at the drop of a hat and leave him footloose again.

"Tell us more, squire," said Pynke with a simpering smile. "Did you visit the land of the headless men that travelers tell of or the country of one-legged giants who use their foot as an umbrella? Did you see the Garden of Eden?"

In a moment of clarity, Tom saw himself as he must appear to this scoffing company who hung around him only for the drinks he could buy them. He had a sudden, sharp vision of Conti, sitting at a tavern table in Constantinople, surrounded by such fools as these, spinning out his yarns of the marvelous land of Vijayanagar while they laughed at him behind his back. Was he only another Conti? How many other travelers had been derided through the centuries as simpletons or as mere boastful drunks? Marco Polo himself had not been believed, and the name "Marco Million" still clung to his memory. But, Tom thought angrily, the things he had seen were real—more wonderful than Conti's tale of streets paved with gems and terrier-size ants who mined gold for the Zamorin of Calicut.

He tried to talk and found that his tongue had gone thick.

"No," he wanted to say, "I didn't reach the Garden of Eden or the kingdom of Prester John, but I saw the ruins of Babylon and the Forbidden City and sailed with the Star Raft and walked through Africa and saw the bloody kingdom of Benin."

What came out must have been garbled—he heard the words "shailed with the straft" hanging in the air—and everybody laughed.

"Have another drink, squire," Aston said.

At that moment Joseph came over and with a worried look at Tom said, "There's some Portuguese sailors from the wine ship just come in, squire. But they're only ordinary garcons—not your sort at all."

"Shend—" Tom mastered his tongue with an effort. "*Send* them over."

There were four of them, swarthy well-knit fellows in patched smocks and wool stocking caps, with open, guileless features. Tom got his speech under control with sheer will-power and greeted them in his sketchy half-remembered Portuguese. Their faces lit up, and one of them managed to return the greeting in English. The others at the table made room for them reluctantly, and Tom ordered wine for them.

The hilarity at the table resumed. The Portuguese didn't understand the reason for it, but they were friendly lads and smiled at each sally.

Tom let the conversation run on around him. He thought he was sobering up a bit—or at least managing his drunkenness better. "Here's to your Prince Henry," he said, lifting his glass. *Um grande navegador.*

They were pleased at that. The one who spoke English toasted Henry the Sixth, and the others aped his pronunciation as best they could.

In short order, Tom had a conversation going in a mixture of English, Portuguese, Spanish, French, and Italian. It worked pretty well, with each of the four supplying words when one of their number got stuck or cooperating to give Tom the word he needed. He drew the mundane particulars of their voyage out of them—where they'd set sail from, the weather they'd encountered, the cargo they carried, what they hoped to load in return. He asked about other voyages and found that two of them had sailed to the Canaries, and one had made regular voyages to the new island called Madeira. The one who spoke English had actually sailed with a grandee named Cabral, who had been the first man to pass Cape Not—Non, they called it—and Tom could hardly believe his luck.

"You went ashore?" he asked. He wondered if, through some miracle of coincidence, this young Portuguese sailor and he had set foot on the continent of Africa at the same time.

The sailor shook his head. "Dom Goncalo Velho thought it enough that he had rounded the cape and proved that it could be done. But a landing's been made since."

The Englishmen at the table had been talking among themselves, having given up on Tom for the time being after he failed to respond to the barbs tossed in his direction. Several of them were gazing dolefully at their empty mugs.

"Say, squire," Pynke hinted, "don't you need another drink?"

Tom made an elaborate show of looking at his tankard in surprise. "I do, at that," he said. He beamed at them drunkenly. "It's time for Master Bagot to buy us a round."

"Excuse me," Bagot said, getting up hastily. He disappeared to another part of the Dolphin.

When next Alice went by, Tom told her to keep the glasses of the Portuguese filled. She gauged the level of the wine in the glasses with a professional eye, and when she returned some time later to replenish it, she brought no ale with her. Aston gave a sour grin and left. Pynke made another try, hinting obliquely at his thirst, but Tom ignored him. Within twenty minutes Tom and the four Portuguese were alone at the table—except for the hedge-priest, who was asleep with his cheek resting in a puddle of ale.

"There was another cape after Non, wasn't there?" Tom asked. "But that's proved to be impassable."

"Bojador," said the one who spoke a little English. His name was Antonio, and he had, Tom discovered, an English grandfather—a foot soldier who had settled in Portugal after serving with the army that John of Gaunt, the duke of Lancaster, had brought to help a beleaguered John the Bastard in his war against the king of Castile.

After an inquiring glance at his compatriots, who returned nothing but benevolent smiles, Antonio went on.

". . . the Bulging Cape. But it was passed last year by Gil Eanes."

Tom clapped him enthusiastically on the back. He called for more wine. "That's wonderful news! But why hasn't it spread through all Europe?"

Antonio looked embarrassed. One of his companions artlessly supplied, "The Venetians. The infante wishes them to learn as little as possible. Already they control the trade in the Mediterranean—and half the world besides. If there is to be trade down the coast of Africa, Prince Henry wishes it to be under the control of Portugal."

"The Venetians send spies," said another of the sailors. "They try to bribe our captains. They want a copy of the *padron*, the map of the world at Sagres that shows all the new discoveries."

"But the English are our friends," said the fourth sailor. "Our *aliados* . . . allies. Prince Henry himself is half English, and so is our king Duarte ... their mother taught them at her knee to love your country."

He broke into a huge smile and raised his glass once more.

Tom, behind his answering smile, sank into deep thought. This Prince Henry must be an amazing man to take such a gamble. He could not know, at this point, of the green lands and the African kingdoms that awaited him past the cruel waste that the Arabs called *sahara*. But if he carried his gamble through, there was gold to be taken out of Africa and ivory. And—remembering the poor miserable creatures sold by their kings to the Arab caravan he had joined—slaves to do the work of a plague-depopulated Europe. The Portuguese, if they had the heart and will to persevere, would have it all for the taking.

"And this Gil Eanes," Tom said. "He landed?"

Antonio looked at his companions for their approval, and said proudly, "He went ashore some fifty leagues beyond Bojador and found a sign from God—Roses of Saint Mary."

"So the infante sent Gil Eanes back—this time with his own cupbearer, Dom Afonso Goncalves Baldaia," said the sailor who mistrusted Venetians.

Antonio nodded. "They went another fifty leagues. And this time they found footprints of men and animals in the sand."

"Proof, you see," said the other sailor, "that men can live there, and that there must be some settlement nearby."

"All Portugal rejoiced," Antonio said. "Gil Eanes is a great hero. Prince Henry gave him estates, titles, gold. He's going to send Baldaia back again, with horses, to push on farther south. It may be that Baldaia's returned already, with his ship loaded with gold."

Tom mused. If the Portuguese were proceeding southward only fifty leagues at a time, they had a long way to go before they reached the part of the coast where gold and ivory could be found, let alone the kingdoms of Benin and the Congo. And at this rate they'd never discover that Africa had a bottom that could be rounded. Prince Henry was in for disappointing times. He needed some encouragement.

"This Prince Henry," he said. "What kind of man is he?"

Tom could hardly sort out the multilingual flood that followed. He gained an impression of a prince of great force and power, one who commanded the devotion and obedi-

ence of those around him and yet was a man with the austere and solitary tastes of a monk. He had been a brave—
even reckless—soldier in his youth, when he had waged war
against the Moors at Ceuta, but he had since acquired the
reflective habits of a scholar, poring over old maps and
books of travel and surrounding himself with astrologers,
mapmakers, and other learned men. He was a mystic who
spent overmuch time on his knees yearning for union with
God, and yet he was a practical man, running his own shipyards and managing with a firm hand the day-to-day affairs
of the juggernaut of exploration he had created.

"One thing that no man can gainsay," Antonio asserted, "is
that the infante is generous to those who can aid him in his
purpose. He rewards well all those who bring him their talents and their knowledge, whether they be Jews or Moors
or some ordinary man with a skill in shipbuilding or navigation."

Tom felt a stir of admiration for the unknown prince.
Henry reminded him a little of Cheng Ho in his single-
minded pursuit of newness and strangeness. Like Cheng Ho
he seemed to have his eyes fixed on the unknown, and like
Cheng Ho he appeared to have the rare capacity to listen to
new ideas.

Tom took a thoughtful sip of his ale, and his eye fell on
the snoring hedge-priest. There would be people at Sagres,
he thought wistfully, who would not mock the tale of his
travels.

By the time the Portuguese sailors staggered off to their
ship, Tom's head was reeling with all they had told him.
Bristol was beginning to feel small to him again, as it had
when he was a boy. Some day, he thought, the seamen of
Bristol would show the world a thing or two but not yet.
Portugal was where things were happening now.

Alice tapped him on the shoulder. He raised his head, and
when the room steadied itself he saw that the tavern was
empty.

"Can you stand, my fine sweeting, or has ale robbed thy
strength?" she said doubtfully.

Tom lurched to his feet. "I can stand well enough, mistress. I'll take you home."

# CHAPTER 17

He returned the next night and the nights that followed to sit with the Portuguese and buy drinks for them. They brought some of their shipmates, and Tom, for a change, was a listener to tales instead of a teller of them. Some of the sailors had sailed with Cabral to the new islands far out in the Ocean Sea that were called the Azores—it was thought that Saint Brendan's Isle or the legendary land called Brasile might still lie beyond. Others knew Madeira, the island of wood, and told him of the fire that had burned for seven years, leaving the land a fertile paradise that grew wheat and sugarcane and grapes. One sailor, a grizzled oldster, had actually sailed with Zarco on the ship that had discovered it. Another, a native of Cape Saint Vincent, where Sagres rose from the cliffs, told him of Prince Henry's School of Navigation, which had become a city in itself, and the exotic folk that swarmed there from all parts of the world. "Majorca," he said, "is where the mapmakers come from; they're all Jews and practice magic. And there are Greeks who worked in the Arsenal of Venice and bring him its shipbuilding secrets."

Tom neglected his former spongers, to their resentment, and there were mutterings about the foreigners who were taking over the Dolphin. Once Joseph had to give a tap of his cudgel to Pynke, the customs searcher, in order to forestall a fight, and after that there was no more trouble.

After about a week there came a night when the Portuguese did not show up. Antonio stopped in for a quick drink with Tom and explained that he could not stay. "We're all loaded," he said. "We sail in the morning. These river tides of yours are tricky, and the captain doesn't want to get caught by them."

Tom, without conscious thought, said, "Take me with you."

"*Não percebo*," Antonio said. "Are you serious?"

"Yes."

"But you're a rich man. We don't have accommodations for passengers. There's only the deck. Why don't you buy passage on a ship where you'll be comfortable?"

"I don't want to wait," Tom said.

Antonio rubbed his chin in thought. "I don't know if the captain would take you. He wouldn't like giving up his own bed."

"He won't have to. Tell him I'll pay him well. If he likes, I'll work the ship and pay anyway."

A puzzled Antonio took Tom to the wine ship, and he explained it all again to the captain, a corpulent middle-aged man named Figueiredo. "I don't know," the captain said. Tom produced a gold noble, and when the captain raised his eyebrows, he added four more to it. "All right," the captain said. "We leave early. Before dawn."

"I'll sleep here tonight," Tom said.

He found a boy on the docks to take his horse back to the manor and penned a note for Hugh. "I'll give you a silver penny," he said. "This paper tells the man you'll deliver it to that he's to give you another one."

Hugh arrived well after midnight, sputtering. "I brought the things you asked for," he said, handing over a bundle wrapped in canvas. "Some rough clothes, a purse of money, that chest with the silk scrolls, and the ivory rods and plates that you brought from . . . from your travels. You can't mean to leave like this!"

"The place will run well enough without me," Tom said. "You'll see to that. And money takes care of itself. I'll write the Medici bank from Portugal."

"Master Tom, Master Tom," Hugh cried, almost in tears. "This is daft! What shall I tell Mistress Margery?"

"Tell her," Tom said, "that the world is wide." He thought

a moment, and added, "And that there is more of it waiting to be found."

"The River of Gold," Baldaia said with a sweep of his hand. "This must be it, finally. Rio de Ouro. The place the Prince predicted, where the caravans come to trade."

He smiled confidently at Pedro, but there had been just the faintest touch of a question in his voice.

Pedro looked out across the rail at the broad inlet. It was several miles wide, framed by a flat stony waste that was almost devoid of vegetation. If it had been the mouth of a river, one would have expected more green on the banks.

"I don't know," he said. "It may be only an arm of the sea. If the sea here were being diluted by fresh water, or if there were silt in it, you'd think it would show color changes."

"You and your colors!" Baldaia said with a snort. "No one can see them but you. I tell you, my friend, this is the estuary of a very large river—you know very well that such waters can remain salty for many miles inland. Besides, there's an incoming tide." His voice acquired a shade of awe. "This may even be the western branch of the Nile that geographers speculate about." He brightened. "We may have discovered a way to sail clear across Africa to Egypt."

"Let's see," Pedro said noncommittally. He had a sailor lower a bucket over the side and draw a sample of water. He tried a mouthful and spat it out. It tasted every bit as salty to him as ordinary seawater.

Baldaia disputed him. He rinsed his mouth from the bucket and pronounced it a shade sweeter. "It's a question of a more refined palate, Pedro, no offense," he asserted. He smiled disarmingly. "After all, it's my profession—I'm the prince's cupbearer."

Pedro shrugged. "We'll soon know," he said.

From amidships came a nervous nickering. There was a shuffle of hooves and warning shouts. The sailors had succeeded in getting a canvas sling under the barrel of the first of the horses, but the beast was skittish and uncooperative.

"It's going to be a job getting them ashore, Dom Afonso," said the coxswain, mopping his brow. Just then a sailor went crashing against the gunwale as the horse lashed out with its hooves and caught him. The sailor was carried into the shade of the stern shelter with what looked like a broken arm. But by then, the terrified horse had been winched off its feet and lowered into the longboat. A sailor stood ready to sooth it, and another tied its reins to a ringbolt. The coxswain climbed down after it, and the boat shoved off for shore.

"Dom Afonso," an excited young voice intruded, "can we go ashore now? The morning's half gone. We've been ready for hours. We ought to get started."

Pedro turned around and saw Hector Homem, closely trailed by young Diego Lopez Dalmeida. Both boys were weighed down with armor and weapons—full steel corselets, greaves, basin-shaped helmets, swords, lances, battle axes, spiked maces. Seventeen years old and from noble families, they had begged the Prince to let them go with the expedition. They had not yet proved themselves, and they hoped for knighthoods out of this voyage. Perhaps the prince had remembered how eager he had been for his own knighthood at Ceuta.

Baldaia laughed indulgently. "Patience, patience. We still have to finish unloading the horses, walk them around, get the stiffness out of their legs. But first, I want you out of that armor. The horses can't carry all that weight in this heat, and neither can you. You're not going jousting. You don't need all that stuff."

"But what if we meet Moors?"

"In that case, speed is your best defense."

Hector's face fell. "To run away? Like cowards? Diego and I have been training with the weapons for the whole voyage."

"Listen to me, *jovem*. The object is to capture a native who we can take back for questioning, not get captured yourselves. What would I tell your fathers? I'm going to allow you a lance and a sword apiece. No armor. You're to follow the banks of the river for three or four leagues, no more, and come back and tell me what you found. If you come upon a solitary native and can capture him without getting yourselves hurt, then bring him back without going farther. But if you encounter armed men in any numbers, you're to turn tail at once. Is that understood?"

"But Dom Afonso . . ." Diego raised a voice in protest.

"Is it understood?"

The youths exchanged a glance. "Yes, Dom Afonso."

"Good. The one thing you *are* going to take is water. I

don't trust the look of this land, and I don't know for how far the river remains salty."

Pedro watched the boys go off to help each other out of their steel shells. He approved Baldaia's good sense. Baldaia came over to stand beside him.

"Good lads, but impetuous," he said. "It goes with being young. It wasn't so long ago that we were like that, instead of being old men of thirty, was it, my friend?"

Pedro thought back to when he had first sailed with Zarco. He had been fifteen then, two years younger than Hector and Diego. He didn't think he had been impetuous. That was for people of the nobility, like Baldaia and the two boys, raised on notions of knighthood and chivalry. Pedro had gone out with his father from an early age to fish and had learned that at sea no one wants to be around a reckless man.

"No, not so long ago," Pedro said.

The unloading of the horses went off without further incident. There were four of them—two for the use of the youthful scouts and two spares. The *barinel* had found good anchorage in a sheltered cove within the sprawling river mouth—if river mouth it was—and Baldaia did not want to abandon it prematurely, before having some indication of what lay up-country.

He had given the cove the name Angra dos Cavallos, Bay of the Horses. It was some seventy leagues farther south than the spot where Gil Eanes had found the tracks of men and camels, far enough for an observant eye to see that this was a transitional landscape. The sandy desert was turning into a wasteland of rocks and boulders, with an occasional twisted, dry shrub poking through. On the horizon Pedro could see a few tortured, leafless trees. But there was no fresh water here to replenish the ship's casks, and neither was the dead growth useful as firewood. The cook had tried some of it in the sandbox, and it had gone up like tinder, singeing his eyebrows. Baldaia had forbidden him to burn any more of it aboard ship.

One form of life, however, was prevalent in the bay— seals. Pedro could see them sunning themselves by the hundreds on the rocks. Baldaia was much encouraged by the sight. "You found these sea wolves on Madeira, didn't you?" he said.

Pedro could only reply, "Yes. But they make their living in the ocean."

By now the two boys, down to their shirts and hose, were pestering Baldaia to let them be off without further delay. They were too impatient to wait for the midmorning dinner the cook was preparing—the only hot meal of the day—but helped themselves to some sea biscuit and a handful of almonds and raisins to take along with them.

Baldaia drew Pedro aside. "They need an older hand to go along and steady them," he said worriedly. "I don't know who to send except you."

"Me?" Pedro said. "I'm no horseman."

"You ride well enough. I've seen you. You managed to keep up with me on the journey from Lisbon to Sagres."

"We never went faster than a traveler's trot."

"That's the idea. With you along at least it'll hold them down to a canter. You're willing to lose some skin off your backside for the good of the expedition, aren't you?"

"All right."

"Good man. Let's go tell them."

The two boys were clearly unhappy at the arrangement. They didn't want to be under the eye of an older person—and a commoner at that. Baldaia salved their pride by telling them that, as pilot, Pedro ought to have a firsthand look at the supposed river to judge its navigable qualities.

"Besides," he said, "Senhor da Costa has fought in the Canaries. He's an experienced soldier when it comes to dealing with savages. You don't know what kind of men you're likely to encounter."

Baldaia gave Pedro his own sword. "I'll find you a lance as well," he said.

Pedro shook his head. "I'll leave that to the *jovems*. I couldn't manage a lance from horseback. It'll be all I can do to stay in the saddle. Besides, as you said yourself, the horses' hooves are our best weapons."

He gave his dinner a last regretful look. It was only salted meat, as tough as leather, and some cooked dry beans swimming in olive oil and garlic, but he was hungry. He settled for a pocketful of hardtack, like the boys, and slung an extra pair of water jugs across the saddlebow in case of breakage.

From the first, Hector and Diego tried to lose Pedro. The fast trot that he tried to hold them to had a way of turning into a gallop, and then Pedro would have to exert himself to catch up, at the cost of a jarred spine and incipient saddle sores. Once they got entirely out of sight, and he found a broken water jug that one of them had jettisoned. He rode at a jolting run to overtake them and gave them a talking-to.

"But senhor, the water's heavy," Hector Homem said with a put-upon look meant for the other boy. "It was slowing us down."

"Water's your best friend out here," Pedro said. On a sudden suspicion he reached over and hefted one of Diego's water jugs. It was too light—only about a quarter full. "You didn't drink that much," he said. "You've been spilling it out as you ride."

"It's my business," the boy said hotly. "Anyway, I'm not thirsty."

"Maybe not now," Pedro said, looking him in the eye until he blushed and turned away.

They cantered along beside him in a sulky silence for the next few miles. Pedro was becoming more and more dubious about the supposed Rio de Ouro. There was no current that he could detect and no river flotsam, only a tidal eddying. He stretched the boys' patience several times by dismounting to taste the water, but it never seemed to get less salty.

A blurred sun the color of an orange climbed higher in a sky that was hazy with particles blowing from the desert to the north. It grew hotter. The pebbled landscape ahead shimmered. Pedro made the boys stop to drink some water and eat some hardtack. Diego's jugs were now empty, and after pretending stoicism as long as he could, he shamefacedly accepted a long swing from one of Pedro's spare jugs.

They allowed the horses to cool out before watering them, and even then the beasts eagerly lapped up all they were given. By the time they finished, two more jugs were empty—about five gallons gone.

"We'd better go easy while the sun's so high," Pedro said. "We'll take it at a walk for the next ten miles, and if we don't find anything, we'll have to turn back and try again tomorrow. We'll need enough water to get back on."

The youths protested. "We're bound to find fresh water if we just follow the river course far enough. Dom Afonso said so."

"We can't take the chance. Country like this sucks the moisture out of a man. Or a horse. You can die of it."

Grumbling, they remounted. The stop had refreshed them. They started to pull ahead of Pedro again. He called to them and got them to wait for him a few times, but it was a losing battle. The gap widened. Pedro saw Diego lean across and say something to the Homem boy. They turned with one accord to look back at him. He couldn't see the expressions on their faces, but they were probably laughing. A moment later they spurred their horses and took off in a cloud of dust.

Pedro urged his horse to a lumbering gallop, but within a very few minutes both of the youthful scouts were completely out of sight. Pedro gave up the chase and dropped back to a canter. He couldn't hope to compete. One thing the *nobreza* were good at was riding horses. They grew up with them.

Sooner or later they'd tire of the game, and he'd catch up to them. Their horses couldn't keep it up for long in this heat, and Pedro had most of the remaining water. He'd dole out a strict ration and then take them back, even if he had to lead their horses by the reins.

The country grew more rugged, with boulders and large rocks littering the plain. Pedro picked his way carefully. A horse could break a leg on ground like this. He hoped the boys hadn't met with a mishap.

Another half-hour's steady riding showed him the yellow dust cloud of their passage hanging in the still air. It had stopped its forward motion and was already starting to settle. Relieved, he urged his horse forward and then, as the scene took shape before his eyes, he broke into a headlong gallop, heedless of risk.

The two youths had reined in their horses and, across a distance of some fifty or sixty yards, were facing a ragged group of men. Pedro counted nineteen of them. The encounter must have happened only moments before, because it was a tableau of arrested motion. Pedro could read surprise and indecision in every line of the desert men's bodies.

They were dark, stringy men, dressed in shirtlike garments tucked up to show long, lean legs. They carried spears and small bundles. They seemed not at all threatening. In a moment they would get over their astonishment and decide what they wanted to do. Pedro hoped that one of the boys would have the sense to say something to them and raise a hand in greeting. There was no particular danger. The boys were beyond range of a thrown spear, and at the first sign of any hostile intent they could follow Baldaia's orders and simply gallop away.

Then, like a bad dream, Pedro saw both youths lower their lances and lean forward over their horses' necks in preparation for a charge.

"Wait!" Pedro shouted without effect. Possibly the youths were too keyed up to hear him. He spurred his horse to a desperate dash, knowing that he was not going to reach them in time to restrain them.

The desert men looked up at his shout and saw what to them would have been a third mounted apparition bearing down on them from another quarter. At the same time, Hector and Diego, with a bloodcurdling battle cry of *"Por São Vicente e Rei!"* flew at full tilt at them.

The nineteen men scattered in a panic and scurried to a pile of rocks. Hector's lance point caught one of them in the side, and he went sprawling. But before Hector could stop his horse's charge and wheel around, the man scrambled to his feet and, despite his wound, managed to scuttle crabwise to the shelter of the boulders. At the same time, Diego, who had missed connecting with anything on his first charge, had cut off one of the fleeing men and was herding him away from the boulder with pokes of his lance. The native backed away, dodging and parrying as best he could, and when he saw his chance he ducked under Diego's lance and thrust with his own spear. It wasn't a very good thrust, but Pedro saw it catch Diego in the foot. The horse reared up, and for a moment Diego had to fight to stay in the saddle. By the time he recovered, the native was in full flight. Diego threw his lance at him. It hit the man in the buttock and knocked him to his knees, but he picked himself up and kept running. The lance hadn't penetrated deeply and had come loose by itself. Diego, with a cry of frustration, drew his sword and pursued his quarry to the base of the piled stones, but his horse could not follow.

When Pedro rode up, the two boys were pacing back and forth on their mounts, shouting for the desert men to come out and fight.

"You did a reckless thing," he told them. "For two of you to attack so large a band."

"One Christian warrior's a match for ten Moors," Hector boasted. "We've brought glory on the expedition." His tone said that Pedro hadn't added much to the glory.

"We don't know that they *are* Moors," Pedro said. "And now we've lost the chance to find out."

"We'll stay here till we catch one," Diego said. "Wasn't that the idea?"

Pedro thought it over. The damage was done. "All right, if we can isolate one and get him without risk," he said. "But what I say goes, understand?" He looked at Diego. "How's that foot?"

"It's nothing—a scratch," the boy said. Pedro could tell from the drained face that he was in pain.

"Let's have a look."

Diego refused to ride a little way off and dismount until Hector assured him that he'd hold the fort for him. Pedro made Diego take off his boot, and saw that the spear had sliced through the leather but hadn't gone much farther. The gash on the instep was oozing blood but didn't look serious. Pedro bound it up for him with a scrap from his shirttail and helped him work the boot back over it. "Doesn't look as if any bones were broken," he remarked. "You're lucky."

The youngster was proud of his wound. He would be able to bear it back home as a badge of courage. "The Dalmeidas don't pay attention to wounds," he said. "My grandfather went on fighting at Aljubarrota with an arrow in his eye."

But the desert dwellers didn't give them much of a chance to fight. The afternoon wore on, and they stayed behind their boulders, flitting from rock to rock whenever Pedro and the two youths tried to outflank them. Once Hector managed to inflict a wound with a lance thrust, but the man got back to shelter. Once a spear came hurtling out of the maze of stones, but it missed its target and went clattering to the ground. Pedro withdrew the pair to a more prudent distance, and the stalemate continued.

"It's getting dark," Hector fretted. "They'll be able to sneak off."

Pedro cast a worried look at the setting sun. "There's no point in staying here any longer," he said. "There are only three of us, and we can't keep them penned up after the light goes, and we can't go in after them by ourselves. We'll have to come back in the morning with more men."

"If only Dom Afonso had let us bring crossbows," Hector lamented. "We could have picked a few of them off."

"Come on, let's get going. You panicked them, but they may get their courage back after dark."

Only one jug of water was left. Pedro gave it all to the horses and hoped it would be enough to get them back safely. At least it would be cooler after sunset, and they wouldn't use up as much water on the return trip. He found a goatskin full of greenish foul-smelling water that one of their adversaries had dropped; no one was thirsty enough to drink it at the moment, but he took it along in case of need later.

The boys issued a final challenge to their unseen foes, shaking their fists at the rocks. "*Covardes!*" they accused. "Cowards!"

"It's only that they've never seen a white face or European weapons before," Pedro said. "When the two of you charged so many, they must have thought you had special powers to be so confident. You may find them braver another day."

They arrived back at the ship about dawn. Baldaia listened to their account and said, "We'll have some breakfast, then take a boat upstream."

"It isn't a stream," Pedro said. "It goes inland far enough, but it's just an arm of the sea."

Baldaia bit his lip but said nothing.

With eight men rowing and a sail rigged, the longboat made good progress inland. Hector and Diego, with the resilience of youth, rode along the bank, pacing the boat, though they frequently darted ahead with impatience and were out of sight for long intervals before doubling back. Baldaia told Pedro that after a night in the saddle he had earned a rest and could consider himself a passenger. But the wind was coming from the quarter, and Pedro decided to handle the gaff-rigged sail himself. All of the sailors were armed, and one of them, a fair archer from Almada, was equipped with a crossbow.

The sun was like a furnace. At about noon the boys returned from one of their forays and hailed the longboat. Baldaia brought the boat inshore, and the boys told him that they were nearing the site of the encounter. Pedro took down the sail and unstepped the short mast. They rowed another mile and Baldaia beached the boat, leaving two men to guard it.

Another mile of walking took them to the place of tumbled boulders that Pedro remembered. They could see where the pebbled ground had been trampled by the horses during the long afternoon. One of the boys exclaimed aloud and pointed out dried blood on the rocks. The sailors spread out and searched the boulders, but the mysterious strangers had fled during the night, leaving behind their pitiful belongings.

Baldaia kicked at a goatskin containing a clay cookpot and some bone tools. "Take these back to the boat," he told a sailor. "We can show them to the prince. But it would have been nice to have a captive."

"Maybe we can still catch them, Dom Afonso!" Hector cried.

"No, they're long gone," Baldaia said. "We'll go back to the ship." His voice turned savage. "At least we'll have some sealskins to show for it."

The slaughter continued for the next three days, until the bay was filled with rotting carcasses and the sea animals, at first trusting, no longer allowed the sailors to approach them. The stink of uncured hides pervaded the ship, and the sailors, their clothes stiff with blood, had become disgusted with their labors.

"Oil," Baldaia said. "It's a pity to waste so much of it. If only we'd known, we could have filled the hold with jars. But those who come after us will know better, eh?"

Pedro nodded to keep the peace, but he didn't see how the prince's cause would be advanced by adding another fishery to those already known. Perhaps a few sealers might be willing to bring their vessels this far from time to time, in hope of returning to Portugal with a sure profit, but they would not open Africa up the way gold and ivory, already collected by the natives and waiting for traders, would have. And the sealers, if they came, would never push on any farther than this ill-named Bay of Horses.

Perhaps something of the sort was passing through Baldaia's mind despite his mulish attempt at justification, because the expression he turned on Pedro pleaded for understanding.

"We'll continue on south tomorrow, eh, my friend?" he said. "Isn't that what the prince says—always a little farther? Perhaps we'll find his river after all."

Fifty leagues to the south they came to a headland with a rock that resembled the prow of a ship. There had been no river mouth, no bay, nothing that looked promising—only more of the same monotonous shore. Baldaia was withdrawn and discouraged. He was ready to give up. Pedro could not fault him—he had gone farther in one voyage than any captain before him. His hope had run out, that was all.

"We'll put in here and have a look before we turn around," Baldaia said. "We can leave a marker."

Pedro made up his mind to persuade Baldaia at least to anchor here overnight. He would plead the need to take navigational readings from the night sky, and he would be telling the truth as far as it went. He would measure the height of the north star with the string and the chip of wood the Venetian chandler, Sandro the gentleman, had given him—the crude instrument that Arabs, so he said, called a *kamal*. It would mean nothing, of course. There was no way to read a latitude off it. You could only duplicate a latitude. It would only mean something if man passed this way again. But it seemed to Pedro that Portugal's southernmost thrust ought to be recorded somehow, even if only by a knot on a string.

The crew was glad of a chance to stretch their legs again. They scoured the shore at Baldaia's behest to look for any sign of human beings, and they were rewarded almost at once.

"Fishnets," Baldaia marveled. "But what are they made of?"

The nets were artfully woven and beautiful to see, but they were not made of any kind of cordage that Pedro had ever seen. He pulled at one to test its pliability. "Strong," he said.

Baldaia picked out the strands with the point of his knife. "It's bark," he said. "They wove it out of bark."

Bark it might have been, but it was as tough and strong as anyone could wish. You could rig a ship with cord like this, Pedro thought.

"But where are the fishermen?" Baldaia said.

"Farther down the coast?" Pedro suggested.

Baldaia looked at him. "No," he said. "I know what you're trying to do. But we're running out of water. We didn't take enough. We were too confident of finding the Prince's river."

It was not the water, Pedro knew. A man can take only so much disappointment, and Baldaia had reached his limit. There would be disappointment in Portugal, too. The nation had sent them out with too much fanfare this time. It was those cursed tracks found by Gil Eanes. There had been too much talk of a river of gold, of kingdoms unreached by the Moors. For all his daring, Baldaia would not have much to show for this record-breaking voyage. There was no river, no gold, no captive whose palpable presence might sustain Prince Henry's expectations. There were only some seal-skins and a few fishnets woven of bark.

# CHAPTER 18

"Leave him alone," Catalina said. "It's no use talking to him when he's like this. He only wants to pick fights and brood about that woman he lost in Madeira."

"He'll get into a fight, all right, if those smart alecks at the next table keep trying to get a rise out of him," Sandro Cavalli countered.

"It's not your business," Catalina said. "You can't blame people for feeling the way they do."

"The hell with the people! When have their wishes ever counted? When Prince Henry gives up on exploration, that's when he'll have some reason to brood!"

Sandro cast an exasperated glance at the table where Pedro da Costa was slouched, sitting apart from his shipmates and staring moodily into his glass. He was halfway to being drunk. When he was drunk enough, he would leave, with or without a fight. It had been the same every night since his return from the Rio de Ouro—a name that had become a joke throughout Portugal. Sandro had managed to pry from him the fact that he had tied a knot in the *kamal* to mark the southernmost point of the voyage, but when Sandro tried to press him about the two of them seeking an audience with Prince Henry, Pedro had shown a total disinterest in pursuing the matter further. "What's the use of it?" he'd grunted. "There's nothing there worth going back for—that's what everybody says."

Catalina responded to Sandro's outburst with a flash of asperity. "You can't deny that the infante's gone cool on the idea. He's looking around for something else to do. They say up on the hill that he's thinking about a war in Tangier."

"There're always people thinking about a war in Tangier. Young Prince Fernando wants one because he's the only one of the brothers who didn't see action at Ceuta, and he feels he didn't win his spurs fairly. King Duarte wants a war because it costs him thirty thousand ducats a year to occupy Ceuta, and he could turn that into a profit if he consolidated his conquest by taking Tangier and was able to expoit the countryside. And all the knights want a war because they're getting fat. Prince Henry's wanted a holy war for twenty years, but he's not going to get one unless the money for it can be raised. The country's in no mood at the moment to be taxed further."

"And in no mood for sending more ships on these wild goose chases," Catalina retorted.

"The money for the expeditions comes out of the prince's private purse."

"And where does his private purse come from?" she replied hotly. "Let me ask you that! You're a gentleman. They still call you O Fidalgo! You don't think about such things. The whole Algarve's his fief and Madeira, too. Ask any fisherman who pays a tithe on his catch. Ask any laundress about the soap fee. Ask Vasques where the profit for every tenth keg of wine goes!"

"It's always been the way," Sandro said uncomfortably. "At least the prince doesn't spend the money on himself. He lives like a monk. He gives it back in charity, widows' pensions, opening up new lands for development. He spends more than he takes in, and that's why he's always in debt." He laughed lamely. "Anyway, I'm not a gentleman anymore—I'm just a poor ship's chandler struggling to make ends meet."

"We'll have a war in Tangier, you'll see," she said with a toss of the head. "The king will go to the Cortes, and the Cortes will give him the funds, no matter what the people say. So you'd better give up on these schemes of yours for getting introduced at court, and stock up on war supplies."

Sandro attempted levity. "Maybe I'll take your advice, *querida*. I'll listen to you and get rich."

"You're rich enough already. To people like me you're

rich. You and your columns of numbers and your double entry. You could buy and sell Vasques."

He took her hand. "Since I'm rich, why don't you give up your job at the Cabra do Mar? You don't have to work here any more; you know that."

It was a bone of contention between them. Sandro's chandlery was doing well enough so that he no longer slept on a cot in back. He had rented a small house in the village, with a couple to do the work. He had persuaded Catalina to move in with him, and despite the poverty of her upbringing, she had taken like a duck to water to the life of a *dona de casa*, managing the house and servants for him as if she had been born to it. But she refused to leave her job as a *tauernera*. "Vasques needs me," she'd said. "The tavern would go under if he had to run it himself. Besides, I've always supported myself, and I'm not going to stop now." And nothing he could say had been able to make her change her mind.

She pulled her hand away. "You can order me around when I'm your wife," she said sharply. "Until then, I'll take care of myself, thank you!"

Sandro started to get angry. "It's true I've never asked for your hand in a blessed marriage, *casamento de bencão*, at the church door, with the sacraments. What do you want from me? You've said often enough that you'd never marry me."

"That's right!" she flared. "I won't marry a man who's consumed by thoughts of revenge, a man still married to the memory of a dead woman—half a man! You're walking through the rest of your life in your sleep! Oh, you know how to make money, as a bull knows how to chew grass, because it's in your Venetian bones, and you breathe and eat and go through the motions of life, and when your body wants to take a woman, I'm there at the cost of a few kind words! But you're no sort of husband for any woman, and you make a poor sweetheart! You don't even share your thoughts. Your soul's like a lump of ice!"

Sandro was silent at that. It was true that he remained bitter, consumed. He knew it all too well, as a man falling from a cliff knows he is dropping without the power to save himself. The news from Venice had been eating at him more than usual lately. Venice was having another war with Milan, and this time Genoa had rebelled against its Milanese overlord, Filippo Maria Visconti, and joined the Venetian-Florentine alliance. Sandro could not help wondering what intrigues Maffeo had involved the House of Cavalli in. As if he didn't need a reminder, his chandlery had received a shipment of Venetian sandglasses, and when he'd unpacked them, he'd found the Cavalli name on the invoice. The signature of the Cavalli head clerk, Ippolito, whom Maffeo had disliked so strongly, was absent, replaced by a name he did not recognize. What other changes had Maffeo made in the business and at the Cavalli palace? His sister, Agnese, would be a matron of twenty-seven, Sandro had realized with a jolt. Had Maffeo made a good marriage for her? Was she happy? His speculations had bumped up against the grim remembrance that Maffeo thought he was dead. He derived a sour amusement from imagining the shock Maffeo would get if he saw the name of the brother he thought he had safely disposed of on the letter of credit paying for the sandglasses, but that was only fantasy; the shipment had been paid for by the Portuguese importer.

He turned a tightly controlled face to Catalina, in which all such thoughts had been extinguished. "I do my best, *cara*," he said.

Catalina relented. "Never mind. I said I'd take you as you are. I must be crazy."

A burst of laughter at one of the tables claimed her attention. It was a large, boisterous party that seemed to be centered around a wiry, yellow-thatched fellow who was as gaudy as a parrot in expensive clothes. He caught Catalina's eye and made urgent gestures asking for refills.

"I'd better go," she said. "It's the Englishman. He spends money like water. Vasques says to keep him spending."

"Who is he?" Sandro asked.

"His name's Tomás—something like that. He's no gentleman, though he's rich as one. He claims to have journeyed to Cathay. Also to have lived in a kingdom in Africa that no one's heard of and to have sailed to the land of spices with Saracen sailors and other such stories. But those freeloaders at his table don't mind, as long as he keeps paying for the drinks."

"What's he doing here?"

"He says he's come to Portugal to see Prince Henry. Another story. No one takes him seriously."

Sandro got up.

"Where are you going?" Catalina asked.

"I think I'll talk to him."

"You're wasting your time. He's only a braggart."

Sandro walked over and slid into a vacant spot at the end of one of the benches. He nodded to one or two of the faces he knew. The Englishman was in the middle of a story.

". . . and the men of this land are very tall and wear the skins of lions and drink the blood of their cattle mixed with milk. They believe that all the cattle of the world were given to them by God, and when they have allowed their neighbors, whom they call Kikuyu, to grow fat for a little while and acquire large herds, they descend upon a village and kill all the men and male children. They stay on in the village until they have consumed its sustenance, and then they club all the women to death and drive off the cattle. Farther south, where it is cooler, are a people called the Hottentot. . . ."

His Portuguese was barbarous but lively and colorful, and with the help of an expressive face and a liberal sprinkling of Spanish and Italian approximations of the words he wanted, he had no trouble making himself understood.

"I beg your pardon," someone said, "but don't you mean hotter?"

"No, the farther south in Africa you go, the cooler it gets."

Another auditor pounced. "There's the flaw in your story, senhor. It's well known that as you proceed south it gets hotter and hotter, as can be told from the fact that people from those climes are burned black. I've seen such black Moors myself as slaves in Venice."

Like all accomplished liars, the Englishman had a quick answer for everything. Undaunted, he replied, "That's only true for the top half of Africa. Once you get past the equator, it's reversed."

"You claim to have crossed the equinoctial line, senhor?"

"Twice. Once going, once coming."

His critic adopted a smug expression. "And how would you know that you've crossed this . . . this *equador*?"

"The skies are different. The north star disappears. Instead, there's a cross in the sky, by which you can tell your direction."

Sandro raised his head at that. The Arab sea captain he had dealt with in Damascus—the one who had given him the *kamal*—had spoken of the place where the north star vanished, the line beyond which the spice ships feared to sail. And old Jaybir, the astronomer, had heard persistent rumors that beyond that place a Frankish cross appeared in the sky to replace the northern constellations. If this Englishman was a storyteller, at least he had not invented the stories—he had heard them somewhere.

The Englishman noticed the look of attention on Sandro's face and appealed to him. "You look like an intelligent man, senhor. What do you say?"

Sandro spoke slowly. "If the world is indeed round, as some people maintain, senhor, then it stands to reason that there would be different skies below the *equator*."

"Exactly," the Englishman said, with a challenging glance round the table. "So that by studying the new stars and making maps of them, the seafarers of the Middle Kingdom can find their way around the southern seas as easily as you or I might find our way through the streets of Lisbon. So that, for example, when sailing *up* the west coast of Africa, which they did not know before, they can tell when they are at the latitude of some place they reached while sailing *down* the east coast, which they have already mapped, and thus measure where they are in relation to the kingdoms of the world."

The scoffer said, "I know something of seafaring, senhor, and I can tell you that it's no easy thing to find your way around the sea, unless you're within sight of a coast you're familiar with. Oh, you can tell your direction well enough by the north star or the sun—by the compass, if you're versed in its use—but only a magician could tell his latitude from the pitching deck of a ship."

The Englishman showed impatience. "The ships of the Middle Kingdom have an officer aboard whom they call a 'sky student'—a sort of astrologer. Surely you know that even in Portugal astrologers have a way in which they can determine latitude."

"Ay—with a heathen astrolabe. I'd like to see one of those mumbling frauds try to use one at sea!"

He drew a round of chuckles from his fellow seafarers at the table.

"They don't use an astrolabe," the Englishman said in exasperation. "They use an instrument they call a 'guiding-star stretch-board' with a set of plaques you hold at a fixed distance from the eye until you find one that fits between the star and the horizon. Another plaque is turned one way or the other until it fits, and a calculation is then made from a table. I'm no scholar, and I don't understand how it was done, but they showed me how to take the measurements myself—and I can assure you that it works!"

To Sandro what the Englishman had described sounded remarkably like the *kamal*, except that you used many plates or boards of different sizes mounted on what was probably a rigid rod instead of one board and a string of variable length in which you tied knots. But the principle would be the same.

He eyed the Englishman, whose face was starting to grow red. This untutored fellow could not possibly have invented it out of his own imagination.

One of the Englishman's self-invited guests saw that the sport had gone too far, and moved to restore a convivial atmosphere. "These yellow men of whom you speak must be rare mariners, from what you said before, Senhor Tomás. Can it be true that their ships won't sink?"

The Englishman was a primitive sort, whose good humor was easily restored. "Oh, I suppose they'll sink if they're damaged badly enough, but it would have to be a real catastrophe. You see, their holds are divided into five or six watertight compartments. If one gets damaged, the others keep it afloat."

"Ingenious! And you say these ships have as many as nine masts and reach a length of more than four hundred and fifty feet—five times the length of our largest Portuguese *nãos*? That in fact they are twice as broad as a *não* is long?"

"That's what I said."

One skeptic wasn't convinced. "It would take a thousand men to sail a ship like that."

"No," the Englishman said soberly, "only five or six hundred."

The other thumped his thigh and laughed. "You're pulling our leg, senhor, admit it."

The Englishman became angry again. "The bunch of you can go to hell. If you don't want to believe me, I can't make you!"

Sandro spoke out. "I, for one, found much of interest in your tale, senhor. I'd like to hear more about these star guide boards you mentioned. I gather that you didn't just hear about them from someone on your travels—you have personal knowledge of them."

"Damn right," the Englishman said belligerently. "I was there myself. I sailed with the Star Raft, rounded Africa, saw it all." He glowered. "D'you doubt me?"

Sandro had his reservations about nine-masted ships that were larger than a Venetian great galley, but he put it down to simple exaggeration. He was willing to credit a ship as large as a *não* or somewhat larger, and perhaps the dimensions had grown as the fellow retold his tales. He said diplomatically, "Not in the least, senhor. What brings you to Portugal?"

The Englishman squinted at him. "You're not Portuguese."

"No, Venetian. Call me Sandro."

"I'm Tom." He held out his hand. He was drunker than he looked, but he carried his drink well. "I was sitting in a corner in England, growing cobwebs, when I heard that a Portuguese mariner had passed Cape Not—Non, they call it here—and I said to myself, that's the place for you, my boy. Then I got here and found that Prince Henry's sailors had passed Cape Bojador as well, but that everybody's gotten tired of exploration because the expedition didn't bring back a shipload of gold. It's the wrong time for them to get discouraged. They haven't even scratched the surface yet." He peered with a drunk's cunning at Sandro. "I could tell them a thing or two about Africa."

"Then you're in luck, senhor. Allow me to buy you a drink. There's someone at that table over there I'd like you to meet."

"'Swounds, this is a novelty—someone offering to buy a drink for *me*," the Englishman said. He lurched to his feet. "Lead on, my friend."

The freeloaders watched him go with faces like cats deprived of their mouse. Catalina, across the room, raised her eyebrows at Sandro. Vasques was going to complain to her about this.

Pedro looked up blearily as they approached. Sandro hoped he wasn't too far gone to talk. He wasn't worried about the Englishman, this Tomás or Tom as he called himself. He had a feeling that Tom could go on talking even after he was lying on the floor with all his limbs paralyzed.

"Tom, I'd like you to meet my friend Pedro da Costa. He's

the pilot who brought Gil Eanes's ship around Cape Non, and brought Afonso Goncalves Baldaia past Cape Bojador."

Tom pumped Pedro's hand enthusiastically. "God's blood, it's an honor to meet a man of your parts. It's a world where everybody sits at home. We need a few more of your stripe."

Pedro suffered his hand to be shaken. The mention of Bojador and Non failed to rouse him from his apathy.

"They've heard of your feat in England," Sandro said. "Tomás came to see for himself."

"You came too late," Pedro said. "The cheering's stopped. Nobody cares about exploration for exploration's sake. All they want is gold."

"There's gold, if that's what they want," the Englishman said. "And ivory and slaves—and eventually spices. You haven't sailed far enough yet, that's all. Africa's big, bigger than anyone knows. So far you've reached only the latitude where on the other side of Africa the Moslems have their holy city in Arabia. You must go twice that far before you reach the great African kingdoms where gold and ivory can be acquired—and twice that far again to reach the bottom of Africa. But once you round that final cape, all the riches of the East will be open to your ships."

Sandro sent a look of apology to Pedro for the Englishman's demented rush, but Pedro had slowly lifted his head to fix his eyes on Tom's flushed face.

"You're very specific, senhor. How can you know?"

Tom suddenly seemed very sober. "I've been there."

The quiet certainty in his voice was more impressive than bluster would have been. Sandro had heard many taproom liars in his day, telling their tales of having visited the fabled kingdom of Prester John, or having slept with dog-faced maidens in a land of headless men with eyes in their chests, but they always sounded like mountebanks at a fair.

"I have some coastal charts too," Tom said. "I took what I could get my hands on. There's one that shows the shape of the southern part of Africa. They're not like our maps, but they make sense to the eye after a while."

"Pedro . . ." Sandro said, his excitement mounting. "Listen . . . we could take this to Prince Henry . . ."

Tom grinned crookedly. "Well, that's a start," he said. "I'll tell you the rest of it, then . . ."

It was a fantastic tale, but the details rang true. Almost, Sandro could see the gigantic ships with their forests of masts and slatted sails, full of treasures and horses and armed men.

Pedro was staring with new surmise at Tom. "When did you sail around the tip of Africa?"

"Two years ago. It took me that long to get home again." He gave another of his lopsided grins. "I didn't stay long, though."

"Two years!" Pedro breathed explosively. "That was when Gil Eanes passed Cape Bojador—and turned back without venturing farther. If only he'd gone on! The two expeditions might have met! What a meeting that would have been!"

"If only Cheng Ho had gone on," Tom said. "He might have met your Baldaia. But the Ming emperors lost their nerve. They gave up too soon. I hope your Prince Henry won't."

For a moment Sandro saw the encounter as the two journeyers before him might have seen it: the two small Portuguese vessels—Eanes's *barcha* scarcely fifty feet long—bobbing about in a limitless ocean; the great Chinese fleet, like a wall of sails, advancing northward; the amazement on both sides, the exchanges of visits, the dawning realization that the way was open between their two worlds; the sense that the affairs of mankind would change, that things would never be the same again.

"We stopped," Tom was saying, "at the mouth of a great river, a river perhaps as great as the Nile itself, which is called the Congo, after a powerful kingdom thereabouts. It was still some hundreds of miles beneath the equator—at about the same latitude as an island called Zanzibar that we encountered off Africa's eastern coast, which gave us the same reading on the guiding star stretch-plates."

"That far?" Pedro was crestfallen.

"There's as much of Africa below the equator as there is above it."

Sandro spoke. "Could this Congo be the River of Gold that appears on the Catalan world map drawn many years ago by the great Abraham Cresques, the father of Jaime of Majorca? Prince Henry sets much store by that map—this would be a piece of information that would indeed make him take notice."

"No," Tom said. "There's another big river farther north that runs through the kingdoms of Mali and Benin and is closer to the coast of ivory and gold where the Arab caravans trade. That must be where the legend of a River of Gold comes from."

"Then it does exist," Sandro said, hitting the table with his fist. "What Baldaia called the Rio de Ouro was only an inlet with bare desert at the end. It was a bad choice of names. It turned the public against Henry. If he could be persuaded that you're telling the truth, it would give him the heart to go on again."

He stole a look at Pedro. Mention of the Rio de Ouro fiasco and the reaction it had caused in Portugal was guaranteed to set him off these days, given the black mood he'd sunk into, but aside from a tightening of the jaw he continued to maintain an even keel. The Englishman's revelations had given his mind something fresh to chew on.

"Yes," Pedro said. "Hope's what we need."

"Hold your horses," Tom said. "You've only ventured a few hundred miles past Cape Bojador so far. You'll sail another thousand miles, and you still won't have reached your gold coast. That kind of disappointment can kill a dream."

"We'll find fresh inspiration along the way. As long as we have some goal to strive for."

The black mood was lifting, Sandro thought. Pedro actually had a smile on his face.

"Africa has a western bulge that may be bigger than all Europe," Tom warned. "The geographers don't even suspect that it exists. I've seen the map of Ptolemy—a lot of nonsense. Your ships, if they find the courage to go on, will find the coast turning east. They'll think they've found the bottom of Africa. They'll be sure of it when the coast continues to trend east. They'll sail a thousand, maybe two thousand miles with their hopes rising, thinking all the time that they've found the way to India. And then their hopes will be dashed. The coast will turn south again. They'll sail thousands of miles more, and the coast will still run south. It's bound to revive all the old beliefs about Africa having no bottom. Disappointed hope is worse than no hope at all. It'll be a worse disappointment for Portugal than this Rio de Ouro that turned out to be no *rio* at all."

"No," Pedro said stubbornly. "It won't happen that way next time."

"We've got to tell Prince Henry's geographers," Sandro said. "Mestre Jaime . . ."

"I tried to see him," Tom said. "They turned me away at

the door. They thought me a charlatan or a madman. My claims were too extravagant. If I'd been more modest—said only that I'd traveled as far as Constantinople or Trebizond and bought a Saracen map that I wanted to sell . . ."

"I was turned away, too," Sandro said, remembering his arrival in Sagres in the rags of a Moor. "I didn't try to see Mestre Jaime, only one of the astrologers."

"You won't be turned away this time," Pedro said, making up his mind. "We'll go together. I'll have no trouble being admitted." His expression turned bitter. "I'm the pilot who brought Baldaia to the River of Gold."

Sandro did not dare say anything for fear Pedro would change his mind. Pedro had been careful enough, Sandro thought, but he couldn't blame him. A pilot's reputation was a precious thing, to be spent more carefully than gold.

At the next table the rowdies who had been heckling Pedro earlier in the evening had finished a long and pointless boasting match about their prowess with the whores of the world and were at loose ends again. One of them had caught the words *Rio de Ouro*.

"Hey, *companheiros*," he said loudly, trying to get a rise out of Pedro, "what piece of property is more valuable than the *Rio de Ouro*?"

"You tell us, Diogo," one of the others said just as loudly.

"The land at the bottom of an outhouse," Diogo replied with a sly glance toward Pedro.

Pedro stiffened. Sandro put a restraining hand on his arm. "Don't let them provoke you."

The idlers at the other table were exchanging guffaws, pleased at Diogo's sally. There were five of them, rough types who might have been henchmen of some *poderoso* of the district. Two of them wore the same badge of household. Their conversation continued for a while, then another of them tried out his wit.

"By God, the prince paid a lot of money to get a bucket of sand. Do you suppose there was any camel dung in it?"

One of them didn't find that funny. "Money that might have been better spent on honest folk," he growled.

"Like us, Estevão?" put in someone else, and there was more laughter. They were looking expectantly toward Pedro's table.

Pedro was doing a good job of controlling himself. "That's the way," Sandro told him. "They're just looking for a fight."

They bought a jar of wine from Vasques and left. "Come with me to my house," Sandro said. "We can talk there."

They woke up the servants when they stumbled through the door, despite their efforts to be silent. Lúcio, the manservant, appeared timidly with a lantern, and Sandro waved him back to bed.

Tom told them some more of his adventures. They finished the jar of wine, and Sandro got another from the wine closet. They were still talking when Catalina came home.

"Well?" she said to Sandro, ignoring the other two.

"I'll be along in a moment," he said, starting to get up and falling back in his chair.

"We're sorry if we caused you any distress, mistress," Tom said, having no better luck in getting to his feet than did Sandro.

She stalked by him without a word. After a while, a door slammed elsewhere in the house.

They stayed up all night talking. Sandro found his tongue loosening. He unfroze enough to tell them something of his adventures on the flight to Granada and of his life as the secretary of the great astronomer, Jaybir al-Sumut, but he steered away from any reference to Marina or his time as a galley slave. Pedro, in turn, described the discovery of the Azores and had much to say about the voyages down the coast of Africa with Cabral, Gil Eanes, and Baldaia, but Sandro was not too thick to notice that he avoided all mention of his part in the colonization of Madeira.

Catalina came to the door two or three times to look in, but she left each time without saying anything. Finally she gave up. Sandro heard the door to the sleeping chamber shut and the bolt fall in place.

In the morning, as the light crept through the windows, Sandro looked at his companions and saw the puffed faces, the rumpled clothes. He looked no better himself, he knew.

"Time to sober up," he told them. "We'll have some food and clean up. Then we can gather our maps and instruments and call on Jaime of Majorca."

# CHAPTER 19

The place reminded Sandro of a wizard's lair, with its piles of parchment scrolls, the smell of dust, the strange instruments hanging from the walls, the cagelike spheres that contained the secrets of the earth and the heavens in their calibrated hoops. He shook off the impression. He'd seen similar chambers when he'd been the slave of Jaybir; there was nothing mysterious about all these objects once you knew what they were for.

The old mapmaker had not yet put in an appearance. "He's not at his best in the morning," the majordomo who had admitted them had said, "but he agreed to see you because Senhor da Costa vouches for you."

While they waited Sandro satisfied his curiosity with a look around. The brilliantly painted panels covered with a spiderweb crisscross of rhumb lines must be a fair copy of the famous Catalan world map made by Jaime's celebrated father, Abraham Cresques. Sandro walked over to it for a closer scrutiny. It was a sensible map with few mythical creatures, and it made an effort to include some of the landmarks mentioned by Marco Polo. A picture of Marco Polo himself was painted upside down in an upper corner with a camel caravan meeting the fabled Kublai Khan.

His eye traveled to the other panels. There were twelve of them altogether. The Christian kingdom of Prester John was there as were the tribes of Gog and Magog, fortunately hemmed in by the Caspian Mountains. Elsewhere a caravan route was shown through a gap in the Atlas mountains, and pearl divers were depicted along the coast of India, as Tom had confirmed.

He searched the rather vague outline of Africa. It was still a continent with no bottom, but along the western coast, just below the level of the Canary Islands, he found a great river labeled "Rio de Ouro" flowing from the east, where it connected with the Nile.

Pedro came to stand beside him. "There it is. That pesky river of gold. He shows it too far north. That's what confused Baldaia."

Tom joined them. "He's got a kingdom of Mali," he said, "but he puts it in the wrong place. And the ruler of Calicut doesn't wear a crown. In fact he hardly wears anything at all. And the pearl divers look like they're bringing up rubies and emeralds. Those don't grow in oysters."

A dry cough sounded behind them.

"So," said a caustic voice, "who are these learned geographers who presume to correct the *mappamundi* of Abraham Cresques?"

The three turned guiltily to face the withering presence of Jaime of Majorca. The prince's cartographer was a small, bent man, frail with age, not at all impressive until you encountered the piercing gaze of the sparrow hawk eyes. He was dressed somberly in black robes and a black velvet cap.

Sandro tried not to be intimidated. More than the others, he was in a position to understand Mestre Jaime's accomplishments. The greatest mapmakers in the world were Catalan Jews of the school of Majorca, and Mestre Jaime, carrying forth his father's towering work, led them all. He had been born Jehuda Cresques, but after his conversion to Christianity was known as Jaime Ribas. It was reported that Prince Henry had paid him an immense salary to lure him away from the King of Aragon.

"You've corrected it yourself, Mestre Jaime," Sandro replied in an even tone. "Unless I miss my guess, the table over there with the cloth over it is your own *mappamundi*, the one that incorporates the infante's new discoveries."

"We don't show that one to Venetians," Jaime said dryly. "Or Englishmen."

"We've not come to obtain knowledge, but to give it," Sandro retorted.

Jaime raised ironic eyebrows. "And at a good price, no doubt."

Sandro hesitated only an instant. "I won't pretend disinterest, Mestre. If the information proves valuable, I'm sure that the infante will wish to reward us."

"Smooth words, senhor. I've heard their like often. Many charlatans come here to Sagres with fancy stories and extravagant claims, having heard of Dom Henrique's generosity. I'm here to filter out the rogues and swindlers for the infante. I warn you, I've heard it all. What have you got that makes you think I'd be interested?"

"Mestre, I was a prisoner of the Moors for many years. I can show you an instrument, simple to use, that will bring a navigator unerringly to his home port." He lifted his head in a direct challenge. "It's one thing to send sailors out to poke into the unknown, giving them a map that purports to show them the way. But they're apt to go more willingly, and sail farther, when they have some assurance that they'll be able to return."

A flare of interest showed in Jaime's deep eyes. He was not only a cartographer but a master instrument maker, who had brought his knowledge of compasses to Prince Henry's artisans.

"I don't doubt that you were a prisoner of the Moors," he said with a contemptuous glance at Sandro's thickened hands. "What could a galley slave, chained to his bench, possibly learn of navigation?"

"Mestre, I was the secretary of Jaybir al-Sumut in Damascus."

Jaime caught his breath. "Where did you hear that name?" he demanded sharply.

"I've told you. I was his secretary. He was no geographer, but I can tell you something of his methods in determining the size of the world and thus putting its cities at their proper distances. You can examine me if you like."

"Don't think I won't. At length. Well, go on!"

Sandro hooked a thumb in Tom's direction. "The Englishman brings you something rarer still—the sure knowledge of Africa's true shape. He's been to Cathay and back."

Jaime was very still for a moment. Then he said, "I should have the two of you thrown out now. But Pedro seems to think there may be something behind your assertions." He turned to Pedro. "Pedro da Costa, I know you to be an honest man and a careful and reliable pilot. The *portolano* sketches you brought back from Bojador and Non were an invaluable aid in filling out the details of Africa's coastline on the official *padron*. But sometimes an honest man can be gullible, especially when victimized by a glib confidence trickster."

Pedro spoke diffidently. "Senhor Sandro explained the use of the Arab instrument to me. The Englishman's information matches. The mariners of Cathay use a different instrument, but it works in a similar fashion."

"They cooked it up between them," Jaime said.

"He's not interested," Tom said. "Let's go."

"Hold!" Jaime held out his hand imperiously. "Give it to me."

Sandro hesitated. If he handed over the *kamal*, he'd have nothing to bargain with. But this was as close to Prince Henry as he was likely to get. The chance wouldn't come again. It was all or nothing. He made up his mind. Contrary to popular belief, he had always found Jews to be more honest than other men. They had to be.

Silently, he unwrapped the small parcel and gave the *kamal* to the old mapmaker.

Mestre Jaime turned the wooden rectangle over in his hands. "Is this a joke?"

"No joke, Mestre," Sandro said.

Pedro said, "I'm a mariner, Mestre, not a learned doctor. I wouldn't know how to use one of your astrolabes. I doubt that even you would find it much use at sea, where the horizon's likely to tilt back and forth. But this Arab instrument's easy to use. I tested it out at Bojador, on the return trip. It brought me in from far out to sea, to exactly the part of the African coast I'd marked on the first trip."

"And how did you mark it?"

"Why," Pedro said, furrowing his brow, "by tying a knot in the string."

"It's crude but accurate," Sandro said quickly. "You hold the string in your teeth and sight with the wood chip to take the altitude of the north star, moving it till it's the right distance from your eye. Each knot in the string represents the latitude of a known port."

"All this without calculations of any sort?"

"It works, Mestre," Pedro said simply.

Jaime chewed his lip. He whirled suddenly on Tom. "And you, Englishman, what have you to show me?"

"I've got myself, Master Geographer," Tom said with an impudent grin. "This body you see in front of you carried me to the world's eastern rim and back. It's sailed below the equator to the tip of Africa, where the eastern and western oceans meet, and it's walked back across the equator again. Surely it's a rare object."

"He sailed with the men of Cathay, Mestre," Sandro said. "He has much of value to tell us. His story is strange, but it hangs together in every detail. He has not the learning to have invented the navigational instrument he described. The mariners of Cathay aren't limited to taking the altitude of the polar star, which is the pivot of the sky. They take the altitudes of other stars, too, at their meridian passage, and make calculations from a book of tables. . . ."

"Let's save time," Tom said. He produced the second of the silk maps he had shown Sandro and Pedro the night before. This one was not star diagrams, but one of Cheng Ho's sailing charts. It was beautifully rendered, the work of one of the Treasure Fleet's shipboard artists, and at first glance appeared to be merely decorative. Mestre Jaime frowned at the unfamiliar conventions of style. Sandro could tell the exact moment when his eye adjusted and made sense out of the shapes.

"You call this a map?" Jaime said.

"As much as that one," Tom said brashly, pointing to the Catalan *mappamundi*. "The difference is that the mapmaker painted what he knew, not what he guessed at."

For a moment Sandro thought that Jaime was going to have an apoplectic fit. The parchment cheeks turned a blotchy red, and his breathing grew labored.

Sandro shot Tom a furious look. "See, Mestre," he said, "here's the final cape at Africa's southernmost tip, and the deceptive bay next to it that gives the impression of a false cape. This thicket of picture writing must be a warning to mariners not to mistake one for the other. And here, this broken line imbedded in more picture writing shows the route. You can see plainly that there's a passage to India."

After a while Mestre Jaime's breathing slowed, and the color faded from his cheeks.

"All right," he said. "You'll answer my questions now, both of us. We'll sort the wheat from the chaff, and if I'm satisfied, I'll take you tomorrow to put it before Prince Henry."

•   •   •

Old Bartolomé's leathery face broke into a smile of pleasure when he saw Pedro. "Pedrozinho," he said. "Where have you been hiding yourself? I've not seen you since the day the prince sent you away with your purse full. Don't you know you're always welcome here? I thought you'd at least drop by once in a while to swap yarns over a cup of wine."

The old soldier was close to eighty now, and had long since been retired from his position as household constable. But he still shuffled around the house, fussing at this and that, to the vexation of his successor. Time had carved him more deeply, bringing out his cords and tendons, and the limp from his old wound at Ceuta had not improved, but his eyes were still good, and he was still strong enough in the arms for light duties.

"A thousand regrets, Dom Bartolomé . . . I didn't want to impose . . . you're looking well. . . ." He turned to include Sandro and Tom. "Allow me to introduce these gentlemen . . . this is Dom Alessandro, a *fidalgo* of Veneze, and Senhor Tomás, from Inglaterra."

"Yes, I know—Mestre Jaime said you'd be here. He hasn't arrived yet. He's slow to get started in the morning. I've told him a dose of rhubarb is what he needs. What's it about, Pedrozinho?"

Pedro said cautiously, "It may be that these gentlemen have some useful information for the infante. About Saracen navigation methods and such matters. Mestre Jaime's offered to place their ideas before the infante. In addition, the *Inglês* is a great traveler. The infante may find something novel in his tale."

Bartolomé sighed. "He could do with a little novelty. He's much distracted these days. But he always cheers up when he has a chance to talk shop."

"He's not in one of his melancholy moods?" Pedro asked. "Perhaps he won't wish to receive us."

"No, no, he'll be glad to see you, Pedrozinho. The prince has mentioned your name, you know, and more than once. He's well pleased with what you've done for him, even if some folks now belittle the accomplishment." He checked himself. "Not that I tolerate such talk in my presence."

"It's the Rio de Ouro, then? The River of Gold that turned out to be no river and no gold."

"If that were all, he'd rise above it. He's never let criticism stop him. No, he's weighed down by family matters—

all this dissension about a new crusade in Tangier—and it saps his energy and prevents him from going forward."

"Perhaps we'll give him new energy, senhor," Sandro put in, "if the information we bring today gives him new reason for going on."

"I hope so, Excellency," Bartolomé said. "I've seen him like this before." He ran an approving eye over Sandro's fine doublet and hose and the belt of enameled silver. Sandro had donned his best suit of clothes for the occasion, and looked, for once, the proper gentleman instead of an ink-stained merchant.

"We're closer to war, then?" Sandro said.

"King Duarte's canvasing all the brothers, and his advisers, for their opinion. He sent for his brothers—the count of Barcelos, too—at Leiria, and they all had it out. Dom Henrique was much agitated when he returned. He feels he's being thwarted again, as when his father refused to let him go on and conquer Gibraltar after the taking of Ceuta. Young Fernando is all for it, of course—he wants to win his spurs in battle. Dom Henrique argued that he and Fernando, at least, be allowed to go with their own armies. King Duarte told him, 'For the love of God, do not excite Prince Fernando!' Prince Pedro's against it. The people are too poor for another war right now, he says—it's only the knights who are at loose ends. Dom Henrique's upset that Prince Pedro opposes him—very upset, seeing that they've always been so close. And now Queen Leonor's all for a crusade in Tangier, just for the reason that Pedro's against it. She's disliked Pedro ever since he married the Aragonese princess and gave her the daughter of her father's rival for a sister-in-law. Dom Henrique's always been her favorite brother-in-law anyway, and so she's telling him that she'll use her influence with Duarte to tip the scale on his side."

He noticed Pedro's urgent signals and drew himself up. "I betray no family confidences. The quarrel's common knowledge."

"An old campaigner like yourself supports a war, I take it," Sandro said with the easy grace of the wellborn.

"I'll tell you the truth, sir," Bartolomé said. "Once I would have been the hottest firebrand of them all. But age cools one off. Now it's all the same to me whether Prince Henry chooses war or exploration, as long as he engages himself again and climbs out of the pit of despondency he's digging for himself."

He turned again to Pedro and said with a worried frown, "It's the old story, *moco*. He's starting to feel unworthy all over again. Perhaps it was the Rio de Ouro disappointment that pushed him over the edge after all. But he thinks he's betrayed Christ by not pursuing the crusade against the Moors with sufficient fervor. He's spending too much time on his knees in his chapel, praying. And I suspect he's scourging himself again as well."

Pedro was chilled at his words. He remembered how frightened he had been long ago, when as a young boy he had glimpsed, as through a crack in a statue of brick, the molten fervor within Prince Henry that had brought him to despair. The prince had felt unworthy then, too. Zarco and Teixeira had pulled him out of it that time. Pedro hoped with all his being that Sandro was right. Perhaps, with this promise of a fresh goal they had brought the infante, they could do the same.

A bustle of courtiers and visitors at the entrance screen to the great hall made him turn his head. The crowd parted to let someone through, and a respectful silence momentarily replaced the chatter. It was Jaime of Majorca, a black intrusion against all the bright colors, followed by an attendant with an armload of portfolios.

He came like an arrow straight toward them, and the attention of the crowd followed.

"Good, you're here on time." He looked them over, and appeared somewhat mollified by the fact that, with hangovers gone and bloodshot eyes cleared up, they looked less disreputable than they had the day before. If Tom's showy doublet, with its garish colors and dagged sleeves, gave him momentary pause, he forebore comment. "You'll remember what I told you," he said. "You'll not say too much. There's no need to go on about giant ships and fleets of hundreds. It's enough to say you sailed on a ship of the east. We don't want to strain the prince's credulity."

"Never fear," Tom said. "I'm the veteran of a thousand taverns."

Jaime gave him a fishy stare and went on to Sandro. "You've brought your Arab instrument with you?"

"Yes. I've whittled a spare. I'll leave it with the prince."

Bartolomé said gruffly, *"Boa sorte, Pedrozinho."*

"Thank you, Dom Bartolomé," Pedro said.

A page boy conducted them to the prince's chambers.

Henry was at the window, staring out to sea. He turned around when they entered, and Pedro was appalled at how haggard he looked.

"Mestre Jaime," he said graciously, walking toward them with his hands out, "and my stout mariner Pedro. Are these the gentlemen of whom you spoke?"

The prince moved stiffly, Pedro noted, and he gave credence to Bartolomé's suspicions about the scourge.

Sandro made an elegant leg. "Vossa Excelência," he said. Tom bumbled his way through a sort of bow. Prince Henry, to his credit, did not blink at Tom's clothes, which must have violated every Portuguese sumptuary law in force.

"Come, rise," Henry said. "I'm told, senhor, that you were a prisoner of the Moors. That seemed to me a good omen, since many years ago another man who had been a prisoner of the Moors, a Spaniard named Morales, was brought to me, and the story he had to tell led to the discovery of Porto Santo and Madeira." He smiled. "Let's hope that your story will lead to something worthwhile too."

"It's not just a story, Vossa Excelência," Sandro said. "I was the slave of a noted astronomer, the great Jaybir al-Sumut, whose reputation is known to Mestre Jaime. Mestre Jaime examined me at length, and I believe I was able to satisfy him in every particular. . . ."

Pedro let Sandro and Jaime do the talking. His attention roved to the prince's worktable. The papers and instruments on it were covered with dust, as though Prince Henry had not been interested in them for a very long time. There was one difference that he was able to pick out—the unfinished ship model that he had seen before had been replaced by another. This one looked complete, even to sails and rigging. Though tall and curved in the stem, it had a straight keel, good for nosing through unknown shallows, and it retained the unobstructed bow of the previous model in order not to interfere with the forward lateen sail. It looked a handy little ship, fast and versatile. But it, too, had been allowed to gather dust.

Mestre Jaime had just finished some long dissertation on the necessity of making latitude determinations along the African coast, and Sandro had interrupted to say, "All well and good, but that we can leave for the geographers to clean up afterward. What's important to sailors is to know where they're going and to have confidence that they can make landfall at a known spot even from far out to sea. Isn't that so, Pedro?"

They were all looking at him. He stopped his day-dreaming with a guilty start. "*Sim,*" he agreed, "it's more important now than ever, since we've weaned ourselves from the mere hugging of coasts and learned to stand hundreds of miles out to sea to pick up the winds home."

"The *volto do mar largo,*" Henry said, nodding, using the name Gil Eanes had given to Pedro's maneuver. "Yes, that changed everything overnight."

The words sounded like the old Henry, but the prince's voice was curiously flat—even listless—as if he were discussing an abstraction of no particular interest to him. Pedro looked to Sandro for help.

"As a practical matter, it's not necessary for a sailor to give a number to a latitude," Sandro said smoothly. "Only to be able to find it again." He produced the *kamal* from its linen wrappings. "This is the instrument the Arabs use. Don't be deceived by its simplicity. I've seen the devices employed by the greatest astronomer of our age, and I swear to Your Grace that it's more useful than any of them."

That earned him a hooded glance of irritation from Jaime of Majorca, but true to his word, the old cartographer threw his support behind Sandro.

"I would not have given credence to his claims, Dom Henrique," he said, "but Pedro da Costa, a steady man and your best pilot, has tested this ridiculous device and found that it may have some merit."

Prince Henry's red-rimmed eyes swung toward Pedro. For the first time there was a glimmer of interest in them. "You've tried it? Is that true?"

"*Sim, Vossa Excelência.*" He was sweating, now that the time had come to say or be silent. "Dom Alessandro tutored me in its use. Already I've fixed the positions of Sagres, Madeira, Santa Maria in the Azores, Cape Non, and Cape Bojador. I found my way back to the exact latitude of Bojador twice without error. If you wish to send me back, I've also fixed the positions of the Bay of Horses and the headland that looks like a galley, where we found the fish-nets."

"And you've said nothing all this time?"

"Vossa Excelência . . . I wanted to be sure. . . ."

Sandro jumped in again and began to explain how the

*kamal* worked. "I've matched all of Pedro's knots, so that they measure out to the same lengths, Vossa Excelência. This one, the first knot, marks the latitude of Sagres itself. I'll leave the instrument with you. You can take it outside tonight and try it out yourself. If you don't arrive at the same knot, I'll eat the thing, string and all."

Prince Henry pursed his lips in thought. Pedro recognized the signs. He'd sat in on some of the prince's conferences with shipwrights, pilots, and craftsmen. The prince often seized the horns of a problem and wrestled it to the ground, leaving the details for others to clear up.

"The string might be replaced by a rigid rod," he mused, stroking his chin. "The plate would slide along it. The distances could be marked by thumbscrews or some other expedient. Such a contrivance would appear more substantial and trustworthy to our mariners. That would remove a lot of prejudice against its use."

Sandro and Pedro looked at each other in amazement at how quickly Prince Henry had grasped the essentials. Tom, who had been chafing in silence until now, took the opportunity to speak.

"The men of the East have done just that, my lord," he said in his atrocious Portuguese, "but they've done it backward, as they do so many other things. The plates stay at the same distance from the eye, but there are many of them, of different sizes, each marked with a number." He cocked his head for a moment and added brightly, "Their compass needles point south, too."

The prince's attention, like a great weight that at last had got moving, swung now toward Tom. "You're the one who claims to have reached Cathay and to have dwelt in the court of the Great Khan."

"The Khans are no more in Cathay, my lord. Things have changed since the days of Marco Polo. The Chinese have thrown the Mongols out of their country. I met the son of the man who did it. The new rulers style themselves emperors and have named their dynasty the Ming, which in the language of the Middle Kingdom means 'bright.'"

Pedro winced. The prince set great store by Marco Polo, he knew. One of his most prized possessions was a rare early copy of the original manuscript that Venice had presented as a state gift to Prince Pedro during his visit there.

But Prince Henry did not at all seem to mind being corrected. "You'll stay and tell me something of your travels?" he said.

"I will, my lord."

Jaime of Majorca said dryly, "Like all travelers' tales, his should be taken with a grain of salt, Dom Henrique. But some of the things he speaks of can be confirmed."

"Marco Polo himself was not believed," Henry said mildly. He gave Tom a magisterial nod. "You'll remember that you're talking to a prince and not abuse my credulity?"

"Yes, my lord." Tom grinned impishly. "Does that mean I'm not to tell you how I crossed the equator?"

It was Jaime's turn to wince. One might as well talk of going to the moon as crossing the equator. "A grain of salt, Dom Henrique," he repeated. "But he might have gained certain garbled facts about navigation in southern climes that are known to the seafarers of the East."

Sandro tried to get the conversation back on course. He tapped the wooden surface of the *kamal* with his finger to bring attention back to it. "The equator's still a long way off, Your Grace," he said. "First we have to get there. Your mariners must be convinced that it's safe to make the attempt. And this will show them the way. The southern skies will be new and strange, that much we know, but this, at least, will guide them as long as the polestar still shows above the horizon. . . ."

Tom was itching to talk. A cautionary glance from Jaime failed to quell him.

"It's not too late to think about what lies beyond that horizon, my lord!" he cried with a sudden passion. "Do you send your ships out only to go so far and no farther? That's not what I've heard. I'm told that you goad your brave sailors to press onward, always onward, to take still another stride so that when a goal is reached, it becomes the starting point for a new goal. I'm told that you do not fear to sail into infinity itself, step by step. Another great prince had such a vision—the Ming emperor called Yung Lo—and he was served by a mariner worthy of his dreams. His ships might have reached our European world and almost did. But the dreams fell into the hands of smaller men. The Mings lost their courage. They left the field to you. If your dream doesn't fail you, it's you who'll change the world now, not them."

And to Jaime's consternation, he reached under his doublet and drew out the silk map. "This shows the way, my lord. Africa ends, finally, and the way is open to the East. . . ."

The prince kept them for hours. Jaime's elderly face grew gray with fatigue, but he gamely declined the prince's invitation to be excused.

"I'll reverse judgment about your marvels and your maps," Henry said to Tom at one point. "I've seen many maps and heard many marvels. It's enough for now that this gives hope."

And then, despite the sternness of his words, he went on to press Tom for details about Cheng Ho's shipyards on the Dragon River and the methods of construction used. "They caulk ships much as we do," Tom said, struggling to recall, "but instead of oakum and tar they use the frayed ends of a sort of bamboo and a mixture of fish oil, bean oil, and lime. They work from drawings, not by eye alone, and the chief designer's name was Chin Pi-feng. They place the broadest beam farther aft than we do, so that the shape of the hull at the waterline is that of a swimming duck rather than a fish, because, as he once explained to me, a fish is entirely in the water while a duck is half in the water and half in the air. . . ."

"Wait," Henry said and sent one of his pages to fetch his master shipwright from the school. When the man arrived, he had Tom repeat it all for his benefit.

He was much interested in Tom's description of the men of southern Africa—the Hottentots and the tall warriors who drank the blood of their cattle. "They're not Moslems, then?" he asked.

"No," Tom replied. "Some worship the powers of nature, some are idolaters. The influence of the Moslems begins to fade out south of the equator because the Arab merchants fear to sail that far. But they ply the sea between Arabia and India."

"Then the Moslems are firmly entrenched in Calicut?"

"Yes," Tom said, grinning as he remembered the Arab merchant colony that had so feared the arrival of Europeans. "But a good dose of your Portuguese cannon would win it for you easily."

There were a half-dozen additional people in the room

now—the master shipwright, another of Jaime's assistants, some instrument makers whom Henry had sent for, still in their aprons. They had only a sketchy notion of what they were there for, not having been present when Tom had begun his story, but the prince addressed this one or that when some point within his scope came up and bade him to listen carefully while Tom or Sandro or Pedro stopped to explain.

Henry was pacing the chamber with nervous energy. The haggard face had lit up in a semblance of its old self. "There's more than one way to serve God," he said. "Christ Himself knows that I've neglected the conquest of the Moors for too long, but perhaps I'm tilting the scales too far in the opposite direction. Surely it must be just as worthy and pious an act to carry the Cross of Christ to new lands." A shadow crossed his face. "There are difficult times ahead," he said, and Pedro knew he was thinking about the impending war in Tangier, "but we can pursue God's purposes on more than one front at a time."

His pacings had brought him to the worktable. He picked up the ship model and blew dust off it. "I've let your masterwork lie idle too long, Mestre Shipwright," he said. "And after all the late hours we've worked to get it just right. Perhaps it's time we started building them."

"*Che carava bella!*" Sandro exclaimed. "What a pretty boat!"

Henry's head snapped around. "What did you call it, senhor?"

Sandro blinked. "Why . . . *carava.* Its lines put me in mind of a kind of Moorish fishing boat one sees in the eastern Mediterranean that goes by that name."

Henry was pleased at the observation. "Yes, you're astute. We've taken some of its lines from Moorish vessels." He might have misunderstood Sandro's lapse into Italian. "Indeed it is a pretty *caravela*," he said, using the diminutive.

The shipwright was beaming. "I can start whenever you say, Dom Henrique. I've got the timbers put aside. I can lay the keel tomorrow, if you like."

"*Bom,*" the prince said. His eyes sought out Pedro, and he addressed him directly. "You'll like this one," he said. "It will do anything you ask of it. You'll notice the sail plan. It will sail with the wind behind it and also sail a lot closer to the wind than a *barcha* or a *não.* Isn't that so, Mestre Shipwright?"

"To within fifty-five degrees or better, if I don't miss my guess," the shipwright confirmed proudly.

"Our mathematicians at the school worked it out," the prince said. "By sailing that close-hauled, our *caravela* will only have to tack three times for every five times a *barcha* needs to tack to cover the same distance. That means better than one-third less distance and so one-third less time at sea."

Pedro matched the prince's broad smile as he saw the implications. "And that means we can go farther out to sea before we have to worry about turning back."

The prince turned to Mestre Jaime. "I put you in charge of sifting through these new ideas of maps and instruments we've heard today. Take the good and see if it can be adapted to our work." His gaze shifted to Tom and Sandro. "What say you gentlemen? Will you help? I want you to take what you know to my school for navigators and work with Mestre Jaime's cartographers and instrument makers. I'll pay you well."

"I don't need the money," Tom said. "But I'll work for you anyway." He grinned puckishly at Jaime of Majorca, who returned him an exasperated expression.

There was a hum of pleasurable excitement from the assembled artisans at the prospect of renewed activity after marking time so long. The shipwright was trying to catch Sandro's eye.

Prince Henry returned his attention to Pedro. "Whatever comes, you'll go exploring again," he promised, "and this time you'll have a ship worthy of the task."

Sandro invited them to his house to celebrate. Catalina relented to the extent of taking a night off from the Cabra do Mar so that she could oversee the preparations for their supper. "It's a slow night anyway," she told Sandro. "I got Ernestina to fill in for me. I ordered a gilded fish, seeing that you invited the Englishman, and I don't trust Generosa to prepare it properly without supervision."

"You don't have to impress the Englishman," Sandro laughed. "He's very natural."

"I don't want him thinking he's better than you are," she said. "He's only born *povo*, in spite of his money."

"You could run a noble household, *cara*," he said. "You're wasting your talents on me."

For some reason the compliment did not please her as he had expected. She turned away and found some excuse to be busy with the table preparations.

The celebration went well at first. Tom did an amusing imitation of Mestre Jaime that made Catalina laugh, and then he won her over by insisting that she sit down with them and have some pastry and a glass of wine. Sandro was full of plans. "I'll have Giraldo take over at the shop for the time being," he said. "Maybe I'll hire another assistant to help him out. The business can afford it."

The three of them had fat purses from the prince with the promise of more to come. Tom had already bought himself two gold chains that clinked together when he walked, given away a fortune to beggars in the street, bought his landlady a bed with a canopy, and now proposed to thank Catalina for the gilded fish by buying her a new gown that, he said, would set off her fine shoulders.

Pedro was enthusiastic about the prince's new ship design, the *caravela*. "Did you see the clean shape of the hull?" he said. "It'll cut through the water like a knife—not like the tubby, round-bellied vessels that we're accustomed to call ships. And the straight keel! That will bring us right up to a beach at low tide. I doubt that it draws more than six feet of water. It's a ship meant for the big ocean, I tell you, not the little seas that we already know!" It was good to see him so animated after the despair of the last few weeks.

But as the evening wore on, Sandro noticed that Pedro was drinking too much. The words got thicker, and there were fewer of them. Sandro tried to draw him out about the *caravela* again and got a glassy stare in return. Once, when Pedro found the wine pitcher empty, he reached out and grabbed Lúcio as he walked past with a tray of cheeses and demanded a refill. Lúcio got it, looking affronted. Sandro shot Catalina a glance, and she shook her head.

At a point where Pedro had sat in morose silence for half an hour, not responding to attempts to bring him into the conversation, Tom said, "Cheer up, *homem*. Why so gloomy? This should be a happy day for you. You have what you want."

Catalina took Tom aside. "No," she said, "he doesn't have

what he wants," and she told him the story of the woman on Madeira.

Tom grew uncharacteristically thoughtful. "Poor bastard," he said. "He's lost her twice, hasn't he? Once to a friend and once to an enemy. He should have fought harder, friend or not. It's no good pining. And he's been pining for ten years. Ten years is a whole life—ask me, I know. When you lose a life, you have to let it go, or it will drive you crazy. He's trying to make a life out of what he started with, and that's not enough. He's following a path that once meant something to him, like a snail going round and round the rim of a bowl on the track it once laid down. He's poisoning himself."

"He knows it's his fault. That's what's poisoning him." Catalina's eyes blazed. "Men! He's not the only one who's poisoning himself!"

Tom was too preoccupied with his thoughts to notice her anger. "You know," he said wistfully, "I have a son in the land of the Mings. At least she was sure it was going to be a son. The soothsayer even told her the color of his hair. Chin-niao, she was going to name him—Little Golden Bird. I wonder if she's told him of me."

Ai-ping, the nursemaid, was agitated. "There's an official all the way from Peking here," she wailed, wringing her hands. "What shall we do? Shall I hide Little Golden Bird?"

"Don't be silly," Lan-ying said. "If someone's come from Peking to see me, he certainly knows about Little Golden Bird. And if he didn't when he arrived, someone from the village would have been certain to have told him when he asked directions. Compose yourself and show him in."

Despite her show of calm, Lan-ying could not help feeling a stab of uneasiness. Who could it be and how had he found her? She had told no one from her former household where she was going, not even Wo. She had lived peacefully in this little fishing village for more than a year now and had almost forgotten about the Yellow Gate.

"Yes, mistress," the girl said, bowing and starting to back out. "But I still think I should hide him. I could cover his head and sneak him out by the back garden."

"Go," Lan-ying said.

"Yes, mistress," Ai-ping said and left, sliding the screen shut behind her.

Lan-ying regretted the sharp tone she had used. Ai-ping was an eighth daughter, a simple girl from the village, but she was a good soul, and she worked hard. There were only four servants in the house. Lan-ying lived modestly, not wanting to call attention to herself, but she made sure that she and Little Golden Bird were comfortable. The jewels she had taken with her were more than enough to provide for them.

"Hsiao Chin-niao, come here," she said, holding out her arms.

The little boy looked up at her, his face wreathed in smiles, and came toddling over. She folded him in her arms protectively. He had lost his baby fat, and looked as if he were going to be wiry, like his father, despite the efforts of the servants to overfeed him. He had a sunny disposition, thanks to the luck of his stars, but he was always getting into trouble if he wasn't watched closely. The blue eyes and the bright, straight yellow hair were startling, but the other children of the village had gotten used to them and thought nothing of them.

The screen slid open, and Ma Huan hobbled in. Lan-ying could see Ai-ping's frightened face behind him, and then the screen slid shut again.

"*Hou,*" the old scholar grunted by way of greeting. "You certainly picked a secluded spot. When I suggested that you retire to Fujian province in the Foochow area, I never thought you'd choose such an out-of-the-way place. It's pure chance I found you. I couldn't wangle your location out of Wo."

Lan-ying was taken by surprise by his appearance. He seemed to have aged a decade in the short time since she'd seen him. His skin was like translucent paper stretched over his cheekbones, and he moved stiffly, advancing with a crippled, crablike gait toward her.

"It's the beating," he said. "I still haven't recovered from it. I was lucky, though. Only twenty-five blows with the jointed rods. Wang Chen, that son of a turtle, ordered it personally. They confiscated the manuscript of my account of the Star Raft's last voyage and burned it." He gave a cackle of triumph. "They didn't know I'd made a copy."

Little Golden Bird chortled with delight. "*Po fu,*" he said. "Uncle."

"He remembers me, at any rate," Ma Huan said, showing his pleasure.

"Why have you come here?" Lan-ying asked, recovering.

"Peking's not a healthy place right now," he said. "I thought I'd better retire to Fujian too. All my old friends are gone. I thought I'd find at least one familiar face." He peered owlishly at her. "How's your cook?"

"You'll find out very shortly. If he's listening behind that screen, he knows that he's to prepare his finest feast, with all the special dishes I taught him."

There was a scurrying and a shadow of movement on the other side of the screen. Lan-ying listened until she could hear a rattle of pans from the kitchen.

Ma Huan cleared his throat. "Cheng Ho is dead," he said.

Her hand flew to her throat. "*Pu shih!*" she said. "Not be!"

"He didn't survive the Hsuan-te emperor by many months," Ma Huan said. "They probably used the same poison on him. They didn't dare execute him publicly. It would cause too much talk. But that turtle's son, Wang Chen, has a long arm. Someone in the Nanking garrison must have been bribed to do it."

"*Pu shih,*" she repeated. Little Golden Bird started to cry.

"The dowager empress will serve as regent for Cheng-t'ung until he comes of age," Ma Huan went on. "But it will be Wang Chen who runs things. We'll have a dictatorship of eunuchs now. The dowager created him. Now she'll have to live with it. They'll poison her, too, if she becomes troublesome."

"Chin Mao was right to go back to the West, then," she whispered. "He knew he could not come back." It was one of the hardest things she'd ever had to say.

Ma Huan's head bobbed in agreement. "He could not have survived. They're erasing all traces of Cheng Ho. His master ship designer, Chin Pi-feng, was executed last month. He was charged with violating the new law against building oceangoing ships. They've burned all of Cheng Ho's charts and records—all those they could find, that is."

"It's all right, Chin-niao, don't cry," she said. The little boy snuggled up to her.

"There'll be no more exploration, ever," Ma Huan said in a voice as dry and brittle as old paper. "It's up to Chin Mao's people now."

# CHAPTER 20

"You'd better come get him," Catalina said. "I don't like the look of it."

She was a little out of breath from having hurried, and she hadn't bothered to fasten the dark cloak she had thrown over her tavern clothes. She stood waiting impatiently in the doorway, not coming into the room.

"What is it?" Sandro asked. "Fighting again?"

"No, he's too far gone in self-pity to fight. A couple of *ladrãos* are sitting with him, pretending to be his friends, making him drunker. They know about the purse he got from the Prince. He carries too much money around. They want to take him out into some dark alley and rob him."

Sandro got up from the table, pushing aside the sketches he had been working on with Tom. "All right," he said. "I'll come. He can sleep here tonight."

Tom got up too. "I'd better come with you. He can be hard to handle in that condition."

They followed Catalina outside. The night was bright enough, with a crescent moon riding a few scudding clouds high in the sky, so that they did not need to take a torch. Sandro's house, though it had a small garden in back, was crowded among its modest neighbors in the dense quarter leading down to the waterfront, not far from his shop.

"He's all right as long as he has something to do," Tom

said as they hurried down the cobbled street, "but when time hangs on his hands, he starts to get broody."

"I thought he was over that," Catalina said. "Then he started in again."

"It's the letdown," Sandro said. "He pulled himself out of his wallow once. Twice is harder."

"What does he expect?" Tom burst out, quickening his step to keep up with Sandro's long strides. "The prince has other things on his mind at the moment. The war in Tangier was a horrible disaster. His brother Fernando's a hostage of the Moors, and they won't give him up until Henry gives up Ceuta, which he refuses to do. Prince Henry blames himself—he said he should have been the one to offer himself in the hostage exchange instead of allowing Prince Fernando to do it. King Duarte's taken to his bed—he's determined to die and fulfill some fool astrologer's prophecy on his coronation day. The country's had a shock. You can't expect Prince Henry to think about caravels now."

"Tell that to Pedro," Sandro said sourly.

"I did. 'The prince will snap out of it,' I said. This setback's only temporary. The caravels are being built. That's the important thing."

"Pedro's no good at waiting. When he has nothing to occupy his mind, he starts chewing over the past."

"Men!" Catalina flung at them. "They're like children. They expect everything to happen at once."

"Things are at a standstill with me, too," Tom said. "They've made their copies of the silk maps and filed them away. I've answered questions about Ming shipbuilding till I've gone hoarse. They listen to my accounts of the voyages, but they don't take notes any more. I didn't bother going back to the school today, and no one sent for me. My feet are getting itchy. I wish I had something to do myself."

"Catalina," Sandro said, "Pedro likes you. Can't you say something to him?"

"What should I say? That he's a fool? That if he feels that way about it, he should go to Madeira and try to take her away from this Lobo? Why don't you say something?"

"He bites my head off if I try."

The lights of the Cabra do Mar showed ahead. The sounds of rough merriment came through the night.

They pushed through the door after Catalina. Across the room an aproned Vasques, looking harried, was setting up a row of winecups. When he saw Catalina, he put his hands on his hips and gave her a fierce admonitory scowl. She made an impolite face back at him and hung up her cloak on a peg. Before going back to work she turned to Sandro and said, "It's those two over there."

Sandro saw Pedro sitting at a table with two men who looked the part of thugs if anyone did. One had lost an ear, either by judicial action or in a fight, and had let his hair grow long to make it less conspicuous. The other once had been slashed down a cheek, and the two edges of the wound had grown together out of line, drawing the corner of his mouth upward to reveal a rodent gleam of teeth.

Pedro was lolling on the bench, having a hard time keeping his head upright, his eyes half closed. One of the cutthroats poured more wine in his glass and tried to give it to him, but got no response.

The two looked at each other, then got up on either side of Pedro and lifted him by the arms. Pedro made no resistance.

Sandro crossed to the table with Tom behind him. "Thank you, gentlemen," he said. "We're his friends. We'll take him home and let him sleep it off."

The one with the missing ear lifted his lip in a snarl. "We saw him first, see? Take a stroll."

"Oh, we couldn't allow you to go to the trouble," Sandro said affably, stepping in close, while Tom circled around to the other side.

The two bruisers looked at Sandro's size and decided not to make an issue of it. They let Pedro slide floppily back to the bench and disappeared.

Sandro caught hold of Pedro before he toppled and hauled him upright. "Pedro," he said. "Can you hear me? Try to stand up. We're taking you home."

"What?" Pedro said blearily. "What's that? Where did my friends go?"

Tom came around to help. "Poor miserable fode," he said. He leaned nearer. "Listen, Pedro," he said, "it's no good going on this way. You've got to do something about it."

Pedro swayed. "You can't talk about her that way," he said and swung a fist. It caught Tom in the mouth. Pedro looked perplexed and promptly went limp. Sandro caught him again before he could fall.

"That does it," Tom said, wiping blood from a split lip. "If

he won't help himself, somebody's got to do it for him." He
smiled jauntily at Sandro. "'Swounds, I'm richer than a man
needs to be. What's money for?"


"I ran as fast as I could!" Inês's neighbor, Jorge Paula,
panted. His face was brick-red from the uphill run. "He's on
his way here now. He's an Englishman, very rich. He must
be a great lord. He hired a whole ship, just for himself, to
take him to Madeira."

"He's coming *here*? To see *me*?" Inês said in alarm. "What
for?"

Jorge fanned himself with his hat. "I don't know. He
started asking around as soon as he landed in Funchal. The
sailors who rowed him ashore said the ship sailed from
Sagres. It was supposed to pick up cargo for Oporto, but he
paid them double. They say he's a little crazy but harmless.
He told them wild stories all the way."

"I don't know any Englishmen. What did he ask?"

"He asked where he could find a man called Lobo."

"Oh!" Inês's face drained.

"Don't take fright. He only knew him by name. Somebody
told him Lobo was long dead. Then he asked where he
could find Lobo's widow, and someone sent him to that
*meretriz* he used to live with. He found out Lobo was never
married to her or anybody else, and she told him the whole
story." He paused in embarrassment. "I'm sorry, senhora."

Inês colored. "It's all right, senhor."

She could not take umbrage at Jorge. He was a good-
hearted soul, not one of the busybodies she'd had to fend off
after the trial. He and his wife had looked after the children
when she'd been locked up, until Mafalda had arrived to
take over, and unlike some others, they had not shunned her
afterward, but had gone out of their way to be nice to her.

"Then he asked for the woman who had been married to
Heitor Honorato . . . he knew Heitor's name, too, and somebody set him right."

Beatriz was at the window. "Mamãe, Mamãe, come look!"

Inês went to see. A man in bright scarlets and greens was
striding up the mountainside, surrounded by swarming children, as if he were the Pied Piper. A crowd of curious
adults, about two dozen of them, followed. Inês could see
the windows of some of her neighbors popping open.

"It's him," Jorge said.

"Fix your dress, Beatriz," Inês said. "And wipe Amélia's face."

The man left the crowd behind at the garden gate. Inês could see one of her neighbors, nosy Senhor Vicente, hanging about in the road.

The Englishman rang the cowbell hanging next to the door, and she opened it. He was a wiry man of medium height with bright yellow hair and pink cheeks that made him look younger, for the first second, than he actually was.

"*Faz favor,* senhora," he said in the worst Portuguese she'd ever heard, "but are you the one who was known as Inês de Faro, who married a man named Heitor Honorato?"

He had a merry, careless face, and she decided to like him. He was no lord, though. The flashy clothes were those of someone trying to show off new wealth, and he had not even one retainer dancing attendance on him.

"That's what I was called," she said.

"I'm a friend of Pedro da Costa."

Her face drained of all color and life. She could not think for a moment, and then she became aware of Jorge Paula standing at the edge of her vision, shuffling his feet and trying out a cough.

"Thank you, Senhor Paula," she said. "It was good of you to come."

The years of exile and hard living had not been able to erase the tone appropriate to the daughter of Dom Martim Alves and Dona Beatriz. She heard her voice, and it seemed to come from somewhere far away.

Jorge heard it, too. He shuffled his feet some more and said respectfully, "Well then, if you're sure you won't need me for anything, *minha* senhora . . ."

"Thank you, Senhor Paula," she said firmly.

He nodded weakly to the Englishman and backed his way out.

The Englishman said to her, "Pedro thinks you're married to this Lobo, whoever he was. Somebody lied to him. He thinks he's doing something noble by staying away from you."

Inês was amazed at how calm and clearheaded she had become. "So that's it," she said slowly. "It had to be something like that."

•   •   •

"You're an idiot," Mafalda said.

Inês continued her packing. She laid out her best gown in the small chest and folded it carefully so it wouldn't wrinkle. "I'm going with Senhor Tom," she said. "He'll give the orders to sail as soon as I make the arrangements with Bernardo and Dionísio to look after things while I'm away."

"And the wine? If it becomes ripe while you're gone? You're risking everything."

"They know what to do. They've been working for me for two years."

Mafalda shook her head. "To pick up and go like this, when he hasn't even asked you himself."

"He didn't know, Mafalda. He still doesn't." She smiled. "Anyway, how could I say no to Senhor Tom? Just think of it! To hire a whole ship to take me!"

"I still say you're a fool. What kind of man would run off and leave you like that—not once but twice?"

"A man who made a mistake twice. The first time he was young and ignorant and thought life would wait for him while he ran ahead a little to catch up to a dream. The second time he was deceived. He meant well."

"Meant well!" Mafalda snorted. "Let him stew, I say. He's been boiling away so long there's nothing left except the charred leavings at the bottom of the pan. You don't need him! You're a rich *fazendeira* now! What's he got for you?"

Inês straightened up. "Should I let the third mistake be mine, *cara*? I've got to go. We'll settle it one way or the other."

Mafalda relented. She put a hand on Inês's arm. "All right then, go," she said. "Don't worry about the children. They'll be fine. I need a vacation from Morales anyway."

"She's here," Catalina said. "I met them at the dock. Tom and I took her to the house and got her settled; then I thought I'd better come by to let you know."

Sandro put down his pen and shoved the ledger aside. "What's she like?" he asked.

"She's beautiful—and a real lady." She looked down at her dress. "I felt shabby in this old thing."

"Nonsense, you look fine. When it comes to beauty, you don't take second place to anyone. Anyway, you've got plenty of fine clothes that I bought you—I don't know why you hardly ever wear them. If you feel that way, why don't you put on the new gown I had made in Tavira?"

Catalina shook her head. "She's quality, you know. You can tell by the way she talks, even if she doesn't put on airs. She sews her own clothes, when it comes to that, but she wears them like *nobreza*. I don't know how a simple fellow like Pedro ever attracted her."

Sandro laughed. "Well, I'd better see this paragon," he said, getting up. He called to his assistant. "Giraldo, will you look after things for a while?"

"*Sim, Senhor Alessandro,*" Giraldo said. "The new shipment of rope is due in this afternoon, but I'll take care of it." He was a muscular, thickset man in his thirties and very reliable.

A few minutes' walk took them to Sandro's house. Tom met them at the door.

"She needs a little time to compose herself. Your man Lúcio's gone down to the dock to fetch her things. Generosa offered her wine to refresh herself, but she refused it. She's drawn as tight as a crossbow string, though she's too proud to show it."

"God grant that we're doing the right thing," Sandro said.

Tom peered into the recesses of the house and lowered his voice. "She's not married, you know. There's nothing in the way."

"What? How can that be? Pedro's let enough slip when he was in his cups for us to piece together the story. 'She'll be better off,' he said. He's been sunk in a quagmire these three years past."

"She never intended to marry this Lobo who murdered her husband. That was only a story that Lobo put about. She stabbed him to death one night when he broke into her house."

"*Meu Deus!*" Catalina gasped.

Tom nodded grimly. "The count of Madeira, Zarco, pardoned her. He ruled that she was blameless. This Lobo was a bad one, by all accounts. He was trying to molest her so as to take possession of her widow's deed, her children, and everything she owned." He raised a pale eyebrow. "A curious custom of law, we'd say in England. But the lady has spirit. She didn't do what was expected of her. She stabbed him with his own knife, it seems. The same knife, the good folk of Funchal like to point out, that killed her husband."

"It's hard to believe," Catalina marveled. "Someone who was raised in the streets like me, maybe—a *tauernera* or a *desmazelada*. That I'd have no trouble understanding. But a gentlewoman like that . . ."

Sandro frowned. "Don't say things like that about yourself," he said angrily. "I've told you before I don't like it."

"Who are you to tell me what I can say?" she snapped back.

Tom intervened before it could go further. "She's all steel underneath," he said in reply to Catalina. "Don't forget that she came to Madeira with the *degredados*. She made something of her farm, all by herself, after her husband died. Zarco's exempted her from remarriage. For now, anyway."

Down the street, from the direction of the waterfront, they caught sight of Lúcio, leading two sailors who carried a heavy, iron-bound chest between them. "Let's go inside," Sandro said.

Tom said, "I'll go get Pedro now. By God's grace, let him be sober."

"He's liable to take a swing at you for interfering in his affairs," Sandro said.

"I'll have to chance that."

Catalina, to her consternation, found herself becoming flustered when she presented Sandro to Inês. The two women had gotten along so well on the walk from the waterfront, after the ice had been broken, and in the few minutes they'd spent together after their arrival at the house. They had chatted together like sisters. But now as she watched her Venetian gentleman with this well-brought-up daughter of a *fidalgo* born, she felt out of her depth.

"A thousand welcomes, *madonna*," Sandro said, in accents he rarely used nowadays. "You do this house much honor."

"You are too kind, senhor," Inês responded.

Catalina listened with a growing sense of exclusion while the two of them exchanged the high-flown inconsequences of the gentry for what seemed an endless interval. Then Inês noticed her discomfort and turned to her with a smile of such warmth that she was immediately put at ease.

"How can I thank you enough, senhora, for discommoding yourself this way for me? Your servants have done everything to see to my comfort."

Catalina realized that the words were intended to convey,

with all the delicacy and tact in the world, acceptance of her status as mistress of the house.

"It's nothing, *dona* . . . please don't think anything of it," she fumbled.

Inês held out her hands. They were work-roughened, with cracked nails. "Do these look like the hands of a *dona*?" she said. "Please, we must be friends."

Catalina took the hands in her own. "Olive oil, that's what's needed," she said. "Olive oil and rose water. I'll see that Generosa keeps you supplied. We'll have them smooth before you leave."

They laughed together. Sandro watched them as if from a distance. A tenseness seemed to go out of him.

Tom arrived with Pedro a quarter-hour later. Pedro's face was pale with strain. His damp hair and a misfastened button were signs of a hurried toilet. He was dressed in a plain but decent russet tunic and woolen hose; he looked quite handsome, Catalina thought.

Pedro and Inês stared at each other wordlessly, with eyes that were wide and hungry, until at last Pedro managed to say, "I prayed every day that I would see you again, senhora, but I had no hope that my prayers would be answered."

"It doesn't matter, senhor," she said unsteadily. "I'm here now."

"You don't understand," he said in a voice that was close to breaking. "It was I myself who denied my prayers."

Her face was as pale as his. "I understand," she said. "Senhor Tom explained everything." She tried a shaky smile that included Sandro and Catalina. "You have good friends."

Tom was fidgeting. He prodded Sandro, who seemed to come out of a trance. His inbred manners came to life.

"I regret that I have to get back, senhora," he said. "I just wanted to assure myself that you were received with hospitality and that your needs were met. I'll return later."

"Thank you, senhor," she said distantly, unwilling to take her eyes off Pedro.

Sandro got a prod from Catalina this time, and with Tom in tow, they departed, leaving Pedro and Inês alone together.

Things seemed to go well in the days that followed. Pedro called early each morning, and he and Inês spent hours together in the little garden, sitting on the twin benches talking, getting used to each other again, and, finally, laughing together. Catalina gave strict orders to Generosa and Lúcio not to disturb them. "Disturb them, senhora?" Generosa said, aghast, spreading a stubby hand on her broad bosom. "Who would think of such a thing? They're like a pair of canaries. It does the heart good to see two people in love like that."

Pedro no longer came to the Cabra do Mar. Catalina arranged with Vasques to take a few nights off, so that she could be available to Inês after Pedro left in case she wanted to talk. She learned much about life on Madeira, and Inês talked at length about her two little girls, though she was reticent on the subject of her husband, the one who had been murdered.

"You've done miracles, to make such a success of your *fazenda*—and from nothing but a wilderness!" Catalina exclaimed during one such conversation. Delicately she did not add, "For a woman alone." She was just beginning to realize how independent and prosperous this mysterious lost love of Pedro's was.

"No, not miracles," Inês said modestly. "Madeira's a garden. It's as fertile as Eden since the great fire burned off the slopes. If you're willing to work hard, there's no limit to what you can accomplish."

Catalina nodded vigorously. "We see the wood. It's beginning to change the look of the whole country. The *fidalgos* build themselves great houses out of timbers instead of fortifying themselves in heaps of stone, with battlements." She laughed. "Sandro says we don't need castles any more, now that the world's beginning to civilize itself."

"That's the miracle—that there was any wood left," Inês smiled. "The fire burned seven years. It kept breaking out from underground, and had to be fought all the time by those who were trying to settle the interior. But God was generous. Somehow great tracts of forest survived."

"*Louvor a Deus,*" Catalina murmured piously.

"But the real wealth of Madeira comes from growing things that weren't there before. The ground yields sixtyfold the grain one could grow in the Algarve. The sugar plantations will soon rival Sicily's. And the vineyards!" Her face glowed. "Such abundance has never been seen! I wish I could describe it to you! We have an early vintage—there's a harvest about Easter each year. I'll have to return before then."

"We thank you for the cask of your wine. Sandro says he's never tasted anything like it. Tom swears he's going to export it to England and make a second fortune."

"You're welcome. It's a small return for your hospitality."

"I wish I could go back with you," Catalina said wistfully. "I wonder what it would be like to start life over again in a place like that."

"Why would you say something like that?" Inês remembered herself. "I'm sorry, it's none of my business."

"No, that's all right."

"Your life here would be the envy of . . . of some of the women I know. You have a good man; you're the mistress of a fine house. . . ."

"No—I'm only a *tauernera* having a run of luck."

"Catalina . . ." Inês took her hands in her own. "Sandro loves you. It shows in his eyes. And I know you love him. You've got to make peace with each other."

Catalina shook her head. "Maybe he loves me. But he doesn't know it. *I* don't know it. He had a wife, you know. When he was a slave. I don't know what happened. I know she died. He blames himself—I think only because he was helpless. He grasped at me as a drowning man grasps at a branch in the water. Perhaps he thought he wasn't good enough for anyone better. What good does it do to talk of loving or not loving? If he were to get rid of his hate . . . if he could bring himself to get married again, it wouldn't be to someone like me. It couldn't be. He'd have to marry someone of his own class . . . there was someone in Venice he was betrothed to before he was taken as a galley slave. I wormed that much out of him. She betrayed him and married his brother. But that's who he pines after, if anyone—" She stopped, made a face at herself. "Forgive me . . . it doesn't matter. . . ."

"It's still not my business, but you're wrong, you know." Inês drew a resolute breath. "You're his wife in every sense—he hasn't given you the name, that's all. You don't have to take an oath in church to be married. The poor would never marry if that were the case. The law says that even the *palavras de presente*, the words of acknowledgment, aren't needed if it's generally known by a couple's friends and neighbors that they're together. Sandro's made that commitment already . . . he's installed you as his *mulher de casa*. He's a tortured man, and who can blame him? He's wrestling with himself to come the rest of the way." She smiled at Catalina. "I know he doesn't want you to work as a *tauernera*."

Catalina smiled back with an effort at gaiety. "Perhaps I'll leave the Goat anyway. Vasques will go wild. But I won't be able to serve the customers when my belly's out to my chin."

Inês opened her mouth, closed it, then opened it again and said, "Catalina, you must tell Sandro right away."

"No . . . I'll go away."

"What's one to do with someone as stubborn as you? Think of the baby."

"And what of the baby? Another bastard of a *fidalgo*, that's all."

Inês let her exasperation show. "Sandro's severed from his past, whatever it was. He's living the life of a small merchant." She bit her lip. "As for class, I'm living proof of how little it counts for anything. It can be taken away from you or given to you. Do you think I care about any of that when it comes to Pedro? Our situation is exactly the reverse of yours and Sandro's, and it matters just as little. Sandro deserves this baby from you. Give him a chance at least."

Catalina was moved. "You're right . . . you're a true friend. Who am I to feel sorry for myself after what's happened to you . . . and to Sandro? I'll tell him about the baby."

"I'm glad." Inês's eyes were moist.

Catalina jumped to her feet. "Why are we so gloomy? I'll get us a glass of wine. What poor hospitality! We were talking about Madeira. Sandro and I will come to visit you and Pedro there some day!"

She bustled at the trestle holding the cask of Madeira wine and returned with two goblets. "What a lucky man Pedro is. To become a *fazendeiro* with all the work of starting up already done for him."

"Oh, he'll work—between voyages, anyway," Inês said, taking the goblet. "It takes a man to manage other men, and I'll soon have to hire more *lavradores*—it's getting to be too much for me to handle with just Bernardo and Dionísio. And I'll need him to deal with the wine lodge. They don't take a woman seriously. Since I showed them the secret of the *estufagem* method for making wine like this, they've built their own wine hothouses, and they don't need me any more." She took a sip of the wine and lowered the goblet. "Besides, I don't know how much longer I'll be allowed to remain unmarried. Zarco's kept his word so far, but I'm beginning to feel pressure from others."

"You've managed fine without having some good-for-nothing forced on you!" Catalina said indignantly. "You've done well for your two daughters."

"I've been allowed to function as *cabeca do casal*, and so I was able to preserve their inheritance," Inês said. "But with the wrong husband, it could be dissipated."

"You'll have no worries on that score, at least, with Pedro. He's a decent sort."

Inês blushed. "He's said nothing yet."

"He will, don't worry. *Santa Maria*, some men are slow!"


But a week went by, and as far as Catalina could tell, Pedro still had not asked, in so many words, for Inês's hand. And though Inês had confided nothing, the atmosphere seemed a little strained. She questioned Generosa about it.

"*Ai*, lady, they're polite enough together, but I haven't heard them laughing these last few days. And he has these long silences."

"You've been spying on them in the garden, haven't you? Didn't I tell you to leave them alone? They know you're there, and it puts them off!"

"No, no, lady, I swear!" She put a hand over her heart and said with injured self-righteousness, "And anyway, didn't you just ask?"

"Anything else?"

"He's not staying as long lately. And this morning he didn't come at all."

"Don't tell me what I know! Didn't I have a peek into the garden when I got back from the market?"

"After she gave up waiting, she went to her room and closed the door. She says she doesn't want dinner. *Ai de mim!* Don't be angry with me! I asked if I could bring her something, but she said she doesn't feel hungry."

"Angry? Don't be an idiot! Why would I be angry?" She patted Generosa's hand. "It's all right, *menina*. Go about your business. I won't be having dinner either. I'm going to the chandlery. But first I'll have a word with her."

Inês was sitting by the window doing her embroidery when Catalina asked for permission to enter. Her hands were always busy. It was the most beautiful embroidery Catalina had ever seen, a cover for a bed. Catalina suspected that it was going to be for her, and she did not know what she was going to say.

"*Bom dia,*" Inês said. Her smile gave no hint that she was in any way troubled.

"I'm on my way to the chandlery," Catalina said. "I thought I'd drop by for a minute."

"Have you told Sandro yet? About the baby?"

"No, I'm waiting for the right time."

"Don't wait too long."

"I won't. I may tell him today, if he's in the right mood."

"I'm glad," Inês said warmly. She sighed. "It's not right that two people who love each other should be at odds."

"Is something wrong?"

"No, nothing," Inês said too quickly.

"Pedro may have been called to the school for navigators this morning," Catalina said. "He's been neglecting his work there lately, as we all know. I'm sure that he'll send word when he gets a chance."

"I'm sure that must be it," Inês said, her needle becoming busier. "He's been so preoccupied these last few days. He must have things on his mind."

"I'll ask Sandro," Inês said. "He'll know what's going on there."

"Oh, no," Inês said. "Don't do that."


"He's getting cold feet, that's all," Sandro said.

They were in the back room of his shop. Sandro was surrounded by crates of supplies that he had been nailing up to fill an order. The cot that he used to sleep on was still there, but now it was his assistant who used it.

"Mother of God!" Catalina exclaimed. "What's wrong with the donkey? He's had all these years to get over his cold feet. Why now?"

"Because he's beginning to understand that she's a well-to-do woman, a woman of property. And he looks at her and thinks she isn't good enough for her."

"He's not poor anymore. He's got his purse from the infante. And there'll be more, once the ships start going out again. When it comes to that, he can put his money into the *fazenda*—she's property-rich, but there's a shortage of gold on Madeira."

"It's not only money. He's thinking about the distance between them."

"Distance? The only distance is between his ears! I've spoken to her about it. She doesn't think she lowered herself from a *dona*. She thinks she raised herself from a *degredada*."

"When he first met her, he thought she needed his protection. Now the old scruples are coming back."

"Men!" she exploded. "They string words together that make fences stronger than steel. What about you? Have you raised yourself or lowered yourself?"

"Catalina . . ."

"Oh, never mind!"

"When you came in, you said you had something to tell me. What is it?"

"It can wait. First I'm going to give somebody a talking-to."


"I thought you weren't going to work this week," Vasques said. "I've got Ernestina filling in, but if you want to put on an apron . . ."

"Stow it." Her eyes searched the room and found Pedro. "How long has he been here?"

"Not long."

"Drunk?"

"No, not yet. He's just starting."

Though it was still early in the day, the Cabra do Mar had a full complement of patrons. The defeat in Tangier and the subsequent paralysis of activity at Sagres and the Lagos shipyards down the coast had put thousands of idle men on the beach. The atmosphere in the tavern was dispirited, not rollicking as in former times; the customers drank to forget or to ease boredom rather than to relax. Pedro looked as glum as anyone else, sitting hunched over the table. Catalina squeezed her way through the maze of benches, ignoring the greetings of some of the older habitués and evading a halfhearted attempt to clutch her. She planted herself in front of Pedro.

"Well, senhor, you're back to old habits, it seems," she drawled.

He looked up slowly. "Catalina."

"Don't Catalina me! On your feet! I want to talk to you, and I don't want to do it here!"

"I'm just having a drink," he said in a surly tone.

"Having a drink? When Inês is waiting for you? In Sandro's house that you've been making so free with."

"Go away. Leave me alone."

"Up, senhor! March!"

He rose to his feet with ill grace and followed her to the back room. Ernestina was there, wiping glasses. "Out," Catalina said. "I want to be alone with this one."

Ernestina raised an eyebrow. "Just as you say, Catalina," she said and left with a sidelong glance at Pedro.

Catalina lit into him without preamble. "You're a donkey! Worse than a donkey, because a donkey knows enough to eat hay that's put in front of it! Why are you making Inês miserable? Haven't you done enough to her? She was only a young girl when you left her to the mercy of an island full of *degradados*. That I can forgive because you were only a young *moco* yourself, still wet behind the ears. Maybe the second time I can forgive because you went away out of respect to her marriage. To a better man than you, you miserable wretch! But I can't forgive the idiot you were to believe what a mad dog said and abandon her again when she needed you most! And why? Because you were thinking of yourself. Feeling sorry for yourself. You weren't good enough for her, you thought. I agree! But that's for Inês to decide! And now God sends you an Englishman with more money than sense to charter a ship and bring her to you and give you one more chance. And you say to God, 'No thank you, Senhor. I'm not worthy of her. I'm only a *moco*.' Well, what have you to say for yourself?"

Pedro's face turned dark red with anger. His neck swelled, and a vein pulsed in his forehead. Catalina watched with interest to see what he would do. She made a bet with herself that he would put his fist through a cask of wine, break his hand, and cost Vasques a pretty penny in spillage, depending on how high in the front of the cask his fist went through.

To her surprise he seemed to deflate, and though his face remained as red as before, it was the red of chagrin.

"I was on my way there, as usual," he said, "and all of a sudden I couldn't make myself go in."

"But why, man, why?"

"You said it." He looked so stricken and forlorn that she felt sorry for him.

"You know what a fool you are?"

He nodded. "It makes it worse, in a way, to have one last chance. I keep thinking of how she saved herself again and again—without me. I should have killed Lobo myself, that day. Instead, I went to the sea as to the arms of a mother. And now I keep seeing pictures of what it would be like if I went back to Madeira with her. Seeing myself sitting at my ease, having the best of everything, while living off her— like her third child. What good would I be to her? Who am I?"

" 'Who am I'?" she mimicked. "I thought you were a man."

He was becoming angry again. "I'm a sailor. I'd be useless as lord and master of a *fazenda*."

"I could shake you!" she erupted. "To moan and carry on about being a parasite! To turn down a woman's gifts! Do you think your silly pride is important? She *needs* you! As a protector, if nothing else. Never mind that she loves you! If you don't marry her, she'll lose the estate . . . maybe not now but eventually. That's the way men arrange things in the world. She's fighting like a she-wolf for her daughters—not just to give you a life of ease with the master's grail in your hand. If you can unbend that stiff neck of yours long enough to marry her, you need have no scruples about stealing her daughters' inheritance. You know what the royal patent for colonies says in such cases. We hear it often enough. The title passes through the female line—whatever part of it isn't squandered by the next husband. It's good for three lives, to provide for widows' and orphans' dowries. All you have to do is keep hands off. Someone else might not be so nice. If you have a son with Inês, you'll have to provide for him yourself—is that good enough for you?"

Pedro stood mute, solid as an ox. Catalina searched for some clue in his face but could find nothing.

She said resignedly, "Never mind all that. Inês is tired. She's done too much. She needs a husband to help her raise the two girls. She wants to give you children of your own, too."

The silence stretched on. Then his sunbrowned, forthright face broke into a smile, and she could have kissed him.

"I'll go to her," he said.

"Then there's nothing more for me to do here?" Sandro said angrily. "Is that what you're telling me?"

Jaime of Majorca sat as stiff as bones in his high-backed chair. Behind him was the glare of an open window that looked out over the sea to the west, and his black gown was edged by the winter light.

"Your part is over," Jaime said. "You have your purse from the prince. You can go back to being a chandler."

"This is poor thanks for what I brought to you," Sandro said, striving to keep his voice down. "Exploration won't be at a standstill forever. Prince Henry's attention will return to it when the echoes of Tangier die down. The keels of the first caravels are laid, even if the work is temporarily at a standstill. The voyages will resume."

"When they resume, there'll be no place in them for Venetians."

"By God, Mestre . . ."

"Exploration's to be a Portuguese enterprise. There are court circles who see great wealth within our grasp, despite the disappointment of the Rio de Ouro." He lifted a gray eyebrow. "Perhaps you find that ironic, in view of the role you played in exciting the infante's hopes. But the fact remains that it's been resolved to impose greater secrecy. I've been ordered to keep the *mappamundi* under lock and key."

Sandro looked across the austere stone chamber and realized what was different about it. The large draped frame that had held Jaime's revised map of the world was missing.

"The Englishman's still welcome here," Sandro protested. "He complains of being neglected, but he isn't driven away."

"England's not our rival on the seas as Venice is. They've always been Portugal's friends and allies."

"They'll wake up one day," Sandro predicted.

"Perhaps they will."

"Well, Mestre," Sandro said, grinning crookedly, "I thank you for being so frank."

"I wouldn't want to hear of you being found with a knife between your ribs," the old mapmaker said.

"You wouldn't care to tell me who my enemies at court are?"

"No."

"What about you, Mestre? Doesn't your patronage count for anything?"

It was Jaime's turn to smile, a thin line. "Jews, Moors, and other outsiders aren't very popular here at the moment, in view of what's happening at Fez. The prince has a very large heart, and we at the school are under his protection, but while he's preoccupied with . . . other matters, I prefer to lie low."

The royal hostage, Prince Fernando, had been transferred by Sala ben-Sala to the city of Fez for safekeeping. It was an unfortunate move, and now the hostage negotiations were threatening to break down. Sala ben-Sala had been adamant in refusing to swap Fernando for his own son, held hostage in Lisbon. "I have plenty of sons," he'd said. "I never particularly liked that one anyway." King Duarte had given in and agreed to surrender Ceuta over Henry's objections. But the vizier at Fez, the malevolent Lazeraq, was like a dog with a bone and refused to produce Fernando for the envoys. In the meantime, Fernando was kept chained in the dark, and now there were reports that he was ill.

"Then why," Sandro asked, "did you send for me, Mestre?"

There was a certain amount of hemming and hawing, and then Jaime said, "There's something you could do for me. It needs a Venetian."

"Well, well," Sandro said, smiling.

"Do you know an Andrea Bianco?"

"I've been away from Venice a long time, Mestre. I know a Bianco family."

"He's chief navigation officer on the Galley of Flanders. But he's also a mapmaker—possibly the finest young mapmaker in Venice. He's had ample opportunity to associate with the Atlantic pilots on the Southampton run and learn from them any reports of sightings and rumors that have come to them. I'm sure he's also heard of the work we're doing here. I've learned that he's made a *mappamundi* that shows land in the Atlantic, west of the Azores, though it doesn't show Africa trending south, as the Englishman claims."

"And you want me to get you a copy, I suppose?" Sandro sighed.

"Yes." Jaime's long fingers twitched. "I'll pay you well. I can invent an errand in Florence that will put you on a Florentine galley that's anchored here now. After that you can find your way overland."

"How devious," Sandro said with an arched eyebrow. "Why don't you just ask for a copy through official channels? Venice isn't as secretive about its maps as Portugal is."

"Why do you think? I'm an old man, but my neck's still precious to me. I'm disliked enough at court without laying myself open to the charge of dealing with Venice on a matter of maps at this juncture. Andrea Bianco will oblige a fellow mapmaker, but this affair will take discretion."

Sandro felt his heart beating faster, but he tried not to reveal his growing excitement to Jaime.

"To go to Venice . . ." he said slowly. "You know I'm under sentence of death there."

"There'd be no tears shed for you in Sagres if you were caught. They'd think themselves well rid of a Venetian spy. And I'd disavow you."

Sandro made another try at resisting the idea. "Venice is having another war with Milan. Spy fever will be high. The lion's mouth in Saint Mark's Square will be stuffed full of anonymous denunciations. If the Council of Ten didn't hesitate to execute its own great *condottiere,* Carmagnola himself, on suspicion of having secret dealings with Milan, you can imagine how the man in the street will be scrutinizing passing faces. If I'm recognized by anyone who once knew me . . ."

"Then you'll have to be careful, won't you?"

Sandro rubbed his chin. "What makes you think this Andrea Bianco will hand over a copy of his *mappamundi* to a Portuguese agent?"

"I told you—we mapmakers are a brotherhood, beyond nations." There was a fever in Jaime's eyes. "Aside from the fact that you'll pay him, he'll see nothing wrong with spreading knowledge."

"What if I spread it in the other direction?" Sandro said wryly. "I may be under sentence of death, but I'm no traitor to Venice. Messer Andrea is sure to ask me about what you're doing here, and about the latest Portuguese discoveries on the African coast."

Jaime's gaze became hooded. "As to that, I wish to know nothing of what you might tell him."

"Even if it violates this new rule of secrecy of which you spoke so vehemently a few minutes ago?"

"I'll remind you that I'm not Portuguese either and so no traitor. And though the dust of Majorca may be on my shoes, I don't count myself Catalan, for whatever that means. My people are strangers in every land. We've been made so." He looked as if he regretted having said so much and went on more softly. "In the spreading of knowledge, one country or another may benefit in the short run, but in the long run the service is to all mankind. And so you and I, senhor, may count ourselves obstetricians to a new age. I have no qualms. Portugal will have its day in the sun, whatever I do. Then it will be the turn of other nations."

Sandro's thoughts had gone far beyond Andrea Bianco while Jaime talked. In his mind he could see the domes of Saint Mark's, the crowded traffic of the Grand Canal, the gilded facade of the Cavalli palace. His emotions churned the images round until they coalesced into the face of Maffeo as he had seen it looming over him on the catwalk of the galley.

"I'll go to Venice for you, Mestre," he said thickly, "but I won't promise to come back alive with your map."


Catalina was humming to herself as she came through the doorway to the kitchen. "Here," she said, thrusting a heavily laden basket at Generosa, "I did the marketing for you. There's a fine fowl in there for Senhor Sandro's supper. I want you to prepare one of his favorite Venetian dishes tonight—perhaps a first course of dry soup with *ravioli.*"

"*Sim, sim,*" said Generosa, taking the basket. "You look happy, senhora."

"Sometimes things go right. Are they together?"

Generosa's wide face shone. "He came a little after you left, senhora. They've been together in the garden all this time. I brought them something on a tray, but they hardly looked at it. Such sighing! Such tenderness!" She lowered her voice confidentially. "I heard the words of marriage, but they're going to get a priest and have a real *casamento de bencão,* too."

"You eavesdropped," Catalina said sternly.

"*Ai de mim, senhora*. Who could resist?"

Catalina allowed herself to smile. "Maybe it's a sign. If donkeys can learn to speak, perhaps wormwood can turn to honey."

"What do you mean, senhora?"

"Is Senhor Sandro home yet?"

"He came in a little while ago. He's upstairs."

She flew up the stairs, telling herself not to hope too much. But perhaps it would be a good idea to tell him about the baby, after all. If he allowed a small part of himself to come out of the shell that had hardened around his natural feelings and found a small thing to love, more of him might follow.

By God, she thought, she'd pull at him, like a terrier with a badger, until she dragged him out all the way!

His back was to her when she entered the room. "Sandro," she said, "I have something to . . . what are you doing?"

He turned around slowly. He had been packing clothing into a small iron-bound travel chest that stood open on the bed. Catalina saw a stiletto, an assassin's weapon, lying on top.

"I'm going to Venice," he said.

"What?" Her legs felt weak and she wanted to sit down, but she kept herself standing with an effort.

"I'll be back in six months at the most. I have an errand to do for Mestre Jaime."

"You can't go," she said, fighting to stay calm. "You've been condemned there. You told me that. You'll be executed."

"I won't be caught. No one will recognize me. I'm older, my appearance has changed. I'll travel incognito. I can disguise myself. I'll be careful."

She shook her head. "You're not going for Mestre Jaime. You're going for revenge."

"No," he said. "That's not true." But his face was growing dark.

"What's that for, then?" she asked, pointing at the stiletto.

"For protection. Travel's dangerous in any case."

Her eyes narrowed dangerously. "Why not a sword, then? A gentleman's weapon?"

"A sword's too conspicuous in Venice. Someone's liable to ask about your right to carry it."

"You're a liar. You're planning to kill your brother."

"Be quiet!" he shouted. "You don't know what you're talking about!"

"Admit it!"

His face contorted with sudden fury. "What of it?"

"And his wife—the highborn lady you were once betrothed to—you're dying to see her, too, aren't you? You've been yearning secretly after her all these years."

"You don't know what you're saying. You're jealous."

"Is she part of your revenge, too? Are you going to take her away with you to Rome or Florence?"

"Catalina . . ." he said. His hand made a reaching gesture, then fell to his side. "I'll do what I have to do in Venice, then I'll come back to you. . . . We'll start over again. . . ."

"No!" she raged. "One way or another, you'll never see me again! You'll die there! Or you'll stay with your milksop lady! Or I won't be waiting for you when"—she thought again—"if you return!"

# CHAPTER 21

The countryside north of Florence was teeming with the hired troops of the opposing *condottieri*. Crossing from Modena to Mantua, Sandro had almost fallen into the hands of the Milanese forces under Piccinino, and after several days of detouring around burned fields and ravaged farmhouses and sleeping under hedges with one eye open, he had counted himself lucky to have met up with an advance guard of the army commanded by Erasmo da Narni—better known as Gattamelata, the "Honeyed Cat"—the renowned *condottiere* Venice had found to replace the executed Carmagnola.

Narni's swarm, like all mercenary bands, was pillaging the surrounding land for what they needed, allies or not, and it had been touch and go for a moment, but the soldiers decided not to rob Sandro, seeing that he appeared to be a Venetian and thus, according to the ethics of the situation, ought not to be harmed.

"You can't go wandering alone, messer," said the captain of the troop, a Savoyard named Vercelli. "There's a big battle shaping up. The Milanese are besieging Brescia, and they've cut off the southern end of Lake Garda. Gattamelata's moved three thousand horse and two thousand foot around the north of the lake and is falling back on Verona. There's a plan to move a fleet of galleys overland on rollers and come to the rescue of Brescia by water. You'd be walking between the jaws of the two armies."

There were some delicate hints, and in the end Sandro paid handsomely for the privilege of proceeding through Ferrara to Venice in the company of a mounted detail that, Vercelli said, was being sent to the Council with dispatches. Sandro did not quibble; they might as easily have taken his purse from him and gone on to find the gold for Messer Bianco that was hidden in the bottom of his chest.

"I'll borrow a sword and helmet as well," Sandro offered, "so that I can lend a helping hand in case there's trouble on the way. Shall we say another ducat for their rental?"

There was a glint of greed in the captain's eyes, and for a heartbeat Sandro thought that he had made the mistake of offering too much in his attempt to seal the bargain. But if Vercelli had started wondering just how much money this big, rugged Venetian, who said he was a merchant, was carrying, he restrained himself.

So far Sandro had not seen a single Venetian among the men in Vercelli's troop—they were everything from Spaniards to Piedmontese—and his luck held when he drew his escort of four men. They accepted the false name he gave them—Balbi—and didn't know enough about Venice to ask him embarrassing questions. As for the rest of his disguise, he had little in common with the eighteen-year-old who had departed Venice so long ago, and his face was further changed by the small neat beard he had grown during the voyage to Italy.

He entered Venice unnoticed, with his borrowed armor and cloak, just one more mercenary among others. But now as they drew closer to the dangerous ground of Saint Mark's Square and the doge's palace, he was wondering how to separate himself from them.

"I'll leave you here," he said, "and many thanks."

The sergeant, a top-heavy, barrel-chested Piedmontese, scowled. "We thought you'd stay with us long enough to have a drink after we delivered the dispatches, Messer Balbi."

Sandro had been the paymaster at every tavern they'd stopped at along the way, though he had paid reluctantly and in small coin so as not to appear too liberal. It was obvious that they hoped to continue to leech off him.

He said, "Many regrets, signore, but my business is pressing." He flipped the sergeant a ducat, the first gold he had allowed them to see. "You and the boys have a drink on me."

The sergeant caught the coin out of the air. "We'll do that," he said, mollified. It would keep them in drink for quite a while, and probably he was regretting not having knocked Sandro over the head after all.

Sandro handed over the sword, helmet, and other accoutrements. He briefly considered buying the sword from them but decided that it would lead to more complications than it was worth. He shouldered his travel chest, exerting his strength to make it appear lighter than it was. He had let no one handle the chest but himself so that they wouldn't wonder why it was so heavy.

He walked away quickly through the crowds along the Molo—but not quickly enough to avoid seeing the bodies hanging from the windows of the doge's palace. It was a timely reminder to Sandro that with Venice at war and the Council of Ten alert to treachery, the Gentlemen of the Night would be working overtime.

He headed for the cheap pilgrim inns in the narrow streets behind the Riva, figuring that he would be less likely to be noticed, or wondered about, among a lot of foreigners. He tried the White Lion first and was surprised to find accommodations scarce despite the war, which might have been expected to keep pilgrims away. The proprietor explained to him that Venice was full of transients this month because of a stopover by the Byzantine emperor, John VIII Palaeologus, and his brother Demetrius, patriarch of Constantinople. The pair were on their way to Ferrara, where the pope had convoked a council that, it was hoped, would unite the eastern and western churches. The pomp and ceremony of the imperial visit had naturally drawn hordes of the curious from the mainland, and a lot of them had been slow to leave.

Sandro finally found a room at the sign of the Flute on a side canal near the Fondaco dei Tedeschi, the big German trading house. It was full of Germans who spoke little or no Italian, which suited him well. The proprietor was a little too friendly and inquisitive, but Sandro's cold manner put him off, and he finally left him alone.

Here, for the next few days, Sandro waited and made his plans. He postponed his business with Andrea Bianco—he wasn't going to announce his presence in Venice to anyone, even under a pseudonym. That could wait till afterward—if there was an afterward. He couldn't go to the Rialto, and he couldn't hang about in taverns and inquire about Maffeo and the House of Cavalli, either. Somebody might go to Maffeo and tell him there was a stranger asking about him. Someone might put two and two together and look more closely at the face under the beard.

At the front of the Flute there were sixty stone steps that went right down to the water. Here, the gondoliers did a thriving business. The Germans were indefatigable sightseers, and it was easy to overcharge them. Sandro went out for daily excursions, never engaging the same gondola twice. He said little, threw in a few German words without overdoing it, made no objections to being overcharged, and if they wanted to assume that he was a foreigner, that was all right. The gondoliers, challenged by his taciturnity, chattered and gossiped a good deal about the *palazzi* they passed. Sometimes Sandro would interpose a laconic question or two.

"That's the Barbarigo *palazzo*, signore. A sad story. They were one of the old families, the real *longhi*, with plenty of money. Then one of them, Nicolò, ran one of the ships of the Galley of Alexandria aground through poor seamanship and failed to go to its rescue. He was fined ten thousand ducats for inhumanity. The family was ruined. The son, Andrea, recouped the family fortunes. He made a killing in pepper. But he keeps his money busy. He never built a *palazzo* of his own. They live in a rented house."

"What's that palace next to it?"

"The Ca' Cavalli. Another old family. Merchants and bankers. Once they had a fine name. But since a son took over, there are rumors of shady practices. They say he's in the slave trade on the sly. Let me think. It was a long time ago, but there was a story that the old man was murdered."

On another excursion he found out about Agnese. "No, there's only the one son living there now with his wife. There was another brother, but he ran away some years ago. Some escapade, I expect. There was a young daughter, too, but she died . . . are you all right, signore?"

"I'm fine, it's just the damp." Sandro blew his nose and wiped his eyes. "I must have caught a chill."

Gradually he established the time of Maffeo's comings

and goings. The Cavalli gondola was still tied up at terce most mornings, indicating that Maffeo was a late riser, and was gone on both of the occasions when Sandro had himself rowed past the palace after midnight, showing that Maffeo had not lost his taste for nocturnal outings. On other nights he saw what windows lights came from at various hours and was able to build up a picture of the house's routine.

There was a new gondolier dozing on the boat landing mornings and late afternoons; old Lorenzo was probably dead by now. But once he caught sight of Bruno. The night watchman was older now, probably in his sixties, and a little white on top, but he still had the same formidable shoulders and the shovel jaw that Sandro remembered.

As for the other servants, he saw no one else he knew. There was a new housekeeper doing the marketing, and she always had a little slave with her. Girolamo Cavalli had never allowed slaves. It was a very different kind of household now. Sandro had no idea if Jacopo was still the major-domo; Maffeo hadn't liked him very much and would not have wanted to keep around someone who had given him orders as a boy, but on the other hand, Jacopo was indispensible.

The lights in the windows told Sandro that Maffeo had taken over the big sunny apartment on the second floor for himself. It was the one that Sandro had wanted to give to Agnese to rescue her from the winter damp and cold of her room on the garden side of the *palazzo*—the one with the defective chimney. It was where Maffeo would be sleeping now with Giuditta—Sandro blotted out the image with grim determination. The second-floor salon opposite, which had been used as an office and sleeping quarters by Girolamo after the death of Sandro's mother, was usually dark, but the lights were lit there for an hour or so before bedtime most nights. Evidently Maffeo was in the habit of repairing there before giving himself over to sleep—whether he drank there, looked over the day's accounts, or what, Sandro had no idea. One thing was sure—Sandro grinned without mirth—Maffeo would want to delay facing Giuditta on those nights when he had visited some doxy. The germ of a plan began to form in Sandro's mind.

Then one day he caught sight of Maffeo himself, and all of a sudden it was no longer the abstract game of a hunter stalking his prey that he had played in his mind all these years.

It was mid-afternoon, and it was by purest chance that Sandro happened to be drifting by the Cavalli palace at precisely that hour. He saw a hired gondola tie up at the Cavalli landing, and two *bravi* climbed out. They were the worst sort of ruffians—flashily dressed and openly carrying arms for which they had no doubt obtained a dispensation from some corruptible Capo di Contrado. A servant came out to see what they wanted, then went back inside. A few minutes later Maffeo came out. He wasn't pleased to be seen with them; he kept looking around to see if any of his neighbors were at their balconies, and then he did a quick survey of the Grand Canal. It was a shock to Sandro to see the distant dot of a face, with the familiar black bar of eyebrow setting off cascades of memory, turned in his direction, but Maffeo found nothing worthy of notice in the tourist gondola and its occupant. He and the *bravi* finished their business quickly, and he sent them on their way.

Sandro found himself shaking with fury. "Take me back to the Flute," he said.

"But signore, don't you want to go on round the *punta*?" the gondolier asked.

"Just take me back," he said. He felt as if there were iron bands around his chest, compressing his lungs and making his breath short.

At the Flute he retrieved the stiletto from under the top layer of clothes in his chest. He wrapped it in a piece of cloth and hid it beneath his doublet, under his left armpit where it wouldn't show and where he could reach it easily. He scarcely paid attention to the locking up of the chest; the gold hidden in its false bottom didn't seem important now.

"Going out again so soon, signore?" the innkeeper said to him. "Aren't you going to stay for supper?"

Some of the other guests looked up at him. The big black dog that was the Flute's mascot and that was supposed to dislike Italians, wagged its tail. Sandro mumbled something or other in refusal and left.

He found a gondola to take him to a point opposite the Cavalli palace, at the entrance to a side canal where stonemasons had been working on a coping. Here he huddled under a broken carving of Neptune and waited, in danger of attracting the attention of a night-watch patrol. He was beyond caring. He was prepared to wait all night and the next and the night after that for his chance.

Fortunately for his sanity, and for his freedom, his opportunity came that same night.

A light drizzle had been falling, restricting traffic along the canal and reducing the chances of him attracting notice. Sandro was soaked to the skin. The compline bells rang, and soon after lights appeared in the second-floor salon. They burned long enough for the lights in the apartment opposite to go out; Giuditta had given up waiting.

Sandro shifted in his niche of stone. The whole house would soon be asleep. He would have to take the chance that Maffeo would remain in the salon until he could smuggle himself into the palace. Otherwise . . .

His mouth tightened as he faced the untidy prospect of having to kill Maffeo in his bedroom with Giuditta screaming, and an aroused household, with Bruno in the fore, coming to Maffeo's aid. Sandro was not afraid of being killed or of being turned over to the night watch—only of being stopped before he could finish the job. But he had seen Maffeo now, and as he felt the iron bands constrict his heart, he knew he could not wait one more night.

And then the light in the salon went out, and he was too late.

Across the dark ribbon of canal, a gondola with a hooded lantern dangling from its prow glided up to the water gate. A moment later, Maffeo came out. It had been prearranged. Whatever business Maffeo was up to tonight, he didn't want his own gondolier knowing about it.

Sandro came back to sanity. The iron band around his chest loosened. He could go back to his original plan. He had thought it all out. It offered the best chance of success. Afterward he wouldn't care if he got away or was caught.

He emerged from his shelter and paid a passing gondola, coming back empty in the rain after delivering a passenger, to ferry him across to San Marco. He circled around to the landward side of the *palazzo* and approached it by way of the rear gardens.

He stopped for a moment behind the twisted trunk of a tree to listen for any sounds of activity from the *palazzo*. The garden was much decayed, a tangle of weeds and brambles; Maffeo had allowed it to go to ruin. His father, when he had been alive, had tried at least to keep it up for Agnese's pleasure.

There were no sounds and no lights showing anywhere. As he had done so many times when he was a boy, Sandro slipped from tree to tree through the garden to the rear portico. The night watchman's alcove was off to one side, but Bruno's habits had not changed. Sandro waited behind the familiar pillar until he was sure he heard snoring from the alcove. Then, on tiptoe, he took the old detour through to the downstairs hall.

He groped his way upstairs in darkness. Maffeo had left not even a candle burning to illuminate the wide marble treads, but Sandro, perhaps with the eyes of memory, could somehow sense the noble frescoes around him—the pious scenes from the lives of the apostles and the bloodcurdling "Massacre of the Innocents" by Master Angelus.

On the landing he felt along the marble bannister until his hand came to the portrait bust of Marco Cavalli, his ancestor, and using it as a guide, he found the bronze knob of the door to the salon. He let himself inside. There was a little more light in here, a gauze of gray coming from the balcony window facing the canal. Dimly the huge square space of the salon rose around him. His father's worktable was still in front of the vast fireplace, and behind it was the tall scrollwork shape of the chair that his father had sat in. It gave Sandro an odd feeling to think of Maffeo sitting there. He walked over to it and settled down to wait.

No, that wouldn't do. He was too far from the door. He got up again and retraced his steps. He fingered the stiletto under his doublet, pondering. There was a bulky curved-front cabinet standing beside the door that would offer temporary concealment when Maffeo entered—long enough for him to spring as soon as Maffeo took a step past it.

Before he could hide behind it, the door abruptly opened and a yellow splash of candlelight made a wedge across the floor. Sandro's hand leapt to the hidden stiletto, but just as he grasped the handle, a woman's plaintive voice said, "Maffeo, is that you in there?"

Too late, Sandro drew back. The woman gasped. Sandro said, "Giuditta, don't scream. Don't you recognize me?"

She almost dropped the candle. "Who . . .?" she squeaked.

"It's me, Sandro," he said quickly. "Don't be alarmed."

She brought the candle closer to his face. "Sandro. . . ? Is it really you? You've changed so much."

"I was a boy, *cara*," he said.

"They said you ran away," she said uncertainly. "We thought you were dead."

"No, not dead. As you can see."

His tension eased a little. At least he had stopped her from screaming, and though the first shock of discovery was over, she showed no immediate inclination to betray him.

He took a closer look at her. The pale light of the candle showed her to be as beautiful as he had remembered her, though perhaps a little more plump. She had the same flawless features, the same arch of brow, the same perfectly etched lips. Her shimmering golden hair was the same; it had been let down for the night and hung loose over her shoulders and bosom. Her breasts, more ample than before, spilled over the low front of her nightdress, and belatedly she drew her robe together and held it closed with one hand.

"But aren't you afraid of me?" he asked.

"No, why should I be?" She gave him an arch glance. "It was very wicked of you to desert me like that, without a word."

"What?" Sandro looked at her in amazement.

"Oh, it's all right. Maffeo told me all about it. Though he wouldn't tell me the name of the man whose wife you seduced. He was too powerful, he said, and he didn't need his enmity. Who was it, Sandro? A senator? A ducal councillor? One of the Savii?" Her eyes glittered with curiosity. "Maffeo said he stuck his neck out to give you the funds to flee Venice—he could have gotten into trouble himself. But you were his brother, and he didn't want to see you stabbed and thrown in a canal some dark night, or hauled before the Council on a trumped-up charge. He was generous, smuggling money to you in exile at great risk—admit it! But then you stopped collecting it, and he thought you were dead."

Sandro, his head spinning, tried to absorb what she had told him. And then he understood. Of course Maffeo would not have told her that he had been condemned as a parricide by the Council of Ten. He would scarcely have advertised the business—would, in fact, have used the great resources of the House of Cavalli to hush it up. Giuditta had no idea that he was supposed to be a murderer. That explained why she had no fear of him.

"What was I to do?" she went on. There was something defensive in her tone now. "You abandoned me. What was I supposed to think? I didn't know if you were dead or alive." Her tone became accusatory. "And besides, why should I remain loyal to you? You were disloyal to me, weren't you? My father was pressing me to marry Maffeo—now that he was head of the House of Cavalli. The old feud was dead. They formed an alliance. It was to everybody's benefit."

Sandro said woodenly, "That's all right, Giuditta. It doesn't matter now."

"Doesn't matter?" She moved closer. He could smell a scent in her hair. "After what we meant to each other? How can you say that?"

The memories came flooding back. Sandro held himself rigid.

She took his hand and put it on her breast. "I'm the reason you came back, aren't I?" she whispered. "Go on, admit it."

"Giuditta . . ."

Carefully she put the candle down on a tabletop. "It's all right," she said. "There's plenty of time. He never comes back before dawn on these nights of his—if then." For a moment her temper blazed. "I've paid him back in his own coin, though. Many times." She felt him stiffen, and she hastened to backtrack. "You're the one I've always loved, Sandro. You must have been thinking of me all these years, too. You're back now, that's what's important. You'll come back in the morning and call on Maffeo in the normal way. Everything must have blown over by now. He'll find some place for you in the firm. We'll have lots of chances to be together."

Sandro felt his dead flesh stir. Why not, he thought. It would give flavor to his revenge to let Maffeo know that he was a cuckold before he died.

He seized Giuditta roughly. His lips bruised hers. She gave a moan and a shudder and clung to him. Their legs tangled and he felt her hands busy on his clothing. He started impatiently to bear her to the floor. "Wait," she breathed. She pushed him away and pulled her nightdress off over her head. "I don't want this showing any signs." She folded the nightdress and put it beside her on the floor. "Come," she said, stretching out her arms.

At that moment there was a tramp of footsteps on the stairs. A voice outside the salon said, "Come on in, *ragazzi*, and I'll pay you off. It's been a cursed messy night's work, but at least it didn't take long." It had not been a woman Maffeo had been visiting this night after all.

Giuditta screamed and rolled away from Sandro. She snatched her nightdress from the floor and was backing away from him, holding it in front of her, when Maffeo and the two *bravi* burst into the room.

"He broke in!" Giuditta shrilled. "He broke in and attacked me!"

Sandro scrambled backward, to where he could have a wall at his back, and felt with his fingers for the stiletto.

"Shall I kill him?" one of the *bravi* said, drawing his sword.

"No, no killings here," Maffeo said in a voice compressed by fury. "They're too hard to explain. We'll cut him a bit and turn him over to the Signori di Notte. The law will take care of him. I'll ask for his eyes."

The *bravi* moved in, grinning with the prospect of sport. They circled around professionally on either side with the obvious intention of pinning his arms. When the first made his grab, Sandro seized him and threw him at the one with the sword.

They went down together. The sword fell with a clatter, but the man retrieved it and was back on his feet in an instant, like an alley cat. The other got up more slowly and moved as if he had hurt his knee. By that time Sandro had the stiletto out. They backed away a little with new respect. They hadn't expected him to be so strong.

"Don't you recognize me, brother?" Sandro said.

Maffeo turned deathly white. "*Il diavolo!* It's you!"

"Yes, it's me. Did you really think I'd be dead by now? Couldn't you feel me hating you?"

"How did you . . . how did you . . ."

"How did I survive? How did I get away? Hate kept me alive, Maffeo, and I flew here on the wings of hate."

Maffeo turned savagely on Giuditta. "What did he tell you?"

"Tell me?" she said, trying to cover herself. "He told me nothing. I told you he broke in and attacked me."

"Shut up, you whore. I'll deal with you later."

"It's true, Maffeo," she whimpered. "He tried to rape me."

His eyes narrowed. "Is that what you'll tell the Signori di Notte?"

"Yes, Maffeo, I swear it."

Maffeo gave the nod to his two bully boys. "We'll kill him," he said.

Sandro gripped his knife more tightly. He was under no illusion that it was any match for two swords.

They approached him again, more cautiously this time. Sandro watched the nervous one, the one with the injured knee, and made him jump by feinting with the stiletto. The other one laughed and said, "No reach, *amigo*, that's your trouble." He proved his point by staying out of range and drawing circles around Sandro's stiletto with the end of his blade, playing with him.

"For God's sake," exploded Maffeo, "finish him off!"

The *bravo* started crowding Sandro, bearing in on him. Sandro kept retreating, back to the fireplace and around the table. He kicked the high-backed chair over and gained a few seconds' respite. The injured one was hanging back a little, pressing the attack more warily. Sandro made him jump again by aiming a kick at his crotch, though he could not have reached it without spitting himself. Maffeo stepped in. "I'll do it myself," he said in disgust, taking the sword from his henchman. "Keep him busy."

The first *bravo* rapped Sandro on the knuckles with the flat of his blade, and the stiletto went flying. The rebounding sword slashed Sandro's sleeve, and Sandro felt a burning pain the length of his arm. The arm went numb— too numb for Sandro to use it to defend himself. At the same time, the second *bravo*, limp or not, made a dive and caught Sandro by the other arm. Maffeo lunged.

Sandro's back was to the window by now. With a violent wrench he broke free and crashed through the delicate latticed panes. There was a scream behind him as Maffeo's blade missed its mark and impaled the unfortunate tough who had been holding him. Sandro took one swift step to the balcony railing, vaulted it with his good arm, and dived into the canal.

He hit the water hard. It closed darkly over his head. He came up choking. When he blinked the water out of his eyes, he was able, blurrily, to see faces at the window he'd broken through. He waited for shouts from Maffeo, but for some reason there weren't any. It didn't matter. There were other faces at other balcony windows along the canal now.

He struck out, one-armed and kicking, for the opposite bank, the Dorsoduro side. When he reached it, helpful hands hauled him out of the water. There were three of them, a patrol of the Gentlemen of the Night.

"Come along, signore," one of them said. "We've got a nice room for you in the Leads."

A key rattled in the lock, and the turnkey entered, stooping under the low slope of the garret roof. He held a lantern over the filthy straw pallet where Sandro lay, and said, "On your feet. Their Excellencies wish to see you."

Sandro stood up stiffly, his joints still sore from the taste of the rack they'd been given some days earlier. "It's an appearance before the Ten, then?" he asked. "Not more torture?"

He had gotten off lightly. He had been stretched only briefly, not enough to dislocate limbs, soon after his arrest—no more than the mild preliminary attentions that were to be expected for any prisoner or witness the Ten wanted to put in a tractable frame of mind. Sandro had given his name freely, and admitted that he was the person who had been apprehended after diving through the window of the Cavalli *palazzo*. "You're Alessandro Cavalli, a son of the house?" he'd been asked, and he'd confirmed that. There had been some whispers out of his sight, and a dungeon lackey had been sent out on an errand. The torture had stopped soon after that, and he had been taken back to his cell. Sandro had been surprised at not having been tortured further, but then he had reflected that it wasn't necessary. He was already under sentence of death, and now that they knew who he was, the present peccadillo for which he'd been arrested would rank as minor by comparison.

The turnkey shrugged. "Be thankful that your catechist saw no point in it."

His answer confirmed what Sandro thought. Venice was a rational state, stern but not wantonly cruel. The real torment would come later, when the eighteen-year-old sentence of death was carried out.

As he ducked through the low doorway, he took a last

backward look at his cell, wondering if he would see it
again. He supposed he had been fortunate, if that was the
word, to be lodged in the Leads—the *Piombi*—rather than
the Wells—the *Pozzi*—where the prisoners waded in sea
water seeping in from the canals, and where a prolonged
stay could be a death sentence in itself. In the Leads, at
least—the cells under the roof of the doge's palace, which
got their name from the lead sheets that covered them—one
only froze in winter and roasted in summer.

"*Vada!* Get going," the turnkey said, giving him a push.

Sandro stumbled through the narrow passage with two
bored guards at his heels. He was relieved, in spite of what
the turnkey had said, to see that they were going left, where
the ducal chambers were, instead of right, which led to the
torture chamber.

The guards conducted him to a rather austere antechamber, where hard benches lined the walls and where there it
was not even a painting to relieve the bare paneled walls.
There they seized him by the arms and hustled him to a
door at the far end. Sandro winced—his wounded arm was
still painful, though it was healing nicely and had been
bound up by the doctor appointed to the torture chamber—
but he knew better than to resist.

They opened the door and thrust him inside. Sandro
stood blinking in total darkness. A hand took his arm and
guided him to a place that might have been the center of a
large room, and left him standing there.

A voice came out of the darkness. "Are you Alessandro
Cavalli?"

"Yes," Sandro said with a sense of hopelessness. "I've admitted it."

The secret trials were generally held in the dark, though
a three-fifths vote of the Council could allow light. Evidently that was not going to be the case this time.

There was a rustling of paper in the obscurity before him,
though no one could have read anything.

"Son of Girolamo Cavalli, who died eighteen years ago?"

"Yes . . . there's no need to go on. I know I've been sentenced to death *in absentia*." His voice took on all the years
of pent-up bitterness. "I suppose it doesn't matter that I'm
innocent. When the egg drops from the basket, as they say,
it's already broken, though it still has a little way to fall. I
never had a chance to defend myself before Your Excellen-

cies, for whatever good it might have done. But I didn't run away. I was taken from Venice against my will."

There were more rustles from the darkness. A cold voice said, "Tell us everything that occurred."

An invisible pen began scratching—the minutes being taken by some clerk who had trained himself to write in the dark. The Council of Ten observed its own legalities. They crossed every *t* and dotted every *i*. But they were implacable, all the same. They never reversed a sentence, not even after death. In one case they had hanged a senator who had been falsely accused, and then the three accusers had been executed and the victim's body exhumed, without apology, for a state funeral. Once they had even beheaded a doge.

Sandro replied in the same legalistic spirit. He would put everything on the record, at least.

"I never killed my father," he said woodenly. "And Monna Tessa had nothing to do with it. He'd been ill for some time. He'd said he wasn't feeling well that day. . . ."

A sense of utter futility washed over him and he almost couldn't go on. He had just realized that the doge's prestige itself was at stake in the old sentence of death. The present doge, as incredible as it seemed, was Francesco Foscari—the same Foscari whom old Mocenigo, on his deathbed, had warned Venice not to elect as his successor—and it had been Foscari, at his father's wake and looking, as always, for votes, who had suggested that the mushrooms Girolamo Cavalli had dined on the night of his death might have been poisoned and that Monna Tessa ought to be put to the torture to find out. Had Monna Tessa, in the agony of the rack or worse, confessed falsely and implicated him?

He forced himself to go on. When he came to the business of the changed will, one of his inquisitors seized on it immediately.

"So on the very day of his death—almost the very hour—your father had a new will notarized that made you, instead of your older brother, his beneficiary?"

"No!" Sandro cried. "Maffeo and I were to have equal shares!"

"But you, the younger son, were to be over him."

"It was for Maffeo's own protection. It was for the good of the House of Cavalli. I would never have killed my father for such a thing. I didn't even want the responsibility—"

He stopped. There was no point in protesting. The charge was unanswerable.

"Go on," said the relentless voice in the darkness.

Sandro collected his thoughts. As briefly as he could, he recounted his abduction, his sale to the Genoese galley captain, his years of slavery, his escape. He was given a few minutes' respite while the Council's chief torturer was brought from the dungeon to testify that Sandro's back was indeed as ridged and scarred with the marks of the lash as any galley slave's.

"Isn't it more likely," suggested a dry voice, "that you were caught and enslaved by Moorish pirates while attempting to flee Venice? Many of our most respected citizens have such scars, including one of our greatest admirals."

"I can only tell Your Excellencies what happened," Sandro said. "What's the point of lying. The sentence is already passed down."

There was more shuffling of papers. Sandro still could not see his judges, but now he had a sense of the space around him and of the tribunal on its dais. In the brief flash of illumination when the torturer had been admitted, he had gained an impression of a row of cowled heads behind a long table and a smaller group, perhaps the clerks, to one side.

"And what of the complaint by the Signori di Notte that brought you here now?"

"What does that matter, either, Your Excellencies? I can only be blinded once, mutilated once, put to death once."

Sandro's mind tried to shy from the thought. The penalties for parricide were infinitely worse than for any other offense in the criminal code, except possibly for treason. He had thought he didn't care about living, but now he discovered that he cared very much indeed about dying.

There was a long, whispered discussion. Sandro remembered the *bravo* who had been wounded in the fight. That would be blamed on him, too. The law said that if a housebreaker caught in the act defended himself with weapons or wounded anyone while fleeing, he lost both eyes and his right hand. He almost would have been willing to settle for that.

"Don't be impertinent," his questioner reprimanded him. "Give your account of what happened."

As truthfully as he could, Sandro described the events of

the night he had broken into the *palazzo*. He held nothing back. It was impossible to incriminate himself further. He was cooked no matter what he said.

There was a pause when he finished. Then a voice said, "No one came forward to press charges. Can you think why that may be so?"

"No, Your Excellencies."

The guards took him back to his cell. Sandro tried to prepare himself; he knew that most sentences were carried out immediately.

The next few hours of waiting were dreadful, but when the door finally creaked open, it was only the turnkey with his supper.

"*Per carità*, friend!" he implored him. "What goes?"

"Nobody's told me anything," the turnkey said, picking his teeth.

He waited through the night, listening for footsteps. They would be those of his confessor, he thought. Surely they would send him a confessor before the executioner's lackeys came to get him. Unless—the thought struck him—they had decided to make a show of it. In that case, confession would be a part of the spectacle—a priest, kneeling at his side as the executioner heated his implements. That would explain the delay; they would wait until morning, and the footsteps he heard would not be those of a priest, but of the executioner's henchmen.

Toward dawn he fell into an exhausted sleep. He was unprepared when the bolts slid back and the door swung open. But it was the turnkey again, by himself.

"Get out," he said.

"What?"

"Get out, you're free to go."

Sandro shook his head to rid himself of the sudden buzzing in it. "But the trial?"

"No sentence was passed," the turnkey said. "If it was, I'd know about it."

"But what of the other sentence, the old one? The *in absentia* sentence of death?"

The turnkey looked at him as if he were mad. "If there ever had been a sentence of death, do you think you'd be leaving this place?"

Sandro grabbed him by the arm. "Have pity on me! *Che succede?* You must know more!"

The turnkey shook him off and turned his face away. "That's all I can tell you. I've said too much already."

Sandro descended the dark narrow stairs that connected with the dungeons below. A silent lackey waited at the bottom to usher him through labyrinthine passages to an inconspicuous door that opened on the narrow side canal leading to the Riva.

He stood blinking in the sunlight, trying to adjust to a world that had turned upside down. The few passersby hurrying past the prison gave him a wide berth. He knew he was unkempt, filthy, his clothes disreputable.

A hiss drew his attention. A man was standing by the door, as if he had been waiting. He was a drab, colorless individual who looked like some minor state official.

"Ser Alessandro?"

"Who are you?"

"I'm nobody. That is to say, I have no existence."

"What do you want?"

The man cleared his throat. "The Council of Ten never makes a mistake. That's a well-known fact. Think what that would do to public confidence."

"Then why did they sentence me to death eighteen years ago?"

He received a bland stare. "There's no sentence against you. There never was. If you could look through the secret minutes for the list of those condemned eighteen years ago, you would not find your name there." He shook his head gently, reprovingly. "You must have been hoaxed. In fact, it's been noted that a crime has been committed against *you*."

The world swam around Sandro. All the years of exile had been for nothing. He might have returned to Venice at any time. Confused images of his life in Portugal came back to him—the court at Sagres, the chandlery, Catalina. Catalina, most of all. He was swept by a sudden hunger for her. No, those years had not been for nothing. They had been his life, not the years in Venice that had never happened.

"A certain Messer Falco, a labor contractor, happened to be arrested this morning," the official went on, looking straight ahead at the canal as if he were not talking to Sandro. "For selling Christians to the Moors. The Gentlemen are now looking for a certain Lombard moneylender."

"And Maffeo?" Sandro said in a strained voice.

"I believe the Gentlemen called on him shortly after lauds

to invite him for a chat with their Excellencies," the official
said distantly. "Oh, don't think it has anything to do with
you—it appears that someone or other put a note in the
lion's mouth denouncing him for treasonable dealings with
banking houses in Milan and Genoa and other such offenses.
It's strange how word gets around. By the hour of prime,
lions' mouths all over the city had been stuffed with similar
accusations. He's even been accused of committing treason
by overcharging the Arsenal during the present emergency
with Milan. It's a wicked world, signore, where if one's enemies learn of one's misfortune, they run to take advantage
of it. And I'm afraid your brother has many enemies. Ah,
well, I have no doubt that he'll have an explanation for everything that comes to light."

He could not think of Maffeo now. He was a Venetian
again. Wonderingly, Sandro said, "What shall I do?"

"Why, if I were you, I'd go home."

# CHAPTER 22

First he went to the Flute. The proprietor, Master Johann, looked askance at his disheveled appearance, but made no comment. One of the German boarders made little sucking sounds of disapproval. Sandro found his travel chest undisturbed. The Flute was as honest as an inn could be. He paid his reckoning and descended the stone steps to the water landing. He had trouble finding a gondolier willing to take so villainous-looking a passenger, but finally one of them recognized him as someone he'd seen before. "The Grand Canal again, signore, as far as the *punta?*" he asked. "No, not to the *punta*," Sandro replied. "Only as far as the Cavalli palace."

The servant who opened the door at the water gate was someone Sandro had never seen before. He was afraid to let Sandro in. The entire household must have been shaken by the raid of the Signori di Notte, and he was taking no chances. He slammed the door in Sandro's face and ran to get Bruno.

Bruno came clanking out with his old sword at his side and a frown on his rugged face. "What's all this? You'll have to leave, or I'll turn you over to the watch—" He stopped.

"Hello, Bruno. *Sta bene?* It's Sandro."

"And didn't I know that?" Tears streaming down his face, the old watchman kissed both Sandro's hands. "We've been talking of nothing else since the night of your visit." A sly humor showed through the tears. "I missed you that night," he said.

"I'm glad of that, old friend."

"I'll go get Jacopo."

He stomped off toward the rear of the house. Sandro noticed how stiff he was.

Jacopo arrived within the minute, straight and dignified in his silk gown. "Messer Alessandro! I never believed that you were dead."

"You're still here, Jacopo?"

"Where would I be? These have been evil times, but someone had to look after the House of Cavalli. I hoped for a little one, whom I could instruct in the meaning of the Cavalli name—there's hope in every new generation—but the signora was not to be blessed." He looked Sandro up and down critically and began to fuss. "We'll get you out of those rags and into a tub. Then I'll lay out fresh hose and doublet for you. We'll move you into the second-floor suite."

"Wait, wait!" Sandro protested. "I'm not master here yet!"

Jacopo's face grew doleful. "Maffeo will never leave the *Pozzi*, except to be hung upside down between the pillars. When everything becomes known . . ." He stopped himself. "Anyway, there's the notarized will. Maffeo stole it from your father's papers the morning after he died—I saw him. But the notary's still alive, and we'll bring him forward now."

"Jacopo . . ." Sandro said. "Monna Tessa . . .?"

"She's still alive. Maffeo got rid of her right away. He sent her back to her village. We'll bring her back."

"I thought . . . I thought . . ."

"No. There was talk of putting her to the question, but Maffeo didn't dare allow that. Who knows what she might have said under torture? He went and fixed it up with his old friend Foscari, who was still only a ward boss then. There was no more talk of poison after that." He shook his head. "They're two of a kind. There are rumors now that Foscari's son's been taking bribes—he's one of the Stocking Club dandies, and he's always in debt. He'll end up between the pillars, too, one of these days, mark my words— doge's son or not."

"Jacopo . . ." Sandro fumbled for the words. "How did Agnese die?"

Jacopo pressed his lips together. "An angel would have wept, Messer Sandro. She died the winter after you disappeared. She was never strong, and the cough kept getting worse and worse in that damp room overlooking the garden. I tried to move her into better quarters. Maffeo and the signora took the best rooms for themselves, but there were others. Your old room was empty. But Maffeo refused to allow it. He said she'd be better off in the back room, and that a young girl ought not to be exposed to some of the sights on the Grand Canal, when gondoliers are paid to look the other way—and she, little saint that she was, never complained. I used to send the serving girls up with warming pans for her, but when Maffeo caught them, he'd send them back, and finally he forbade it. He said it was too wasteful of charcoal."

"But why? Why would he do such a thing?"

Jacopo shrugged. "At any rate, let's get you settled. I can move the signora by tomorrow."

"No, let her stay where she is." Sandro could not have brought himself to move into the second-floor apartment or the salon that had been used in later years by his father. "I'll move back into my old quarters."

"It's not ready," Jacopo protested. "It needs a cleaning. There's lots of work to be done."

"I'll sleep in Agnese's old room tonight. I'd like that. I can stay there until things are put in order."

Jacopo nodded in understanding. "I'll see to it."

"In the meantime I'll do some housecleaning of my own. What happened to Ser Ippolito?"

"Maffeo got rid of him, too. He was too honest to go along with the funny business at the firm. He was kicked out without a pension. He's living in poverty in the Cannaregio district. There's a new *fattore* now, a Lombard."

"Not any more," Sandro said. "Find Ser Ippolito for me. Bring him here as soon as you can. We're going to get the House of Cavalli out of the slave trade and the rest of the dirty business."

"I'll have him here tomorrow," Jacopo said.

Sandro put his hand on Ser Jacopo's shoulder. "Don't worry, old friend, we'll restore the Cavalli name."

Giuditta secluded herself in the second-floor apartment. She had her meals brought to her by a serving maid. Sandro rarely saw her. When they passed each other on the staircase, they exchanged a mumbled formal greeting, and that was all.

In any event, he was too busy at the warehouse with Ser Ippolito to think much about Giuditta. The old *fattore* was in the winter of his years, as bleached and sere as old canvas, but he was still lively as a cricket, and his mind had lost none of its sharpness.

"It's not only the secret dealings with Genoa, when Genoa was our enemy," Ippolito said in a dusty voice, "or the dealings with Milan of late. It's all those years of selling munitions to the Moors, to be used against Christians, that will count against him. Oh, I know that everybody does it, and the export laws are winked at. But once you're in the dungeons of the doge and the process of inquiry has begun, everything's dredged up against you. They'll single Maffeo out for that, too. The meat grinder must be fed its meat."

"Were you the one who put the denunciation in the lion's mouth?" Sandro said quietly.

The knobby little man drew himself up. "No. There was no need for me to do it. They're standing in line for the job."

In the midst of untangling the affairs of the House of Cavalli Sandro found time to carry out his mission for Mestre Jaime with Andrea Bianco. He took an immediate liking to Bianco. The mapmaker was a vigorous, stocky man of about his own age, with a naval officer's forthrightness. He was overwhelmed when he learned that Mestre Jaime had taken an interest in his work. "Of course I'll make a copy of my *mappamundi* for the mestre," he said at once. "I'll be leaving soon on this year's voyage of the Galley of Flanders, but I'll squeeze it in somehow, even if I have to hire draftsmen to do the dogwork." A thought struck him. "We could deliver it together, Messer Cavalli. Our fleet will put in for several days at Sagres, on the way to England. Will you be returning to Portugal to wind up your affairs there?"

Like everybody in Venice he knew the gossip about Sandro's return from the dead. It was the talk of the Rialto. For days, Sandro had received a stream of bankers and fellow merchants at the Cavalli palace, all of them eager to find out what the state of affairs was at the House of Cavalli, and what future direction the firm would take. Sandro had done nothing to feed the stories, but there was nothing he could have done to keep them from spreading.

A shadow crossed Sandro's face as he thought of Catalina's ultimatum to him. If Bianco noticed it, he could not have imagined its cause, and Sandro could not have explained to another Venetian gentleman why a diversion with a tavern wench in another country should be important to him.

"Yes, I'll go back," he said. "But there's so much to do here first. I don't know if I can finish in time to sail with you."

"Try to manage it if you can," Bianco urged him. "If you're going to undertake a long and arduous journey by sea, there's no better way to travel than on a Venetian state galley. But you must know that. I'll book you passage with me, on the flagship, and as a nobleman you'll dine at the head table with the *capitanio*." He laughed. "I'd join you there, but there's a new rule that the chief navigator presides at a separate table over those officers and notables who don't happen to be noble—as an act of courtesy so they won't feel left out. At any rate, on the Galley of Flanders you'll be safe from pirates and other annoyances."

Sandro forced a smile. He had lost his taste for traveling on galleys after experiencing two years at the wrong end of a whip. The voyage from Sagres to Florence had confirmed his resolve to confine his future travel to sailing ships. But he supposed that if he had to endure a journey by galley again, a Venetian galley would be preferable. At least Venice's oarsmen were free; they were even allowed to do petty trading of their own at the ports of call.

"I'll see what I can do," he said.

Monna Tessa arrived the following day, burdened with hampers, chest, baskets of eggs, cheeses, and even a brace of squawking chickens that she had brought with her from her village. "Praise the Virgin that you're alive," she said, "and the wickedness that took you from us will be punished." She looked at him critically. "Who's been feeding you? You haven't been eating well, and you haven't been getting your sleep. I'll have someone's hide!"

"It was the prison food, Monna Tessa," Sandro said. "And the journey by sea and overland. I was well taken care of in Portugal, and as to the meals I'm served here since I returned, I have no complaints, though there's none that can compare with yours."

"We'll see about that," she proclaimed. "I'm going to the

kitchen to have it out with that woman who's been lording it over this household since I left, and then we'll decide if she stays and what place we'll find for her. And another thing—we'll have to do something about the little slave girl. The Cavalli house has never had slaves, and it never will again as long as I'm here!"

"As you say, Monna Tessa."

Her manner softened, and she gave him the old warm, square-toothed smile that he remembered. "You're a man now, signore, and you can do what you want. So don't mind the grumblings of an old woman."

She shook her head to herself and marched to the kitchen to do battle.

Sandro saw to the legal paperwork that afternoon and the slave, a little Tartar girl of ten or eleven who had been given the name Ghirigora, was freed the same day. A place was found for her with wages all the time, and she was soon following Monna Tessa around all the time, aquiver with adoration.

Nothing was heard about Maffeo. His arrest and imprisonment were supposed to be secret. But secrets were hard to keep in Venice. It was noticed and whispered about which of his associates disappeared at night, and witnesses, including those who had been examined under torture and then released as being unculpable, told their stories in whispers to their families, and the whispers were repeated and spread. Sandro went to the ducal palace once or twice to ask about Maffeo but was turned away with a warning not to interest himself in state affairs.

Finally one day Ser Jacopo came to Sandro with a face that was somber even for him. "The ducal palace sent a message. The examination's finished. Sentence has been passed. What's left of him will be displayed between the pillars tomorrow. As a means of making amends for what you've suffered, and because of your father's name, they're putting aside the usual rules and allowing a visit by relatives."

It was indeed unusual. The Council of Ten not only rigorously excluded relatives from its proceedings, but maintained strict secrecy about sentencing. Ordinarily the first inkling anyone had about a sentence was the appearance of the corpse in the Plaza or dangling by one leg from a palace window.

A sliver of ice penetrated Sandro's heart. "What's the sentence?" he asked.

"The most severe. The flesh to be torn from him, castration, disembowelment, burning. Only when he's dead is he to be beheaded."

Giuditta refused to go. She went into hysterics. "No, no," she wept, "I can't see him! I can't talk to him! I don't want to look at his face!"

Sandro took Jacopo aside. "I'll get my cloak. Have the gondola made ready."

"After what he did to you? You came here to kill him."

"It's over. He's my brother."

Maffeo was unable to get up. His limbs had been dislocated, for the second time during his examination, and this time it had proved impossible to reset them in the sockets. He stared up at Sandro with smoldering eyes in a face that was pulled so tight over the bones that Sandro hardly recognized it.

"Hello, brother," he said. "Have you come to gloat?"

"No," Sandro said.

Seeing Maffeo broken by the rack, Sandro could no longer hate him. Within him, where the hate had always been, was an empty place. It provided a curious sense of relief, like the empty socket of an aching tooth that at long last has been pulled.

"Last night," Maffeo said, "they tried one last time to get me to admit that I poisoned our father. The death sentence was already certain, they told me, and I could spare myself further pain. I told them I couldn't confess to something I hadn't done."

"Maffeo . . ." Sandro said.

"Falco and the Lombard die beside me tomorrow. Neither of them was any good under torture. Between the two of them they confessed to enough, both false and true, to sentence me to death twenty times over."

"Why didn't you confess, then? I know it was only the old story of poison that you invented to deceive me with come back to haunt you. But even if it's not true—"

"But it *is* true," Maffeo said. "That's the one reason why I couldn't confess to it."

"You're lying," Sandro said. "Even now, you're trying to make mischief."

"Ah, my brother understands me at last. You never did before."

"Stop it now, Maffeo. Give yourself peace. There'll be a priest. Make your confession."

"When the priest comes, he'll find me repentent. I'll confess to everything else. But I'll tell him I'm innocent of the poisoning—that you did it after all."

"Do you hate me so much, then?" Sandro could only feel pity.

Maffeo had a coughing fit that brought a froth of blood to his lips from something that had been broken inside. When it was over, he said, "Yes."

He tried to wipe his lips, but his crippled arms wouldn't reach them. Sandro took his handkerchief and did it for him.

"It's all right, Maffeo," he said. "I forgive you."

The sunken eyes glared at him. "But I don't forgive *you.*"

Sandro got up to go. By some curious trick of perception, he seemed to be seeing Maffeo at a distance, as if through the wrong end of a telescope, a little figure of twisted sticks on a straw pallet.

"Tell me one thing," he said. "Why did you keep Agnese locked away in an unheated apartment?"

"I knew she wouldn't last the winter," Maffeo said in a detached voice. "I kept the doctor away from her, too, because I knew he'd order me to move her to a sunnier room. I would have deprived her of proper food, on the pretext of diet, except that she never had any appetite anyway."

"Why?" Sandro asked. "Why would you do such a thing to our sister?"

"Because she knew too much about the night of your disappearance. She was watching through her window when Falco's men took you in the garden and stuffed you in a sack."

"Dear God!"

Maffeo smiled peacefully up at Sandro. There was more blood on his lips. "I kept her quiet by telling her the same story the Lombard told you. I said it would put you in great danger if anyone knew. But I didn't rest easy until she was dead."

Sandro thought of what was in store for Maffeo tomorrow, and found that he still could not hate him. "Good-bye, Maffeo," he said. "God have mercy on you."

"I don't want His mercy," Maffeo said. "I'll scream in His ears until the end."

They kept him sitting in the room with the hard benches for over two hours. Finally someone came out to see him. It was the colorless man who had been waiting for him outside the prison door, the one who had said that he had no existence.

"I hear you've been making a nuisance of yourself. Are you trying to get yourself locked up again?"

"I came to plead for mercy for Maffeo," Sandro said.

"The sentence has been passed. It has to be carried out. Every item of it."

"Behead him first," Sandro said.

The nonexistent official raised a thinning eyebrow. "An easy death for him? He murdered your father. He as good as murdered your sister. He would have murdered you, except that he was too weak, and his accomplices overruled him for the sake of their pocketbooks. As it was, he put you in hell. Don't you want revenge?"

"He wants to scream in the ears of God," Sandro said. "I'll deprive him of that. That's revenge enough."

"Curious." The official looked at him as if he were an inanimate object, like a chair. "You're a fool, you know that?"

"I want to see the doge," Sandro said. "It's my right. I demand it."

The official sighed. "We've had enough scandal out of this. Their Excellencies have done everything in their power to contain it. You're becoming an inconvenience."

"The ax," Sandro said. "That's all I ask. No one will know the difference. When the populace sees the body hanging between the pillars, they'll see that everything prescribed for parricides and traitors has been done. Public policy will be preserved."

The official shook his head in disbelief. "Wait here," he said.

This time, Sandro was kept waiting three hours. The nonexistent man finally appeared, looking exasperated. "You're very persistent," he said. "Their Excellencies are very annoyed with you. He'll be beheaded. First."

•   •   •   •

In the next few days, Sandro kept himself busy. He worked at home; he did not want to go to the Rialto. That would have required passing the Plaza of Saint Mark's and the present object lesson between the pillars, feeling the stares of the curious on him, enduring conversation with his peers about the day's prices and rates of exchange. Ser Ippolito came faithfully each morning, and together they untangled the knots of the business that Maffeo's deviousness had tied over the years.

"Slaves," said Ippolito. "There's still a balance of twenty-two of them left over from a shipment that was rerouted to Crete for transshipment to the African market. Dregs—the old, the sick, the untrainable. Unsalable, most of them."

"We'll pay off the factor for his loss of commission and set them free. They can't go home, I suppose. If they were bought at Tana, their homes lie beyond the Mongol lands, in the hands of those who sold them in the first place. We'll bring them to Venice, those who want to come. We'll get them settled somehow, one by one."

"It will be costly to the firm," Ippolito said, pursing his lips.

"Is there money enough in the various accounts?"

"Yes."

"Maffeo's shady schemes put it there. We'll spend some of it to make things right."

Ippolito nodded. "Next, the cloth purchases through the Cappello brothers at London and Bruges. We owe twelve hundred ducats. If we cash in the Balbi bills of exchange in London, we'll realize a profit of an additional five percent by the time it gets back to the Medicis in Florence. . . ."

Andrea Bianco continued to press him about taking passage on the Galley of Flanders, but Sandro did not see how he could be ready to leave in time. He put Bianco off again. The *mappamundi*, however, was coming along splendidly. Sandro followed its progress in the workshop of the copyist whom Bianco had engaged at his expense and was intrigued by the suggestion—based on God knew what reports and rumors Bianco had heard on the Atlantic run—that there was more land waiting to be discovered to the west. What Prince Henry would make of that could only be imagined.

Giuditta gradually recovered her composure, though she refused to accompany Sandro to the Church of the Miseri-córdia after he had persuaded them to accept Maffeo's remains for interment. "It's the shame," Ser Jacopo apologized for her. Within a week she was commandeering the Cavalli gondola for visits to the Borgo palace, saying that she needed the consolation of her family. The fine clothes she wore on these occasions had nothing of mourning about them—splendid gowns of silk and damask, trimmed with pearls and jewels, that must have cost Maffeo a pretty penny. Sandro noticed that she passed him on the stairs more frequently, and that her greetings were less stiff. Once or twice there was the suggestion of a sad smile, and he could not help feeling sorry for her. She was going to have to live with the stigma for the rest of her life. Her presence in the Cavalli palace with the brother of her late husband was growing untenable. It was not proper. But Sandro could not bring himself to say anything.

He was using the salon for business now, as his father had. One day, he supposed, it would be used for entertainment again, but the time was not yet. He was uncomfortably aware of the apartment on the other side of the landing, across the yawning well of the staircase.

On a sunny spring afternoon, at about the time of day that Ser Ippolito usually packed up his ledgers and sheafs of correspondence and left, Sandro was surprised to see Giuditta come into the salon. He had become accustomed to having her avoid him. She had on her most fetching gown, a blue velvet with a low, square neck, and she wore a little cap with pearls that set off her golden hair.

She waited, immobile, while Ippolito gathered his papers and gave him a barely perceptible nod as he saluted her and let himself out.

"*Buon giorno, signora,*" Sandro said, a little stiffly.

"You don't have to be so formal, Sandro," she said with a wan smile. "We're past the time for that, aren't we?"

"Giuditta, then," he said.

"That's better." The smile curved higher, then diminished again. "It's been terrible, hasn't it? Everything that's happened."

"Yes," he agreed.

"It's been terrible for me, as well. I'm a victim too, you know. Perhaps more of a victim than you are. You, at least, are vindicated. Everybody sympathizes with you. You're making a fresh start, wiping out the past. But sometimes I feel as if I'll have this black cloud over me forever."

"People will forget," he said.

"I never loved him, you know. He treated me badly. He only married me because I was a Borgo and to get back at you. I don't know what you ever did to him—"

"Nothing," he said. "I did nothing."

"I know," she said quickly. "I know that. You weren't at fault, and neither was I." She moved closer to him. "Listen to me, Sandro. We can take up where we left off. We'll put all of this behind us. Remember that night on the canal, the things you said to me? We'll start from there."

He stood very still. She was close enough for him to smell the rose water in her hair. Her words called up the memory of a boy in a gondola, playing a lute. A pleasant enough boy. Sandro could see his face very well, but he found that he didn't know him.

She saw the way his jaw was working. "I know you're thinking of Maffeo. It's only natural. You can't help remembering that I was his wife. But it was you that I loved. I was forced into the marriage by my father. He and Maffeo together saw the advantages of an alliance between the Casa di Borgo and the Casa di Cavalli." She pouted a little, with a provocative flutter of eyelashes. "If you care for me so little, *mio caro*, you can at least think of the practicalities. The alliance can continue, to your advantage."

"Giuditta . . ." he said uncomfortably.

"I admit it. I was dazzled by the Cavalli wealth, the name . . . I was only a young girl. But I was never a real wife to him, only another possession. I never knew about the things he did. I had nothing to do with that regrettable business of Agnese. Remember, I was a newcomer in this house. I was young and inexperienced. I only knew there was a sick girl in the garden room. I used to go in and visit her sometimes. The servants will tell you that. She liked me . . ."

Sandro turned to stone. He could almost hear Agnese's bright chatter, how she had seen Giuditta in church and thought how beautiful she was, how interested she had been in his courtship.

Giuditta sensed the churning emotion behind the ice of his expression. "Ah, *caro*, how can you be so cruel to an innocent woman. Not even a little word, a smile? I know how much you hate Maffeo, but it has nothing to do with us."

"I don't hate him."

"Well, then . . ."

Her smile was triumphant. She put a hand on his arm. She was very beautiful in the blue gown, but he remembered that he had seen her naked not long ago, when Maffeo had still been alive.

He removed her arm from him. "No," he said. He forced his voice to calmness. "I'll see that a settlement is made on you. You need have no fears on that score. You're lucky. The Council might have confiscated everything, sent you into exile, as they did Carmagnola's wife. You can stay here until you can make other arrangements."

Her face twisted, became ugly. "You can't do this to me! It's mine! It belongs to me by right! I won't see it all go to some other woman, after they start swarming around you! The Casa di Borgo will dispute the inheritance! My family will tie up the Casa di Cavalli forever in legal claims!"

Sandro turned to go. Her voice became more strident at his back. "My brothers will take revenge! You'll live to regret this! I'll see you a galley slave again!"

He made his escape. The salon door closed on the tirade behind him.

Giuditta moved back to the Borgo palace the following day. "You'll send for the lawyer this afternoon," Sandro said to Ser Jacopo as they watched her gondola depart, riding low in the water from the weight of her piled belongings, "and we'll see about drawing up the papers for a pension for her."

Bruno was packing up the rest of the things that were to be sent along later to the Casa di Borgo. There was hardly room to move about on the boat landing. *"Che tigre,"* he said, mopping his forehead. Neither Jacopo nor Sandro reprimanded him.

"I'll go to see Messer Bianco this morning," Sandro went on. "I'm going to tell him that I'll be sailing with him on the Galley of Flanders after all. You'll have to run the affairs of the household by yourself until I get back."

"It's all for the best," Jacopo said. His eyes followed the wallowing progress of the overburdened craft down the Grand Canal. "You could never have married her, the Borgo name or not. But however that may be, you can't deny that the House of Cavalli will need a great lady at its head."

"It has one," Sandro said.

# CHAPTER 23

On a late summer day in Sagres, with a fresh wind blowing from the sea and the sun like a badge in the sky, a Venetian gentleman came into the tavern of the Cabra do Mar. The patrons goggled to see him; what was a *poderoso*, a great man, like that doing in a dive like the Goat, with its clientele of sailors and wharf rats?

He was a tall man with an aristocratic bearing, splendidly attired in a tight silk doublet that emphasized his breadth of shoulders and powerful chest, fine camlet hose, a rakish velvet cap with a gold medal to set it off, a jeweled belt appropriate to his rank, and a heavy gold chain that was worth a fortune in itself.

He looked around the tavern and seemed disappointed at not finding what he was after. His eye fell on Vasques, and he strode across the room toward him.

"By God, now I know who it is," said an old-timer nursing a drink at the corner table. "It's O Fidalgo."

"Tell us something we don't know, Matos," another said. "Anyone can see he's a somebody."

"No, no," Matos said. "I mean it's the chandler they used to call O Fidalgo because of his ways. I worked beside him when he was a dockworker."

"You're off your head," scoffed the other.

But Vasques seemed to recognize him too. "Senhor Sandro, is it you?" he burbled. "I can't believe my eyes."

"Listen, where's Catalina?"

Vasques appeared about to embrace him—or pummel him—but a look up and down at the noble costume and the jewels intimidated him, and his hands dropped to pluck at his apron. "I knew the Galley of Flanders anchored a little while ago, and I thought I might expect some sailors or oarsmen later on. But you, senhor! And like this!" He stumbled and caught himself. "Of course I knew all along that you were a man of quality. How could anyone mistake it? But tell me, how does it happen that—"

Sandro cut him short. "Later, Vasques, later. Where's Catalina?"

Vasques gave him a mournful look. "She's not here anymore."

"She left, then?"

Someone else was at his elbow. "So you're alive, after all. Catalina didn't expect ever to see you again."

Sandro turned and saw Tom of Bristol. The Englishman was grinning like a dissolute cherub. From the rosy glow on his cheeks, he'd had more than a few.

"You've returned just in time," he said grandly and unsteadily. "But you've missed all the fun. Portugal has a new king—a six-year-old. Poor Duarte pined away over the hostage business with Prince Fernando until he died. Prince Pedro wrested the regency away from Queen Leonor, and there was almost a civil war, but Prince Henry talked sense into both of them. He had a busy time of it, but now he's free to go exploring again. The new ships are ready. Pedro's come back from Madeira with Inês to take charge of the new expedition. We'll see him off, you and I, with a drink for old times."

"Tom . . . for God's sake . . . Catalina . . . Do you know where she went? Where can I find her?"

Tom beamed happily at him. "Why, at home. Where else would she be?"

Generosa opened the door and screamed when she saw him. "O senhor!" she cried. "Ai, ai!" She dropped to her knees and tried to kiss his hand.

"It's all right," he said. "Go back to your work. Is the senhora here?"

A movement at the end of the hall answered him. His

breath caught as he saw the slim, straight figure silhouetted against the light of the window there. He thought he saw her sway, but then she was coming toward him with those long-legged, decisive strides that a woman of his class would have thought unladylike.

He moved toward her, but they stopped short of each other, as if a fence had suddenly sprung up between them.

"Hello, Sandro," she said. He had expected fire, but she was subdued, almost wary.

"Hello, *cara*."

He drank in the sight of her. Her face, usually too mobile for people to think of it as beautiful, was in a state of watchful repose that made it possible to see the fine structure of it, the splendid bones, the symmetry. She was wearing one of the good dresses he had bought for her—one that he had never seen her wear before. It came to him that her carriage was just as fine in it as that of any great signora of Venice.

"You look very grand," she said. "You didn't have to come back, you know. Giraldo's been taking care of things at the chandlery. He'll have a nice balance to show you. And your instructions have been followed about the bills here."

He waited for a moment after she finished. "Maffeo's dead," he said.

"Your brother?"

He nodded.

"So you've had your revenge," she said quietly.

"No. That's not the way of it." He sat her down on a bench and poured out the story. At the end, as he told her of the final mercy he had obtained for Maffeo, he saw tears spilling down her cheeks.

"You've never spoken to me so freely before," she said.

"I've never felt so free."

She touched his face with her fingers. "The hate's gone, isn't it?"

"Yes," he said.

"I could tell." She gave him a big wide smile. "I don't care what anyone says. A *tauernera* can kiss a *fidalgo* . . . what do they call them in Venice?"

"Signore," he said. "Just signore."

She threw her arms around his neck and they kissed, warmly, without thought, as they had in the best of times. "You've found redemption, signore," she whispered in his ear. "When you found mercy in your heart for your brother, you redeemed your soul."

"You mustn't talk of redemption," he said. "It's blasphemy. You can't know. Only a priest can grant absolution."

"Then I'm a priest," she said. "You're absolved. I know."

There was a silence. Then Sandro said, "You told me you wouldn't be here when I returned—if I returned. Why did you change your mind?"

"Ah, Sandro, it was bread cast upon the waters. I had a talk with Pedro, and Inês had a talk with me. She's very kind. She persuaded me that I had a reason."

"What reason?"

"Come with me. I'll show you."

She took him by the hand and led him to the kitchen. Generosa was sitting on a stool, rocking a baby back and forth in her lap. "It's almost time to feed him," she told Catalina. "It's disgraceful that the mistress of the household should be tied down to a *bambino* like a nursing sow. He should be sent out to a wet nurse."

For a moment the old Catalina with the fiery temper flared. "Never would I send my child out to nurse! What, to have him raised on the milk of a *balia*! Give him to me!"

She took the child from Generosa. He was large and sturdy, and he broke into a toothless smile when Catalina picked him up. She cooed at him, her outburst forgotten.

"This is your son, Sandro. I gave him a Venetian name— Aldo."

Sandro, his eyes wide with surprise and delight, gave Aldo his little finger. The baby gripped it with surprising strength. Sandro smiled at him and got a smile in return.

"Inês told me it would be unfair of me to take him away when you had provided a house," Catalina said. "She said he deserved something from his father for as long as it was offered, no matter how I felt about it."

"I'll be returning to Venice with the Galley of Flanders in the fall," Sandro said. "I'll close up the house then. I'm going to give the chandlery business to Giraldo."

Catalina's expression did not change. "That's all right. I don't expect anything. Vasques wants me back. I can take Aldo with me."

"We'll marry here, though, in the presence of our friends. At the church of Saint Catherine, above the harbor, I think.

We'll have the sea voyage for our honeymoon. But I'm afraid we won't have much privacy on a Venetian galley."

She looked at him in astonishment. "Go back to Venice with you?"

"Of course. I can't leave my wife and son in another country."

She wrapped her arms more tightly around the baby. "No," she said. "I couldn't."

"You said I'd never speak the words. I've spoken them."

She shook her head violently. "No, Sandro, we're too far apart. You're a great signore of Venice, and I'm what I am."

"What you are is worth a thousand painted ladies on balconies," he said. "You'll be a great lady in Venice. The House of Cavalli will see to it."

"How could I fit in, in a place like that?" she said feebly.

"You'll have my majordomo Jacopo, and my housekeeper Monna Tessa, and the rest of my household to help you. You'll preside over the House of Cavalli, and the House of Cavalli will get the better of the bargain. No one will dare say a thing."

"No . . . no . . . how would I act?"

"As yourself, signora." He laid a big hand over the hand that was cradling the baby and said, "Listen to me, Catalina. It's a different world in Italy and everywhere else. In Venice and Florence and Bologna and Rome there are many ladies of great houses whose origins are recent and honest. As a foreigner, without a provincial accent to burden you, you'll be better off than most of them." He grinned at her and the baby. "As for moving from class to class; don't forget that I've been a galley slave, a household servant of the Moors, a common laborer, and a small waterfront merchant. We'll face down the snobs together."

The baby gave a small belch.

"You see," said Sandro. "You're the mother of the next head of the House of Cavalli."

There was terror in her face. "All right," she said. "I'll go where you go."


The shore was thick with people for miles. From the top of the promontory a tide of local folk could be seen lapping around the base of the cliffs in the narrow band between rock and water, and there were still more crowded along the edge of the heights, looking down. All Sagres and the surrounding villages had turned out to watch the new caravels depart.

There were two of them riding at anchor only a little way out, sleek graceful vessels that were obviously thoroughbreds among the tubbier foreign vessels scattered around the point, waiting for a southerly breeze. The caravels with their huge triangular winglike sails would use whatever wind they found.

"Almost time to go," Pedro said.

Behind them the church bells tolled. Catalina gripped Sandro's arm more tightly.

"How far will you go?" Sandro said.

"Farther," Pedro replied. "Always farther. Isn't that what the prince always says? Some day there won't be any farther to go."

"Inês will stay with us until you return," Catalina said. "We don't sail for Venice until fall. We'll keep the house open till then."

"We thank you for witnessing our marriage," Sandro said.

Tom grinned. "Two masses in one week. My soul's well saved."

Together they turned to watch Prince Henry's party coming down the steps of Saint Catherine's church, where the Bishop had presided over a special mass for the success of the voyage. The prince looked older, his face lined with his recent sorrows, but his tread was lively. His brother, Prince Pedro, in uneasy tandem with the widowed queen Leonor, was the effective ruler of Portugal until little Afonso reached his majority, and in a change of heart about the value of exploration, he had promised Henry all support.

"Perhaps, if life is kind, you'll come to visit us on Madeira," Inês said. "Pedro will one day grow too old and fat for the sea, and he'll have to stay home."

"I won't get fat on Maderia," Pedro laughed. "I'm glad to be going to sea so I can have a rest."

"It's not impossible," Sandro replied. "When Aldo is old enough, I may send him to the prince's school of navigation here at Sagres for seasoning. Perhaps by that time they'll be accepting Venetians."

"No," Catalina said. "He's going to be a Venetian banker, like his father."

"What happens here," Sandro said seriously, "is going to

affect the price of pepper on the Venetian exchange. And many other things. If a new route to the East is discovered, the old arrangements among nations will vanish overnight. Venice will have to keep up with the changes or find itself left behind when the world opens up. Aldo had better know the seas our profits depend on, the new seas as well as the old. I'll be keeping an eye on Pedro and those like him, if only to protect Aldo's heritage."

Tom said, "I've been offered a post at Sagres, you know, now that things are moving ahead again. I think it's to keep my mouth shut."

"Are you going to accept?"

"Not on your life. I've been here long enough. I'm going back to England. We're seafarers ourselves, you know. I'll tell my tales again. Perhaps this time I'll shake up the merchants of Bristol. They might be induced to finance an explorer of their own. There have always been rumors of an island called Brasile somewhere to the west. I have plenty of money. Maybe I'll invest, too. I might even go along myself."

The prince's procession, bearing banners before it, started down the winding path to the sea. Pedro said his last good-byes and fell in behind it with his shipmates.

The caravels spread their sails to the wind. From the cliffs above, the people watched until the brave ships dwindled to invisibility, sailing out into what was no longer the Sea of Darkness.

*The saga of the bold men and courageous women who sailed in search of a new and fabulous world continues in . . .*

# THE DISCOVERERS

*Turn the page for a preview of The Discoverers by Paul King, on sale in Fall 1994, wherever Bantam Books are sold.*

# CHAPTER 1

CONSTANTINOPLE, 1453

The huge cannon boomed with a thunder so loud that all who heard it quaked in fear. A flash of light and a cloud of smoke poured from the mouth of the cannon as a two-hundred-pound stone shot hurtled, black against the sky, toward the walls that surrounded the city. The heavy ball struck with terrible effect, knocking holes in the defenses, turning the mortice into powder, and shattering sections of the palisade, sending jagged wooden shards flying in every direction to strike down hapless victims.

"Ayiieee! We are all going to be killed! We must surrender! We must surrender! I don't want to die!" one of the Genoese defenders shouted. He stood and began to run along the top of the wall, screaming in terror, his nerves finally shattered by weeks of battle.

"Stop him! Someone stop that man!" Captain-General Giovanni Giustiniani shouted, pointing at the berserk soldier. Giustiniani was the commander of the Genoese element of the Christian defenders of Constantinople. "Someone pull him down!"

Giustiniani's warning came too late. With a whistling rush of wind, a Muslim longbowman's arrow made a hundred-yard flight to bury itself in the terrified defender's chest. Grabbing the arrow, the victim tried to pull it out, but he only succeeded in breaking it. He held the shaft in his hand and looked, as if surprised, at the blood that began pouring from the broken shaft still lodged in his chest. He stood there for a moment longer, then pitched forward, falling outside the wall.

An Islamic warrior, brandishing his curved scimitar and using the cover of heavy cannonading, dashed toward the wall to sever the head of the fallen Christian soldier. He started back toward his own lines, making the loud, distinctive ululation of victory. He was almost to safety when the arrow of a Christian crossbowman found its mark and sent him sprawling facedown in the sun-baked, blood-soaked dirt. The slain Christian's severed head rolled like a ball from the fallen Muslim's hand.

For two months now the mighty Islamic army of Mohammed II had been laying siege against the badly outnumbered defenders of Constantinople. Never before had such powerful engines of war been used in battle. Every day the Turks bombarded the city with frightful effect. Every night, as the Christians worked desperately to repair the walls damaged by the day's heavy cannonade, bonfires burned brightly in the Turkish camp. The sultan's warriors were using the firelight to build new firing platforms even closer to the palisade so that they might move their cannons and ballistae inexorably forward.

Then, on the fifty-third day of the siege, the sultan rode through the sprawling camp of his huge army to announce that the final great attack against Constantinople would take place very soon. He promised his soldiers of the Faith that after the fall of the city, in accordance with the customs of Islam, they would be allowed three days of unrestricted sacking and pillaging.

"All treasure found in the city will be fairly distributed among my faithful warriors," the sultan declared.

The proclamation was met with a shout of jubilation: "There is no God but Allah, and Mohammed is His Prophet!"

That night the sultan's army was in a state of high excitement, shouting and singing to the music of pipes and ouds. Then, at midnight, their celebration abruptly ceased, and all the fires were extinguished. The sultan had commanded that the soldiers prepare themselves for the battle to come with one full day of rest and atonement.

The next day, for the first time since the siege began, stillness reigned outside the walls. The great cannons were silent; there were no shouts of challenge and no barrages of flying arrows. Some inside the walled city even expressed hope that the Turks had conceded and were now getting ready to withdraw.

But most knew better. Most understood that the moment of truth had finally arrived. That night the soldiers kept particular watch and strengthened the defenses against the final onslaught. However, as only the engineers and a few guards were needed for this task, Captain-General Giustiniani released the rest of his men long enough to join with the people of Constantinople in one last great outpouring of piety.

Almost as if in open defiance of the Prophet, who according to legend hated the sound of bells, the chimes of every church in Constantinople began to peal. Against this resonating background the faithful Christians began their procession through the city's streets, bearing upon their shoulders the icons and relics of their religion. They passed along the length of the wall, pausing to invoke the blessings of all the saints upon those spots where the Turkish bombards had done the most damage. Those in the procession, Greeks and Italians, Orthodox and Catholic, sang hymns and repeated the kyrie eleison as they paraded through the city, winding up in the Church of Holy Wisdom.

Among the Italian defenders of Constantinople were Venetians and Genoese. These two city-states, both maritime powers, had put aside their age-old enmity long enough to come to the aid of Christendom's easternmost citadel. And though many of the Italians were truly motivated by the holiness of their mission, it was not insignificant that the fall of Constantinople would give the Muslims undisputed control of the eastern Mediterranean and the Black Sea—a disaster that would cut off the trade that had made Venice and Genoa wealthy.

After the procession of the defenders through the city, emperor Constantine arrived at the church, along with his courtiers, senators, and archons, all arranged according to their rank and position.

The Venetian Council of Twelve was there, as were the Venetian nobles. They, like the emperor and his court, were dressed in ceremonial silks and velvets. Giovanni Giustiniani, the captain-general of the Genoese forces, came with his officers. The military men were fresh from the ramparts, and many wore the gleaming armor of soldiers and sailors of high rank.

The crowd of worshipers was swelled by huge numbers of Constantinople's ordinary citizens, those from the middleclass down to servants and slaves. Their homespun clothes were mingled with the colorful garb of the highborn.

It had been five months since many of the more pious Greeks had attended mass, because they believed that in the union of the Eastern and Western churches the liturgy had been defiled by the Latins and renegades. On this evening, however, the only people absent were those defending the city wall. Priests who had previously maintained that the union of the Orthodox Church with Rome was a mortal sin now came to the altar to administer communion alongside their Catholic brothers. The cardinal was there with bishops who had not previously acknowledged his authority. Everyone made confession or took communion, without regard as to whether the bread was leavened or unleavened, not caring whether it was administered by Orthodox or Latin. The images of Christ and His saints looked down upon the worshipers as the priests in their splendid vestments moved through the solemn rhythm of the liturgy.

All present confessed their sins in a murmuring chorus. Some said the words in Latin:

"*Comfietor Deo omnipotenti, beatae Mariae semper Virgini, beato Michaeli Archangelo, beato Joanni Baptistae, sanctis Apostolis Petro et Paulo, omnibus sanctis, et tibi, pater, quia peccavi nimis cogitatione, verbo et opere:*

*mea culpa, mea culpa, mea maxima culpa. Ideo precor beatam Mariam semper Virginem, beatum Michaelem Archangelum, beatum Joannem Baptistam, sanctos Apostolos Petrum et Paulu, omnes Sanctos, et te, pater, orare pro me ad Dominum Deum nostrum."*

Others spoke in Greek.

Everyone heard the same words, regardless of language:

"I confess to almighty God, to blessed Mary ever virgin, to blessed Michael the archangel, to blessed John the Baptist, to the holy apostles Peter and Paul, to all the saints, and to you, Father, that I have sinned exceedingly in thought, word, and deed, through my fault, through my fault, through my most grievous fault. Therefore I beseech blessed Mary ever virgin, blessed Michael the archangel, blessed John the Baptist, the holy apostles Peter and Paul, all the saints, and you, Father, to pray to the Lord our God for me."

One of those making confession in Latin was a young Genoese, Giovanni Ruggi. A sailor rather than a soldier, Giovanni was one of the many who had been taken from their ships two months earlier and put on the palisade to strengthen the defenses.

Standing beside Giovanni and making her confession in Greek was Iole Zarous, the daughter of the merchant in whose house Giovanni was being quartered. Soon after his arrival Giovanni and Iole had become lovers, this despite the enmity often found between Greeks and Genoese and despite Iole's father having spoken out against it. But with Constantinople in its last hours, Zarous seemed less inclined to interfere with his daughter's happiness, however brief it might be, and he had made no protest tonight as he watched his daughter and the young foreign defender leave his house and join the procession to walk hand in hand to the church.

Now, standing in the nave of the church during communion, Giovanni and Iole shared a tiny crumb of the sacred Body of Christ and declared to each other, in this holy assembly, that their love was eternal. Giovanni took something from his pocket and held it out to Iole. It flashed in the light of the thousand candles, glowing as if it were made of candlelight itself.

"Let this be a pledge of my love for you," he said, fastening the clasp around her neck.

"Oh! It is a chain of gold!" Iole said, holding it up between her thumb and forefinger to examine its beauty. She looked at Giovanni with eyes sparkling with joy and wonder. "But no, Giovanni, how can I accept such a marvelous gift? It must have cost a fortune!" She reached around to the clasp to remove it.

"Had I seven fortunes, I would give them all to you," Giovanni replied, putting his hands on hers to stop her from removing the chain. "Please, you must keep it. Don't you like it?"

"I have never seen anything so beautiful."

"Then you will not take it off?"

Iole smiled up at him. "It will stay around my neck until the day I die," she promised solemnly.

"Citizens, behold!" someone shouted. "The emperor speaks!"

Emperor Constantine moved down to the transept crossing, and as the people began to gather around him, he addressed them:

"My friends," he said, his voice trembling despite his attempt at composure, "you have heard the roar of the huge cannon that the Turks have employed against us. You have seen the damage their mighty engines of war have inflicted upon our walls. You are aware of the vast army lying just outside our gates. And yet, despite all that, the Turks will not prevail, for we have God and our Savior.

"My loyal Greek countrymen, you know that a man should always be ready to die for his faith or for his country or for his family or for his sovereign. But I say to you now that you must be prepared to die for all four causes. For is there a man among you who doubts the perfidy of the infidel sultan who has brought on this war to destroy the true faith and to install his false prophet in the seat of Christ?

"And you Italians, gathered here in this great and noble cause, know you now that one hundred, nay, *five* hundred years hence, men will write stories and women will sing songs of your faith and your courage.

"To all I say: Let our spirits be high. Be brave and steadfast. For with the help of God, we *will* be victorious!"

"Soldiers, sailors, warriors for Christ!" Giovanni Giustiniani shouted. "We will never surrender to the Turks!"

The cheers of the military were joined by those of the citizens. The sounds of defiance still echoing from the mosaic ceilings of the enormous domed church, the great carved doors were thrown open, and the worshipers began to leave, returning to their homes or duty stations.

As Giovanni Ruggi and Iole Zarous walked through the night, their way was guided by golden patches of candlelight spilling through windows. Overhead, the vaulting darkness was filled with brilliant stars, some so large and bright that it seemed as if Giovanni could reach up and pluck one down. Countless others, not as brilliant, dusted the blackness with what seemed to be luminous powder.

"Why must you go back to the wall?" Iole asked. It was not the first time she had posed the question.

"You know why," Giovanni answered. "To defend against the infidel."

"Infidel or heretic, what does it matter? Some in our city say better a sultan's turban than a pope's miter," Iole said.

"Surely you can't believe there is no difference between the Holy Father in Rome and the sultan!"

"The sultan threatens our religion less than the pope," Iole insisted. "In the cities already under his control the Greek priests are free to serve the Christians and without defiling the liturgy. Only the bells are forbidden.

The Turks never molest the poor people so long as they pay their tributes. And it is said that the tributes paid to the sultan are less than the taxes imposed by the emperor."

Giovanni stiffened. "Iole, why do you talk so? That is the talk of a defeatist."

"It is the talk of reason," Iole insisted. "If the emperor and the Latins have their way, the city will be sacked and our people slaughtered."

"What would you have us do? Throw open the gates to the invaders?"

"Yes! It is known that the Koran says a people who surrender shall be shown mercy."

"Mercy? I would rather die at my post than throw myself upon the mercy of the Turks!"

Iole began to weep. "But, Giovanni, that is exactly what will happen. You *will* die at your post, and so will thousands of others—not only the soldiers who defend us, but the citizens of the city as well. And for what? To defend the emperor and the pope?"

Trumpets sounded, calling the defenders back to the wall. Giovanni turned to Iole and put his hands on her shoulders. "Beloved, I must go now."

"You go to die," Iole said.

"If so, I have the Church's promise that I will be taken directly into heaven. And with the life I've led, that sounds like a good bargain," Giovanni said, smiling and trying to make light of it.

"I am serious," Iole said. "If you go to the wall now, you will die. Come with me. Wait in my house with me. When the city falls, we will throw open the doors and invite in the Muslims. They will not harm us."

"No! Hide from them! Do not let them in!" Giovanni pleaded. "They will be drunk with bloodlust. Do you really think they will follow the teachings of the Koran? Those who surrender to them will be surrendering their lives."

The trumpets sounded a second call, and Giovanni, feeling like an animal caught in a trap, looked toward the wall. "I must go," he said. "But promise me—please, promise me!—you won't surrender yourself to the Turks. You'll hide until they are gone."

"If you insist," Iole said. "But if you are killed, my fate will not matter to me. I would not want to live."

"I won't be killed," Giovanni said. He pulled her to him and smelled the scent of flowers in her hair. "I promise you, I will not be killed. A soldier knows such things."

"I love you," Iole said.

"I will come for you, my darling," Giovanni vowed. "Win or lose, after the battle, I will come for you. I will take you with me. Promise me you'll wait for me."

"I will be there for you."

"You, sailor! Did you not hear the trumpets?" a passing officer shouted.

"I'm coming!" Giovanni replied.

He broke the embrace, walking away to join the others. But Iole reached for him and he reached back. Their hands joined a moment longer; then they slipped apart until only their fingertips touched. Even through that tiny connection Giovanni could feel the love, and the anguish, of his beautiful Iole.

"Now, sailor!" the officer ordered. "Your comrades need you."

"I will come for you, Iole!" Giovanni shouted the promise over his shoulder. "Wait for me!"

"I love you, Giovanni! I love you!" Iole called.

Giovanni started running toward the wall. When he reached the end of the street he turned for one last look back and saw Iole still standing in the patch of light, her hand still extended toward him as if she could draw him back to her.

A double line of walls surrounded the city. Those who were to defend the outer palisade would take their places, then have the sally ports of the inner wall locked behind them—ensuring that they would fight until they fell. It was being said of those on the outer wall that they were now without sin. Giovanni Ruggi was one of those who took his position there.

Suddenly the Turkish camp, which had been quiet for so long, exploded with a horrifying noise. For as far as Giovanni could see in either direction around the wall, raging Turks were rushing in with their attack, screaming battle cries, while drums, trumpets, and flutes added to the din.

All over Constantinople church bells began to peal in a prearranged signal that the attack had come, though such was the noise of the fighting that the signal was scarcely needed. The defenders on the walls prepared to meet the enemy, while inside the city, old people, women, and children crowded the churches.

Giovanni fitted a bolt into his crossbow and watched as the mass of shrieking humanity surged toward the wall. Spotting one particularly large fellow brandishing a scimitar over his head and shouting encouragement to those around him, the Genoese raised the bow to his shoulders, took aim, then shot. He followed the flight of his bolt and saw it plunge into the big man's neck. The man dropped his scimitar and put his hands up to the wound, clutching at the bolt, trying to pull it out. Blood spilled between his fingers, and then he pitched forward.

"Fight for Christendom!" an officer near Giovanni shouted, but his rallying cry was cut off by an arrow that had been loosed by a longbowman from within the ranks of the attackers.

Giovanni shot again, but he let out a curse of frustration when he saw this bolt harmlessly hit the ground.

Leading the Turkish attack were the bashi-bazouks, the sultan's irregular troops. There were thousands of them, including many from Christian Europe, such as Slavs, Hungarians, Germans, and even a few Italians and Greeks. These men of no scruples were willing to fight against their fellow Christians for the money the sultan paid them.

Behind the bashi-bazouks were the janissaries, the sultan's most elite forces and his own personal guard. Their purpose in this attack was to keep the mercenary bashi-bazouks from retreating.

The bashi-bazouks were handicapped by their numbers. There were so many of them that they got in each other's way, and as they bunched up against the bottom of the wall, they were easily killed by stones, bolts from crossbows, and Greek fire.

"Giovanni, the ladder!" someone shouted, and Giovanni looked over to see a red-bearded man just reaching the top of a scaling ladder. Grabbing a lance, Giovanni thrust it into the man's chest; then he and two of his comrades took hold of the shaft and pushed hard, propelling the ladder backward and disposing of three other attackers with it.

"Swordsmen! We need swordsmen here!" Giovanni shouted, and a handful of men brandishing sabers answered his call, rushing along the top of the wall, stepping over the bodies already littering the walkways. They hacked and stabbed at the scaling attackers as each new threat was presented.

The fierce fighting continued for two hours before the bashi-bazouks were allowed to withdraw. At first the defenders actually thought they had been victorious, and a few even started to cheer.

"Hold your cheers," Giovanni said, wiping the sweat from his face and pointing toward the hill across from the Civil Gate of Saint Romanus. His comrades, seeing what Giovanni was seeing, groaned; a few began to weep.

A second attack was suddenly launched, this one by the Anatolian guards—a much larger army, better uniformed, better disciplined, and better armed than the bashi-bazouks had been. Cannons boomed, and the walls trembled and shattered under the assault. A large hole was opened, and the Anatolians began to pour through.

"To the defense!" someone shouted, and Giovanni jumped down from his position on the palisade and joined the other Christians who had gathered at the breach in the wall. The Anatolians coming through were slaughtered by the score and eventually beaten back.

When the Anatolian attack was defeated, the sultan brought forth his own guard, the janissaries. If these most elite regiments of his army were also beaten back, the siege would fail, and the Turks would have no choice but to withdraw.

The beautifully uniformed janissaries moved in, pelted by arrows, stones, javelins, and shot. Despite the hail of missiles launched toward them, their ranks remained unbroken. Wave after wave of the powerful soldiers rushed up to the walls, tearing at the stones with their bare hands and hacking at the beams that supported them.

The battle continued for over an hour, with the janissaries unable to make any headway. By now the Christians had been fighting for over four hours without so much as a moment's respite. Giovanni felt his muscles aching and his breath coming in ragged gasps, but he knew he couldn't rest; if he did, it would be the end.

He saw one of the Turks raise a firearm, and he reached for a bolt to load his crossbow, only to discover that his quiver was empty. A half-full quiver was on the body of a soldier beside him, so he dropped to one knee to take out one of the missiles. As he loaded his crossbow, the Turk discharged his gun. There was a flash of light, a puff of smoke, and a loud bang, and then the ball whizzed by Giovanni's ear. He heard it hit something—or someone—just behind him. At that same moment he was able to raise his crossbow and shoot. When he saw his bolt plunge deep into the Turk's chest, he let out a small cry of victory.

"Friend, I am shot," he heard someone say, and when Giovanni turned to see who had spoken to him, he gasped in alarm.

Captain-General Giustiniani was standing just behind him, weaving back and forth. The Turk's ball had struck the Genoese commander. Giovanni groaned in anguished frustration. If his quiver had not been empty—if he had been a second faster in getting off his shot—this would not have happened.

"We need help here!" Giovanni shouted. "Call for a surgeon! The commander has been hurt!"

Giustiniani sank slowly to the ground, then pulled his hand away from the wound and looked at the blood pooled in his palm. He coughed, and more blood oozed from his mouth. He looked up at Giovanni and smiled sadly.

"I fear there is little a surgeon can do for me now, my brave fellow," he said. "I am done for."

"It is my fault. I should have shot the Turk more quickly," Giovanni said, despairing.

Giustiniani started to laugh, and again he spewed out blood. "Do not berate yourself. You killed him. I can die happy now, knowing that my slayer has already died."

One of Giustiniani's bodyguards knelt beside his commander, examined him for a second, then looked up. "He cannot stay here. We must get him away from the field of battle."

"How are we to do so?" another asked. "The inner gate is locked. We're trapped on the outer wall."

"No, we aren't."

"You know a way we can get out of here?"

The soldier grinned broadly and held up a key. "A good soldier is always prepared. Let's get him out of here."

Giovanni watched as they carried the wounded commander toward the locked gate. After they opened it, they made no effort to close it again, and a few other defenders decided to leave, then others still, until suddenly a mad rush of Genoese soldiers was pouring through the gate and fleeing the battle, running through the streets of the city toward the harbor.

"Wait!" Giovanni shouted to them. "Wait, stand here with me! Victory is nearly ours! We only need to beat them back one more time!"

Giovanni reached for one of the soldiers, intending to grab him and hold him fast, but no sooner did he get his hand on the soldier's arm than there was a sudden burst of color and light before his eyes as something crashed into the back of his head. He went down.

# THE DREAMERS

## Paul King

The adventure begins...a saga of the bold men and courageous women who sailed in search of a new and fabulous world.

1418. As this century of discovery opens, Prince Henry of Portugal is putting his wealth into a search for a fabulous lost island somewhere west of Africa. On this daring voyage a fisherman's son will witness both miracles and despair on a perilous, dark sea. Young Alessandro Cavalli of Venice will also meet his fate on the watery deep after a brother's betrayal leaves him chained to an oar as a galley slave. And teenaged apprentice Tom of Bristol is running for his life when he stows away on an ocean-bound ship...as the magnificent adventure of exploration begins with *The Dreamers.*

---

Available at your local bookstore or use this page to order.
☐ 29242-0 DREAMERS  $5.99/$6.99 in Canada
**Send to:  Bantam Books, Dept. DO 46**
        **2451 S. Wolf Road**
        **Des Plaines,  IL  60018**

Please send me the items I have checked above.  I am enclosing
$_____ (please add $2.50 to cover postage and handling). Send check or money order, no cash or C.O.D.'s, please.

Mr./Ms._____

ddress_____

City/State_____Zip_____
Please allow four to six weeks for delivery.
Prices and availability subject to change without notice.    DO 46 1/94